Praise for *A Quilt for Jenna,*
the first book in Patrick E. Craig's
Apple Creek Dreams series…

◇◇◇

"Patrick Craig writes with an enthusiasm and a passion that are a joy to read. He deals with romance, faith, love, loss, tragedy, and restoration with equal amounts of elegance, grace, clarity, and power. Everyone should pick up his debut novel in Amish fiction, turn off the phone and computer and TV, and settle in for a good night's read. Craig's book is a blessing."

Murray Pura
author of *The Wings of Morning* and *Ashton Park*

"A good storyteller takes a fine story and places it in a setting peppered with enough accurate details to satisfy a native son. Then he peoples it with characters so real we keep thinking we see them walking down the street. A great storyteller takes all that and binds it together with, say, a carefully constructed Rose of Sharon quilt and the wallop of a storm of the century that actually happened. *A Quilt for Jenna* proves Patrick Craig to be a great storyteller."

Kay Marshall Strom
author of the Grace in Africa and Blessings in India trilogies

"A touching tale of three people who have lost their way. In *A Quilt for Jenna*, Patrick Craig deftly contrasts the peaceful Amish lifestyle with the harsh World War II Guadalcanal battlefield, tied together with a lovely message of sacrifice, humility, and forgiveness. I was entranced."

Sarah Sundin
award-winning author of *With Every Letter*

The Road Home

The Road Home

PATRICK E. CRAIG

HARVEST HOUSE PUBLISHERS
EUGENE, OREGON

Cover by Garborg Design Works, Savage, Minnesota

Cover photos © Chris Garborg; Bigstock / Jan Marijs, VibrantImage

Author photo by William Craig—Craig Propraphica

THE ROAD HOME
Copyright © 2013 by Patrick E. Craig
Published by Harvest House Publishers
Eugene, Oregon 97402
www.harvesthousepublishers.com

Library of Congress Cataloging-in-Publication Data
Craig, Patrick E.
    The road home / Patrick E. Craig.
        pages cm. — (Apple Creek dreams series ; bk. 2)
    ISBN 978-0-7369-5107-4 (pbk.)
    ISBN 978-0-7369-5108-1 (eBook)
    1. Amish—Ohio—Fiction. 2. Foundlings—Fiction. 3. Family secrets—Fiction. I. Title.
PS3603.R3554R63 2013
813'.6—dc23
                                                        2013005873

Printed in the United States of America

13 14 15 16 17 18 19 20 21 / LB-CD / 10 9 8 7 6 5 4 3 2 1

To my wife, Judy,
who over our twenty-five years together
has shown me that the Lord truly sets the solitary in families

ACKNOWLEDGMENTS

Thanks to Nick Harrison, my editor and strong advocate for the
Apple Creek Dreams series,

and to

Steve Laube, for his wisdom and guidance through the sometimes
treacherous and always challenging shoals of publishing novels, and
for encouraging me to write this series in the first place.

Contents

◇◇◇

A Note from Patrick E. Craig

◇◇◇

What connexion can there have been between many people in the
innumerable histories of this world, who, from opposite sides of great
gulfs, have, nevertheless, been very curiously brought together!

CHARLES DICKENS
BLEAK HOUSE

WHEN I WAS A PASTOR, I once counseled two young people who wanted
to get married. She was a Christian, but he was not. Like the character
in this story, his name was Jonathan. My wife and I spent many days
with this precious young couple, doing our best to share the Lord with
Jon, but he seemed impervious to the pressing of the Spirit.

One day, Jon and Sherry were telling us about their lives, how they
had lived in so many different places and done many different (often
wild and dangerous) things before finally coming to California and
meeting—by coincidence, they said.

Suddenly something occurred to me. I drew a rough map of the
United States on a piece of paper and had Jon and Sherry put a dot on
all the places they had lived before they met. Then I had them connect
the dots. Both of their meandering trails led to one spot—a little town
in California. Then I took the map and I said to Jon, "Do you know
how I know God loves you?"

He looked at me strangely and then said no, he didn't. I traced his journey with a pencil as I said, "I know He loves you because over the years, He led you through all these places in your life, watched over you, and kept you safe so that at this time in your life, He could bring you to California and give you Sherry to love."

Well, I saw the penny drop. Jon stared at the map and then at his lovely fiancée and then at the map again. A huge smile broke on his face and he said, "I guess God really does love me."

Coincidence? Some say coincidence is God choosing to remain anonymous; others say coincidence simply means you're on the right path. Often in writing, coincidence is regarded as a weak literary device—a quick way to advance a plot or move characters from one place to another without the need for a clever story line. But when we look at our own lives—especially those of us who believe God is real and that He has a plan for us—don't we discover a lifelong thread of "coincidences" that have moved us ever onward toward a specific purpose for our lives? And if God is the author and finisher of our faith, would He use a weak device to write our story?

The Road Home is a story about God's desire to fulfill His intention in people's lives. In particular, in Jenny, who, though surrounded by a loving family and a satisfying life, is still a mystery to herself and to her adoptive parents, and also in Jonathan, a young man seeking answers to the questions we have all asked in our own lives. This is a story based on what some would call coincidence, but the truth is, there is really no such thing as coincidence.

For if God is working all things together for good, then each moment, each event, each step, is somehow governed by His plan. And as for Jenny and Jonathan, the story of their lives brings them both to a little town called Apple Creek, where they pass through a series of "coincidences" that in the end...

Well, I'll let you read the story and find out.

Part One
APPLE CREEK AGAIN

◇◇◇◇◇◇◇◇◇◇◇◇

THERE'S SOMETHING ABOUT AN AGRICULTURAL TOWN that's unique and wonderful—a deep link to the land, which brings a sense of being settled and permanent.

All the bright days of youth in such a place are held in the mystery of God's eternal circle of life and death, winter and spring, summer and fall. The cycles of the seasons dictate the deepest feelings in the hearts of those who live there, with days marked not by events, but by smells and colors and sounds and all the other sensory signals.

The temperature of a morning's rising can tell you everything about the day ahead, be it the coolness of a daybreak in spring; the heat of the long, languid days of summer; the crisp bite of a fall day; or the chill of winter that pushes you with icy fingers back under the welcoming warmth of a lovely down quilt.

The lilting chirp of a robin outside an open window or the haunting call of the Canada geese heading south can manifest the procession of days more surely than any calendar. The solemn silence of a winter night, with your feet softly crunching on the snow as you make your way toward the light in the window ahead, or the grinding of the machinery and the smell of the thick harvest dust…these things mark the passage of time and bind one surely to the beloved land and the life so graciously granted by the Master of the vineyard.

Apple Creek, Ohio, is such a place. It's especially beautiful in the fall. The leaves of the Buckeye trees turn bright red, and the green, spiked pods that hide the horse chestnuts split open and drop their beautiful brown seeds on the ground. Children pile the leaves into forts and arm themselves with the shiny brown nuts against the trespasses of intruders from down the street.

Mornings come armed with the warning bite of winter yet to come, and the air is alive with the promise of families gathered at festive tables and the wonder of frosty nights that delight the heart with cathedrals of starry splendor. Soon the soft snow will blanket all living things in the quiet death of winter, but not yet, for it is harvest time, and the cycle of life is at its peak.

The fields surrounding the village are ripe with bounty, and the air is heavy with the fecundity of the yearly progression coming to its fullness.

The rest of the world changed greatly after World War II and the Korean War, but Apple Creek remained much the same. Even as the nation wandered into the disaster in Vietnam, the Amish community in Wayne County remained above the growing conflict and social revolution that would follow.

It was as though Apple Creek had been captured in a backwater eddy of time and now slowly drifted in a lovely continuity of days while the main current of civilization rushed by into an unknown and frightening future.

The Amish in Apple Creek were connected to the land, and the land was forever. The fields stretched to the horizon, and the days were like the fields, reaching back into the permanence of the past and extending forward into a future that they knew held the same tasks, the same demands, the same feasts, and the same succession of birth, life, and death. And yet they were not afraid of death, for they had their God and His promises, they had the land and its harvest each year, and they had the children, who were their inheritance and also a down payment on the continuance of their lives. And above everything, they had the simplicity of their way. And it was enough…for some.

CHAPTER ONE

Jenny

◇◇◇

"Du Schlecht'r!"

"Jenny Springer! You should not say such bad words! You should be ashamed."

Jenny's face burned as she reached behind the quilting frame with her left hand and pushed the errant needle through the quilt to complete her stitch. The finger of her other hand, showing a tiny red drop where she had pricked herself, went into her mouth. She stared angrily at the quilt she was working on. The design was awkward, and the edges of the pattern pieces were puckered where she had attempted to sew them together.

"Oh, Mama, I will never, ever be a quilter like you. I just can't do it."

Her mother's shocked expression softened somewhat, and she put her arm around the girl's shoulder. "Quilting is a gift from God, and it's true that you don't yet seem to have the eye for it. But you're gifted in so many other ways. Don't be disheartened. Sometimes you're a little *eigensinnig und ungeduldig*, and these qualities do not fit well with quilting. You must learn to still your heart and calm the stream of thoughts rushing through your head."

Jenny reached behind her head and rubbed her neck. She took a deep breath and stuck the needle back into the pincushion with finality.

"I need to stop for a bit, Mama. This quilt is making me *vereitelt*!"

Even in her present state, Jenny was a lovely girl of nearly twenty. Her reddish gold hair framed a strong brow and deep violet eyes that could flash with annoyance in an instant or radiate the most loving kindness a moment later.

Jerusha Springer reached down and enfolded Jenny in her arms. "*Sie sind meine geliebte dochter,*" Jerusha whispered softly into the curls that refused to be controlled by the heavy hairpins and happily tumbled out from under the slightly askew black *kappe* on Jenny's head. Jenny turned on her stool, and her arms crept around her mother's waist. She held on as though she would never let go.

"Are you ever sorry that you got me instead of Jenna, Mama?" Jenny whispered.

Jerusha paused before replying. "I was given Jenna, and then I was given you, my dearest. Jenna was a wonderful little girl, and your papa and I were blessed beyond measure by having her. When she died, we didn't know how we would ever go on with our lives. But God in His mercy sent us a wonderful child to fill the emptiness in our hearts. That child was you. Sorry? No, my darling, I will never be sorry that you came to us. There will always be a place in my heart for Jenna, but now I have you to love and hold. I couldn't hope for a better *dochter.*"

Jenny clung even tighter to her mother. Her mother's arms had always been a safe haven for her since the day Jerusha rescued her from the great snowstorm so many years ago. Jerusha had kept Jenny alive by holding the child next to her heart all through the long nights until Papa and Uncle Bobby had rescued them. That was the earliest memory Jenny had of her mother. The calm, steady beat of her mother's heart comforted her, and it was always in this place of refuge and life that she felt the most secure. But today, even in her mother's arms, she couldn't still the turmoil in her heart. She pulled away from Jerusha and began to talk in a rush.

"Mama, don't you ever wonder where I came from and who my birth mother was? Maybe I'm the daughter of criminals or murderers. Maybe there's a bad seed in me that will come out someday. It makes me afraid sometimes."

Jerusha stroked her daughter's hair. "There are some things we can never know, and you must not worry or fret about them. 'Be careful for nothing—'"

"I know, I know, Mama, but sometimes I do worry. I would never want to do anything that would bring shame on you or Papa. But sometimes I think that I'll never find real peace until I know...and yet that's impossible."

Jenny released her grip on her mother and grabbed up a scrap of material. She wiped another drop of blood from her finger, crumpled the cloth, and threw it down.

Jerusha took a breath and then answered. "You are so *standhaft* in all your ways. Many times your papa and I have had to pick you up and dust you off when you went too far. But that same quality has helped you to overcome difficulties. The accomplishments in your life are proof of that."

Jerusha reached over and softly stroked Jenny's cheek. "You're a *gut* student. No one in our community has such a grasp of the history of our people as you do. Someday you will be a teacher who can pass down to your children the things that keep the Amish separate and distinct from the world."

Jenny looked away and shrugged her shoulders. "I don't think I will ever have children, Mama."

Jerusha stiffened, and a fleeting frown passed over her face. "Why not, my darling?" she asked quietly.

"I don't think any man could put up with me, for one thing, and for another, I think I'm just too independent. I'm not sure I could ever submit to a husband ruling over me."

Jerusha's mouth tightened slightly. "If I were true to our *ordnung*, I would tell you what my grandmother told me when I was a girl, and insist that you follow it," Jerusha said. "She used to say that marriage is not built first on love but on the needs of our community and our faith."

"But, Mama…" Jenny said.

"Let me finish, *dochter*," Jerusha said quietly. "I loved your father very much before we were married, and someday that may happen for you. You'll meet a man whom you will love so deeply that you will gladly surrender everything of yourself into his care and protection. I used to be so bound up in my quilting that I thought there was no room in my life for love or marriage. But the first time I looked into your father's eyes, I was lost forever." Jerusha's face softened, and she smiled at a secret memory.

"Why, Mama! You're blushing," Jenny laughed. "I can understand why you lost your heart to Papa. He's a handsome man."

"Did I hear someone talking about me?" Reuben Springer came into the room. His face was stern, but there was a smile behind his eyes.

"Papa!" Jenny broke free from her mother and ran to her *daed*.

Reuben took the girl into his arms. "This is always the best part of my day, when I come home to my girls," he said as he kissed his daughter on the forehead. "I used to have to bend down so far to reach you. Now you're all grown up."

Jerusha smiled at him, a tinge of pink in her cheeks.

"I can still make you blush, eh, Mrs. Springer?" he asked.

Jerusha turned away with a reluctant smile.

A frown passed over Jenny's face like a small dark cloud, and her father noticed it.

"What is it, *dochter*?"

"Jenny was asking me about her birth parents," Jerusha said. "Not knowing about her past troubles her."

"Jenny, you mustn't concern yourself with things that can't be known," Reuben said. "When your mother found you, there was no identification or any means to discover who you were. The police found a man's body in Jepson's pond the next spring, but he had been in the water far too long to make a clear identification. The car was stolen in New York, so there was no way to trace the man. You must be content with the wisdom of God. He sent you to us because He knew you needed us and we needed you. That's all we need to know."

"But, Papa, sometimes I feel like a stranger, as if I don't really belong here." Jenny saw the pain in her father's eyes and stopped. "I'm sorry, Papa. I didn't mean it exactly that way. I don't know why it's so important to me to find out these things, but it is. Sometimes I think I'll never be who I'm supposed to be until I find out who I really am. It doesn't help that I'm so stubborn."

"Your Mama was just as stubborn when I first met her," Reuben said. "Even twenty-four years later, I feel the sting on my face where she slapped me the first time I kissed her."

"Husband!" Jerusha exclaimed as her cheeks once again turned rosy pink.

Reuben smiled at his wife and then looked at Jenny. His voice took a sterner tone. "Your mama has changed over the years, and you will change too. For the good of our family, you must put these things out of your mind."

Jenny felt a small flash of anger at her father's words. She wanted to speak but wisely stayed silent. Then she decided to take a different approach.

"Papa, maybe if I did know, I could be more peaceful inside and not be so much trouble for you and Mama. Maybe if you helped me to find my birth parents I could be a better *dochter* to you and—"

Jenny's papa stiffened at her words. "Jenny, I love you very much, but I am still the head of our home, and until you're married and under the care of your husband, I will decide what's best for you. There's much in the world that you're too young to understand. God has entrusted me with your care and safety for a good reason. The man you were with may have been your father, or he may not, but judging by what the police found in the car, he was not a good man. There were drugs and alcohol—"

"But what if he wasn't my father and he just kidnapped me or—"

"*Dochter*! That's enough! I know what's best for you. Asking questions that can't be answered will only cause you heartache and sorrow. I want you to put these wild ideas behind you. We will not discuss this further!"

Jenny stared at her father, and he stared back at her. She started to speak, but her mother placed her hand on Jenny's arm and squeezed a warning. "Your father is right, Jenny. You must listen to him and obey. Now, is anyone hungry, or should we go on working on this quilt?"

Jenny took a deep breath, looked at her masterpiece, and smiled ruefully. The star design she had labored over for so many hours was crooked and wrinkled, and the colors she had chosen clashed.

"I think we'd better have dinner, Mama. I don't think there's anything I can do to fix this mess."

"Well, let's go then," Reuben said. "I need kindling for the stove, and Jenny can go out and close in the chickens."

"All right, Papa," Jenny said, still stinging from Reuben's rebuke. "Do I need to bring in any *milch*, Mama?"

"Yes, dear," Jerusha said, "there's some fresh in the cooling house."

When Jenny had banged out the back door, Jerusha turned to Reuben. "She's so impetuous. I worry there'll come a time when she crashes into a predicament we can't get her out of. But you must not be so hard on her. She's still young."

"I know. But young or not, her curiosity worries me," Reuben said. "She's headed for disappointment if she keeps searching for answers that don't exist. I want to keep her from that as long as I can."

Jerusha nodded. "I want her to be happy, but in my heart I'm afraid that if she does somehow find her birth parents, she'll want to be with them more than with us. And their way would be so different from ours. The world out there is filled with danger, and I don't know if she would be able to understand it. I'm afraid for her, Reuben."

"I'm afraid for her too, Jerusha," he said quietly, taking his wife in his arms. "And that's why I want her to forget about her past. I'm trying hard not to crush her spirit, but the girl doesn't think things through. She thinks she's all grown up, but she still has many *kindisch* ways about her. There may soon come a day when she goes her own way, and the thought of what she might choose…"

Jerusha felt a momentary chill grip her heart, and she pulled herself deeper into the circle of Reuben's arms.

CHAPTER TWO

Memories

◇◇◇

JENNY HEARD THE SCREEN DOOR SLAM behind her as she bolted out of the house. The noise brought her up short, and she deliberately slowed her pace and took a deep breath. She had read about rockets, and she thought they described her perfectly. She was always going full blast and leaving a trail of fire behind her. Her mama said that young ladies should be dignified and demure in their behavior, quiet and plain in all their ways, but somehow that was not for her. She tried her hardest, but she just seemed to go at life like an angry goat, and there was nothing she could do about it.

Jenny looked up at the sky as the red, purple, and pink of an Apple Creek sunset spread in glorious abandon across the deepening blue. As the sun dropped into the west, small clouds caught its last rays and reflected them downward to wash the trees with hints of golden glory. The sight made Jenny catch her breath. Across the sky to the east, the stars began to appear one by one, and as they did, they twinkled and sparkled in the indigo velvet like diamonds on display. A shooting star trailed low on the horizon and disappeared behind the trees.

Jenny felt the familiar tightness in her chest growing. She had felt it often in recent days, and sometimes it was so strong that she could hardly breathe. She forced herself to inhale slowly and deeply. She thought about her papa's words and wondered if she should just forget about all the nonsense whirling around in her head. On the other hand, she didn't like being treated like a child. She was old enough to make her own decisions.

Why does he treat me that way? I'm just like that star shooting across the sky. I love Apple Creek and my home, but sometimes I feel like I'm standing back and watching everything from the outside. If I hadn't gotten lost, if Mama hadn't found me…if things had been different, what would my life have been?

Jenny walked slowly down the path to the cooling shed to fetch the milk. The Springer farm stretched out before her. She could smell the hay that Papa had just put up in the barn, and with the smell came a rush of memories—being carried up to the hayloft in her papa's strong arms, sliding down the big pile of hay and collapsing in a heap at the bottom, lying in the hay and watching the pigeons scrabbling along the highest beams. She sighed.

The cows mooed mournfully and the sheep bleated at her as she went by. The big Rhode Island rooster glared at her from his perch on the woodpile as his hens scratched for bugs in the dirt of the pathway. She grabbed up a stick lying by the path and began to herd the chickens back into their pen. The rooster jumped down and angrily defended his flock but eventually surrendered and meekly led the hens inside.

Summer in Apple Creek had come to an end, and the nip of fall was in the air. It was harvest time, and the men were working from dawn to dusk in the fields, bringing in the crops and putting them up for the winter. Soon Jenny would be spending her days with her mother and grandmother, canning the fruit and vegetables, cooking and salting the meat, and getting ready for the long, cold days ahead.

Once more the unwanted thoughts began to crowd into her head, and she felt a sudden chill pass over her. What would her life be like if she weren't an Amish girl? Maybe she would be an *Englisch* girl getting ready for college or living in a big city. Since the car she was found in came from New York, maybe her birth mother still lived there. Maybe she was from a rich family, and they had been looking for her all these years and…She stopped short in the path and stilled her thoughts, wondering why she couldn't be content with the life she had right in front of her.

Life for the Amish was an endless cycle that was intimately connected to the land and the seasons. Planting in the spring, tending the fields through the long summer, harvesting when the air grew crisp, and then waiting out the days when the snow blanketed the ground— quilting, sewing, reading the Bible, or just sitting before a roaring fire. And of course there were the winter feasts and family get-togethers. These things had been the routine of Jenny's life, and in her younger days it had been enough.

She loved her home and especially her parents. They were so good to her, and she knew they loved her deeply. Her mama was a wonderful quilter, and her quilts were known throughout the Amish community and even out among the *Englisch* in the village and throughout Ohio. Once, when she was younger, she had asked her mama why she didn't sell her quilts in some of the big *Englisch* stores or offer them in catalogs.

"There was a time I thought I wanted to do that," Jerusha answered. "I was angry at God because I blamed Him for taking Jenna away. I was going to use my quilts to get out of Apple Creek and leave God and this Amish life behind. I was running away, but He put me right in the middle of a terrible storm. Then He showed me how wrong I was, how prideful and arrogant and faithless. And when I surrendered to Him, He led me to you to show me how much He really did love me."

"But, Mama, your quilts are so beautiful. You could be famous, and we would make lots of money."

"Yes, but when I was in that cabin, struggling to keep both of us alive, I remembered what my grandmother taught me when I was first learning to quilt. She had told me, 'You're too proud, Jerusha. This gift is not for you, but for those you can bless with your quilts. It is God working through you to touch others, and not to be held for yourself. You can't take this gift and use it to bring attention or recognition to yourself.'

"I realized that God has given me this gift to bless others and not myself. Now I make the quilts for people in our village who really need them. It's my way to thank *du lieber Gott.* So, Jenny, we won't worry about your mama being rich and famous. What need do we have for money? We have each other and your *daed* and the land and the Lord. That is enough."

Jenny remembered the question she had asked her mother. "Has God given me a gift that I can use to bless people, Mama?"

Jerusha took the girl in her arms and held her close. "Your very life is a gift and a blessing to your papa and me and to many others. God has given you a quick mind and courage and determination. Soon He will begin to open doors for you to walk through. When He does, you mustn't hesitate, but you must do exactly as He says. Then you will discover who you are to be and what your place is in this world."

Jenny realized she was standing in the middle of the path, lost in her thoughts. She wondered what someone who might come down the path would think about finding her standing stock-still and silent in the dark. She walked to the cooling shed and went inside. The ice blocks, cut from last winter's frozen pond and packed in sawdust, had kept the insulated building cool all summer, and Jenny often slipped in there on hot days to refresh herself. She usually loved this place, but tonight it seemed cold and dark. She looked around at all the produce and goods her family had set aside, some of it especially for the holidays that would soon mark the end of the harvest season. She found the milk in the metal can, poured some out into the pitcher she had grabbed on her way out of the kitchen, and went back outside.

Jenny looked up at the night sky again, and suddenly her heart was filled with love for this place, for her parents, and for the ways of her people. In that quiet moment she decided she needed to put all the wondering behind her. She needed to get on with her life. The mystery of where she came from would just have to remain an enigma forever. She was Jenny Springer, and she was thankful for such a wonderful home. This is where her life was, and nothing could take her away.

Jenny turned and went back to the house. There! That was settled forever…no more thinking or dreaming—and then a thought popped unbidden into her mind. *What if I'm the daughter of a rich family and stand to inherit millions? Or what if my real father is a famous musician or—*

"Jenny, stop it!" she cried out loud.

From inside the house her mother's voice called out to her. "Are you all right, Jenny?"

Jenny felt her face burning. *Wonderful! Now I'm talking to myself. The people in the village all know I'm pushy. Shall I now add* verrückt *to their opinion?*

"I'm fine, Mama. I'll be right in." *I must get hold of myself! This is the reality of my life. I will never find out where I came from or who my birth parents are, so I should just make up my mind to give up this hopeless dream!*

◇◇◇

When Jenny crawled into bed that night she couldn't rest. She drifted in and out of sleep, tossing and turning. She tried praying, but that didn't help. Finally around midnight she slipped into a troubled sleep. Her dreams were filled with strange places and people. She felt as if she were flying, and then a scene took shape in her mind. She was in the backseat of a car, and she was very cold and hungry. The man driving the car was drinking out of a bottle as the car sped down the highway. He was yelling and singing and weeping, and the car was swerving and jerking.

"Jingle bells, jingle bells, jingle all the waaayyyy."

Terrified, Jenny clung to the door handle with all her might. Suddenly the car swerved off the road. It started to run up on a bank, but the man twisted the wheel and the car shot back onto the highway.

"Mama, Mama!" Jenny screamed.

The man reached back and tried to grab her. Jenny held on to the door handle and screamed again. She felt the man's hand gripping her shoulder and pulling her toward him. She looked into his eyes. The pupils were like little pinpoints, and they terrified her. An evil grin spread across his face as he clutched at her.

"You want your Mama?" he asked. "I'll send you to her right now."

The man was turned toward her, not watching the road. The car shot off the road and over a bank. Everything seemed to go into slow motion. She felt the car lift off the ground and begin to roll over in midair. There was a sickening crash, and then they were sliding down a steep bank. Everything moved so slowly, and the man's screams were low-pitched, as if someone were playing a recording too slowly. The car hit a tree and some rocks, but because everything was moving so slowly, it was all like a strange dance. Finally the car came to rest on its side at the edge of what looked like a snow-covered meadow.

Jenny had been thrown down between the front and back seats and then onto the side door, and she lay there, unable to scream or cry, frozen in terror. The man struggled around in the front seat, and his movements made the car roll over on its top. He fell heavily onto the roof and cried out. She was buried underneath the seat cushions and some clothing. The front seat had broken loose, and when the car rolled over, it fell down on the passenger side, blocking access to the back of the car. She saw his legs thrashing around and heard him groaning. Then she saw his hand try to reach around the broken seat, but he couldn't get to her, so he started kicking at the front passenger door until it finally opened. A blast of bitter wind came in and chilled her to the bone. The man crawled out onto the snow, and as he did, the wind blew the door shut.

Jenny groaned and tried to make herself wake up, but she couldn't move or make a sound. She slipped back into her whirling dream. The car was upside down, and she was lying on the roof. She could see the man's legs outside the window. He had gotten up and staggered to the back door. Now his feet were next to the window. She heard him pulling on the handle and swearing. She lay terrified as he began to kick at the window. She could just barely hear him mumbling incoherently. The window didn't break, and then she could see him step back.

She saw him walk away from the car, and then she saw a piece of metal lying a few feet away. She watched him as he bent over to pick it up. Suddenly a hole opened up under his feet, and he fell into it. There was a big splash, and then he was up to his neck in water. He tried to pull himself up, but the edge of the hole kept breaking off. His face was only a few feet away from hers, and as she looked out the window of the car, she saw him sink beneath the surface.

He came back up, and with one arm he grabbed the edge of the hole. He looked right into her eyes, and then she saw his face turn into a skull, and his bony skeletal fingers reached for her. Just as they touched the car door, the edge of the hole broke, and the man disappeared under the water once more. There was a thrashing underneath the surface, and more water splashed out. Then, finally, everything was quiet, and the surface of the water became smooth and still.

Jenny felt the cold creep into the car. Then somebody was with her in the car, and she felt as if she were being covered with warm feathers.

She turned to look, and she wasn't in the car anymore. She was lying on a bed in a small room. A woman was lying on the bed with her. Jenny tried to cuddle up to her and get warm, but the heat was gone from the woman's body. The man who had drowned was sitting in a chair in the corner of the room, weeping. Ashtrays full of half-smoked cigarettes and empty bottles were scattered around the room. On a stand by the bed was a spoon with some brown liquid and a piece of cotton in it. The woman had something tied around her arm. Jenny was crying. Suddenly the woman's eyes opened, and she looked straight at Jenny.

"I'm sorry, Jenny," she said quietly. "I didn't mean for all this to happen. I just wanted the pain to stop."

The woman looked up at the ceiling. "Dear Jesus," she prayed, "please look after my little girl."

Then everything began to get all mixed up. She was back in the car, and then she was being carried through blinding snow. She was freezing, and then she was wrapped in something warm and soft. Now she was somewhere in a dark room. She was being held next to a warm, beating heart, and she felt moisture dropping on her face. She opened her eyes and looked up into the beautiful face of another woman. The woman was holding her close and weeping. Her body was shaking with sobs. It was Mama! And then as she looked, Jerusha's face turned into the face of the woman in the small room. The other woman's skin was cold and blue. Her eyes opened, and she looked at Jenny.

"Jenny, come find me. I'm lost, so lost," she said, and then the skin began to melt off her face, and she was just bones and the bones were death, and Jenny fell into the water, and the man who had drowned came up from below and grabbed her leg with bony fingers and began to pull her down, down, down...

Jenny sat up in bed and screamed. "Mama, Mama, where are you? Come find me, Mama!"

There was the sound of hurried footsteps in the hall, and Jerusha rushed into the room, holding a lamp. "Jenny, darling, what is it?" she asked as she came to the side of Jenny's bed.

"A dream, Mama, a horrible dream," Jenny sobbed.

Jerusha put the lamp on the stand by the bed and sat next to Jenny. She took the girl in her arms and kissed her forehead. "I'm here, my darling, I'm here."

Jerusha held Jenny close, and Jenny felt the beating of her mother's heart.

Chapter Three

Johnny

◇◇◇

JOHNNY THE CANDYMAN WOKE UP out of a deep sleep and sat straight up in his bed, moaning and holding his head in his hands. Strange images and faces and…horses, yes, horses and plows, like a weird kaleidoscopic farm movie, were all mixed together in his mind. Finally his dazed thoughts cleared, and he opened his eyes. As he slowly came back to reality, he shrugged and thought, *The drugs. It was the drugs I took last night.*

Johnny rubbed his eyes and looked around the room. The walls were brightly painted with clashing primary colors that strobed and flashed and made his head ache. Large posters of Martin Luther King and Mahatma Ghandi were pinned on the wall over the bed. The room was decorated in the quasi-Edwardian mode that was all the rage in the Haight-Ashbury.

An overstuffed brown, furry couch and a brass floor lamp with a shade fringed with strands of tiny golden beads sat against the wall. An expensive oriental rug lay on the floor. The stale smell of incense, Gauloise cigarettes, and patchouli oil permeated the room. On the back of the bedroom door was a hand-lettered poster advertising one of Ken Kesey's acid trips. The letters seemed to swell and pulse—more of the lingering effects of the acid, he guessed.

His precious Gibson twelve-string guitar leaned against the wall, its case lying open on the floor beside it with a few dollars from his most recent panhandling foray still inside. His fingers ached from the hours of mindless strumming that had passed for music among his friends the night before.

The sound of automobile traffic rose up from the street outside. His bed was a mattress on the floor next to the wall, so he turned over on his knees, grabbed the windowsill, pulled himself up, and looked out through the tall window of his second-floor flat. Traffic was bumper-to-bumper headed west. It was time for Sunday morning football at Kezar Stadium, and a line of cars inched along as the straight folks drove down Haight Street to see the hippies. Unfortunately for the drive-bys, the hippies had been partying Saturday night, and very few of them were out on the street Sunday morning.

Johnny crawled off his mattress and groped his way to the pile of clothes heaped on the floor. He pawed through until he found the pieces that comprised his favorite outfit. He took hold of the couch and pulled himself up slowly, his head aching. He stood there for a minute until the whirling sensation passed. Then he pulled his clothes on. A thin cotton embroidered shirt, torn bell-bottom jeans, and green suede Beatle boots completed his attire. He stumbled over to the closet, pulled his leather-fringed jacket off a hanger, and put it on. He went to the mirror and stared at his pale complexion for a few moments.

Sheesh, look at me. I've got to get out more.

Then he ran his fingers through his long dark hair, pulled it into a ponytail, and fastened it with a rubber band. He looked at the orange headband on the dresser with the button that read, "Give us this day our Daily Flash" pinned to the knot, but he decided to forego wearing it this morning. His body was still wrestling with the effects of the drugs, and he really didn't feel like a "daily flash" at the moment. As he stared at the bleary-eyed face in the mirror, he wondered why he thought tripping on LSD was so great.

He thought back to last night's "freakout." After the LSD had come on, Fat Freddy, one of his roommates, sat down in the corner and started asking, "But what does it all mean?" over and over until he had almost driven Johnny crazy. And then there was Lisa, the girl from Seattle, who liked to writhe like a snake on the floor when she got stoned. At one point Johnny got his guitar, and they sat in a circle and jammed until late into the night, everyone moaning and chanting along with the strumming.

Then there had been a big fight over whether they should listen to a Jefferson Airplane album or just turn on KMPX and lie on the floor. The party had ended up being a bunch of strange people doing weird stuff and playing loud music. That was supposed to be enlightenment? At one point it had gotten so loud that Johnny had yelled at them to shut up and peace out. Then someone suggested doing a flaming groovy, and they almost set the ceiling on fire.

Johnny opened the door and peeked down the hall. None of his roommates were up yet, and he was glad of that. He had made a bit of a jerk of himself by reproving his roommates' obnoxious behavior, and he really didn't want to face them this morning. Instead, he headed quietly down the stairs and out the door. There was a good breakfast place on Haight Street, and he wanted some strong coffee to wash the bitter taste out of his mouth and some decent food to help him feel better.

The air outside was crisp and cool as he went down the stoop onto the street. His Volkswagen bus was sitting at the curb. It had been dark blue when his father bought it for him back in Levittown, but now it was covered with green and orange Day-Glo flowers and glued-on pictures of the Beatles and Timothy Leary.

As he looked at the van, he remembered the day he had decorated it and how tripped-out he had been. These days, instead of feeling excited and high on life as he had then, he felt weary and anxious. He stared at his bus for a minute, shook his head, and then headed down the street past the Unique Men's Shop. Mnasidika, a clothing store, was closed and dark, and the Psychedelic Shop next door was shuttered.

People were starting to crawl out of the various pads they had crashed in the night before. As Johnny passed them by, he noticed that they all looked like weird, hairy rodents, scratching their lice-ridden heads and blinking at the strange yellow ball in the sky. He walked by the free clinic and noticed the sign in the window.

"Closed. Free penicillin shots on Monday at nine a.m. Free food today at the Diggers tent in the Panhandle."

The cafe at the foot of Clayton Street was just opening, and Johnny went in and saw an empty table toward the back. It was September in San Francisco, and Indian summer was in its full glory. The sun was streaming in the front windows, and the bright light was hard on his eyes. He grabbed a menu from the rack by the cash register on his way to the table, and once he was seated, he scanned it quickly. Crash Landing with eggs, toast, hash browns, bacon, and hot coffee looked really good.

He took a quick look in his wallet to make sure the two twenty-dollar bills were still there, and then he caught the eye of the waitress. She shuffled over and took his order. He peeked at the two twenties again. He could hardly believe he was down to his last forty bucks. What had become of all the gigs he was going to get?

Johnny the Candyman had arrived in San Francisco in the early spring of 1965. Even out in the wilds of Long Island, he heard that there was a Beat revival going on, led by the likes of Ken Kesey, Neal Cassady and Marty Balin. Johnny was an aspiring folksinger who read *The Catcher in the Rye* and *On the Road* in high school and became enthralled with the concepts of alienation, teenage angst, and rebellion.

His father, a successful businessman, was never around much, and after Johnny found out about the mistresses his dad kept in two different cities, he shut his father out of his life.

His mother solved her anger issues with martinis and garden-club meetings and more martinis, so Johnny was on his own for most of his teen years. When President Kennedy was assassinated in 1963, Johnny felt that any possibility for society to move away from the straight Eisenhower suburban lifestyle had disappeared forever. He started listening to the Beatles, Bob Dylan, and the Byrds, took up the guitar, smoked some pot with his high school friends, and decided that the conventional life he was living in Levittown was a dead-end street. So in the spring of 1965 he packed his bags, liberated two thousand dollars from his mother's bank account, and headed west in his van to San Francisco.

Now, as Johnny waited for his breakfast, he rested his face in his hands. Six months in the City and this was it? This was what he came across the country for?

He thought back to last night's party. Sure people wore different clothes, had longer hair, but they still played the same mind games as the people he left in Levittown.

Was there someplace he could go that was simpler? He remembered that National Geographic magazine someone had left at the Laundromat. The feature on Alaska was intriguing. Maybe life would be better there? Maybe they could use his musical talents, if San Francisco couldn't. Well, it was a good idea, but it would have to wait. Thirty-six dollars wouldn't get him very far. So now he was having his breakfast with a big question mark in his fuzzy mind and thirty-six dollars left in his wallet. His reverie was interrupted by a strident voice.

"Candyman, my main man, what's happening?"

Johnny groaned.

"I heard you guys were trippin' big time last night. You should have let me know. I'm always up for a good time!"

The person Johnny was not too excited about seeing was short and swarthy with two days' growth of beard and long, dirty hair pulled back in a ponytail. He had on a leather jacket with bikers' colors on a vest over it. The patch on the back of the vest read, "The Death Heads" in red letters surrounding a grinning skull over crossed bones.

"Hey, Shub," Johnny said. "It wasn't really that big of a deal, more like a last-minute kind of get-together. We split some acid and smoked a little pot. Nothing great."

"Well, let me know next time," Shub grumbled. "Mind if I join ya?"

Noting that Shub had already slid into the chair across from him, Johnny acknowledged his new tablemate with a nod.

"Say, Candyman, how you fixed for bread these days?" Shub asked.

"Funny you should ask, Shub," he replied. "I'm getting ready to split town, and I'm a little short."

"Well, I got a way for you to make a few hundred if you're interested," Shub said with a crooked grin.

"What do I have to do?" Johnny asked suspiciously.

"Not a whole lot, my man," Shub said. "Just give me a ride to Pacifica and back. I have a transaction to make, and I can't do it on my bike, if you know what I mean."

Johnny lowered his voice. "You doing a deal or something?"

Shub answered in a whisper. "This is the big one, Candyman. The gold mine, the mother lode. I got some guys who want to buy a bunch of LSD, and I happen to have twenty grams."

"Where did you get that much acid?" Johnny asked.

Shub gave Johnny a conspiratorial wink. "Never you mind, my man. Are you in or not?"

"Okay, I'm in, but I need a hundred up front, and I stay in the car while you do your business," Johnny said. "What time do you need me?"

"Seven o'clock tonight, corner of Fell and Stanyan."

"I'll be there," Johnny said.

"Cool," Shub said as he pulled out a roll of cash and slipped Johnny five twenty-dollar bills. "Now that we've got that settled, I have a question."

"Ask away," Johnny said.

"How come everybody calls you Candyman?"

"My real name is Jonathan Hershberger," Johnny said. "When I first came to town I was tripping with some freaks who wanted to call me Hershey Bar. I didn't particularly appreciate that, so I straightened them out. They decided to call me Candy Bar instead, then Candy, and then the Candyman. And that's the story in a nutshell."

"Hershberger, huh? Sounds like some kind of a weird sandwich. Is that Jewish?"

"Don't really know," Johnny said. "I'm not exactly sure what it is— maybe German or something."

Shub started to get up from the table, and then Johnny found himself blurting out a question. "Say Shub, can I ask you something?"

Shub paused and then slid back down in his seat. "What is it, my man?" he asked.

Johnny paused. "Do you know anything about farms?"

"Farms?"

"Yeah, farms. I'm not sure if it happened when I was tripping or after I went to sleep, but this morning when I woke up, I remembered something about farms and horses, and I don't know exactly what was going on, but it was so real."

"Yeah?"

Johnny paused, and then it came out in a rush. "I was walking behind a team of horses, driving an old-fashioned plow, of all things. I've never even seen a plow except in pictures. I could smell the dirt as it broke up and turned over beneath the blade. As I watched the plow, it was like the clods were trying to escape, but they just broke apart, and the blade turned them under. Other guys were there with me. They were dressed in old-fashioned clothes, and the older men all had beards. They wore boots, but I was barefoot—I could feel the ground under my feet, pushing up between my toes."

"Yeah? And then what happened?" Shub asked.

Johnny swallowed. He didn't like sharing himself with other people, but he felt like he needed to tell someone about this. "The dirt between my toes was almost comforting. Then as I walked, my legs began to sink in, and I felt the strangest sensation. It was like roots began to grow out of the bottom of my feet into the ground. And as they grew, I began to feel...I dunno, empty or lonely. What do you think that was about?"

Shub stared at Johnny with a strange, sad look on his face. "Wow, that's heavy, man," he said slowly. "You know, I kind of understand what you're talking about."

"What do you mean?" Johnny asked.

"I grew up on a farm in eastern Washington State," Shub replied. "When I was a kid, I used to go walk out in the fields after they were plowed. I'd walk way out until I couldn't see any roads or power lines. I'd take off my shoes and walk in my bare feet in the dirt. It was like I was connected to the land or something. I really loved that place."

"Why did you leave?" Johnny asked.

"I don't really know," Shub said sadly. "I just kind of drifted away."

Shub sat quietly for a minute and then pushed away from the table and stood up. "Behave now," he said with a crooked smile. "See you tonight."

Then Shub walked away, and as he watched him go, Johnny had an empty feeling in his heart.

CHAPTER FOUR

The Long and Winding Road

◇◇◇

AT SEVEN O'CLOCK, Johnny pulled up at the corner of Fell and Stanyan, and Shub climbed into the van with a large leather briefcase in his hand.

"Let's go, my man," he said, and Johnny headed for Nineteenth Avenue.

The drive was uneventful. Johnny followed Highway 1 until they came to a motel on the south side of Pacifica near Devil's Slide. They pulled into the parking lot, and Johnny stayed in the van while Shub went inside.

"Keep the motor running," he said as he climbed out. "I don't trust these guys." He opened his jacket to show Johnny the butt of a revolver in the inside pocket.

"Wait a minute, Shub," Johnny said. "I didn't know there were going to be guns involved."

"Listen, kid," Shub growled. "When you're dealing with this much money, you always come prepared. Don't worry. I'll be out in about five minutes, and we're outta here."

Johnny sat in the van and watched as the fog rolled in from the ocean. The yellow streetlamps became fuzzy glows, barely visible in the dark. Cars whizzed by, headed down the coast or into the city. The neon motel sign flashed on and off, on and off, the green letters flickering strangely in the mist.

A sudden chill ran down Johnny's back. He tensed for a moment but then relaxed and stretched his shoulders. The van's engine puttered quietly away. Johnny's ears perked up when he thought he heard raised voices. At first they were indistinct. He rolled down the window to hear better, and then he heard someone shout, "He's got a gun!"

Then Johnny heard a gunshot, followed by more yells. The door of the room burst open and Shub came running out, followed a few seconds later by a tall man. Shub ran to the van, pulled open the passenger door, and tossed in the briefcase.

"Take off, Johnny! They're on to me!"

Shub started to climb in when three more shots rang out. Shub jerked violently and fell forward onto the seat. His fingers opened and closed stiffly as if he were testing them. He lifted his head and looked at Johnny.

"I...I just want to go home..." he said, and then his eyes glazed over. Shub slid out of the car and collapsed on the pavement, clearly dead.

There was a yell and another shot, and a bullet hit the van, shattering the passenger-side mirror. Johnny jammed the van in gear, tore onto the highway, and headed back to the city. He looked in the rearview mirror and saw a car chasing him.

Johnny sped up, swerving in and out of traffic. He looked in the rearview mirror again and saw that the car was only half a block behind. On and on he drove, the car behind him in hot pursuit—all the way into San Francisco, past San Francisco State. There he saw his chance. Up ahead, a Muni trolley car was starting to cross Nineteenth. Knowing they always blocked traffic when they made the turn from Ocean Avenue, Johnny swerved the van in between the trolley and the edge of the street with inches to spare. In the side-view mirror, he saw the car try to swing around the end of the trolley, but it ran out of room and slid off the street onto the Muni tracks. Johnny glanced back again and saw two men jump out of the car onto the tracks. Then he was gone up Nineteenth.

He rocketed through Golden Gate Park, made an illegal right turn onto Geary, and headed for the Haight. As soon as he got home, he raced upstairs, threw his stuff into a suitcase, grabbed his guitar, stopped long enough to blurt out a story about a family emergency back in Levittown, and then he was gone, leaving his astounded room-mates staring after him.

In twenty minutes he was on the Oakland Bay Bridge heading north on Highway 80 toward Sacramento. An hour later he crossed the Yolo Causeway outside the state capital. Somewhere near Rocklin, the narrowness of his escape finally hit home. He started shaking uncontrollably, partly from the cold and partly from a delayed response to what had happened back at the motel. He pulled over to the side of the road to put on a sweatshirt under his leather jacket, and then he kept on going.

Soon he passed Auburn and started winding up toward the top of the Sierras. The dark canyon walls closed in on him, and the lights of oncoming cars flashed in his eyes over the top of the center barrier. Truckers in their huge eighteen-wheelers steamed by him, crowding him toward the side of the road as they jammed their way up the mountain toward Reno.

Johnny's insides were churning. At one point he realized that tears were rolling down his face. He pulled over at a rest stop and sat with his arms and head on the wheel, sobs shaking his body. After a while he felt calmer, so he pulled out onto the road and pushed on.

The hours crept by as the underpowered Volkswagen labored through the mountains. Finally he saw a faint brush of light in the eastern sky ahead of him. The light slowly grew around him, and as it did, he began to feel better. By dawn he had topped Donner Summit and was headed down the eastern side of the Sierras. At Truckee, he turned off the interstate and pulled into a truck stop downtown. He filled up with gas and then parked the van and walked into the restaurant.

Johnny ordered breakfast, but he didn't eat much of it. He couldn't get the image of Shub's eyes out of his mind—the way the light had died in them when he was shot. There was a news rack with copies of the San Francisco Chronicle next to the register, so he bought a copy and read it while he drank several cups of coffee. He didn't find anything in the paper about Shub's death, so he folded the paper and headed out to the car.

Then he remembered the briefcase Shub had tossed into the van. He opened the passenger door and found it under the front seat. He picked up the briefcase, wiped some blood off with an old rag, and opened it up. Inside were three large plastic bags filled with white powder. There was also a brown paper bag wadded up and shoved in next to the bags. Johnny pulled out the paper bag and opened it up.

It was filled with money. A *lot* of money. There were big wads of hundred-dollar bills, fifties, and twenties all bundled together. He stared in disbelief and then looked around to see if anybody was watching him. Seeing no one, he began to count the money. There were a lot more hundred-dollar bills than he thought, and when he finished counting, he sat numbly staring at the pile. The bag held fifty thousand dollars!

Johnny started the van and drove out of the restaurant parking lot and down the block. He turned onto a shaded side street and pulled up in front of an empty lot. He looked in the rearview mirror to see if anyone had followed him, and then he opened the bag and looked at the money again. Johnny wondered why Shub still had the LSD. Had Shub tried to steal the drugs back?

He opened the plastic bag and smelled the white powder. Then he licked the tip of his little finger and stuck it in. He took a tentative taste. There was none of the slightly metallic taste of real LSD. The powder was sweet. Then he knew what had happened. The powder was sugar. Shub was going to rip them off, and they must have asked to taste the stuff, so Shub pulled his gun and took the money. What a fool! But now what? Johnny had fifty thousand dollars that belonged to some drug dealers.

Johnny stuffed the money and the powder back into the briefcase, pushed the briefcase under the backseat, and laid his knapsack in front of it. He drove slowly out of the neighborhood and kept going until he found a freeway entrance.

As he pulled up to the signal directing traffic onto the interstate, a thought occurred to him. What if they were still after him? Fifty grand was a lot of money, and it wasn't likely they'd just let it go. He tried to go over in his mind how they could know where he was.

Maybe they saw my license plate.

Then it came to him so clearly he almost laughed. "It's not like my van is inconspicuous," he said out loud. "Duh."

This was a no-brainer. They could easily find out where he lived. Anybody in the Haight could tell them where the van parked every day. All they would have to do is pull a gun on his roommates, and they would spill his family history all the way back to Adam. With that much information it wouldn't be hard to locate his father and mother in Levittown. Hershberger was an unusual name in his upscale neighborhood.

Johnny's stomach tightened into a hard knot. Beads of sweat formed on his forehead. He was freaking out, and rightly so. What could he do now? Where could he go?

Suddenly the brazen blast of a car horn crashed into his panic. His heart jumped into his throat, and he looked in the rearview mirror. A

pickup had pulled up behind him, and he could see the driver pushing hard on his horn and motioning at him.

Is it them?

Then Johnny glanced up and saw that the light had turned green.
He put the van in gear and rolled ahead and onto the freeway.

The next several hours slipped by as Johnny kept heading east. His
only thought was that he had to get home. By two o'clock he was
exhausted. He pulled off the freeway at Burmester and drove a few
miles into Tooele, a little town outside Salt Lake City. After he got
some gas at a decrepit little station, he drove next door to a motel,
where he booked a room. He was getting his things out of the van
when it occurred to him that he should be prepared to leave in a hurry.
He grabbed the briefcase, pulled a change of underwear and his shaving kit out of the knapsack, left the rest of his things in the van, and
went into his room.

He looked around the small room. There was a doorless closet to
his left. He set the briefcase inside and then slumped into the chair by
the bed. The room smelled of stale cigarettes. Any shag from the worn
and dirty rug had long since been scraped off. The early afternoon sun
forced its way through bent and dusty Venetian blinds. The queen
bed had a worn brown blanket and two pillows. There was an ancient
TV with a set of rabbit ears sitting on a dresser in the corner. Paint was
peeling off the walls in places, and curtains hung loosely from plastic rings. An old swamp cooler rumbled and clanked from the bathroom window.

Johnny let out a sigh and sat on the edge of the chair, his head in
his hands, wondering how in the world he had ended up in this place.
The day before he was just a broke hippie on Haight Street, and now
he was on the run from drug dealers.

Finally, Johnny got up, went to the small bathroom, and washed
his face. Then he pulled the curtains over the windows, slipped off his

jeans, and crawled into bed. As soon as his head hit the pillow, he fell into a troubled sleep.

◇◇◇

When Johnny awoke, the room was pitch black, and for a moment he panicked, not remembering where he was. The darkness of the room and the stale smells crushed down on him as if someone were standing on his chest. He gasped for breath, jerked up in the bed, and almost cried out. Then it came back to him that he was in a crummy motel room in Tooele, Utah, and the reality of the past two days flooded in on him, accompanied by a deep sense of hopelessness.

He swung his legs over the side of the bed and knocked his knee against the bed stand. In the darkness, he fumbled for the lamp and finally found the switch. He had to turn it three clicks before the light came on. The small clock by the lamp read three a.m. He had slept almost ten hours, but he didn't feel rested. He did feel hungry, but he couldn't imagine finding a restaurant open at this hour in this tiny town.

He got up and went into the bathroom. He stood in front of the mirror and looked at himself. The face that looked back was haggard, and the eyes were bloodshot. He turned on the tap, filled his hands, and plunged his face into the cold water. He did it three more times until he felt the cobwebs leaving his mind.

Johnny took a shower in barely lukewarm water that spurted rudely out of the rusty shower head. He reached out of the narrow stall, grabbed his razor out of the shaving kit, and gave himself a blind shave. When he was finished, he dried himself off and went back into the bedroom and dressed. Then he grabbed the briefcase, left the room key on the stand by the bed, turned out the light, and went to the door. Johnny cracked it open and peeked out.

The neon sign in front of the hotel flashed a strange orange-pink light on the courtyard. There was only one other car, an old Chevy, parked down the row. The sky was overcast, and he couldn't see the moon or any stars. A few crickets chirped from the vacant lot next to the motel. Nothing stirred, and there was no traffic on the street. Far off in the distance he could hear compression brakes as a big truck slowed to take the exit off the interstate. The sound carried across the flat desert and fractured the silence.

The motel office was dark, and a green neon vacancy sign glowed in the window. He slipped out, shut the door behind him, and walked through the passage by the ice machine, stopping at the vending machine to buy four Mounds bars and a couple of bottles of Fresca. Then he walked toward the alley behind the motel. His van was parked where he had left it, and he climbed in. The knapsack was still where he had left it, and he slipped the briefcase under the seat and made sure it was well hidden.

Satisfied, he took a deep breath, started up the van, and drove onto the street. In a few miles he came back to Burmester and turned east onto the freeway. He drove awhile, lost in his thoughts, and then he began to pay attention to his surroundings. Off to his left was a deep darkness, and he couldn't quite figure out what it was. Then as a car passed him going west, the opposite side of the road came into view for a moment, and Johnny realized he was looking out over water. It was the Great Salt Lake. He remembered driving past it on the way to San Francisco and thinking it was one of the dreariest places on the face of the earth.

Another car passed going west, followed by a string of cars. He could see the waves of the lake lapping against the bare dirt shore. A dead stump sticking up out of the water came into view. Then the clouds over the lake opened up a bit, and the dim new moon faintly lit the bleak landscape, touching the waters of the lake with a ghastly illumination. The starkness of his surroundings and the events of the past few days crowded in on him, and fear gripped him. He saw Shub's eyes, dead, like this horrible place, and he almost ran off the road. His breath was coming in gasps, so he pulled over to the side of the road.

Get it together, Johnny! Do something! Get a grip on yourself.

Suddenly a thought came to him—a thought he'd never had before. He could pray, couldn't he? If there was a God, now was the time to get His help.

"God, if You're real, I need Your help. I don't know what to do or where to go. I've never asked for Your help before, but if You can hear me, I need it now."

Johnny sat silently behind the wheel. His breathing quieted, and the pounding of his heart slowed. A big truck roared by, and the wind shook his van.

Chapter Five

Close Call

◇◇◇

JOHNNY KEPT DRIVING. The second day he made good time. The third day, his tiredness and some bad weather slowed his progress, but on he drove.

By the time he approached Cleveland, he was exhausted and wanted to stop, but during the past two days a fear had grown in him that if he stopped, the drug dealers would find him and kill him. An obsessive thought took over his mind. *If I can make it to Levittown, I'll be okay. I just need to get back to my own room and my own bed.*

Johnny knew it was foolish thinking, but he couldn't help himself. The highway stretched before him, and the monotony and fear wore on him. He was totally beat and knew he would never make it to New York by that night. The sky had been overcast all day, and the gray clouds and drizzle matched his mood. The landscape in this part of the country was unsightly and grim. He drove through factory towns with their ugly strip malls and rundown row houses. The air smelled of sulfur and coal smoke. He imagined that this was what hell must be like.

Since his one unsuccessful attempt at prayer, he hadn't tried again. Instead, his thoughts had become dark and morbid, filled with Shub's dead face, gun-wielding crooks, and visions of his own death.

As dusk approached, he passed the turnoff to Akron, and he could feel that his fingers had locked on the wheel of the car. He knew he had to stop, so he started looking for a motel. He saw an exit with a Best Western sign below the turnoff arrow. He pulled off the interstate, turned at the first light, and followed the frontage road until he came to the motel. Interstate 80 was right across the street. Only a dirty, trash-strewn median strip and a chain-link fence separated the motel from the continual stream of roaring traffic.

He pulled in and drove up to the office. His knees ached, his back was stiff, and he had to unclench his hands several times before they loosened up. He had an odd thought that he might never play the guitar again.

Johnny pushed his way through the swinging glass door and walked up to the counter. The clerk was sitting in a chair in front of a messy desk reading a newspaper. A half-smoked cigarette smoldered in an ashtray next to him. The clerk continued reading for a few more minutes. Just when Johnny was about to say something, he put the paper down, got up, and shuffled to the counter. He was a greasy old man with sparse, stringy gray hair, and his unpleasant smile revealed the spaces where two teeth were missing.

"What can I do you for?"

"I need a room," Johnny said.

The clerk went to a board hanging on the wall and got down a key with a big green tag. "Twenty-five in advance," the old man said as he glanced out at Johnny's van. "Which way you headed?"

Johnny paid the money without comment, and the old man shut up and handed over the key. Johnny walked back outside and got in the van. Cash always seemed to answer an inquisitive clerk's questions. He drove the van around to the back of the building and found his room. The parking space in front of it was empty, so he pulled in.

Johnny got out of the car and started toward the room, but then

he remembered that he hadn't asked the clerk about nearby restau-
rants. He locked the van and started back around the building. As
he turned the corner, he looked down the row of doors toward the
office. A brown sedan was parked in front of the office door, and a
man sat behind the wheel apparently waiting for someone. Johnny's
heart leaped into his throat. He jumped back behind the corner of the
building and snuck another glance. Inside the office, a tall man was
questioning the clerk. Was it the same tall man he had seen in Pacifica?
From this angle, Johnny couldn't tell.

The clerk was shaking his head, obviously answering a question
from the tall man. Then the man reached in his pocket and pulled out
a green roll, peeled off a bill, and handed it to the clerk. Johnny saw
the clerk take the bill and then point in his direction. He jerked back
behind the corner but not before he saw that the tall man *was* the man
from the motel in Pacifica. They had found him!

They must have gotten information from his roommates and then
come after him. It would have been easy to catch up to him. With two
guys, they could have driven straight through, checking motels on the
way. They obviously figured out he was headed to Long Island. And
the way his van was painted, it wouldn't have been too hard to track.
Heading home was the worst thing he could have done. He should
have gone north to Portland or Seattle. Too late now.

In a panic, Johnny ran back to his van, jumped in, and started it up.
He looked around. The parking lot in back of the motel opened out
onto a side street. He drove out slowly, crossed the lanes, and headed
into an alley on the other side. He maneuvered down the alley, looking for a way of escape.

There was a large open door in the side of a building about halfway down, and he pulled into it. It was the lower floor of a large parking garage. He turned around inside, pulled up behind the wall, and
stopped the van. Then he got out and carefully looked out the entrance

scl-s

toward the motel. From where he was he could see the door of his room. The brown sedan pulled up in front of his room, and two men got out. The tall man walked up from the direction of the office. Johnny saw them move to both sides of the door and pull their guns. Then the tall man pulled out a key, opened the door, and rushed inside.

The men were inside for just a moment and then came out quickly. The tall man went to the driver's side and pointed toward the freeway. The car sped off in the direction of the freeway entrance. Johnny broke into a sweat. He obviously had to go another direction.

Johnny drove slowly out of the parking garage and turned onto the street in the opposite direction from where the brown sedan had gone. He turned out onto the frontage road and headed down the street, looking for a freeway entrance.

In a couple of blocks he saw the sign, turned onto the freeway, and headed west. He watched the signs, looking for an exit north or south. In about a mile he saw a green sign that said INTERSTATE 77 SOUTH, AKRON, 1 MILE. The gloomy clouds had grown thicker, and a heavy drizzle was falling. He found the Akron exit and took it, heading south.

Within a few miles the wind picked up, and the sky opened. Torrential rain began to pour down. The lights of the cars coming toward him were blurs through the rain-covered windshield as the wipers labored to clear the water away. The van jerked as the wind struck it, and Johnny had to fight to stay on the road. He knew the men wouldn't have to go too far to figure out that he hadn't headed east. He had to get off the main road. As he drove through the rain, his heart was pounding, and his hands gripped the wheel until the knuckles turned white. In spite of the cold, he could feel sweat pouring off him.

"Help me, Jesus!" The words were torn from his constricted throat. "Help me, help me!"

Just then he saw a sign ahead. OH-21s, MASSILLON.

He jerked the wheel and took the exit at about forty-five, the worn tires of the van shrieking and protesting. In about ten minutes he saw another sign. OH-585s, WOOSTER.

Again he took the exit and headed toward Wooster. He was on a two-lane country road with crossroads coming in from the left and right. He turned off onto one that headed into a forested area. He kept going, looking through the rain for something, anything, a place of safety.

Up ahead he saw a break in the trees. A dirt road led into the woods, and he turned onto it. A hundred yards ahead of him were some buildings, but he couldn't see them clearly in the darkness. He drove slowly toward them and then pulled into a clearing.

In front of him were several ramshackle structures, including an old barn, some sheds, and a house that was falling down. He passed a faded sign that read FOR SALE, ACREAGE. The rain was blowing sideways now, and Johnny saw a few shingles tear off the house and disappear into the dark. An old windmill, just visible in the glow of the headlights, spun madly in the gusting wind.

Just ahead of him, the wide barn door was open and hanging on one hinge. The whole place was rundown, desolate, and clearly abandoned. He drove carefully through the open barn door and into the wide main floor area. He climbed out of the van and went back to the door. He could tell it had been hanging open for a long time, and weeds had grown up around it. He stepped out into the pouring rain and tried to pull it loose. It took some doing, but he finally worked it free and swung it closed. He stood in the dark, soaking wet. His heart was still pounding, and he was shaking from the cold.

Outside, the wind howled, and the rain beat down on the barn roof. He got his knapsack out of the van, rummaged around in it, and found his flashlight. It was an old Boy Scout flashlight he'd had for years, and a sudden memory came to him of happier times in the woods, sitting around campfires and laughing with other Scouts.

He turned it on and shined the beam around. He could see that the place was empty except for a few old saw blades and some strange utensils still hanging on the walls. As he shined the light up into the loft he heard the rustle of wings. He jumped.

Above him, a small flock of pigeons rose up in the beam of light from the rafters where they had been sitting and circled around the inside of the roof before settling back down on their roost. Rain was pouring in at the far end of the barn through a hole in the roof.

Johnny got out some dry clothes from his knapsack. Once he was changed, he looked around again. Some firewood was stacked in a bin on one side of the main room, and more dry wood and old boards were lying around. He gathered some up and piled them by the van. He searched through his knapsack until he found some matches and then built a small fire and pulled a couple of logs up next to it. He laid his wet clothes over the logs to dry and then looked in the car for some food. There were a couple of candy bars left and some chips and a warm can of Fresca that he had picked up at a gas station stop. He pulled a stump up by the fire and sat down. He sat by the flickering flames, munching on the chips and contemplating his close call.

Maybe if I meditate on my mantra I'll peace out.

Johnny sat down on the floor and assumed the position—legs folded and ankles crossed, hands resting on his knees with the thumb and first finger together and the last three fingers out straight. Then he began chanting the word he had learned from the guru who had lived next door in the Haight.

"Shrang, shrang, shrang…"

He chanted the word for a few minutes, but he couldn't settle into the relaxed state he normally found when he meditated. Instead, the barn seemed to grow darker, and a shiver went down his spine. Quickly he stopped.

Whoa! What was that?

Johnny looked around. He felt almost as if someone had come into the barn.

Then, without knowing why, he remembered that just before he found this hiding place, he had called out to Jesus.

That's interesting. I haven't said Jesus' name for years, not since Sunday school.

He lowered his head and spoke quietly. "Jesus, if it was You who helped me escape and find this hideout, thank You."

Then, for the first time in days, Johnny felt better. It was as though warmth slowly crept over him, and he felt his muscles finally relax.

A thought occurred to him. *Hide the money!*

Johnny stood up and looked around the barn. He grabbed one of the boards and broke it so it had a sharp point on it. He went to the pile of firewood and took several pieces out until the floor of the bin was exposed. The floorboards had rotted from sitting under the wood, and he easily broke through them. Under the floorboards the ground was dry and hard. Johnny went back to the van and got the briefcase and the sack.

I'm almost out of money. Maybe I'll borrow just a little from the stash.

Johnny counted out a thousand dollars and put it in his wallet. Then he put the paper bag back into the briefcase and closed it. He shoved the case under the floor of the bin and laid a few short boards over the hole. He stacked the firewood back up, being careful to leave the area as undisturbed as possible. He felt a little better, but he was still troubled. He needed help. He decided that in the morning he would drive to the closest town and turn himself in. Then the police could protect him or maybe capture the dealers.

Johnny threw another piece of wood on the fire and pulled the stump he was sitting on closer to the flames. Outside, the wind howled and the rain continued to pour.

CHAPTER SIX

Connection

JENNY SPRINGER WALKED DOWN LIBERTY STREET in Wooster toward the Wayne County Public Library. She had always been good at history and had recently completed an ambitious undertaking, detailing the historical roots of her family and their arrival in Apple Creek more than a hundred years earlier. The magnitude of the project caused her teacher to think Jenny might be of service to the Amish community by continuing her research.

At first her *daed* objected, but then Jerusha intervened, pointing out that one of the goals of Amish education is to teach children how to be valuable members of the Amish community. Reuben had finally given his consent, though with some misgivings.

Jenny loved the library and was so earnest in her studies that finally Mrs. Blake, the librarian, suggested she take on her current position as a research assistant, specializing in local history and genealogy. For two years Jenny went twice a week to Wooster. When she was baptized into the church, Reuben wanted her to quit her job, but some of the elders of the church saw value to the Amish community in her position and asked Reuben to reconsider. He did so reluctantly, and Jenny continued working at the library.

Jenny usually looked forward to her days at the library with great anticipation. The library had an exceptional department dealing with local history. Often she would spend the whole day in the basement, poring over the dusty tomes, organizing long lists of birth records, and tracing and detailing the influence of the Amish on Wayne County and the rest of Ohio. The hours would fly by, and finally Mrs. Blake would come to the top of the stairs and call down to her that it was closing time.

But there was no joy in her heart today. Today her thoughts were dark and gloomy, and she couldn't put the images from last night's nightmare out of her mind. The sky was overcast, there was a chilling bite on the fall wind, and it felt like it might rain. The day matched her mood.

In the morning after the big storm, Johnny Hershberger awoke slowly beside the burned-out fire, wrapped in an old blanket he had dug out of the back of the van. A chill had crept into the barn. In the dim light he could see the remains of the storm sailing by in a glowering sky through the hole in the barn roof. His hair felt greasy, and hunger gnawed at his belly. He dug through the knapsack to see if he had anything left to eat, but all he found was an empty potato chip bag. He got up, kicked at the fire to make sure it was out, and then packed his stuff into the van. He fired up the engine and drove slowly out of the barn. Leaves and tree limbs littered the clearing leading to the road. On the horizon, the sun was beginning to peek through the gray mass of clouds that still roiled overhead.

Johnny drove out to the road and turned back toward the main highway. When he got to the intersection he looked for directions.

Across the road was a sign that said WOOSTER, 4 MILES. He turned onto the road and headed toward town, making sure he remembered the turnoff so he could find his way back.

Soon he approached the outskirts of town. He saw a sign that said CITY CENTER. A man was walking along the sidewalk, so he pulled over and asked him the way to the sheriff's office. The man took one look at his van, pointed vaguely toward the next street, mumbled something unintelligible, and walked off, shaking his head.

Johnny turned onto Liberty Street and headed in the direction the sign pointed. After a few blocks, he saw another sign that said HOSPITAL, and below it, WAYNE COUNTY SHERIFF. He came to a red light and stopped. It changed to green, and he started to turn left off Liberty when someone stepped off the curb right in front of the van.

Without looking at the light, Jenny had stepped off the curb. She didn't see the vehicle making a left turn onto Walnut Street from Liberty. The driver honked his horn and swerved to avoid her, and the van screeched to a halt as it rammed one of its tires into the curb. The driver leaned out the window and yelled at her. "Hey, watch where you're going! I almost hit you."

"Well, if I remember correctly, pedestrians have the right of way!" Jenny called back.

"Yeah, they do if the light is in their favor," he said pointing toward the signal.

Jenny looked back at the light. The left turn arrow was green, but the pedestrian light still said WAIT. She felt herself wanting to say something nasty, but realizing she was in the wrong, she mumbled, "I'm sorry, I wasn't paying attention," and walked on.

"Wait a minute, are you okay? I guess I should have been more careful, even if the signal was in my favor."

He opened the door and got out. Jenny stopped and looked back. "I'm fine. A little startled, but fine."

For the first time, Jenny looked at the driver. He was tall and trim, and his long hair was pulled back into a ponytail. He wore a leather jacket with fringe hanging down, bell-bottom jeans and some kind of green boots. Then she saw that he was driving a blue Volkswagen van and that his van was covered with strange pictures pasted on the metal in a collage. There were flowers and strange foreign-looking men in very awkward positions. The largest picture was pasted on the driver's door. It was of a white-haired man in a white jacket with the words "Turn on, tune in, drop out" written below it. She looked back at the young man. She realized that he was very good looking, but his most striking feature was his eyes. They were deep sea-blue, and she could see a hint of a smile behind them. She felt herself being drawn into those eyes and had to pull herself back with a start.

His eyes—they are just like Papa's!

Jenny noticed that the young man was staring at her *kappe*. His eyes traveled down, taking in her face, and then her plain wool coat with the hooks instead of a zipper, and then the high-top laced shoes.

"Excuse me," he said. "Are you in a play or something?"

"What?" Jenny asked.

"A play," he said. "You're dressed like you're in a play."

"Right," Jenny retorted, feeling both a blush and an irritation rising up within her. "I'm one of the starving pilgrims and you must be Squanto, the Indian who saves us. But wait! The Indians didn't wear green boots or drive decorated trucks, so you must be one of those beatniks I've heard about. But I don't remember any beatniks at the first Thanksgiving, so I guess you're not in the play after all."

The young man smiled. "Whoa! Slow down! Beatniks dress in black and play bongos. I guess I'm what you folks would call a hippie, but in San Francisco I felt a little more local. Right this minute, I feel about as local as a fish in a tree."

He was trying to be smart, but instead he came off sounding very foolish. Jenny didn't miss the opening.

"Well, perhaps you should get a paint job for your truck and maybe trade in that jacket and those boots for a pair of overalls and some work shoes. Then maybe you'd feel a bit more local. And by the way, I'm Amish, and I dress this way every day, if it's any of your business."

The young man shrugged off Jenny's barbed remark and smiled again. "Listen, this isn't going well. I've never met anyone who is… Amish, and I didn't mean to offend you. Look, let's try another approach. I just got into town, and I've got a problem. I'm trying to find the sheriff's office. A guy down the street gave me directions, but they weren't really clear, and I'm wandering around in circles. Can you tell me where it is?"

Jenny pointed up Walnut Street. "You're not too far away. It's right up there on the corner of North and Walnut." She looked the young man over once more and then offered her assessment. "You're not in San Francisco, you know. I would make sure you don't have any of that stuff you hippies like to smoke before you go up there. My Uncle Bobby—*Sheriff* Bobby—doesn't take kindly to strangers who break the law."

"Your uncle is the sheriff? I thought the Amish were all pacifists."

"Well, he's not my biological uncle, but he's a very close friend of the family. He and my papa fought in the war together." *Why am I telling him this? Why was he so nosey?*

The young man cocked his head and looked at her. "Your dad is an Amish war vet?"

"Well," Jenny said, "it's actually none of your concern, so it doesn't really matter, does it?"

"Hey, it's okay," the young man replied softly. "I'm not trying to pry. It's just interesting, that's all. Can we start again?"

He stuck out his hand. "I'm Johnny Hershberger. I just happened to be driving through Wooster and almost ran you down…"

Jenny could feel his eyes study her face.

"…and I'm a great believer in destiny. What's your name?"

Jenny hesitated for a minute. She was put off by the young man's brashness, but the fact that his name was Hershberger appealed to the historical researcher in her. She put out her hand hesitantly and took his.

"I'm Jenny Springer. I'm from Apple Creek. It's interesting to me that your name is Hershberger—that's my mother's maiden name."

"Is she Amish too?" Johnny asked.

"Well of course she is," said Jenny with a toss of her head. "What else would she be?"

"I'm sorry, that was a dumb question. Of course she's Amish. It's just that I'm a Hershberger and I'm not. Amish, that is…not Amish."

"Well, that's obvious," Jenny said with a small smile, momentarily forgetting her irritation. "Still, all the Hershbergers I know are Amish. Don't you know anything about your family history?"

"Not really," Johnny replied. "My dad never talked about it, and my mom was too occupied with her club socials to ever sit down with me and talk family history. So I'm pretty much clueless about the previous generations."

Jenny looked at Johnny. She knew she could help him find out about his family. It would be so easy. *Wait a minute—I don't even know who this man is.*

Suddenly she realized that she was still holding his hand. She pulled her hand back abruptly, and then she felt herself blush. She looked down so he wouldn't see her face.

"Did I upset you?" he asked seriously, but she could hear the laughter in the question. "You seem to be blushing."

"It's just that I'm not used to holding hands with every strange man I meet on the street, especially after he's tried to kill me with his stupid truck."

"It's not a truck, it's a van," Johnny laughed.

Jenny felt the irritation rising up in her again. She turned on her heel and headed toward the library.

Johnny started after her. "Wait, I'm sorry. Please don't go."

Just then a big delivery van tried to turn onto North Street and almost hit Johnny's van, which was blocking the way. The driver slammed on his brakes and honked impatiently and rolled down his window.

"Get that hippie wagon out of the way," the driver shouted, looking at Johnny with a jaundiced eye.

Johnny hesitated, wanting to go after Jenny, but then he shrugged his shoulders, turned back, and climbed into the van.

"Hey, peace out, brother," he shouted out the window, making the peace sign with his two upraised fingers.

"I'll peace you out, you freak. Why don't you go back to the Worst Coast where you belong? You won't find it very comfortable around here. Now move that van before I shove it the rest of the way off the street."

"Okay, I'm moving it, I'm moving it."

Johnny started the van up and backed off the curb. He pulled out of the way of the delivery van, and as he did he noticed a distinct vibration from the front end of his van. He watched the belligerent truck driver move past him, and then he got back out of his van to check his front right wheel. He knew something must have bent when he ran up on the curb. He got down on his hands and knees and looked behind the wheel. He couldn't see anything obvious, but he knew that something needed fixing. He decided that after he went to see the sheriff, he would find a mechanic—if the police didn't put him in custody first.

He stood and then remembered Jenny. He looked down the street where she had gone, but the strangely dressed girl was nowhere to be seen.

CHAPTER SEVEN

Old Friends

◇◇◇

BOBBY HALVERSON PULLED UP in front of the plain brown concrete building and turned off the motor of his sheriff's cruiser. It was a crisp fall day, and last night's rain had washed the air clean. Bobby got out of the car, walked up the steps, and headed through the wide glass doors. He was a well-built, trim man of forty-eight with a thick shock of sandy hair. He couldn't be described as handsome, but his face was genial and friendly, and smile wrinkles surrounded his eyes. He walked with the upright bearing of a soldier, which made him look taller than his six feet, and except for a slight bulge around the middle, he was in good shape. His service revolver hung at his hip, and his khaki pants were pressed and neat. He wore a brown bomber jacket with a Wayne County Sheriff's Department badge sewed on the shoulder and a beige Stetson hat. As he walked down the hall toward his office, friendly faces popped out of cubicles and small offices.

"Mornin', Sheriff."

"How's it goin', Sheriff?"

"Hi ya, Bobby! How are you today?"

Bobby answered each of the queries with a tip of his hat and a smile.

After ten years as sheriff, he still hadn't gotten used to all the fuss. He turned the corner past the reception area and walked into the spacious corner room that was the office of the sheriff of Wayne County, Ohio.

Bobby closed the door behind him and looked around. The room was large and bright with windows on all the outside walls. A big dark mahogany desk covered with books and stacks of paper faced the door. A large chair sat behind the desk, and another one sat in front of it for guests. A heavy gun safe and a filing cabinet stood against the wall by the door. Next to the safe was a tall bookshelf made of cherry wood. A picture of his mom and dad as well as photos of some of Bobby's favorite spots around Wooster and Apple Creek sat on the shelf in front of the books.

The middle shelf had a built-in case with glass doors. In the case, on a board covered in black velvet, was a red, white, and blue ribbon with a five-pointed gold star hanging from it. A small brass plaque was mounted below the star. He walked over and read the words again. "To Sergeant Robert Halverson, for distinguished gallantry in action against an enemy of the United States."

Next to the medal was a faded black-and-white Kodak picture. It was stained and smudged, and one corner had been folded over and was almost torn off. In the picture were three tired-looking Marines in combat fatigues with a grizzle of beard on their faces. They were dirty and battle worn. One of the men was Bobby. The man in the middle was tall and dark-haired, very stern looking, with piercing eyes. His helmet tilted rakishly to one side of his head, and the strap hung loosely by his face. Next to him stood the tallest of the three men, a big, powerful-looking man with a crew cut and the triple chevrons of a master gunnery sergeant on his uniform sleeve. He was so tall he had to lean down to get into the picture. He had one hand on the shoulder of the man in the middle and a Thompson submachine gun cradled in his other arm. Bobby and the dark-haired man both held rifles with large scopes mounted on them. The caption on the white space under the picture, written in pencil, said, "Marine Sniper Scout Platoon 4, Guadalcanal, August 1942."

Bobby looked at the photo for a minute or two and then slowly drew to attention and saluted. He stood and held the salute silently for a moment and then turned back to his desk. He pulled off his leather jacket and hung it on the coatrack in the corner and stuck his hat on top. He smiled to himself and sat down in the comfortable chair. As he sat there he had to resist the impulse to put his feet up on the big desk.

Even though he had been sheriff for ten years, he still felt a little out of place as a peace officer. After he was mustered out of the Marines, Bobby came back to Apple Creek and slipped into his old routine. He got his construction job back and tried to settle into his old patterns. But he hadn't really fit in anywhere until this job came along. He had never intended to run for any office, but he was well liked and well known throughout Wayne County, so when the sheriff retired in 1955, the local businessmen, especially around Wooster, Dalton, and Apple Creek, drafted him to run.

He had stiff competition from the man who had been the old sheriff's chief deputy, but just when the race seemed to be going to his opponent, help came from an unexpected quarter. Bobby had been a good friend to the Amish folk in Wayne County for many years, and though they didn't often vote in elections, a surprising number of the local Amish registered and voted for Bobby. It was enough to turn the tide, and Bobby Halverson was elected sheriff.

In the ensuing years, Bobby became one of the most popular sheriffs in Wayne County history and for good reason. He was a war hero who was fair and impartial in his dealings with people, yet he was not afraid to step in when force of action was needed. Bobby prided himself in the fact that he had never shot anyone. Instead, he had often been able to defuse unpleasant situations with a smile and a slap on the back.

The only trouble he ever really had was when he was first elected and some small-time gangsters came to Wooster to set up their operations. Bobby proved to be harder to handle than they had figured, and after they cooled their heels in the local jail for a few weeks, they left town. After that things stayed fairly peaceful in Wayne County.

Bobby had also been smart enough to keep his opponent in the election—a big, gruff ex-serviceman named Bull Halkovich—on his staff as chief deputy. Bull was good natured, he liked Bobby, and he took his defeat with grace. Bobby relied on Bull to show him the ropes, and the two men became a good team and, in due time, close friends.

Bobby started going through a stack of paperwork on his desk. This was the part of the job he liked the least. He was most effective when he was out in his cruiser, keeping an eye on things and dealing with people face-to-face.

He looked at the first case on the top of the stack and stifled a yawn. "Well, you pay your money and you take your choice," he said out loud and started in. Two hours later he was halfway through the stack when the intercom on his desk buzzed.

"What's up, Jill?" he asked, glad for the diversion.

"Someone to see you, Boss," answered his receptionist.

"Who is it?" Bobby asked.

"It's an Amish gentleman," Jill replied coyly.

Bobby brightened, knowing it could only be one man, especially on this particular day.

"Well, send him in, Jill" Bobby said with a laugh. "Don't keep the poor man cooling his heels."

A moment later the door opened and Reuben Springer walked in.

"How'd you get over here from Apple Creek?" without looking up from his paperwork.

"Same as always. Henry Lowenstein brought me," Reuben answered gruffly.

"Don't you think you're old enough to get your own car?" Bobby asked as he laid down his pen and looked up.

After all the years Bobby had known him, Reuben Springer still looked the same. The guy could have been a movie star. Reuben stared intently at Bobby, and then the stern features cracked into a wide grin, and the two men started laughing.

"It's good to see you too, you old barn rat," the man said as Bobby stood up and walked around the desk.

The two men gripped hands firmly and looked at each other. As they did, something passed between them that is shared only by men who have faced great trials together. The man pulled Bobby into a bear hug and then put his hands on Bobby's shoulders and looked him over.

"You're still taking nourishment, I see," he said. "Maybe a bit too much. Your mom still as good a cook as ever?"

"Well, Reuben," Bobby said, "I must admit that it's awful hard to pass on a second piece of her strawberry-rhubarb pie, if that's what you mean. It's good to see you too, especially today."

"September thirteen, nineteen forty-two. Twenty-three years ago today. Some things aren't easy to forget," Reuben said as he glanced at the picture in the case.

The two men walked over to the bookcase and looked at the faded picture. Finally Bobby spoke. "It seems like a lifetime ago, doesn't it?"

Reuben was silent for another moment, and then he spoke, his voice breaking. "Ed Thompkins was a real man and a real soldier. He taught me many things, and in the end he laid down his life to save us both. If he hadn't jumped on that grenade, neither one of us would be standing here."

Bobby stepped over to the desk and opened the bottom drawer. "I never drink on the job, but I thought today it might be all right to offer a toast. Care to join me?"

"Well, it's not usually my cup of tea, but considering the day and the man, I will," Reuben said.

Bobby pulled a small bottle of brandy and two glasses out of the drawer. Reuben smiled again. "So you think you know me well enough to bring an extra glass, do you?" he asked.

"Yep," said Bobby.

He poured two small shots and offered one to Reuben. They stood silently in front of the case for a moment and then Bobby lifted his glass. "Here's to you, Gunnery Sergeant Edgar Thompkins, good soldier, fighting Marine, and our friend. Semper Fi!"

Reuben lifted his glass in salute, and the men drank the toast. Reuben handed his glass to Bobby and smiled. "It's a good thing nobody walked in just then," he said. "I'm sure they would have found it very interesting to come upon the sheriff having a drink with one of the local Amish."

Bobby smiled and motioned Reuben to the chair in front of the desk. "You can stay a bit, right? It would be good to catch up."

Reuben nodded and sat down. Bobby sat in his chair, and the two men sat for another quiet moment.

"How's Jerusha?" Bobby asked. "And Jenny?"

"The girls are doing well. Jerusha is still as beautiful as the first day I saw her, and Jenny is growing up into a delightful woman."

"Is she still as rambunctious as ever?" Bobby asked with a smile.

"Jenny does tend to rush in where angels fear to tread, but she's been a joy and a great comfort to us since Jenna died," Reuben said. "I love her like my own flesh and blood. I've always been amazed when I remember the way God sent her to us. And I will never forget the part you played in finding the two of them in that storm."

"Does that mean you're going to buy me lunch today?" Bobby asked with a grin.

"Is there a serious bone in your body?" Reuben asked.

"Sure, but in this job, I try not to wear my heart on my sleeve. I think you know that besides my mom and dad, you, Jerusha, and Jenny are the only family I have. And that girl is precious to me too. Is that serious enough?"

Reuben sighed. He loved this man more dearly than a brother, but Bobby wasn't one to reveal his deepest feelings very often. Reuben's thoughts went back to the fall of 1950, when he and Jerusha were separated after Jenna's death and Bobby had been a loyal and steadfast friend. He had searched for Jerusha for three days in the middle of the worst storm Ohio had ever seen. And when Jerusha had found Jenny lost in the storm and the Springers adopted her, Bobby had transferred all the love he had focused on their first child, Jenna, to Jenny.

"Twenty-three years ago, we were heading up to the top of that ridge on that hellhole of an island to fight the decisive battle of that whole campaign," Bobby said. "If the Japanese had gotten past us and retaken Henderson field, we might not be sitting here today."

Reuben winced and then moved past the memory.

"Still bother you to think about it, Reuben?" Bobby asked.

"*Es ist schwierig, es zu vergessen*," Reuben said. "It is difficult to forget. I used to have bad dreams about it, but in the last few years the whole scene seems to have faded from my memory, for which I am grateful. I don't know whether it's because I'm getting older or if I've just figured out how to block it from my thoughts."

"For sure it's because you're getting older," Bobby said and then smiled. "Actually, Reuben, I have had the same dreams. I don't think it's something you really ever get over."

The two men sat silently for a moment, remembering the horror of the battle, the explosions, the cries of wounded and dying men, and the Japanese soldiers coming at them in wave after wave.

"Ever since I figured out that I needed to trust God instead of just following the rules, I've found a great comfort in my faith," Reuben said. "How do you deal with it?"

"Now, Reuben, you know where I stand," Bobby said. "I've always been glad that you've found solace in your church. But I just have never quite figured this whole God thing out. I'll probably wait the rest of my life and then be a death-bed penitent."

"I pray that you'll come to faith before then, my friend," Reuben said, holding Bobby's gaze.

"Come on," Bobby said as he jumped up and grabbed his coat and hat. "Let's go have some lunch. I'll drive."

"Ha-ha," Reuben said. "Very funny. By the way, Bobby, I have something important to talk to you about over lunch. It's about Jenny. I'm in need of your help."

CHAPTER EIGHT

Come Find Me

◇◇◇

JENNY WAS WATCHING FROM THE LOBBY of the library as the young man in the blue van drove past. For some strange reason she wanted to run out and stop him. Her meeting with Johnny Hershberger had been strange and disconcerting. He had made her feel uncomfortable and nice at the same time. She remembered looking into his eyes and starting to lose herself in them. She still felt the touch of his hand on hers, so she shoved the offending member into her pocket and tried to scrub the memory off against the wool lining.

"What's going on?" she asked out loud. "I'm having crazy dreams, I'm remembering weird things from my childhood, I'm telling everything about my life to complete strangers…"

A library patron, hurrying past, gave Jenny a very strange glance.

…*and now I'm talking to myself!*

She stopped her thoughts and took a breath. She felt as if her life were spiraling out of control, and she realized that it might be a good idea to pray. But the idea made her uncomfortable when she remembered that she hadn't prayed in a week, so she quickly bowed her head and whispered. "Lord, I'm feeling a little *verblüfft*, and I need Your help, I guess. Can You give me some help here please? Amen."

Jenny looked up and looked around. No one had noticed her praying, but it hadn't been much of a prayer anyway. She glanced back out the glass door. The blue van was no longer in sight, and she didn't know which way it had gone.

She turned and walked toward the little desk that Mrs. Blake had given her in the back of the building. She decided to bury herself in her work all day and not think of the things that were troubling her anymore. She came to her desk, pulled off her coat, and hung it on the rack beside her cabinet. She pulled out her chair, sat down, and attacked the stack of historical material on her desk. But even as she worked, two images kept coming to her mind. One was a pair of sea-blue eyes that drew her deep into their unknown depths, and the other was a woman's face.

The woman's words echoed in Jenny's head. "Jenny, come find me. I'm lost, so lost."

◇◇◇

Later that afternoon, Jenny was still sitting at her desk. She had tried to work on a project with a fast-approaching deadline but hadn't been able to make any headway. Her thoughts kept drifting back to the dying woman. Jenny remembered her face being beautiful. She had long black hair, and her eyes were deep and dark, almost black.

Maybe that wasn't my mother. My eyes are violet, not dark.

As Jenny tried to recall everything she could about the woman, the words kept coming back to her. "Jenny, come find me. I'm lost, so lost," she whispered to herself.

Jenny wondered what that meant. Why was she lost? Where was she lost from? Then Jenny remembered something Papa said about the car where Mama found her. The car was from New York, and the police found a man in the pond with the sunken car. She thought about the man and wondered if he was her real father. Jenny didn't like the thought. The man had tried to hurt her. She decided to look through the old newspaper files at the library for stories that could tell her more about the dead man.

Jenny put her unfinished project back in the file folder and then carried it with her up to the front desk. Mrs. Blake was checking in returned books. She was an older lady with white hair and pointy Harlequin glasses that hung on a chain around her neck when she wasn't putting them on her nose to peer at the paperwork in front of her. Jenny waited while Mrs. Blake finished checking in a copy of *Swiss Family Robinson*. Mrs. Blake looked up from her work and noticed Jenny standing there.

"Hi, sweetie. Do you need something?"

"Mrs. Blake, is anyone using the microfiche this morning? I need to do some research on my project, and I have to check the old newspaper and magazine files."

Jenny felt a small check in her heart. Great—now she was lying to her friend. Maybe Papa was right. Maybe the whole pursuit of her past would only bring heartache. She felt a surge of guilt about lying to her papa and to Mrs. Blake, and she wondered where else her newly acquired sin would take her.

The librarian smiled and said, "No one's using it right now, honey. You can have it until someone comes in and asks for it."

Jenny's need to know about the dead man in the car that night overpowered the quiet voice in her spirit, and she took the key to the microfiche room from Mrs. Blake's hand and headed down the hall. In the room she placed her folder by the reader and then went over to the wall of filing cabinets where the film was kept.

Now how did that all go? The big storm was in the fall of 1950. The police located the car in the pond the next spring, and while they were removing it, they found the man's body.

She decided to look through the files for articles from early 1951 in the *Daily Record*, Wooster's local paper. She pulled all the film for the months she wanted and then sat down at the reader and began to work. It took her about an hour, but at last she found an article in the April 4 edition of the paper.

Local Police Locate Dead Body in Jepson's Pond
BY BOB SCHUMANN

The Wayne County Sheriff's Department discovered a dead man in Jepson's Pond near Dalton. The body was in a severe state of decomposition. Police were unable to take any fingerprints, and no means of identification was found, so the identity of the man remains a mystery.

The body was located while officers were removing a sunken car from the pond. According to sources in the department, the car had been in the pond since the Thanksgiving Day storm. Local resident and war hero, Bobby Halverson, reported the sunken car in November, but authorities had to wait until the ice melted this month before they could send divers to investigate. While searching the pond for the car, the divers came upon the remains of the dead man.

Halverson told this reporter that he and Reuben Springer, a member of the Apple Creek Amish community, found the car on the ice while searching for Springer's wife, Jerusha, who was lost in the storm, but that they did not know about the man in the pond.

The car slid into the pond when the ice broke as the two men were retrieving a battery from the vehicle during their successful rescue of Mrs. Springer.

In an unusual addendum to the story, it was also learned by this reporter that Mrs. Springer found a small child in the car two days earlier. She took the little girl to the abandoned cabin near the pond during the height of the storm and kept her alive while awaiting rescue. The identity of the child was unknown, and it remains to be seen whether the man found in the pond was any relation to the little girl or if there was even any connection between the man and the car.

In the meantime, the child was first given to the State Child Welfare Agency and then, following the Springers' application, placed in foster care in the Springer home. Mr. Springer is also well known in the area as a winner of the Congressional Medal of Honor on Guadalcanal during the Pacific campaign before returning to the Amish faith after the war.

Mrs. Springer is an Amish quilter of some renown in Wayne County.

Jenny read on. There were a few more details about the make of the car, and then she saw that the reporter had put in the license plate number—SN12-66. Jenny looked to see if there were any follow-up articles and found one written a month later.

Dead Man's Identity Remains a Mystery
BY BOB SCHUMANN

An investigation concerning the identity of the dead man found in Jepson's Pond in April has proved fruitless. Police investigators working out of the Wayne County Sheriff's Department have been unable to find any clues concerning the man or what he was doing when he drowned in the pond.

The officers believe the man was probably driving the car and was involved in an accident that caused the car to slide off the road and onto the frozen pond. Skid marks, broken trees, and pieces of the car led from Highway 30 to the pond.

When they traced the license plate, officers discovered that the car was reported stolen in New York, and efforts beyond that have reached a dead end. Police also discovered empty liquor bottles and unknown substances sealed in plastic bags in the car. It is believed that the substances were illegal drugs.

Meanwhile, the girl who was found in the car by Mrs. Reuben Springer remains in foster care at the Springer home. The girl's name is Jenny, and the Springers report that she is doing very well. The Springers have applied to the courts to adopt the child, and local agencies support their application. Mrs. Springer says they are only waiting for any relatives to come forward and claim the child, but at this point, none are forthcoming.

Jenny leaned back in the chair and took a deep breath. A terrible fear that the man might be her father crept into her heart. She had always been afraid that she was a bad seed, that there was something in her that would cause her to disgrace her mama and papa. Jenny went back to the first article. The license plate was the only clue that showed promise. No identification, no fingerprints…it all seemed hopeless to Jenny. Suddenly the words of the woman in her dream came back to her so strongly she could hardly breathe.

Jenny, come find me. I'm lost, so lost.

Jenny put her face in her hands and quietly wept. After a few minutes, she sat up and wiped her eyes with the sleeve of her dress. Jenny could feel a resolve building in her heart.

"I'm going to find my real mother. I just have to," she said out loud. "But where do I start?"

Then she had an idea. Maybe Uncle Bobby could help her! He was the sheriff. He could reopen the investigation and maybe find out where the car was stolen and who owned it. Maybe the real owner of the car would know something. Another thought came to her, and she jotted down a note to call Mr. Schumann, the man who wrote the articles, to see if he had discovered anything else.

Jenny realized she had to solve this mystery, or her life would never be right. Regardless of what her papa had said to her, she knew she had to do this. If she didn't, she would struggle with the questions her whole life. She had to find out who she was.

Jenny checked her purse. She had a few dollars and some change. Quickly she packed up the microfilm and replaced it in the file. She went to the front desk and told Mrs. Blake she was taking a break. Then she took her notes and left. A row of phone booths stood along the curb in front of the library, and she went into one. She thought about calling Uncle Bobby but remembered he was having lunch with her papa. So she picked up the phone book hanging on a chain from the wall and looked up the number of the *Daily Record*. She dialed it, and a woman's voice answered.

"The *Daily Record*, how may I assist you?" the woman asked.

"Hello. Does Mr. Bob Schumann still write for the paper?" Jenny asked.

"Mr. Schumann retired a few years ago, but he drops by from time to time. He's what we call our editor emeritus. And you're in luck because he happens to be here today. Let me connect you."

After a moment's silence, a gruff voice said, "Bob Schumann here."

Jenny hesitated. She knew that if she started down this path, she would have to go wherever it took her, and a momentary fear of the future and what might happen to her family choked her up.

"Hello, Bob Schumann here," the man said again.

Jenny took a deep breath and plunged ahead. "Mr. Schumann, my name is Jenny Springer. My parents are Reuben and Jerusha Springer. Fifteen years ago you wrote an article about a dead man who was found in Jepson's Pond and a little girl who had been rescued from the car the man was driving. I'm that little girl."

"Well, for goodness sake," Schumann said, his voice softening. "That was a long time ago. Quite an interesting story. Say, how did you know the man was driving the car? There were so few clues as to his identity, the police could never even definitely connect him with the car."

"I remember that night," answered Jenny. "The man was driving the car, and he wrecked it when he tried to reach back and grab me. Then when he tried to get me out of the car, he fell through the ice."

"You say you remember?" Schumann asked. "You were only four years old. How can you remember that far back?"

"Mr. Schumann, I don't know how I remember, but all I know is that over the past few days, the details have become more and more clear in my mind," Jenny said. "But the man is not the issue. Somewhere to be found in this whole mystery is the identity of my birth mother. It has become very important to me that I find out who she is and why I was alone with that man in the car that night. I don't know if he was my father—he might have been—but I do know that my mother was associated with him somehow and that she was very, very sad about something in her life. And I can't rest until I find out what it was that caused her so much pain."

"What did you say your name was?" Schumann said.

"I'm Jenny, Jenny Springer. You wrote about me being placed with my mama and papa—Reuben and Jerusha Springer—and about my adoption."

"Oh yes, Jenny. Did they adopt you?"

"Yes they did, and they have been wonderful parents. But now I need to know more."

"Yes," Mr. Schumann said. "That story always bothered me. There was never a conclusion to it, and I like to have conclusions to my stories.

It was maybe the one story of my career that I never got the answer to my questions. Jenny, we need to talk."

"I'm working at the library today," Jenny said. "We could meet now, if you're available…in the microfiche room?"

"I'll be over in fifteen minutes."

CHAPTER NINE

Roadblocks

◇◇◇

BOBBY AND REUBEN WALKED INTO EILEEN'S on the Square in down-town Wooster. The waitress who met them at the door smiled and grabbed two menus.

"Hi ya, Sheriff," she said with a quick wink. "Any place special you two want to sit?"

"Over by the window would be fine, Jolene," Bobby answered.

They made their way to the back of the restaurant, Jolene leading the way like a pilot dolphin. As they passed tables, people nodded and smiled, reached out to shake Bobby's hand, or nodded at Reuben.

"People here know you, Reuben," Bobby said.

"That's from growing up here. I used to cut a pretty wide swath through Wooster when I was younger."

Jolene got them to their table, dropped the menus and, after asking whether they wanted coffee, headed off to the kitchen.

"Do you ever miss those days, Reuben?" Bobby asked, setting down the menu.

"What days?"

"You know, the days when you were cutting a wide swath through Wooster," Bobby said.

Reuben looked at his friend and smiled. "Bobby, you became my friend at a very difficult time of my life," he said. "I wouldn't be baptized, my family wouldn't speak to me, and I was pretty sure that God didn't even exist. I was finished with being Amish. When I joined the Marines with you, I did it because I believed you when you said that everyone had an obligation to stand up and defend the country that provided them with blessings found nowhere else on earth. I don't regret serving my country. What I deeply regret is killing the men I faced across those trenches. They were men just like you and me, and they deserved to live out their lives with their wives and children."

Reuben reached into his pocket and pulled out his wallet. In the back section was a piece of paper. He pulled it out. It was a photo of a young Japanese man in the uniform of the Imperial Army. He was standing beside a lovely Japanese woman. She was dressed in a traditional kimono and holding a small boy. The man was stiff, very military in his bearing, and looking straight at the camera. The woman was looking up at the man, and it was plain that she loved and admired her husband.

"I found this picture on the body of the sniper I killed that day you and I and Thompkins were on patrol. This man had a family—a wife who obviously loved him and a son who grew up without ever knowing his father. Bobby, this man could have been me or you or any of us who fought in that war. I've kept it with me all these years to remind me that it's wrong to kill other men. I've never been able to forget the surprised look on his dead face when I turned him over on that jungle floor. So no, I don't miss any of that. And as for the wide swath I cut, some of it with your able help I might add, I just chalk that up to sheer stupidity. And if you think about it, I'm sure you'll agree with me."

Bobby smiled ruefully and then glanced around. "Don't tell any of my old drinking buddies, Reuben, but I have to admit you're right. The only good thing about the good ol' days is that they're gone."

Jolene glided back to the table with two cups of hot coffee. She put them down on the table and then pulled a pad out of her apron pocket and a pencil from behind her ear.

"What'll it be, boys?" she asked.

Bobby picked up the menu. "You're going to have to give me some more time. We got to talking."

"Sure, take your time," Jolene said, and then she left.

Both men perused their menus for a few moments. Bobby peered over his and asked, "So, what was it you wanted to talk to me about?"

Reuben closed his menu and looked over at Bobby. "I need to ask you some questions about the car Jerusha found Jenny in, and I need to find out what you know about the man they discovered in the pond."

"That's a long time ago, and remember, I wasn't sheriff yet." Bobby said, looking back at the lunch menu.

"Well, did you ever do any investigation? I mean, just out of curiosity? After all, you're as close to her as a biological uncle."

Jolene returned, pencil and pad in hand.

Bobby handed her his menu. "Hot turkey sandwich with a side of fries, Jolene, and I'm fine with the coffee."

Reuben nodded. "Sounds good, Jolene. That's what I'll have also."

Jolene picked up the menus and headed for the counter to put the order in.

Bobby turned back to Reuben. "Since you ask so direct, the answer is yes, I did do a little investigating. I was reorganizing the old sheriff's files, and I came across that folder, so I sat down and read through it. As I remember it, the car was stolen in New York. The owner was contacted, but since it was totaled and had been in the water for five months, he didn't want the car back, so it went to the junkyard and was scrapped.

"The police and sheriff's departments had gone over the car and made some interesting discoveries. There were several glassine bags in the glove compartment that had stayed sealed under the water. The bags contained an unknown substance. The lab boys determined that it was heroin. I believe there were also some empty bottles. That, along with the hypodermic needle in a nice little kit, convinced the investigators that whoever was driving the car either used or sold drugs and drank a lot. Not a lot to go on."

Reuben interrupted. "What about the man in the pond?"

"I was coming to that," Bobby said. "The investigators can't be sure that the man in the pond was even connected with the car. More than likely he was, but there's nothing to link the man and the car together."

"Was there any identification, anything that could be traced, that would help determine who the man was?"

"None," Bobby replied. "The only thing that was unusual was a pretty spectacular tattoo—the kind you see the Navy boys sporting, with two flags on each side, the Statue of Liberty in the middle, and the words 'God Bless America' on the top. It was pretty deteriorated, but it was big enough to figure out what it was. Still, he would have to have a criminal record with the tattoo listed as an identifying mark to be able to trace him with it. And that's a needle in a haystack because there were probably thousands of guys with that tattoo. As far as fingerprints, his fingers were mush, and it was impossible to get any prints from him. The whole story is pretty much a dead end, really."

Bobby paused for a minute and then asked a question. "So, my old friend, why do you want to know all this? I thought it was a closed case as far as you and Jerusha were concerned."

"Yes, it is all in the past. Jerusha and I seldom think about it."

"What then?" Bobby asked.

Reuben looked down at the table. "It's Jenny. She's been pestering us with questions, and the whole issue of who she really is has become of great importance to her. Her head is filled with all kinds of fantasies about the possibilities."

Just then Jolene returned with lunch balanced on her arms. She bent down and slid the first plate of turkey in front of Bobby and then handed Reuben the other one.

"Hot plates," she said with a grin.

"Didn't seem to bother you any," Bobby said.

"I'm a tough old biddy," Jolene answered as she headed off.

"Back to Jenny," Bobby said.

"I think Jenny is going to ask you to help her find out about the man and the car," Reuben said slowly.

"What if she does?"

"I'm asking you not to help her. I'm afraid for Jenny. She's headstrong and determined, and this crazy idea of hers could lead her to places she doesn't need to know about. If she comes to you, I'm asking you to put roadblocks in her way, to hedge her in. The world isn't for Jenny. She belongs with us, with her Amish family, in Apple Creek. I've seen what's out there, and I know that the plain way is best, especially for Jenny."

"But, Reuben," Bobby said, "she's almost grown up. You can't run her life forever."

"Our way is different from the *Englisch* way. We want our girls to be safe and secure while they're at home and unspoiled when they marry. As long as Jenny is under my roof, I'm responsible for her. When she marries, I will hand that responsibility over to her husband."

"Can I remind you of something, old friend?" Bobby asked quietly.

"I know what you're going to say. Yeah, I do feel most secure when I have rules to follow. Call it a weakness if you want, but to me, it can also be a strength. But, in spite of what you might think about me, I'm not trying to impose my rules on Jenny for the sake of having my own way. It's because she's my daughter, like flesh and blood to me. I love her very much, and to the extent that I can, I want to keep her from the pain."

Bobby looked at Reuben. There were tears brimming in his eyes. Reuben quickly wiped them away with his sleeve.

"Okay, Reuben," he said, "I'll do what I can. But Jenny is head-strong. I may not be able to keep her from finding things out on her own."

"I'll worry about that part," Reuben said. "I'm only asking you to intervene if she comes to you. I'm not asking you to lie, I'm just asking that you not volunteer information or lead her down a path that will start her thinking. She's a very intelligent girl, and if she gets on a scent, she is relentless. I know it's awkward for you because I also know how much you love her too."

Bobby took a bite of his turkey and sat silently chewing it. "If Jenny asks, I'll only tell her what she could read in the newspaper. After all, she works at the library, and if what you say is true about her determi-nation to find her birth parents, she's probably already way ahead of me. I won't volunteer any information, but that's about all I can do."

"That's enough for now," Reuben replied. "And I thank you for your help."

Bobby poured some cream into his coffee and stirred it thought-fully. "Sure, Reuben, it's not a problem. I want the best for her too."

CHAPTER TEN

A Helping Hand

◇◇◇

JOHNNY DROVE SLOWLY AROUND THE BLOCK and then circled it again, trying to find that Amish girl he had almost hit. After a while he gave up and turned the van back onto Walnut Street and headed in the direction Jenny had pointed. She had said the sheriff's office was at the corner of Walnut and North. After he had driven a few blocks he came to North Street and saw the building across the street.

Johnny pulled up to the curb. He wanted to get out and go in and tell the first person he saw about what had happened in San Francisco, but the possibility of being put in jail himself dampened his enthusiasm. He started to open the van door but paused, debating whether he should really do this. Things seemed a little less urgent in the daylight.

As he sat there he heard a car pull up behind him. His heart jumped, and he looked back. A big man in a large Stetson hat, dark sunglasses, with a gun on his hip was getting out of a sheriff's cruiser. The man walked slowly up to the van and stood by the window as Johnny rolled it down.

"Yes, officer, can I help you?"

"Got any ID, son?" the sheriff asked.

"Idee 'bout what?" Johnny asked.

The officer stared at him impassively.

"It's a joke, officer," Johnny said as he reached into his coat pocket for his wallet. He opened it, took out his New York driver's license, and handed it to the officer. He noticed that the big man had a nametag that read Bull pinned to his light-brown shirt.

Appropriate!

"You're a long way from home, son. Which way are you headed?"

"Well, actually, officer, I'm headed to Nashville," Johnny lied. "I've got some gigs down there playing with a band."

"I didn't know they had any psycho-dylic bands in Nashville." The officer attempted to smile at what he obviously thought was a joke, but the expression was more frightening than friendly.

"Oh, don't be fooled by this outfit, officer," Johnny smiled. He lied again. "I've been out in San Francisco, and I wore these clothes while I was playing in the coffeehouses. This is not really my thing."

"Well, if it's not your thing maybe you should change it to a more inconspicuous thing because you certainly attracted my attention, young man," Bull said. "We don't see many folks dressed like you or driving such an artistically decorated vehicle around here. If you pass muster with me, I would suggest you follow your dream and head on down to Nashville. Not a lot of tolerance around here for hippies."

"Have I done something wrong, officer?"

Without looking up from Johnny's license, the sheriff pointed silently to a sign on a pole next to the van. NO STOPPING AT ANY TIME.

"Wait here while I run your ID."

Johnny watched as the big man walked back to his car. The fear of the police among the drug users in San Francisco caused a familiar paranoia to close in on him. It occurred to him that he might be going to jail whether he wanted to or not. In about five minutes Bull came back. He handed Johnny's license back through the window.

"Well, no warrants or tickets as far as I can tell, but then we don't have access to all the modern tools. Now like I said, Wooster is a small town, and you might not fit in here very well. Nashville seems like the place for you, and I would go there ASAP. I'm not going to give you a ticket because that would mean you would have to stick around for traffic court, so a big window of opportunity to move on just opened up for you, son, and if I were you, I'd drive through it."

"I would like to, officer, but I have a small problem," Johnny said. "You see, back down the street a girl in funny clothes stepped out in front of me while I was making a turn. I don't think she was watching where she was going, and I had to swerve to keep from hitting her. I ran up on the curb, and I think I bent my suspension. Do you know a shop where I might get it looked at?"

Bull looked at Johnny suspiciously.

"The best shop is Dutch's in Apple Creek. It's about eight miles. Can you make it?"

"I think so," Johnny said. "How do I get there?"

Bull pointed back down Walnut. "Go down Walnut to Liberty and turn left. Then turn right on Bever Street. That'll put you on 302 South. Keep going until you see the Apple Creek sign. About a block past that is a Quonset hut on the left. That's Dutch's place. He'll get you fixed up."

"That's interesting, officer," Johnny said. "The girl I met back there said she lived in Apple Creek. She was Amish, but she said her uncle was the sheriff. Are you her uncle?"

"Oh, no," Bull smiled, "that would be my boss, Sheriff Bobby. And the girl must have been Jenny Springer. Real pretty, right?"

"Amazing," Johnny said. "But she didn't seem to like me much."

Bull laughed out loud. "Bad luck, boy. One of the things we've all learned in Wooster is not to get on Jenny's bad side. She's a real sweet gal most of the time, but she doesn't take much to fools. Not to say that you're a fool or anything. Oh, and speaking of funny clothes…"

Bull looked at Johnny's outfit and smiled again. Then he motioned back down Walnut Street. "Dutch closes early these days, so I'd get going if I were you. Good luck."

Bull turned and walked back to the cruiser. He was laughing. Johnny could hear him say something about Jenny Springer and laugh some more. Suddenly Johnny felt very out of place. He turned the engine over and put the van in gear. Bull pulled out and passed him. Johnny could see that he was still laughing.

Johnny headed out of town, trying to remember Bull's directions. Back down Walnut, left on Liberty, right on Bever, and follow the road to Apple Creek.

◇◇◇

The countryside was beautiful, but Johnny wasn't able to admire much of it as he slowly nursed his van along the road. It was a lovely day, and a nip of fall was in the air. The smell of fallen leaves and wet earth and freshly burned wheat stubble, something he remembered from his childhood adventures to the farm country around his grandfather's place at South Hampton, wafted in through the half-open window. Then Johnny saw something that grabbed his attention.

Up ahead on the right-hand side of the road, a group of men were working together in a large hayfield. They were harvesting and baling the hay, but they weren't using tractors or gas-powered machinery. Instead, a team of horses pulled their baler through the field. A man out front with a horse-drawn hay cutter was mowing down the greenish-brown hay. Behind him, another piece of machinery was raking the hay into long rows. And at the end of the line, a big machine was being pulled by four horses. It was scooping up the hay, baling it, and then dumping the bales onto a large flatbed wagon following close behind.

But it wasn't the machinery that attracted Johnny's attention. It was the men operating the machines. They wore straw hats with wide brims and overalls or jeans with blue shirts. None of the men had mustaches, but most of them had beards.

Johnny pulled over and got out of the van. He walked to the fence and stared at the scene. There were men of all ages in the group. An old man with a long white beard operated the cutter. Behind him younger men with dark beards drove the horse teams as boys walked alongside them. It seemed to Johnny that the men were teaching the boys as they moved through the field, pointing to the row of hay and calling the boys' attention to the teams of horses and machines as they walked. It was strange, but these were like the men he had seen in his vision or dream or whatever it was that night in San Francisco.

Johnny watched intently as the long file of machines turned the corner of the big field and came along the fence line. They obviously had just started working this particular field because they only had a few swaths cut and baled. As they passed close by him, Johnny heard some of the men singing.

"Lassen Sie ihn, der gelegen hat, seine Hand auf dem Pflug nicht sehen sich um! Presse zur Absicht! Presse Jesus Christus! Derjenige, der Christus gewinnt, wird sich mit ihm von den Toten am jüngsten Tag erheben."

Without knowing why, Johnny waved at the men. A man in a black hat waved back at him. Then the emptiness that had been so poignant back in his flat in San Francisco filled his heart again. Suddenly, powerfully, a realization swept over him—nothing about his life and how he was living made any sense. The only thing that was real for him in that moment were the men and their horses and machines and the land they were working.

The smell of the fresh-cut hay rose up to him, and the hot sun beat down on his face. To his surprise, Johnny found tears in his eyes. Why, he didn't know. Maybe he was crying for the lost dreams of his youth, or for the foolishness that had gotten him into such a mess, or for the fact that he had never really known his father. Soon, great sobs were torn out of him, and he clung to the fence to keep from falling. His head was down, and he didn't hear the approach of the man with the black hat until he was standing next to him.

"Are you all right, son?" a quiet voice asked.

Johnny looked up with tears streaming down his face. He wiped his eyes with the back of his sleeve and then tried to answer.

"I…I don't know what happened to me. I was just watching you harvest this field and listening to the song and it was so beautiful and it just touched something in my heart…" Johnny choked up for a minute and then went on. "Who are you and why are you using horses and…"

The man smiled at him and put a hand on his shoulder. "We are the Amish, the Plain people. We don't use modern tools because they're of the world, and we have separated ourselves from such things. We live the simple life, and that's what keeps us faithful to our God."

"Amish. Of course! I met a girl today who said she was Amish, but I didn't really know what that meant except I know that the Amish don't get drafted."

"Ah, the draft. Yes, that's true; we don't fight in wars. Jesus tells us it's wrong to kill other men."

"What does the song mean…the one you were singing?" Johnny asked.

"Let him who has laid his hand on the plow not look back. Press on to the goal! Press on to Jesus Christ! The one who gains Christ will rise with Him from the dead on the youngest day."

Johnny looked into the kindly face and the soft eyes of the man, and suddenly a longing to be safe came over him. He felt more tears rolling down his cheeks. In the distance he heard a man's voice calling.

The man squeezed his shoulder. "Maybe you have troubles that you should give to Jesus Christ, my boy. If you do, He will help you." Then the man looked away at the group passing by. "I must go then. The men need my help. God's blessing on you."

The man turned and walked away, and Johnny wanted to jump over the fence and run after him and join the men as they worked and sang, but instead he just stood looking after the retreating figure.

About a half-hour later, Johnny pulled up in front of Dutch's Garage in Apple Creek. Inside, he found a thin man with bushy eyebrows bent over a bench. He was dressed in blue mechanic's overalls with a welder's cap on his head. The place smelled of oil and metal, and a large stove made out of two fifty-gallon drums stacked on top of each other stood in the middle of the shop. The stove was glowing red. The man looked up and smiled when Johnny walked in. He put down the part he was working on and stepped out from behind the bench. He picked up a rag and wiped some kind of grease off his hands as he walked over.

"What can I do for you, hoss?" he asked.

"I think I need some work done on my front-end suspension. I ran up on a curb, and I think I bent something. A sheriff named Bull over in Wooster was kind enough to send me here. He said that Dutch's place was the best, so I guess you're Dutch?"

"That would be me," Dutch said, offering a grimy hand. "And you are…?

"Johnny, Johnny Hershberger."

Dutch gave him an odd look. "So Bull Halkovich sent you my way. He's a good friend. How is Bull?"

"Well, it wasn't exactly a social call. He was trying to run me out of town, but I couldn't get very far with my van banged up."

"Okay, let's take a look," Dutch said.

They walked out to the van, and Dutch got down and looked under the front end. After a few minutes he popped back out.

"Yep, the tie bar is bent. You must have banged it good."

"Can you fix it?" Johnny asked.

Dutch fixed a stare on Johnny. "Son, I can fix anything. That is, if I have the part. I don't keep parts handy for this here German-made car since I mostly work on American cars. But I can make a few phone calls and get the part shipped over here. Shouldn't be more than a couple of days."

"A couple of days?" Johnny frowned. The fear of the drug dealers came back over him.

"Got any money, boy?" Dutch asked.

"Sure. Do you want a deposit?"

Dutch took off his cap and scratched his grizzled head. "Well," he said slowly, "given that I don't know you, that would probably be a good idea. How about fifty dollars? Oughta cover the whole shebang."

Johnny fished the money out of the pocket of his striped pants. "Are there any motels in town that are close by?"

"Sure, the Bide-a-Wee is just down the street. Nice rooms for a real good price. I think Jonas has a weekly rate too." Dutch said. "There's a restaurant right across the street. And if you have need of transportation, I got a loaner out back. Seein' as how I'll have your truck and all."

Dutch looked the van over. He gave Johnny another one of his curious looks. "You wouldn't be needin' a paint job, would ya? Twenty-five dollars, and she's as good as new. Scrape all that hoo-haw right off and paint her a nice inconspicuous blue."

"I'll think about it, Dutch," Johnny said. "It would probably be a good idea to keep a little lower profile out here."

Dutch smiled in agreement.

Chapter Eleven

Bitter Words

◇◇◇

Jenny watched from her desk as the man picked up the key to the microfiche room and headed there. When he went inside, she slipped quietly up the hallway and followed him in. He was waiting for her and stuck out his hand.

"Hi, Jenny. I'm Bob Schumann."

Jenny took his hand and shook it. He was a nice-looking older man with white hair and a pleasant smile. He had on an Ohio State jacket and a Cincinnati Reds baseball hat pushed back on his head. The smile wrinkles around his eyes belied the gruffness she had sensed on the phone. A briefcase sat on the desk behind him.

Jenny went to the files, pulled out the filmstrips, and handed them to Schumann. He sat down at the reader and quietly perused the two articles. Then he turned to Jenny.

"I remember when I wrote this story. It was a real mystery in nineteen fifty-one, and the fact that there was heroin in the car was a huge deal back then. Nowadays, with all the stuff going on in San Francisco and New York, the drug angle isn't so exciting. It's always bothered me that all the leads in this story were dead ends."

"What can you tell me about the man?" Jenny asked.

"Not much more than what's here," Bob said. "They did an autopsy, and the cause of death was drowning. The only possible identifier they found on him was a large tattoo."

"A tattoo? That wasn't in the story," Jenny said.

"I made a sketch of it at the coroner's office when they let me view the body, but the police chief made me leave it out of the article. Seems that it was a popular tattoo with the servicemen during the war, and the sheriff didn't want anything bad reflected on our local vets, what with the heroin and the empty liquor bottles they found. It didn't seem important at the time, so I pulled it."

"Describe the tattoo to me," Jenny said.

"Very large, located on his left shoulder," Bob said. "Well here, let me show you."

Schumann opened the briefcase and rummaged among some papers. He pulled out a sheet with a rough drawing in the middle. The picture was of a large, ornate tattoo of the patriotic type common among servicemen. The Statue of Liberty was in the center, surrounded by four flags, two on each side. Above the tattoo it said, "God Bless America," and right under the statue were some Roman numerals.

"Notice the number under the statue. When I compared it to other tattoos like it, they didn't have a number. I've always remembered it, maybe because it was like a palindrome."

He wrote the number in larger letters beneath the drawing: IVIII IIIVI.

"Is there any significance to the number?" Jenny asked.

"I didn't find any at the time."

"Didn't you say that the tattoo was popular with men in the military?" Jenny asked.

Schumann nodded.

"Well, what if it's some kind of identifying number like a dog tag or a social security number?"

Schumann's eye's brightened, and he pulled a pair of reading glasses out of his pocket and perched them on his nose to take a closer look. After a minute he looked at Jenny over the glasses.

"You know, Jenny, you may have something there," Schumann said. "The Navy issued commission numbers to officers. By the end of the war there were at least three hundred sixty thousand of them. Most of the ones over a hundred twenty-five thousand were issued at the beginning of the war."

Jenny looked at the Roman numerals. "What if these numerals actually represent a large number, and it was the only way to write it in this form. Let's see. One, five, three, a break, and then three, five, and one. What if the number is actually this?" She wrote down the number.

Schumann stared at Jenny's figures. "Jenny, you could be right. It would fit the pattern of naval commission numbers. Our boy could have been a Naval officer!"

"Where could we find a list of those numbers and who they were issued to?" Jenny asked.

"War Department or the VFW. You'd have to know somebody who's a vet."

"My papa won the Congressional Medal of Honor. Do you think that might give him access to some of these records?"

Bob Schumann smiled. "Say, young lady, if you ever decide to leave the Amish faith, I could get you a job at the newspaper. You've got the makings of a good investigative reporter."

"Well, Mr. Schumann, I probably wouldn't have to leave the faith to write for you. I'm a history intern here at the library and have already written several articles about the local Amish and their contribution to Wayne County and the state of Ohio. I'm putting together a book that I'm hoping to publish someday. You might find some of the information of interest to your readers. But first I have to solve the mystery of my birth mother."

"Jenny, you've got a deal. You're a self-possessed young woman, and I would very much like to see some of your writing."

"Thank you, Mr. Schumann. Now, is there anything else we can find out from the information you came up with?" Jenny asked.

Schumann turned back to the reader and scanned the article again. "There might be a lead in the license plate number," he said. "The Department of Motor Vehicles would have a record of the registered owner at the time. Perhaps they might have some information about the car or have an idea who stole it. That's about all there is. But we have two leads here to follow. The man who helped rescue your mama in nineteen fifty is now our sheriff. He could probably get you access to the DMV records."

"Our family is still very close with Sheriff Halverson. In fact, I call him Uncle Bobby."

"Well, there you go! This is looking more promising. I'm sure a young lady with your determination can find the answers to these questions."

Jenny smiled at Schumann. "Thank you so much for your help. You've given me some hope."

"Glad to help," Schumann said. "Please keep me updated on what you find out. I would certainly like to print the end of this story. I'll give you a byline." The older man stood up and extended his hand again. "Good luck to you, Jenny, and may the Lord bless you in your endeavors."

"Are you a Christian, Mr. Schumann?" Jenny asked.

"Who isn't?" the old man replied with a smile. Then he strode through the door and was gone.

◇◇◇

Jenny waited on the curb in front of the library. She had come away from her conversation with Bob Schumann with two important clues. Now she had to figure out how to get her papa to help her track the possible naval commission number. Getting Uncle Bobby's help with the license plate would be easy.

She thought about the woman who had come to her in her dreams. An unshakable certainty settled on her, and she knew that the woman must be her birth mother. *Mama, I'll find out what happened and put this mystery to rest.*

Just then Henry pulled up at the curb. Her papa was sitting in the front seat, so she climbed in the back.

"And how was your day, *dochter*?" Reuben asked.

"Just fine, Papa. I was doing some historical research today and found some very interesting facts."

"*Das is gut*," Reuben said as he turned to look at her. "Perhaps some-day you can chronicle some of the information you've gleaned. I'm sure our people would be interested in reading about their history, and per-haps it could set to rest some of the misconceptions about the Amish."

Jenny looked back at her papa. He was usually very skeptical about her research, and she wondered what had made him more open today. She hesitated and then spoke again.

"Yes, Papa, I'm sure it would be of value. I was thinking perhaps I might write some small articles about our customs and background and submit them to the local paper."

Jenny watched her father's face for any telltale negative responses. His jaw did tighten for just a moment, but then he said, "That might be something we could talk about. I would like to read some of your work if you don't mind."

"Why, Papa! I would love to show you some of my writing. Mama has seen it, but you have never seemed to be interested."

"I know, Jenny, and perhaps I've been remiss in not encouraging you more. I know that you were an excellent student in Amish *schule*, but I must admit I was a bit skeptical when you desired to continue your education. It's just my way, and I'm sorry for not showing more appreciation for your talents."

Jenny didn't know what to say. Her papa had seemed to resist her internship at the library, but Mama had convinced him that it was a safe way to work out her natural curiosity, so he had acceded to Jerusha's request and let Jenny go forward. Now he was actually encouraging her. What was going on here? It wasn't like him. She felt a small hope growing that he might let her follow up the leads she had uncovered.

Henry dropped them at their lane, and as he drove off, Reuben and Jenny walked together up to the house. The afternoon sun did little to take the chill out of the air, and the breeze carried the smell of fallen leaves and moist dirt. The fall was fully on them, and the harvest nearly done.

Off in the distance Jenny could see the rest of the Springer farm laid out like a beautiful quilt. There were the hay fields with the stacks of bales. Behind the house was the orchard with the luscious Gala, McIntosh, and Golden Delicious apple trees. The faint scent of grounded apples flavored the air, a smell that always comforted Jenny. Out past the barn the cornfield started. The rows stood tall and green with the first touch of light brown and gold touching the leaves. The silken tassels on the ears had turned dark—proof that the golden kernels were ripe and sweet beneath the husks. Beside the house was her mother's kitchen garden with ripe red tomatoes, leeks, onions, herbs, beans, squash, and cucumbers climbing their stakes and racks in wild abandon.

Jenny took her father's hand in hers as they walked, and she let her heart fill with the beauty all around her. She looked up at her papa, so tall and strong beside her, and the love that welled up in her heart gave voice to her feelings.

"It's so beautiful here, Papa. Thank you for having me as your daughter and raising me in this place."

Reuben was silent, but she felt his hand squeeze hers in quiet assurance. Jenny hoped she would never do anything to hurt Papa. She wanted to be a good daughter above everything else.

They went up onto the porch and into the house. Jenny heard her mama's voice, beautiful and clear, floating from the kitchen, borne aloft on the aroma of roast beef, boiled potatoes, string beans, and carrots. She was singing *Das Lobleid*, the hymn of praise, and the words comforted Jenny's troubled heart.

Lässt loben Ihn mit allen unseren Herzen! Weil Er allein würdig ist!

While Reuben went to the washroom to clean up, Jenny went into the kitchen. Her mama was setting the table for the early evening supper.

"Jenny, just in time. Can you put the applesauce in a bowl and get out the beets and pickles? I just put the biscuits in, and we'll be ready to eat in about ten minutes."

Jenny helped Jerusha put the food on the table. Along with the main course there was butter and jam, peaches in syrup, and Shoofly pie. Jenny liked her pie with maple syrup, but Reuben and Jerusha preferred fruit and thick cream on top.

Reuben returned, and the three of them sat down to eat. Jerusha was a wonderful cook, and the food was delicious.

Reuben spoke up. "I've never been able to decide which of your graces I appreciate the most, wife. When I kiss you, I'm sure it's your beauty. When I watch you quilt, I know it's your talent. But when I sit down to the table, I realize without a doubt it's your cooking."

Jerusha didn't miss a beat with her reply. "It's well understood that the way to a man's heart is through his stomach, so that doesn't surprise me at all, husband."

Jenny enjoyed the loving banter between her parents and decided this might be a good time to broach the subject of her conversation with Bob Schumann.

"Papa, today I spoke with Mr. Schumann, a man who used to write articles for the *Daily Record*. I talked to him about perhaps publishing some of my articles on the Amish way of life and history. He was very interested and asked to see my writing. I would like your permission to show my articles to him."

"Yes, I would be willing to permit," Reuben said. "But first I would like to read them for myself."

"Certainly, Papa. I'd be happy to have you read them and tell me what you think."

"That's wonderful, dear," Jerusha said. "I'm so glad you're finding a way to use the gift God has given you."

"Oh, Mama, we did talk about this before, didn't we?"

Her mother nodded. "Yes, we did indeed."

Jenny decided to go all the way with her request. "Papa, there was something else I talked about with Mr. Schumann."

Reuben glanced up at her, and then her words came out in a rush. "Mr. Schumann was the one who wrote the article about finding me in the car in the storm and about the dead man they found in the pond. He shared some information with me that might help in solving the mystery of who my birth mother was, but I need your help. You see—"

Reuben put his utensils down and looked straight at her. His words came at her like knives. "Jenny, I told you that the matter of finding your birth mother is closed. I explained my reasons. If you pursue this, it could lead to serious consequences. I will say this one last time. The issue of your birth mother is not to be spoken of in this house again. If you don't promise me that you'll obey me, I'll have to tell Mrs. Blake that you can no longer work at the library."

"Reuben!" Jerusha exclaimed.

Reuben looked at Jerusha sharply, and she looked down at the table.

Jenny felt anger rising up in her, but she held her peace. *Let it go, Jenny. This isn't the place to fight the battle.*

"Jenny, I want your promise now." Reuben's voice was quiet, but Jenny could hear the finality in it. She clenched her jaw so that she wouldn't say something sarcastic. She took a deep breath and then spoke.

"Yes, Papa. I promise." *There, I said it. I hope I won't become a liar.*

Reuben relaxed. "*Gut.* I will accept your promise. I trust you won't break your word to me. That's enough now. Let us go on with our dinner."

Then silence lay heavy on the Springer home.

Chapter Twelve

Friendship

◇◇◇

Jenny walked down the main street of Apple Creek to the bus stop with a heavy heart. Since her tense words with her papa two days before, things had been on edge in the Springer household. She loved her papa, but her need to know the truth was consuming her. She stood waiting for the bus, her world filled with gray clouds even though the autumn sun was shining brightly. She didn't see the young man who came out of the restaurant across the street, but he saw her and walked toward her.

"So we meet again."

Jenny looked up into those troubling sea-blue eyes that had bewildered her that day in Wooster.

He looked different, and then she realized why. He wasn't wearing the fringed jacket or the green suede boots. Instead he wore a plain brown wool jacket and loafers, and jeans and a pullover turtleneck had replaced the striped pants and tie-dyed T-shirt. His hair was still long, but it was pulled back and he was a lot less...noticeable.

"I took your advice," he said with a smile.

"What?" Jenny asked, startled.

"I took your advice about the clothes, and I do feel a bit more local."

"Oh, the clothes," Jenny said as she pulled at her coat sleeve. "Well, I'm glad I could be of help."

"Say, Jenny, um…it's Jenny, right?"

Jenny nodded cautiously.

"I'm wondering if you can help me. The other day you said that your mother's maiden name was Hershberger, like mine. I've been thinking about that. I remember my mother once saying that my family originally moved from Pennsylvania to Ohio a long time ago. I'm not sure how we ended up in New York, but it's not so far from here, so that's not a stretch. Then you told me that all the Hershbergers you know are Amish. I didn't really know what that meant until I saw some Amish men working in a field not far from here. Here's my question. If my family is originally from Ohio and named Hershberger, shouldn't they be Amish too? I mean, how many different kinds of Hershbergers can there be?"

The historian in Jenny began to take over. "Well, uh, Mr. Hershberger—"

"Please call me Johnny."

"All right, Johnny. I happen to work as a historical and genealogical staffer at the Wooster library. I research the history of Wayne County and its families. If you have a family tie to Ohio, I could probably locate it for you."

"Really?" Johnny asked. "If you could, I would be very grateful. I…I'm not sure how to say this, but when I saw the Amish men working in the field, it touched me inside. I felt a connection, and my life suddenly seemed very complicated. It's probably just because I have my own difficulties right now, and it seems that there are a lot of things I could get rid of in my life. Simpler would probably be better."

For the first time, Jenny really took in the young man standing next to her—not just his features, but something of who he was. She looked into his eyes and didn't see anything that frightened her. Then she said something that surprised her.

"Maybe God is trying to tell you something."

"What?"

"I said, maybe God is trying to tell you something. If you have all these troubles, maybe God is showing you a way out of them. He does that, you know."

Johnny had a strange look on his face. "You know, the Amish man in the field said the very same thing. The thing is, I'm not so sure I believe in God, although I've found myself asking for His help in the past several days, especially when I found myself in…shall we say, a delicate situation."

"How about if we just say you're in trouble and be honest," Jenny said.

"Boy, Bull was right. You are direct." Johnny laughed.

"Bull?"

"Yes," Johnny said. "Officer Bull, in Wooster."

"How do you know Bull?"

"I met Officer Bull the other day after I almost ran you over. He encouraged me to get out of town. It was all very much like a scene from a Western. He also said he worked for your uncle, and he said you were very direct, especially with foolish people."

"Yes, he's my uncle's chief deputy, and sometimes he takes himself a bit too seriously. He also tends to give out information that he should keep to himself." Jenny frowned, took a deep breath, and mastered her desire to walk away.

"Well, would you?" Johnny asked.

"Would I what?"

"You know, help me find out about my family?"

"My papa wouldn't like me to be seen with a strange *Englisch* boy," Jenny said.

"But I'm an American," Johnny said, puzzled.

"Oh, no," Jenny laughed. "I didn't mean you were from England. We call everyone who isn't Amish, *Englisch*."

"Will you help me? Even if I am…English?"

Jenny paused before answering, torn between her fear of making her father angry again and the eager expression on Johnny's face. Finally she decided. "All right, I'll help you. Do you still have your van?"

"It's in the shop getting the suspension fixed, but I do have a loaner. I can drive you to Wooster."

"No, it wouldn't do for me to be seen riding with you. My family and friends wouldn't understand. Besides, I have work to do first. Just meet me in Wooster at the library in three hours. I should be done by then."

"Where's the library?" Johnny asked.

"Half a block away from where you tried to kill me," Jenny said, but the bite was gone from her voice.

Just then the bus pulled up, and Jenny got on. She waved and smiled. "See you soon."

Then the door closed and the bus pulled out, belching a black cloud of diesel smoke.

◇◇◇

Johnny went back to the motel and hung out in his room. He tried reading the local newspaper he found outside his door that morning, but he couldn't stay focused, so he played his guitar for a little while. The hours crept by until finally it was two thirty. He went outside and climbed into the brown Dodge Dart Dutch had loaned him. It was pretty funky inside, but it ran like a top. Dutch obviously knew his stuff.

As he drove by the field where he had watched the Amish men, he pulled over, hoping for a glimpse of them, but the field was empty except for four large haystacks covered with canvas tarps. He pulled back onto the road and drove on, thinking about the powerful feelings that had swept over him that day.

First he had dreamed about the men, and then he had actually seen them. The whole thing was way too weird. A new thought came to him. Maybe God actually was trying to show him something. He sure seemed to be answering whenever Johnny asked Him for help.

Surely it's just a coincidence, or maybe my karma at work.

Thinking about his karma didn't seem to raise the mystical excitement he had once felt as he sat listening to the guru next door going on and on in his high-pitched, singsong voice about karma and dharma and the great wheel of life. Now when he thought about it, it all seemed like just a bunch of gobbledygook.

Johnny pulled up in front of the library and walked up the stone steps. He walked inside and looked around. A familiar smell brought back a not-so-pleasant memory of childhood days in Levittown when he had gone to the library to escape from his father's indifference and his mother's drunken ramblings. Then he spotted the front desk and went over to it. An older white-haired lady looked up from her work.

"Can I help you?" she asked.

"Yes, I'm looking for Jenny Springer."

The woman's face took on a slight look of surprise.

"May I ask what for?" she asked with an unfriendly smile.

"She's going to help me with a genealogical project regarding my family history," Johnny said.

The woman gave him the once-over, pointed down a hallway, and went back to her work. Johnny walked toward the back of the building until he came to an alcove off the main hallway. Jenny was seated at a desk with a stack of papers in front of her. She looked cute in her black *kappe* with the errant golden curls peeking out—a little out of place in a library, but still cute.

"Hi there," Johnny said.

Jenny looked up and then glanced at the clock on the wall. "You're early. You'll have to wait a few minutes while I finish this project for Mrs. Blake."

She went back to her work, and Johnny took a seat in a chair on the opposite wall of the hallway. He looked around. There were lots of pictures and information on the walls, and through a large open door at the end of the hallway he could see shelves stacked with books and what looked like bound journals and three-ring notebooks.

In about ten minutes, Jenny closed the notebook she was writing in and put it aside.

"Let's get started," she said. "Sit over here."

Johnny moved over to the chair Jenny pointed out. "Where do we begin?" he asked.

"Tell me everything you know about your father's side of the family, as far back as you can remember."

Johnny started in. "My dad's name is Ronald Hershberger, and his father's name was Peter." Johnny paused, and then he went on. "Peter's father was Jonas, and I know my mom told me what my great-great grandfather's name was. Let me think. Oh yeah, Joshua—his name was Joshua. But that's as far back as I know."

"That will help," Jenny said. "Wait here. I have to grab some record books. We have the biography and genealogy master index here, and it's quite helpful. I'll be right back."

Johnny sat waiting until Jenny returned with a stack of documents and books.

"Can you remember any birthdays or dates of death?"

"Well, my dad was born in nineteen twenty-one—September twelfth to be exact. My grandfather Peter died five years ago in April of nineteen sixty. I remember because the cherry trees were in bloom back home. I don't know much more than that. Oh, one thing, my

birth name was Jonathan, but my dad didn't like it so he started calling me Johnny when I was a kid. I think I was named after someone,
but I'm not sure."

Jenny opened a large notebook. "I've traced my side of the family back to the large wave of Amish settlers that came to Pennsylvania
in seventeen twenty-eight and even further back to the Hershbergers
and Springers that lived in Europe. Let's see if we can find a connection from my side of the Hershberger line."

She began to read. "My grandfather Hershberger is Jonas, his father
was Ezekiel, and his father's father was Joshua. My great-great-great
grandfather was also Joshua, and his father was Jonas."

Jenny paused for a moment. Then she began scanning through the
pages. After several minutes, she looked up.

"This is very interesting. My great-great-great grandfather, Joshua,
had a brother named Jonathan, but I don't see him in any of the Amish
genealogies. Maybe there's a connection there."

Jenny pulled out an official-looking volume.

"This is what we call the BGMI. It has exhaustive records of most of
the families in the United States. This is the volume for Ohio and the
Northeastern United States."

Jenny looked in the index and then leafed through several pages
until she came to an entry. Her face took on a slightly bemused look.

"Here it is. Jonathan and Joshua Hershberger. Twin brothers who
moved to the Ohio River valley with their family before the Revolu-
tionary War."

She read further. "Jonathan had a son named Matthew. Matthew
had a son named Jonas. Jonas had a Joshua, Joshua had a Peter, and
Peter had a Ronald. And then came you, Jonathan Hershberger, born
in Garden City, New York, April twenty-seventh, nineteen forty-three."

Jenny smiled at the amazed look on Johnny's face.

"That's right! April twenty-seventh!"

"That was easy," she said. "It seems that you and I are very, very, very distant cousins."

"You mean my family is originally Amish?" Johnny asked.

"From what it says here, I'm presuming so. Most of the Hershbergers I've encountered in the history books between seventeen twenty-six and eighteen hundred were originally from Switzerland. They were Anabaptists, either Mennonites or Amish, who came to Pennsylvania when William Penn proclaimed religious liberty and offered land to willing settlers. There were slight variations of the spelling of the name, but they were all from the same family. So when you told me your name was Hershberger, I guessed that somewhere back in the seventeen hundreds, your ancestors were Amish from Switzerland.

"And there's more. When I was researching my family, I came across an old volume written by one of my family members. It's called *The Family of Jonas Hershberger*, and it tells the story of the Hershberger family starting when they came to Pennsylvania and continues after they moved out to Ohio in seventeen fifty-three. Let me get it."

Jenny left again, and when she returned, she had another bound volume. This one was thinner and a bit dusty.

"I've read through this one, and I think it has the answer to your questions, Jonathan."

"You're the first person who has ever called me that. I rather like it," Johnny said.

"Let's see, it was back several chapters after the genealogy in the beginning."

Jenny turned several pages until she came to a piece of paper stuck between two pages. "That's right, I marked it. This is really interesting."

"Before you get into the story, can you give me a little background?" Johnny asked. "I mean, I know nothing about the Amish, where they come from, or what they believe."

"Yes," Jenny said. "It's important that you have a backdrop to the story, or it won't make any sense to you."

Jenny turned back a few pages in the volume. "Yes, we'll start here."

Then Jenny began to tell Johnny the story of his family.

Chapter Thirteen

A Meeting

◇◇◇

"Jonas Hershberger arrived in Pennsylvania with his father, Mathias, and his mother in seventeen twenty-eight, when he was three years old," Jenny began. "His father bought land from William Penn outside of Lancaster, Pennsylvania, and established a prosperous farm. Do you know who William Penn was?"

"Yes," Johnny said. "He was the Quaker who started Philadelphia. He's on the Quaker Oats box."

"Actually, he started more than just Philadelphia. In sixteen eighty-two, Penn bought all of Pennsylvania from the British Crown to start a colony. He needed settlers to populate his colony, so he went around Europe, especially Holland and the countries along the Rhine River, asking people to come. Thousands of Amish and Mennonites came to America and purchased land from Penn for their farms. Our ancestors were among them.

"Jonas grew up on that farm with his ten brothers and sisters. He was the youngest son, and since there was not enough land to be shared between all the brothers, he left Pennsylvania in seventeen fifty-three when he was twenty-eight years old. Jonas and his wife settled along the

Ohio River near what is now Wheeling, West Virginia, but it was still Ohio territory then. They eventually had three sons and two daughters."

"Whoa, Jenny," Johnny interrupted, laughing. "This is incredible. Where did you learn all this?"

"It's all here in this book by my great-grandfather, Ezekiel," Jenny said. "I've read it so many times I almost have it memorized."

"You're really into all this history stuff, aren't you?" Johnny asked. "How come?"

Jenny hesitated. "You'd have to know my own story to understand."

"Will you tell me?"

Jenny had been so absorbed in telling Johnny the story that she hadn't noticed he had pulled his chair close to hers and was leaning on the desk, almost touching her. Distracted, she reached to turn the page of the book and brushed her hand against his. To her astonishment, a strange sensation ran up her arm. Flustered, she stood up and accidentally knocked the book off the desk onto the floor, along with some of the papers she had been working on. She knelt down to pick them up and knocked her head against Johnny's knee. Her black *kappe* came off, spilling the long, golden curls that escaped her bun out onto her shoulders. She felt her face burning.

A surprised Johnny smiled and tried to pick up the book. When Jenny looked up at him, she was transfixed by his eyes. Then suddenly, surprisingly, she was crying.

Johnny stared down at her, perplexed. He wanted to comfort her, but his hands hung like lead weights, and so he sat still, not knowing what to do.

Jenny got up and went into the restroom across the hall. She closed the door and stood for a long time, sobs shaking her shoulders.

What's wrong with me?

She remained there until her breathing quieted and her heart stopped pounding.

There was a quiet knock on the door. "Jenny, are you okay?"

"I'm fine, I just got *ferhoodled* for a minute."

"*Ferhoodled*?"

"It's an Amish word. It means flustered. I'll be out in a minute."

Jenny wet a paper towel and washed the tears off her face. She straightened her *kappe* and then looked in the mirror. Her face was pale and her eyes sad.

She opened the restroom door and peeked out. Johnny was sitting next to the desk. He stood up quickly.

"Gee, I'm really sorry if I said something to upset you," he said. "I didn't mean to."

"*Ja, wohl*, it wasn't you," Jenny said, returning to her chair. "It's something personal I'm struggling with. Sit down and let me finish the story about your family."

As they sat down at the desk, Jenny looked at the book and then back at Johnny again. His face was kind, and there was concern in his eyes. Then she was talking in a rush of words.

"I'm not really a Hershberger. I don't even know if I'm Amish or who I am."

Johnny looked puzzled. "What are you talking about?"

Jenny sat with her hands in her lap and her shoulders hunched. The story began to spill out of her.

"I'm adopted. I was rescued from a car wreck when I was a little girl. My mama found me. The man who was driving the car died and didn't have any identification. The car had been stolen and there were drugs in it. The police tried to find out who I was but they never did. My parents took me in and later adopted me. Lately I've been having the same dream over and over about the wreck and the man and about a sad woman who I think is my birth mother. And I'm also starting to remember things, little details about the time before I came here."

Jenny saw the quizzical look on Johnny's face, and she wondered why she was telling him all this, but she went on.

"I asked my papa to help me but he thinks I'm better off to put it all behind me. I think my mama and papa are afraid that if I find my real parents I'll leave Apple Creek. I'd never do that, but this need to know the truth is gnawing at me. I'm not the happy person I used to be and I don't think I will be until I find out who I really am."

"Is that why you are so interested in history and genealogy?"

"I think so," Jenny answered tentatively, gaining a little composure. "I've always had an interest in history, but lately it's become an obsession. I met the newspaperman who wrote the story about the car crash, and he gave me some ideas about how to continue the search. But my papa and I had a huge fight about it, and now he's angry with me. I love him so much, but sometimes he can be very set in his ways."

"Look, if there is anything that I can do to help you, I will," Johnny said. "I don't think it was just a coincidence that I almost ran over you. I believe in fate, don't you?"

"It's God who directs our paths, not an impersonal fate," Jenny said stiffly.

"Whatever you want to call it, I just feel like it's no mistake that we met, and my offer stands."

Jenny smiled as best she could. "I'll remember that, and there may come a time when I will ask you."

What am I doing? This man is an Englischer. *I shouldn't even be talking to him. His ways are not our ways!*

"Go on with the history," Johnny said. "If you think you can."

"Yes, I can. But before I read from the book I need to finish giving you some background. Jonas brought his wife west to Ohio. Back then this area was the most beautiful wilderness. There were several Indian tribes living here. The most notable were the Delaware, a fierce tribe who had been pushed out of their lands to the east by the white settlers and who had been on the warpath for many years, starting with the beginning of the French and Indian war. By the time Jonas arrived in Ohio, the war had been going on for seven years. The French had suffered serious losses, but the Indians still roamed the woods attacking outlying homes and small settlements. Jonas and his wife settled near what would become Fort Henry and started a family. Soon a small community of Amish believers settled around him."

"Wasn't that kind of dangerous, living out there without any guns?"

"Oh, the Amish had guns," Jenny said. "They just didn't use them to kill people. Besides, some *Englischers* came to the same area and eventually built a fort. They didn't have the same reservations about shooting their enemies."

"I guess people make a lot of assumptions about the Amish without knowing what they're really like," Johnny said.

"Yes, they do," Jenny replied tartly. "And one of the assumptions they make is that the Amish don't mind being interrupted."

Johnny looked at Jenny in surprise. Jenny tried to muster a stern face, but they both burst into laughter.

"You are a real contradiction, Jenny Springer."

"I'm sorry, Jonathan, it's just my way. I'll try to be nicer."

"I like it...when you...when you call me that," Johnny said, suddenly awkward.

On an impulse, he reached out and took her hand. She tried to pull back, but he gripped her hand, and then just as quickly, she stopped resisting. She looked at the floor, blushing.

"Please, don't," she said quietly, but she didn't try to pull away. "I don't even know you, and I'm Amish. We don't allow such behavior except when people are courting."

It was Johnny's turn to blush. He pulled his hand back. "I'm sorry, I just feel like we could be good friends. Now go on. I'll stop interrupting you."

"Where was I?"

"Jonas had just arrived at the farm in Ohio with his wife," replied Johnny.

"Yes, at the farm…" Jenny opened the book, found the place she had marked, and began to read.

"Over the years, after he arrived in seventeen fifty-three, Jonas had three sons and two daughters. Two of the sons were twins—Joshua and Jonathan—and the other son was named Christian. The daughters were Ruth and Miriam. His wife was named Martha. They lived in relative peace until the twins were seventeen years old. Then came the event that changed the history of the Hershberger family forever.

"On June nineteen, seventeen seventy, the young people of the neighborhood gathered at the home of Jonas Hershberger to have a social. They remained until late in the afternoon. After the young folks departed, the family retired. About that time the dog made an unusual noise, which awakened Christian, the youngest son. He opened the door to see what was wrong and received a gunshot wound in the leg. He realized in a moment that they were being attacked by Indians and managed to close and lock the door before the Indians could enter. In an instant all the family were on their feet. Ten Indians were outside near the barn.

"Several guns and plenty of ammunition were at hand. Jonathan and Joshua, the twins, picked up their guns and were about to defend the family, but the father, Jonas, firmly believing in the doctrine of non-resistance and remaining faithful in this hour of severest trial, refused to give his consent. In vain the sons begged him, but he told them it was not right to take the life of another, even in defense of one's own. Jonathan ever after claimed that the family could have been saved as he and Joshua were excellent marksmen and the Indians could not have withstood a solid volley of musketry."

Jenny looked up from the book. Johnny was staring off into space as if he weren't even in the room.

"Jonathan, are you listening?"

Johnny's eyes jerked spasmodically and then focused and came to rest on Jenny. "While you were reading, it was like I was there," he said slowly. "There in the house with them. It was so real, just like my dream."

"What are you talking about?" Jenny asked.

"The night before I left San Francisco, I had a dream…I guess you could even call it a vision. I was with men in a field, and they wore strange clothes. They had beards but no mustaches and straw hats, and they were working in a field, and I was with them. The earth was cool on my feet because I wasn't wearing shoes, and then I felt, I don't know, like roots growing out of me, down deep into the ground. I guess I woke up then, and when I did I had the emptiest, loneliest feeling."

"That's what Amish men look like," Jenny said.

"Yes, and when I was driving into Apple Creek, the first day I was here, I saw them. They were working in a field outside of town, and they were using horse-drawn equipment and singing. I stood by the fence and watched, and I felt that intense loneliness again, like a deep sorrow for something I'd lost. And then, all of a sudden, I was crying. Then a man came over, and he said if I was in trouble, I should ask God for help. What's happening to me?"

This time Jenny reached out and took Johnny's hand. She looked at him for a long time before she spoke. "I think we are the same, Jonathan," she said.

"The same?"

"Yes," Jenny said quietly. "Neither of us knows who we are. We're both searching, and I know the answers are right here in front of us, and yet they're just beyond our reach. We're both lost."

Johnny's hand was warm in hers. She looked at him, adrift in his sea-blue eyes, and she remembered her mother's words. *Someday…*

you'll meet a man whom you will love so deeply that you will gladly surren-
der everything of yourself into his care and protection.

"Tell me the rest of the story," Johnny said quietly.

Jenny came back to herself. She took her hand from his and opened the book.

"It will be hard. I've read it before, but of course I didn't know that Jonathan was your ancestor. Now it makes sense, and maybe you'll find the answers to your questions here. But I think they may be hard answers."

Johnny took a deep breath. "I want to know."

Jenny glanced up at the clock. "It's almost five o'clock. I'll miss the bus home."

She shoved the book into the desk drawer and then jumped up and grabbed her coat from the wall hook.

"Wait, you can't go! You have to finish the story!" Johnny stood up and tried to take hold of her arm, but she eluded his grasp and hurried away.

"I'm here twice a week," she called over her shoulder. "I'll be back on Thursday. Meet me at noon."

And then she rushed down the hallway and was gone.

CHAPTER FOURTEEN

The Way

◇◇◇

JOHNNY SAT IN THE DODGE DART in front of the library. It was eleven thirty-five on Thursday, and he had been up since six that morning. He knew he was early, but he was eager to see Jenny again, and there wasn't a lot to do in Apple Creek on a Thursday morning.

He got out to stretch his legs and then got back in the car. He turned on the radio, spun the knob, and dialed in a station from somewhere in Indiana. The announcer was droning on about crop yields and weather reports, interspersing his dialogue with overly hyped commentary about the big sale down at the local Chevrolet dealer and the senior special at a place called Frenchie's Restaurant. Then two little girls came on and sang a song about another local business.

> For every heating problem
> Be your furnace old or new
> Call Boyle Fuel Company
> And they'll solve them all for you
> If you need coal or oil, call Boyle
> Fairfax eight, one-five-two-one,
> fairfax eight, one-five-two-one

He tried switching stations to see if anyone was playing some modern music, but the closest he got was Eddy Arnold singing "Make the World Go Away." With a sigh, he turned off the radio and slumped down in the seat. He had been thinking about Jenny and nothing else for the last two days. His dangerous situation somehow seemed like a distant memory, pushed aside by the powerful feelings the girl evoked in him.

What has gotten into me? This girl is like someone from a different planet. She's bossy and outspoken and emotional…and beautiful and smart…

Johnny climbed back out of the car and slammed the door shut. It was the fourth time he had gotten out since he arrived at the library. He stood on the curb and watched traffic, trying to count how many Buicks went by. Eventually he gave up and walked up and down the library steps to get some exercise.

Finally it was almost noon. He looked down the street and saw the bus approaching. His heart started racing, and his palms began to sweat. The bus pulled up, the door opened, and Jenny got out. She had her wool coat on and her black *kappe*, and Johnny felt as if an angel had stepped off the bus. A question he had never asked himself in his whole life crossed his mind. *Am I in love with her?*

They stood for a moment, their eyes locked. A pink blush appeared on Jenny's face, and a faint smile lifted the corners of her mouth. Johnny instinctively reached for her hand and then pulled back, remembering what she had told him about proper Amish behavior. He didn't know what to do with his hands then, so they hung limply at his side as his eyes drank in her face. After what seemed like forever, he broke the spell.

"Hi, Jenny."

"Hello, Jonathan."

Jenny looked down at the ground and they both stood, awkward and silent. The bus pulled away with a belch of smoke. Then she spoke again. "How are you today?"

"I'm fine. I've been looking forward to hearing more of the story. It's kind of cold today—are you warm enough?"

"Yes, thank you for asking," she replied and then stood silent again.

Johnny searched for something else to say. *This is ridiculous. I'm Johnny the Candyman, breaker of hearts, conqueror of San Francisco women. What in the world is happening to me?*

"Well, maybe we should go inside," Jenny said.

"Okay," Johnny replied.

They walked up the steps together, the tall, long-haired worldling and the little Amish girl. Johnny snuck a glance at her out of the corner of his eye. She looked sad but so beautiful.

They pushed through the big glass doors, and Jenny stopped at the front desk to say hello to Mrs. Blake and remind her that she was helping Jonathan with some historical research. Then they walked down the hall to Jenny's desk. They were silent except for the click, click, click of their shoes on the tile floor.

The sound echoed in the wide hallway, and Johnny felt strange and disconnected as the events of the past days began to push their way back into his mind: Shub's death, the flight from San Francisco, the close call with the gang near Cleveland, and then meeting Jenny and seeing the Amish men. Now he was in a library in Wooster, Ohio, of all places, walking with a wonderful, sweet girl who had somehow captured his heart.

When they came to Jenny's desk, Johnny walked around and pulled out the chair for her. She flashed a little smile at him and sat down. Jenny pulled the book out of the drawer, and Johnny drew up one of the chairs standing by the wall.

"Where were we, do you remember?" she asked.

"The Indians were attacking the house," Johnny replied.

"That's right, the massacre."

"Massacre?" Johnny asked.

"Yes. I'm sorry you have to hear this, but it will explain to you how your branch of the family ended up outside the faith," Jenny said quietly. "Let me finish and you'll see."

Jenny opened the book to her marker and began reading.

"When Jonas refused to defend the family, Jonathan became outraged with his father and denounced him as a coward. His brother, Joshua, defended our ancestor and took his side, choosing to follow the Amish way with Jonas. Jonathan disregarded them both and said he would go to the *Englischers* who lived nearby and bring help. He went to the back door of the house and, after looking to see if he was being watched, slipped out, promising to return as quickly as he could.

"Meanwhile, the Indians continued to fire rifle shots into the walls of the house. Not meeting with any return fire, the braves grew bolder in their assaults. They took turns running past the front of the house and firing their rifles into the log walls. These acts of bravery seemed to delight them, and they filled the air with whoops and screams.

"Finally, the Indians started a blaze and then produced some torches with which to set the house on fire. As the fire took hold on the roof, the family took refuge in the cellar and endured the smoke as long as they dared. When the flames began eating through the floorboards above their heads, they attempted to escape through the cellar window. They were quickly captured.

"To their horror, they saw that after Jonathan slipped out to go for help, he had been discovered, overpowered, and dragged back to the house. The Indians tormented the entire family and finally killed the girls and the mother.

"A few months before the attack, several Indians had come to the farm pleading for food, but Mother Hershberger had denied them and

forced them to leave. This seems to have caused grave insult to the Indians and most likely was the cause of the attack, as the Indians of the
border were known to be implacable in their hatred of any who might
insult or dishonor them. But for this unkindness, the Hershbergers
might have remained unmolested, but as there had been several other
incidents along the border that spring, it is impossible to know.

"Jonas was carried into captivity along with his two twin sons. The
younger son, Christian, was deemed unfit for the journey because of
his wounds and was killed."

Jenny laid down the book. Johnny sat in absolute silence. After a
few moments he spoke. "How did your grandfather Ezekiel find out
about all this?"

"Jonas, Jonathan, and Joshua were prisoners for five years. Jonathan was taught the warrior oath and eventually adopted into the tribe,"
Jenny explained. "Jonas and Joshua refused to learn the Indian ways
and were made slaves. Jonas lived out his days as a slave but kept his
faith, and ultimately he was able to help his son Joshua escape. Jonas,
however, was killed in the attempt.

"Joshua returned to the white settlements and rejoined the Amish
community. He wrote down all that had happened in a journal and
passed it down to his sons. Ezekiel used Joshua's journal to write the
story."

"What happened to Jonathan?"

"While he was a captive, his skill as a marksman and his cleverness
as a woodsman made him a favorite with the Delaware," Jenny said.
"He learned their craft and cunning and absorbed their tracking skills
and woodland knowledge. As an adopted son, he was given a certain
amount of freedom, and he bided his time until the opportunity to
escape presented itself.

"One day he was hunting in the woods with several other braves.
He and two braves were far in the lead. He turned on them, killed

them, and took off running. The other Indians chased him through the woods for three days. He finally stumbled into Fort Henry and was saved by the garrison there. The story of his exploit became legendary on the border.

"After he recovered, he lived in the woods. He became a border-man—a hunter of Indians. He killed them whenever and wherever he could find them. The Indians referred to him simply as *Nènhilëwès*—the Murderer."

"Did he ever reconcile with his brother?"

"The book says that before Jonathan died, he forgave his father and brother. It did not say whether he ever came back to the faith."

"He had children," Johnny said. "Does it say what his wife's name was?"

Jenny picked up the BGMI and reopened it to the section she had marked. She perused through the lists.

"This is interesting," she said. "Jonathan married Ruth, but there is no record of Ruth's family history."

"How could that happen?" Johnny asked.

"Ruth may have changed her name. In those days, many Indian women married white men, and they usually took a white name."

"Do you think Jonathan married an Indian girl even though he hated them so much?"

"It's quite possible," Jenny said. "That's the only reason I can think of that there would be no record of her before her marriage to Jonathan."

"Wow," Johnny said. "This is really getting trippy. First I don't know who I am, and then I find out I'm of Amish descent and maybe Indian too!"

"I'm glad I could help," Jenny said as she closed the book.

Johnny saw a tear running down her cheek. "What is it?"

"Well, you found out who you are, but I still don't know who I am."

Johnny put his hand on Jenny's shoulder. "I think we were meant

to be friends. I promise to help you find out about your past, whatever that takes."

Jenny looked at him, and then suddenly they were in each other's
arms. Jenny felt his heart pounding, and his embrace was a place of
safety, like the memory of her mother's heart beating next to hers. A
sensation unlike any she had ever known engulfed her, and she was
burning and freezing at the same time. His arms tightened around her.

"Jenny…" he whispered in her ear. "Jenny."

And then another voice whispered in her heart. *This is the road home.*

CHAPTER FIFTEEN

Conflict

◇◇◇

JENNY GOT OFF THE BUS at the stop near the lane that led to her house. Her heart was heavy and yet bursting with the newfound realization that she loved Jonathan. She couldn't understand it or even explain it. He hadn't tried to kiss her; he had only held her closely against his chest. Yet she had known in those few moments that she belonged nowhere else but in his arms and by his side for the rest of her life. But how could that ever happen?

She trudged along the highway deep in thought, her emotions a roller coaster, until she came to the head of the lane. The familiar path stretched before her. Everything she knew and loved, everything that was safe and familiar was here. There were the fields that her *daed* and *grossdaddi* before him tended. The buckeye trees that she loved rose in fall splendor along the lane, their leaves painted golden red by the brush of September frost. The sheds where she had played as a child, the barn where she helped her mama milk the cows, the cooling room where she would hide for hours on hot summer days, dreaming among the jars of milk and fresh vegetables—all of this was in her soul, part of her, the core of her life. This was all she had, and always it had seemed enough.

But today, the loveliness of the trees, the familiarity of the fields and livestock, the safety of the small house with her mother's curtains hung in the window, all of it seemed to have dimmed as though she were seeing it through a mist, faded and gray. Today the glow in her heart didn't come from her home and her family and all things loved and familiar. It came from a love for a man. Jonathan's face came before her, and the warmth of his embrace enfolded her again. The knowledge that love had found her, unheralded and unasked for, was a miracle unlike any other she had ever known, and she had to stop and catch her breath at the wonder of it.

She came to the front porch and looked at the steps up to the front door. There was the rocking chair where her mama would sit in the cool before sunset, reading the Bible. There was the bench where her *grossdaddi* rested in the evening, sipping lemonade, while she sat silently next to him with her hand in his, feeling the hard calluses and the strength of his hand. There was the chair where her papa sat, so handsome and so quiet, looking stern and formal but letting her into the secret place behind his eyes where the smile that could steal her heart lived.

She felt a great emptiness in her heart, and she slumped down on the steps and began weeping, her head whirling and her heart pounding. She heard the door open and her mother's steps on the porch behind her.

"Jenny, my girl, what is it?"

Jenny turned and saw her mother bending down to her. She rose and went into Jerusha's outstretched arms, and her sobs kept time to the beating of her mother's heart.

◇◇◇

That night at dinner Jenny sat silent as Reuben and Jerusha went over the events of the day. She hadn't said anything to her mother about Jonathan. She had only stayed in the comfort of Jerusha's arms until her weeping had quieted. Then silently she had gone into the house and to her room. Jerusha had watched her go, knowing with a mother's intuition that she should hold her peace, that Jenny wasn't ready to talk. So now they sat at the table, the corn and biscuits growing cold on Jenny's plate as she picked at her food.

After a while Reuben noticed Jenny's silence. "What ails you, *dochter*?" he asked. "Are you not feeling well?"

He didn't see the warning glance from Jerusha, so when Jenny didn't answer, he pressed on.

"Jenny, are you sick?"

Jenny looked up, her face stricken. She felt as though every nerve in her body had been stripped bare, and his words were like burning swords piercing her.

"Reuben," said Jerusha, "Jenny's not herself. Perhaps she just needs to rest."

"Maybe she's spending too much time at the library," Reuben said while he carved his meat. "Maybe she needs to come back to our ways and forget this foolishness that only gives her heartache."

"What do you know?" Jenny said quietly.

"*Entschuldigen Sie mich*?" Reuben said, an incredulous look on his face.

"Jenny, can you go fetch some cream for the fruit?" Jerusha asked, sensing a storm on the horizon.

Jenny ignored her mother's plea and repeated her response, this time looking directly at her father. "I said, what do you know about it?"

"You shall not speak to me in such a way," Reuben said slowly.

"That's what you always do, Papa," Jenny retorted, and her words bit like sharp teeth. "You shut me off, turn away, and never listen to what I need or want. I'm a woman now, and I need your support. But you're not there for me, ever. You only want what you want."

Reuben looked at his daughter, the sudden broadside catching him unguarded and unprepared.

"Reuben…" Jerusha said, seeing her husband's jaw set and knowing it could only bode ill for her daughter. But he laid his knife and fork down and went on.

"Is this about your birth mother again?" Reuben asked. "Because I've told you what I want in this matter. I've told you to put this behind you and go on with your life. I've said what I want, and in my house, that is what will be done."

"In your house?" Jenny found herself choking on the words. "I live here too, Papa. Or am I not part of this family? Am I just some stranger you've taken in to ease your conscience?"

Her words struck a place in Reuben's heart that hadn't been touched in many years. "*Sie haben die kühnheit* to say such a thing to me?" he hissed. "I have loved you and cared for you as my own daughter."

"Have you, Papa?" Jenny choked out. "If you had, you would know that this ache in my heart, this need to know, won't hurt me, it will only help me. I'm not Jenna, Papa! I'm Jenny. But your hard heart will kill me just as surely—"

"*Gott im Himmel!*" roared Reuben, slamming his fist on the table. "How dare you say such a thing!"

Jerusha sat absolutely still, all the blood drained from her face.

Jenny went on, the words pouring out. "There's something else I need to say to you, Papa. I'm going to go on with my search with or without your help. This need to know who my birth mother and father are will always be between us until I find out and am whole again. If you really understood me you would know that finding out about my past is the key to my future. Unless I unlock it I'll never know who I am."

Reuben rose from his chair. "You will not do this," he shouted. "I forbid it!"

"You can't stop me!" Jenny shouted back.

Reuben took control of himself with great effort. His next words were like ice. "I can and I will."

Jerusha rose halfway from her chair and leaned forward with her hands on the table, shaking like a leaf in the wind.

"Jenny, Reuben, please don't speak this way to each other!" she cried with tears streaming down her face. "Please, we are a family! We love each other."

"If Papa really loved me, he would hear my heart," Jenny sobbed. "And there's something else." She paused, knowing that the next step would carry her past the limit of her father's endurance and out into an unknown land where all safety and security would be stripped away, but she pressed ahead.

"I have met a boy…a man," she said simply. "And I am in love with him."

"What boy?" Jerusha asked. "What family is he from? We have never seen you with a boy at the gatherings."

Jenny took a deep breath. "He is not Amish."

Reuben sat down as though he had been shot. "An *Englischer*! Jenny Springer, have you gone *verrückt*?"

"No, Papa, I'm not crazy," Jenny choked out as she put her head down in her arms and began to weep.

Reuben turned to Jerusha. "You see, wife?" he said, his words cutting. "You see what happens when we give her freedom? We let her take that job at the library because we thought it would benefit our community, and what does she do? She goes out into the world, associates with the *Englisch*, fills her head with wild ideas, and then gives herself to an *Englischer*. I warned you what would happen if we let her work at that library. And now the day has come when this mistake has born its fruit. This will not be…it cannot be. It must be stopped and stopped now."

Reuben rose from his chair.

"Where are you going, husband?" Jerusha asked.

"To fetch the bishop and the elders," Reuben said coldly. "There is only one way to deal with this."

"Reuben, no—please don't do this," Jerusha cried. "There are other ways. Jenny will come to her senses. We must give it time—"

"No, Jerusha, time has run out."

Reuben took his coat and hat from the peg by the door, put them on, and went out into the night.

For Jenny, the hours that followed were a dim nightmare. Her father returned shortly with the *bisschop* and three *völliger dieners* of the church. She sat silently while her father repeated the story to the men. They listened intently, and then the *bisschop* spoke.

"Jenny, you have sinned against your father and against the *ordnung* of our church. You must repent of these things and do as your father tells you. You must also swear that you will never see this *Englischer* again."

Jenny looked up. Her mother sat with red eyes and a tearstained face, looking shocked and bewildered. Her father stared at her as though he didn't know who she was. A great weariness filled her soul and her heart broke. But still the voice spoke to her heart. *This is the road home.*

She looked at the stern faces of the men in front of her. She knew what her words would bring, and yet deep in her heart, she sensed somehow that the Lord was leading her, as dark as the way seemed. She heard words coming out of her mouth as though she were listening to someone else speaking.

"I will not stop looking for my birth mother, and I will not give up Jonathan." There! She had said his name.

"Oh, Jenny," Jerusha said, and she put her face in her hands and wept silently.

Her father's face fell, and his shoulders slumped.

The *bisschop* spoke. "Then we have no choice. I pronounce the *bann* on you, the *meidung*. From this time until you recant, you are to be shunned. You will have no relationship with the members of our community. You will not attend church services. You will eat at a separate table from your parents. You will not speak to them. They may speak to you only to instruct you as to your responsibilities at home. You will discontinue your work at the library. This *bann* will last for six weeks. If you repent, you will be received back with open arms. If you do not and your rebellion continues, it can only lead to permanent *meidung* and full excommunication from your church and your family.

"You are a baptized member of the Amish church of this section. You have a great responsibility to the community and to your family to stay separate from the world and keep yourself pure. If you choose to follow other paths, you will only divide yourself from the ones who are your family, your friends, and your hope of salvation. We love you and hope you will repent, but that is up to you."

The men rose and filed silently out of the house.

Chapter Sixteen

Shunned

◇◇◇

Jenny lay facedown in her bed. She felt like fine china after a monstrous earthquake. She clenched her fists and did her best to choke back her sobs. She was determined not to let her papa know how much he had hurt her.

This room—her room—had been her refuge all her life, the only place on earth where she felt totally safe. Every night when she was growing up she knew that her big, strong papa was right in the next room sleeping. That knowledge had kept her secure through all her years. Now her room felt like a prison, and the man in the next room was no longer the father she knew but a strange, stern, warden who was unwilling to release the keys that would unlock her future. How had this happened to her? She was not a sinner to be shunned! She was Jenny Springer, who loved her mama and papa and had always been a good Amish girl.

She got up and paced the room. There, beneath the window, was the oak chest her papa had made. Her bed, too, had been made by his hands and rubbed with mineral oil, and its smell had become woven into the fabric of her childhood. She lay again on the bed, her thoughts stirring her emotions like milk in the churn. This quilt beneath her had been handcrafted by her mother. Now it was damp with tears.

She rolled over on her back and stared at the ceiling. Then she got up again and went to look in the mirror on her dresser. Her face was red and her eyes puffy. A fist of fear clutched her insides. She was tempted to cry out, to call her mama, to confess, repent—anything to free herself from this torment. And yet somewhere inside her was the still, small voice beckoning her on. *This is the road home! The answer lies somewhere out there, and only you can find it.*

A great resolve rose in her heart. She would find her birth mother. Jonathan would help her. She lay back down on the bed, pulled the quilt around her, and closed her eyes. A great weariness came upon her. Her eyes jerked open. She stared at the ceiling. Her eyes blinked closed, once, twice...

Tomorrow I will go. Tomorrow I will go. Tomorrow...
And then she slept.

◇◇◇

Reuben and Jerusha sat in front of the fireplace. A cheerless flame flickered on the hearth. The lamps didn't seem to keep the darkness away. Reuben looked at his wife with troubled eyes. Finally he spoke. "I sat here once, years ago, and had the same *schwierigkeiten* in my heart," he said. "It was when I came home during the storm and you were gone. I was sure you'd left Apple Creek forever, and my heart was broken. The life was gone from this house. Then when Bobby came and told me you were lost in the storm and probably dead, I felt fear. Not the kind of fear I had in the Pacific, but the kind of fear that comes from knowing your life is over, yet you will go on living. I lost Jenna and then I lost you. The only hope I had was to go with Bobby to find you, to do something, to try and fix it. But this! This is something I don't know how to fix."

"Perhaps, then, it's not for you to fix, husband," Jerusha said. "Perhaps only Jenny can fix it. Perhaps she must find the answer."

"How is it that someone who isn't my blood can be so much a part of me?" Reuben asked with an anguished look. "Jenny has been my daughter since the moment she told us her name and I knew God had given her to us to comfort us and to be ours. And yet now I feel like I've never known her."

Reuben put his face in his hands. "Is Jenny right?" he asked, his voice muffled. "Did I kill Jenna?"

Jerusha looked at Reuben and then came to his chair and knelt before her husband, laying her head in his lap. She felt his hand reach out and softly stroke her hair.

"We all make mistakes," she said. "Some are inconsequential, and we escape with nothing more than a scare and a reprimand. Others can follow us throughout our lives. I know you've carried the burden of Jenna's death. I see it in your eyes when you look at Jenny. I see the love you have for her, and I know you have a deep fear that you will lose her too.

"But you must remember that our times are in God's hands, not ours. Jenna was with us for four years, and then God took her home. I know someday we will see her again. In the meantime, He has given us Jenny, who needs us to guide her far more than Jenna ever would have. It's time for you to surrender to God's grace in this matter and forgive yourself, for I have forgiven you, and I know that the Lord has too."

Jerusha felt her husband's hand shaking. She looked up at his face. Tears were running down his cheeks, and his shoulders were heaving with silent sobs.

"Reuben," she said softly. "You're a good man, kind and gentle, and I know how much you love Jenny. Perhaps there's another way to reach her. We must pray for guidance."

Reuben reached down and pulled Jerusha up onto his lap. Her

arms slipped under his as he held her, and they sat that way until the fire flickered out.

◇◇◇

The first flush of dawn was creeping over the eastern hills when Jenny awoke. For a moment she lay still, wrapped in her mother's quilt, peaceful and warm. Then the events of the night before flooded back into her mind, and she felt as if a giant hand reached into her chest and squeezed her heart with an unmerciful grip. She was to be shunned! How could this be?

Jenny sat up and swung her legs over the side of the bed. She was still dressed. She clutched the quilt around her shoulders for a few moments and then quietly stood up, went to her closet, and found her knapsack. Then she went to her drawer, opened it quietly, and took out some underwear and socks and stuffed them in the bag. She knew she would need to buy different clothing for her journey in order to blend in with everyone else.

In the top drawer was a small green wooden box. She opened it and lifted out the top section. In the bottom of the box lay a bundle of bills. It was all the money she had earned and saved from working in the fields and babysitting. She counted just a little more than two hundred dollars. *That won't get me very far, but I have to start somewhere,* she thought. *I'll see Jonathan. He said he would help me.*

Jenny changed into a fresh dress and pulled on her boots and then her coat. She took a last look around at the four walls that had bound the small world of her childhood. A sudden fear gripped her. *What am I doing?*

She looked at her *kappe* sitting on the dresser. She started to pick it up and then paused. A pair of scissors was lying there, and she picked them up instead. She took a deep breath, pulled back her shoulders and grabbed her long hair. She breathed a prayer, closed her eyes, and quickly began to chop away the hair. After a few minutes she had shaped what remained of her hair into a short, curly, boyish cut. She took one look at herself in the mirror and then picked up the knapsack. She went to the window and quietly lifted the sash until there was room to crawl out. Quickly she set the knapsack out on the porch and crept through the window. She stood on the porch for a moment and looked at the house. Everything she loved and knew lived here in this house—her mama and papa, her memories, her faith.

Will I ever come back here? she wondered.

Then she turned, stepped off the porch, and quietly walked away.

Reuben rose later than usual. He had lain awake long into the night, praying quietly. He had continued praying until at last he felt he had an answer. Now he arose and walked quietly to the door of Jenny's room. He knew what he needed to do to help his daughter. Softly he knocked on the door.

There was no answer.

"Jenny, can I come in?" There was still no answer. He gently opened the door and looked quickly around the empty room. On the dresser sat Jenny's green box with the lid off and the box empty. The window was open, and the morning breeze ruffled the curtains where Jenny had made her escape.

Chapter Seventeen

The Bargain

◇◇◇

Johnny sat in his room at the Bide-a-Wee Motel in Apple Creek. He had packed his bag and set it on the bed. His repaired Volkswagen van was parked outside. When he picked up the van from Dutch, he had noticed that it ran a lot better when he started it up. He asked Dutch about it.

"Well, I know you didn't ask, but I put a tune-up on her," Dutch said. "You seem like a nice young fella, and I hate to send you on your way with the possibility of breaking down somewhere between here and Nashville. Oh and don't worry, the fifty bucks covered it."

"How did you know about me going to Nashville?" Johnny asked.

"Apple Creek is a small town, son." Dutch smiled, showing a gap where a tooth was missing. "Word gets around, especially if you tell your story to Bull Halkovich. He checked in to see if I was facilitating your 'soon departure.'"

After thanking Dutch, Johnny went back to the motel, fully intending to leave after he packed his things. But he couldn't get Jenny off his mind. He wanted to ask Dutch where Jenny lived, but he remembered that Jenny wasn't even supposed to talk to the "English," as she called them. He didn't want to get her in trouble, so he sat in the motel room, strumming his old Gibson guitar and thinking. He tried to write a song, but he could only come up with a verse that was more of a chorus.

> Tonight I sing this song of love
> You're the one I'm dreamin' of
> Tonight, hold me tenderly
> Come so easily
> Into my heart, tonight

Nothing more came to him, so he played listlessly for a while and then set the guitar down. He thought about driving to Wooster to see if she was at the library, but then he remembered she worked only on Tuesdays and Thursdays, and today was Friday.

Johnny thought about what had happened with Jenny. He remembered her body pressed against his and the way he felt when she whispered his name. He hadn't kissed her, but a whole book could have been written about what passed between them. Something about the way she called him Jonathan made him feel, for the first time in his life, that he belonged somewhere.

Now his thoughts tumbled over themselves as he reflected on the absurdity of the situation. He was hiding out from a gang of drug dealers. He had discovered that his ancestor was an Amish man who quit the church after his family was massacred, and who might have married an Indian girl. He had fallen in love with an Amish girl who was forbidden to see him.

I'm sitting in a motel in a little village called Apple Creek, for goodness sake, and I can't call her or go to her house. Every car that passes makes me jump. I don't even know who I am anymore. How in the world did all this happen to me? Just last week I was tripping out on the streets of San Francisco, and my only problem was paying the rent. How did my whole life change in a week?

The incongruity and the hopelessness of his circumstances crowded in on him, forcing him to decide. He couldn't stay in Apple Creek. He had to go get the money, find a place to hide out, start a new life, and forget this had ever happened.

He got up, put his guitar back in its case, and gathered up his belongings. He looked around the room to see if he had left anything, picked up the room key, and started to leave. Just as he reached for the doorknob there was a soft knock on the door. He jerked his hand back and quietly put his things down and went to the window. He pulled back the curtain a little bit and took a quick look out behind the shade. Someone was standing at the door, but he couldn't see who it was. From the side it looked like a girl wearing jeans and a sweatshirt under a light jacket, but he couldn't see her face. She had short, curly, red-gold hair. He opened the door a crack.

"Yes?"

"Jonathan, it's me."

"Jenny?"

He opened the door. It was Jenny, but she looked completely different. Instead of being tucked up under a *kappe*, her hair was short, the curls framing her face. She had on new jeans and wore a plain blue sweatshirt under a denim jacket. On her feet were a new pair of low-cut white tennis shoes. She looked at him apprehensively.

"Can I come in?" she asked.

"Of course..." He reached out and took her hand, pulled her inside, and closed the door.

They stood there, not speaking, the silence dreadful and wonderful.

Her eyes dropped, and a slow flush crept up her cheeks. She looked back up at him, a tremulous smile starting on her lips. Time seemed to slow down as he became aware of tiny details—the little mole on her earlobe, the cupid bow of her mouth, the deep violet color of her eyes. He had to draw her into his arms. As he did so, her hands crept around him, and he felt her strength as she pulled herself into his embrace. And then Jonathan Hershberger knew that he had found what he had always wanted—someone to be his, someone to belong to, someone to love.

◇◇◇

Reuben stood in the middle of Jenny's empty room. The dresser drawers were empty, and Jenny's prayer *kappe* lay on the dresser next to the amputated locks of her long hair. He looked in the closet. Her knapsack, coat, and shoes were gone. Reuben turned back to his bedroom and shook Jerusha awake.

She looked up at him with a question in her eyes. "What is it, husband?"

"Jenny's gone," Reuben answered.

Jerusha slipped out of bed and ran to Jenny's room. It was as Reuben had said. She sat down on Jenny's bed and put her hands over her face. Reuben stood helplessly in the doorway. After a few moments Jerusha looked up. "What shall we do, Reuben?"

"Jenny's going to try to find her mother. I'm afraid my response to her didn't have the effect I hoped for. Instead it seems to have made her more determined than ever to find the answers to her questions. We must find her before she makes any more foolish decisions."

"But what if she's already left town? What do we do then? She's taken the money she saved, and that will at least buy her a bus ticket."

"She may not need a bus ticket," Reuben said. "The *Englischer* she met may have a car. They're probably leaving together."

"She said his name was Jonathan. Is there any way to find him?" Jerusha asked.

"She either met him in Wooster or here. Maybe Bobby knows something. Not a lot of strangers come our way, and Bobby keeps a watchful eye on his town."

"She also said that a newspaper reporter gave her some clues that she could follow up on. Can we talk to him?"

"That's probably a good idea. If we can find out what she knows, maybe we can discover where she plans to look."

Reuben placed his hand awkwardly on Jerusha's shoulder. A terrible picture came to him. He was standing in the emergency room in Wooster. Bobby was with him. The door from the ICU opened, and Jerusha came out. She looked at him with terrible anger, almost hatred in her eyes. She walked slowly toward him until she stood in front of him. She began to strike him on the chest with both hands. Reuben pushed the picture out of his mind and spoke to Jerusha.

"I promise you, Jerusha, I'll do everything in my power to find her and bring her home. I will not lose her like I lost Jenna."

Jerusha looked at him, but this time there was no anger in her eyes. Instead of striking him she embraced him.

◇◇◇

Jenny felt so safe in Jonathan's arms. She held him as though she would never let go. Finally he pulled back and looked at her. "What happened to you? Your hat, your clothes—and your hair! What did you do to your hair?"

Jenny grimaced and pulled at the short curls by her ear. She took a deep breath. "I got into an argument with my father last night. I said some horrible things to him, and then I told him about you. I told him that I…" She stopped.

"That you what?"

Jenny looked into his eyes. "I told him that I had met you and that…I was in love with you."

Johnny pulled her close again and whispered, "Jenny…you love me?"

"Yes, I do."

Johnny let out a sigh and kissed her forehead. "What did he do?"

"He called for the bishop and some elders, and they placed me under a temporary *bann*, the shunning, like I told you about. I'm an outcast unless I repent. But if I do repent, it means I have to stop looking for my birth mother. It also means I can never see you again. I can't do either of those things."

"But, Jenny, that means you can't be Amish anymore, doesn't it?"

Jenny took a deep breath. "Yes, eventually it would mean excommunication and complete ostracism from my family and my faith."

"Are you really prepared to do that?" Johnny asked quietly.

Jenny moved back a step and lifted her head defiantly. "I've given my heart to you. Don't you want me to love you?"

Johnny saw the fear in her eyes. He stepped toward her and took her hands in his.

"Jenny Springer, I don't know how it happened or why it happened, but in just these few days I've come to love you as I've never loved anyone in my life. You're so beautiful and smart and I want to be with you always. I've never believed before, but as I look at you and hear you say you love me, I almost can believe there's a God and that He must love me very much to bring me here to meet you."

Johnny saw relief and joy flood Jenny's face. Then the awesome obligation they had taken on by declaring their love struck them. Suddenly they were both shy, not knowing what to say.

Jenny broke the spell. "Jonathan, I've also come to ask for your help."

"Is it about finding your birth mother?" Johnny asked.

"Yes. I know I'll never be whole until I know who I am. I think I know where I need to start. I've had a dream...or maybe it's just a memory from when I was very little, about the time of the car wreck. In my memory...or dream...my mother spoke to me. She was very sad and said we had to go to New York. And then she said the name

Robert. I don't know what it means, but I know I must go to New York."

"New York is an awfully big place. Are you sure?"

"Yes I am," Jenny answered. "I have some clues we can follow. And I have two hundred dollars. I don't know what to do exactly, but somehow I believe that God is trying to show me something…the way to find my mother. Will you take me?"

Johnny looked at Jenny for a long time. He thought about the fifty thousand dollars he had hidden in the barn. If things didn't work out in New York, it would be a simple thing to forget about the crooks, come back and get the money, and then disappear with Jenny.

"Yes, I'll take you. And don't worry. I have some money too."

Even as he spoke he felt guilty hiding the truth from her. He felt his jaw clench. His discomfort didn't escape her notice and a look of uncertainty passed across her face. Then she spoke hurriedly.

"If we're going, we need to leave very soon. My *daed* will be looking for me. I told my parents your name, and it won't take long for Uncle Bobby to figure out who you are. All he has to do is ask at the library. You haven't exactly kept a low profile."

Johnny thought about the van sitting out in front of the room and he realized how stupid it was to have it decorated in such a noticeable way. He should have taken Dutch's offer and let him paint it. Too late now. They'd have to make do and try to leave undetected.

"Okay, I'm ready. Do you have anything else?"

"Yes, my knapsack is outside by the door, but I don't have much."

Johnny picked up his guitar and backpack and looked at Jenny. "Are you sure about this?"

"No, but I have to go, even not knowing if it's right. All I know for sure is that I love you."

"Okay then, I'm going to make a bargain with you. I'll take you to New York, and we will follow the clues you have as far as we can. I'll do my best to help you, but when and if we exhaust the leads and we start getting low on money, I'm going to bring you home.

"But, Jonathan, I—"

"Look Jenny, I know you think that God is somehow leading you to do this. I'm afraid I don't have as much faith as you, so I have to go on what's real. You've got to promise me that when you see we've come to the end of possibilities, you'll take it to mean that God didn't really tell you to do this and let me bring you home."

"But, Jonathan, what about us?"

"That's something we'll have to work out after you get this out of your system. Is it a deal?"

Jenny slowly nodded her head.

"Let's go then," he said, gathering up his things and heading for the van. Jenny climbed in while Johnny went to the office, paid his bill, and dropped off the key. He came back, got in, then looked over at Jenny.

"Are you ready?"

Jenny looked out the window at the small village she had grown up in. She had never been farther than Wooster or Dalton in her whole life, and the idea of leaving gave her a chill.

"Let's go quickly, Jonathan. Please."

Johnny started the van and drove out onto the main road, heading out of town. As he drove by Dutch's garage, Dutch was rolling up the front door. He watched the brightly colored van go by. He also noticed who was sitting in the passenger seat.

"That's interesting," he said aloud to the old gray cat rubbing against his legs. "That was Jenny Springer with that boy."

He thought about what he had seen, and then he walked into the shop and picked up the receiver from the phone sitting on a cluttered desk by the back wall.

CHAPTER EIGHTEEN

Trouble

◇◇◇

JOHNNY HEADED EAST ON HIGHWAY 30 toward Canton, Ohio. When he got to Canton he turned north toward Akron, caught Interstate 70, and followed it until it intersected with Interstate 80. They had been driving for a couple of hours when he began to have some misgivings. What was he doing? The guys who were following him knew he was from Long Island. His roommates in San Francisco must have ratted him out. The gang had almost caught him once before. They would no doubt be on the Interstate somewhere looking for him.

He glanced over at Jenny. She was looking at him, and when their eyes met, she blushed and looked down. He knew he was putting her in danger, but he didn't know what else to do. The situation was crazy. Here he was with an Amish girl he had only known for a few days, headed for New York to find her mother, who was probably dead. What could they possibly do in New York? It was such a big town. How had all this happened? He broke the silence.

"Jenny?"

"Hmm?"

"Are you sure you're okay with all of this? I mean, it's kind of a

strange situation we're in. We've known each other for only a few days, and in that time you've been disciplined by your church, you've split with your parents, and you're heading to New York with a guy you barely know to find your mother, who you haven't seen for fifteen years. How are we going to do this?"

Jenny looked at Jonathan again. The muscle in his jaw was working, and his teeth were grinding on each other.

"Why are you doing that?"

"Doing what?"

"Grinding your teeth."

Johnny realized his jaw was clenched, his shoulders were tight, and his hands were gripped on the wheel. He tried to relax. "I'm just a little uptight about all this."

"Why should you be…uptight?"

Johnny stared out the window. Outside a light mist of rain sifted down onto the glass from a dull, gray sky. Johnny fumbled with the knob that turned on the wipers. It stuck as usual, and he had to twist it hard until the wipers went on. The slow swish, swish of the blades locked into the rhythm of his breathing. The weight of his secret suddenly became more than he could deal with. He looked back at her.

"Jenny, there's more to my story than you know. I probably should have told you, but I had no idea we would be running away together. I didn't know I would fall in love with you."

Jenny turned on the seat to face him. "What didn't you tell me?"

Johnny took a deep breath. He looked out at the countryside that was sliding away behind them and then he spoke. "I'm in trouble, Jenny."

"Trouble?"

"Yes. I…I got involved in some things back in San Francisco. I mean I didn't really do anything. I just drove a guy I know over to a place where he was going to do some business."

"What kind of business?"

A hot flush crept up Johnny's neck. It puzzled him. He had been so free back in San Francisco. "Whatever turns you on" had been his mantra. But now, with this girl who had lived all her life in the simplicity of a world without drugs or rock music or pop philosophy, he felt laughable and foolish.

"I…well…"

"What kind of business, Jonathan?"

"Okay. Give me a chance here, because I feel really stupid telling you this. I was with a guy who was going to sell some acid to some other guys."

"Acid?"

"LSD. It's a drug that makes you have hallucinations."

"Why would you want to do that?"

"Sell acid or have hallucinations?"

"Have hallucinations…well, both."

"Well, back there, taking an acid trip seemed very hip and romantic and adventuresome. Now I think it was just a big waste of time. But let me finish. I drove this guy out to a town south of San Francisco to meet some guys who were going to buy the drugs. It was a way for me to make a couple hundred dollars. I didn't know there were guns involved."

"Guns?"

"Yeah, guns. It turned out that the guys he was dealing with were big-time crooks. I think they were from the East Coast and were trying to move in on the scene out in San Francisco. They were real gangster types with suits and guns. And I also didn't know that Shub—that's the guy I was with—was going to try to rip them off."

"Rip them off of what?"

Johnny had to smile. She was so innocent.

"What's so funny?"

"It's just that…well, it's like we live on the same planet, but we operate in two different universes. I guess I need a translator. 'Rip them off' means that he was going to steal their money. He didn't really have any acid. It was just sugar."

"But that's dishonest. How could you be part of that?"

"That's a good question, Jenny. I didn't know he was going to do what he did. I was just along for the ride."

"Well then, why are you in trouble?"

He took another deep breath. "When he was in the motel doing the deal, they must have found out he was trying to rip them…trying to cheat them. I guess Shub pulled his gun and took their money. He tried to run back to the car so I could help him get away, but they shot him."

"You mean, with their guns?"

"Yes, with their guns."

"Did he get badly hurt?"

"Jenny, they killed him. He died right there where you're sitting."

Jenny groaned. She looked down at the seat where Shub had fallen in those last moments.

"They…they *killed* him?"

"Yes. But that's not the end of the story. When Shub ran out to the car, he threw a bag into the van. The drug dealers were shooting at Shub and the van. They shot out your side mirror. They thought I was in on the rip-off, so they tried to kill me too. I managed to get away, but they chased me almost back to the place where I lived. I knew they would find me eventually, so I packed my bags and left town that night.

"I was headed back to Long Island to my mom's house, and after a few days on the road I stopped at a motel west of Cleveland. They showed up at the motel. They must have found out where I was going from my roommates because they had followed me all the way."

"Why were they following you if you left town?"

"I have their money." There, he said it.

"Their money?"

"Yeah. Before Shub died, he tossed a bag into the van. It had fifty thousand dollars in it."

"Fifty thousand dollars!"

"Yes."

The look in Jenny's eyes made Johnny feel sick. She looked away. After a few minutes she looked back at him.

"Can't you give it back and just be free of them?"

"Jenny, you don't understand. I saw them kill a man. I took their money, although I didn't know I did until later. They don't want to leave any witnesses to their crime. If they find me, they will kill me. I was going to the sheriff's office in Wooster when I almost ran over you. And then everything changed and I thought I'd go to jail if I told your uncle and I wanted to find out more about you and then everything happened with your dad and here we are."

Jenny sat silent for a few moments looking out the window. When she finally spoke there was sadness in her voice. "If these men find you and kill you and I'm with you, won't they kill me too?"

Johnny stared straight ahead. Outside it had really clouded up and a few larger drops of rain began to slap down on the windshield. The worn-out wipers did their best to push them away. Jenny asked the question again. His spine felt like ice, and the muscles in his jaw started moving again.

"Probably."

"Probably? You mean my chances of living are not very good, don't you? What were you going to do if they found us? How could you put me in danger? You're grinding your teeth again."

"I'm sorry, Jenny. I didn't mean to put you in danger. All this happened so fast."

"All this?"

"Yes, meeting you and falling in love with you and leaving Apple Creek."

Jenny stared straight ahead and then spoke with measured words. "If you really loved me, you would never have put me in danger. I don't think you know what love is, Jonathan."

Her words cut him like someone had laid a bullwhip on his back. He stared straight ahead as they drove on in silence. After a long time she spoke again.

"Jonathan, I think I've made a mistake. Not about loving you, because I know I can't change what I feel for you. My mother once told me that one day I would find a man who I would surrender my heart to. I didn't believe that could happen, but when I met you, it did. I can't do anything about that. But I made a mistake in not listening to my papa. This desire to know my birth mother has blinded me to everything I already have. I thought I could go with you and find the answer to my questions and everything would be all right.

"I was so angry with Papa, but now I know that I've hurt him terribly. He warned me that my quest would lead me into trouble, and he was right. Now I'm scared—scared because I love you so much, and scared because I don't know you and don't know if I can trust you. I want to be with you forever, but how can I? Can you tell me Jonathan? Can you tell me what I should do?"

With that Jenny put her face in her hands and burst into sobs.

◇◇◇

Just outside of DuBois, Pennsylvania, a young man sat in an old Chevy truck in a gas station parking lot. He was facing the interstate and watching the cars. Suddenly he perked up. A garishly painted blue Volkswagen bus had just passed, headed east. The man climbed out of his truck and walked over to the bank of phone booths next to the station. He picked up the receiver and dialed the operator. When she came on, he asked to make a collect call and then waited. In a moment someone came on the phone at the other end.

"Mr. Moretti?" the young man asked. "Yeah, this is Frank Williams, over in DuBois. Yeah, that's me. Say, I saw that blue Volkswagen you asked me to look out for. Yeah, going east on 80. Where are you now? Stroudsburg? Well if you head west you should pick him up in less than an hour. He's just putting along, so he should be easy to spot. An extra fifty? Thanks, Mr. Moretti. Say, what do you want this guy for? Okay, okay, keep your shirt on, I was just asking. Yeah, I'll be at Johnson's gas station working tomorrow. You can drop it by anytime. If I'm not here just give it to Pete, he's the owner. Yeah, you're welcome, Mr. Moretti. Anytime."

The young man hung up the phone and headed for the restaurant next to the station, where he decided he would have the T-bone steak tonight.

◇◇◇

Johnny drove on down the interstate. He looked over at Jenny as she continued to sob, and he felt completely helpless.

After a while, Jenny composed herself and lifted her face. They drove on without speaking for a long time. Finally Johnny broke the silence.

"What do you want me to do, Jenny? I'm so sorry I got you into this. Maybe I should just take you home."

"Right now, home sounds very good to me," Jenny said with a small smile. She wiped her eyes with the back of her sleeve and then pulled herself together and looked at Johnny. "But I made a decision back in Apple Creek when I told you I loved you. I'm going to stand by that." Jenny paused and then went on. "We're on our way, so let's keep going and see what…"

At that moment she was interrupted by the sound of a car horn honking. Johnny looked to his left. A brown sedan had pulled even with the van. The window on the passenger side was rolled down, and a man holding a gun was signaling for Johnny to pull over.

An electric shock went down Johnny's back. He knew he couldn't outrun their car, so he looked ahead for a place to get off, pulled over, and came to a stop. The car pulled into a spot in front of them, and two men leaped out and ran back to the van. A tall man with a dark face came to Johnny's side and motioned for him to roll down the window.

"Hi ya, Candyman. Isn't that what they called you back in Frisco?" the man said with a grim smile as he held the gun tightly. The other man was standing by Jenny's door with his gun just below the window.

"Now, I want you to keep quiet and do exactly what I say," the man continued. "Luis is going to join you, and we'll just follow along. There's a rest area just up the road that's a perfect place to have a little talk. Now move."

Johnny looked at Jenny. Her face was as white as a sheet. The man called Luis opened the slider door and climbed in the back. Johnny pulled out on the freeway, and they drove to the rest area with the brown sedan following. It was raining when they pulled in, and the parking lot was empty. The tall man got out of the sedan and walked up to the van. He opened Johnny's door and motioned him out of the car. His gun was pointed right at Johnny's stomach.

"Where's our money, Johnny?" The man's voice was sibilant, like a snake.

"I don't have it."

"Sure you don't. Shub tossed it in the van. Where is it?"

Johnny glanced over at Jenny. She sat looking at him, her eyes begging him to do something.

"I was afraid, and I stashed it back in Wooster, at an abandoned farm. If you don't believe me, search our stuff. It's not here."

There was a rustling sound from the backseat as Luis quickly went through their bags.

"It ain't here," he said.

"Well, we'll just have to take a little ride back to Wooster then."

Suddenly Jenny blurted out. "My uncle is the sheriff of Wayne County! He will catch you. You have to let us go."

"The girl's got a point, Sal," Luis said. "We can't take her back there if her uncle's the sheriff. It's a small town, and someone might recognize her."

"She's not going back," Sal replied. "She's going to stay with you while Maxie and I take the Candyman back to get the money. She'll be our guarantee that Johnny boy won't try anything stupid. He was a stranger in town, right? We'll just look like tourists. Get her out of here and take her up to Moe's. We'll join you there when we have the money."

"Leave her out of this," Johnny said. "She knows nothing about all this."

Sal laughed. "You're a bit late on that score, Candyman. She's in it now." He jammed his gun into Johnny's midsection and then nodded to Luis. Luis got out, opened the passenger door, and pulled Jenny out.

She looked over at Jonathan. "Just get the money, Jonathan. I'll be all right. Just get it and come back for me."

Luis led Jenny away.

"Jenny! I'll come back," Johnny called after her. "Don't fight them."

Sal smiled and waved the gun toward the van. A short, dangerous-looking man joined them and climbed in the back.

"Let's go, Johnny boy. You got some drivin' to do."

CHAPTER NINETEEN

Missing

◇◇◇

BOBBY HALVERSON HEARD THE BUZZ of the intercom on his desk. With a sigh he pushed aside the files for the case he had been working on. Paperwork wasn't his cup of tea, especially when it involved Randy Culberson's new shed being eighteen inches closer to the street than the setback allowed, which was a cause of great offense to Maxine Schuster, who lived directly across the road.

"What is it, Jill?"

"Dutch Peterson on line one."

"Thanks."

Bobby picked up the phone. It was always good to hear from the best mechanic in Wayne County. Dutch was getting a little slower now, but he could still make a tractor run like an Indy 500 racecar.

"Dutch, old buddy, what's up?"

The voice on the other end of the line sounded troubled. "Hey, Bobby, I think I better tell you about something."

"What's that, Dutch?"

"Well, I been fixing the van of a hippie kid who came in here a few days ago with a damaged tie-rod. Seems he bent it when he ran up on a curb to keep from running over someone."

"And…"

"The someone he almost ran over was Jenny Springer."

"So did Jenny get hurt? I don't understand."

Bobby could hear Dutch sigh. "Let me finish, hoss," Dutch said. "This kid picked up his van and left town today. I seen him driving out."

"Probably a good thing," Bobby said. "We don't have a lot of patience with hippie types."

"Yeah, but, Bobby, Jenny was with him when he left."

"What?"

"Jenny Springer was with this kid. His name was, uh….Johnny… Johnny…wait a minute, I got the bill right here. Oh yeah, Johnny Hershberger."

"Hershberger! You say he was a hippie, not an Amish kid?"

"Let me finish," Dutch said. "When I saw Jenny this morning, she was dressed in regular clothes. She weren't wearing her little hat either. And her hair was short! I almost didn't recognize her. And I think the boy got in some kind of trouble while he was here because Bull Halkovich dropped by to make sure I expedited his departure from town. What do you think it means, hoss?"

"I don't know, Dutch. I'll call Reuben and check it out. Thanks for letting me know."

Bobby hung up the phone. Every day since he and Reuben had lunch together, he had been thinking about Jenny. She was certainly an impulsive girl—and now this. Something bad must have happened between her and Reuben. He clicked the intercom button.

"Yes, Sheriff?"

"Jill, can you call Hank Lowenstein for me and ask him if he can go next door and bring Reuben or Jerusha over to the phone?"

"Right away."

Bobby put down the phone and waited. In about ten minutes the intercom buzzed.

"Yeah, Jill."

"It's Reuben Springer."

Bobby grabbed the phone. "Reuben, I didn't expect to hear from you. Thought you'd be out working."

"Not today, Bobby." There was a great weariness behind Reuben's voice.

"Reuben, what's going on? Is Jenny in trouble?"

There was a pause. Reuben was a very private man, and Bobby knew he didn't like to air his dirty laundry. "Come on, Reuben, this is Bobby. What's going on?"

"Jenny's gone," Reuben said. "We had a fight, and we said some terrible things to each other. I got really angry with her, and she laid into me."

"Was it what you talked to me about? About her birth mother?"

"Well, yes, but there was something else. She told us that she had fallen in love with a boy, an *Englischer*. We had to do something, so I had the bishop come…"

"What did you do to Jenny, Reuben?"

There was another long pause. Bobby thought Reuben was stonewalling him, but when Reuben answered, Bobby could hear the pain in his voice.

"Jenny was placed under a temporary *bann*, Bobby."

"You mean she went under the *meidung*, the shunning?"

"Yes, that's what I mean."

Bobby breathed out a long breath. "Well, Reuben, I hate to say this, but I think you overreacted, and now it's backfired on you."

"What do you mean?" Reuben asked.

"Dutch Peterson saw Jenny leaving town with the young man she told you about. They were headed east."

"What!"

"Apparently they left town this morning. But here's the strange part. Dutch said she wasn't wearing her Amish clothes. And her hair was cut off."

The silence from Reuben's end was deafening. Then Reuben spoke. "Bobby, can you help me with this?"

"I'm not sure what I can do, Reuben. Jenny's nineteen. She can basically do whatever she wants. Unless the kid she's with has a record or some warrants, I have to stay out of it."

"Can you at least check on that?"

"Sure, Reuben, I'll make some calls, and I'll talk to Bull. I guess he had some kind of a run-in with the boy. By the way, his name is Hershberger."

"Hershberger?" There was genuine surprise in Reuben's voice.

"Yeah, Johnny Hershberger," Bobby replied. "I found that a bit odd too. All the Hershbergers I know are Amish. Look, Reuben, I'll find out what I can, and then I'll either come over or have Hank come bring you to the phone."

"Thanks, Bobby."

The line went dead. Bobby flicked the intercom switch again.

"Yes, sir," Jill said.

"Is Bull around?"

"Sure, he's in the break room grabbing a cup of coffee."

"Have him come in here, would you please? And have him bring his report on Johnny Hershberger."

In a few minutes there was a knock, and then Bull Halkovich came in carrying his ticket book.

"What's up, Bobby?"

"Did you run into a kid named Johnny Hershberger in the past few days?"

"Yeah, the hippie kid with the freak-o bus."

"Freak-o?"

"Yeah, well, it was all painted and had pictures of weird guys pasted on it. A regular sideshow at the circus."

"What do you have on him?"

Bull leafed through the ticket book.

"Here we go. The van had New York plates, 6S-5844. I ran them but didn't get any hits, so I let him go. He said he was a musician. He'd been in San Francisco, but he was on his way to join a band in Nashville. I…uh, I encouraged him to be on his way."

"You mean you ran him out of town?" Bobby said with a chuckle.

"Well, sort of. He bent something in his suspension running up on a curb. That's the funny part. He did it to keep from hitting Jenny Springer, and I guess she gave him an earful. I sent him over to Dutch to get it fixed. Dutch had the van for two or three days. What's it all about, Bobby?"

"Dutch called me to say he had seen the Hershberger kid headed out of Apple Creek. Jenny Springer was with him."

"Jenny? That's strange. What would she be doing with that weirdo?"

"I'm not sure. I know you didn't get a hit on the plates, but our resources are a little limited here. You said he was coming from San Francisco? Would you mind calling out there and seeing what you can come up with? And maybe check the registration on those plates again."

"Sure thing, Boss." Bull picked up his pad and left.

Bobby sat tapping a pencil on the top of his desk.

The three-hour drive back to Wooster had been uneventful. Johnny was driving, and Sal sat in the passenger seat. Sal hadn't spoken two words the whole time. Maxie was sitting in the back. He had also been silent, but the bulge under his coat spoke volumes. Johnny's thoughts were in turmoil. Jenny was clearly in danger, and he could do nothing. Suddenly a thought occurred to him. Silently he began to pray.

God, if You exist, I'm asking for Your help—not for me, but for Jenny.

She's in real trouble, and I can't help her. I need to get away from these men. Please help me. I don't know who else to ask.

After he prayed, Johnny felt his heartbeat slow down. The beads of sweat on his forehead dried, and he felt a strange calm. And then he knew what to do.

◇◇◇

Bobby was thinking about Jenny and what kind of a disagreement would make her leave Reuben and Jerusha. *It must have been a dilly*, he thought just as the intercom buzzed, startling him.

"Yeah, Jill."

"It's me, Boss," Bull said. "I called the boys out in Frisco and got some information you need to hear."

"Come on in, Bull."

In a minute, Bull came in holding a notepad with some hand-written notes on it.

"What's up?"

"I checked with the San Francisco sheriff's department, and it seems Johnny boy is a wanted man."

"Really?" Bobby asked.

"Yep. He was involved in a shootout at a motel just outside of San Francisco about a week ago. I guess one of the residents at the motel was awakened by gunfire and peeked out his window. He saw a hippie van just like Hershberger's tearing out of the parking lot, and shortly after that another car went after it. They left a dead guy in the parking lot."

"How do they know it was Hershberger's van?" Bobby asked.

"The witness just happened to be an ex-cop. He was able to describe the van in detail. He also remembered both license plates, out of habit I guess. Sure enough, the plates on the van were from New York—6S-5844. The other plates were newer but also from New

York—AX-3636. The van is registered to Ronald Hershberger of Levittown, New York. The other car—a Lincoln—is registered to Moretti Trading Company, Brooklyn, New York. Looks like our boy is involved with some bad people."

"Bull, put out an APB on the van and the Lincoln in case they're still in the county. I'll call Emmett over in Stark County and have him do the same there."

"Right, Bobby. I'm on it."

◇◇◇

Johnny drove into Wooster in the early afternoon. Sal finally spoke. "Okay, Mr. Candyman, where's the dough?"

"At a farm outside of town. I only remember the street I came in on, and I don't know this town so I have to backtrack my way out of town. I have to go down Walnut and then out Liberty."

Johnny turned on North and headed west. In a few blocks he saw what he was looking for on the right—the big brown building that housed the sheriff's office. He drove slowly by, hoping. *Bull, if you're ever going to be observant, now's the time!*

Johnny turned south on Walnut and then turned left around the block, hoping to make one more pass before Sal and Maxie caught on.

"Hey, what are you doing?" Sal asked suspiciously.

"I turned the wrong way back there. I have to go north out of town on Walnut. Just bear with me."

Johnny felt Maxie's gun barrel against his neck.

"Just don't try anything funny," Maxie said.

Johnny turned onto North and went by the sheriff's office once more. As they did, a sheriff's patrol car passed them going the other way. Johnny's hopes rose, but the officer kept driving.

Then they turned north on Walnut and headed out of town. Johnny's heart sank.

◇◇◇

Once again the intercom buzzed.

"Yeah, what?"

"Boss, you won't believe it, but our boy just drove through town. Tony Garrison was on Walnut Street, and the van passed him going the other way. It looked to Tony like they were headed north, so he went up to the intersection, turned around to follow them and called me pronto. He said Jenny's not with the kid, but there are two men in the van with Hershberger. What do we do?"

"Tell Tony to stay with them but far enough back so they don't catch on. Grab your cruiser and your shotgun and meet me out front. We're going hunting."

◇◇◇

Johnny drove slowly out toward the farm. He knew without a doubt that as soon as he handed over the money, Sal would kill him and probably bury him right there. No one would ever know. And Jenny would surely be killed too. Desperation grew in Johnny's heart.

What do I do now, God?

He was turning onto 585 when he looked in his rearview mirror and saw flashing lights.

His heart jumped. It was a sheriff's cruiser.

Sal put his gun in Johnny's ribs.

"Pull over but don't say nothin'. If you want to live and you don't want to see this cop dead, play it straight."

Johnny pulled over and waited, but the cruiser just sat behind them. Then two more sheriff's cruisers pulled up across the road, and another roared past and took up a position in front of the van. Bull got out of one of the cruisers, and a smaller man who was carrying a rifle got out of the other. The two took up positions behind their cars with guns leveled. A voice came over the bullhorn from the cruiser behind them.

"You, in the van. Put your hands in plain sight and step out of the car."

Sal swore and shoved the gun in Johnny's stomach. "Roll down the window."

Johnny rolled it down and Sal shouted, "If you don't want me to kill this guy, let us go."

"Bull, they have Jenny!" Johnny shouted.

Sal grabbed Johnny's head with his free hand and turned it so the police could clearly see his gun now pressed against the back of Johnny's head. Johnny closed his eyes.

"Back off, Sheriff!" Sal screamed. "We're driving out of here. Do what I say or the kid dies and so does the girl!"

"Throw the gun out and step out of the car," came the voice from the bullhorn. The sheriff with the rifle took aim at the car.

"Okay, Sheriff, I warned you!" Sal shouted.

He pulled back the hammer of the pistol with his thumb. Suddenly there was a crack of a rifle and Johnny felt something hot zip by his ear. It struck Sal's hand, and the gun flew away. Sal screamed and grabbed his injured hand. Maxie leaned forward, threw his gun out the window, and raised his hands.

"Now climb out and lay facedown on the ground. All of you."

The three men climbed out and stretched out facedown on the ground in front of the van.

"Lock your hands behind your head."

Johnny heard footsteps running toward them, and then strong hands jerked him to his feet. He found himself staring into the eyes of a very determined-looking man. The badge on his coat said "Sheriff." When the man spoke to him, Johnny could tell that he wanted an answer, fast.

"Where's Jenny?"

◇◇◇

A half-hour later a police cruiser pulled up in front of the Springer home. Bobby Halverson got out, walked up on the porch, and knocked on the door. Jerusha Springer answered, her face pale and drawn.

"Bobby, what is it?"

"Hello, Jerusha," Bobby said. "Is Reuben home too?"

"He's out at the barn. Come in while I go fetch him in."

Bobby went inside and stood with his hat held in front of him while Jerusha went out the back door to find Reuben. He glanced around. It had been a while since he had visited the Springer home. The last time was last Thanksgiving. Bobby remembered it as a pleasant time. The conversation had turned to another Thanksgiving during the Great Storm of 1950, when Jerusha had found Jenny and he and Reuben had rescued both of them from the storm. The Springer family had been close-knit and loving that day. Obviously a lot had happened since then.

Just then Reuben came in with Jerusha. He walked up and gripped Bobby's outstretched hand.

"*Guten tag*, Bobby. You have news?"

"I'm afraid it's not good, Reuben. We found the Hershberger boy, but Jenny wasn't with him. He was with a couple of tough characters with guns. I haven't sorted out all the details yet, but the Hershberger kid told me a pretty troubling story about a drug deal gone wrong and fifty thousand dollars the bad guys were trying to get back."

"But what about Jenny?" Jerusha cried.

Bobby paused. "She's being held captive until the guys we captured come back with the money. It doesn't look good. This brand of criminals doesn't like to leave any witnesses. I'm sure once they have their money…"

Jerusha gasped and sank down in a chair. Reuben took Bobby by the arm with a steel grip.

"Are you telling me that Jenny is in danger of being killed?"

"It doesn't look good, Reuben. She's in danger."

"What can we do?" Reuben asked as he let go of Bobby's arm.

"Our only hope is to get the guys we caught to talk. They need to tell us where Jenny is, and then we have to try to get her back. I've got them down at the station, but as of now, they aren't talking. Johnny Hershberger has told us everything he knows, but I'm not sure how to proceed from here."

"Bobby, are they going to kill my girl?" Jerusha asked.

"I don't know, Jerusha. It's not a good situation."

Jerusha stared at her husband. She got up slowly and turned to leave.

"Where are you going, wife?" Reuben asked.

"I must pray for Jenny. It's the only hope I have left."

Part Two
THE KEY

◇◇◇◇◇◇◇◇◇◇◇◇◇

PRAYER IS A WONDERFUL GIFT that God has given His children. As we pray, we must believe that God has placed a force in our hands that can shake the very heavens and bring His power down to earth in our hour of need. But speaking our supplications is only half of prayer. The other half, and the most important, is listening to what God speaks to us.

CHAPTER TWENTY

The Prisoner

◇◇◇

JERUSHA KNELT BY THE BED AND PRAYED. She began without words, but then they came as she wept, begging God to help. And then when she was finally drained and exhausted, a thought came to her. *This is what I did before Jenna died. I cried out to You, but I didn't listen when You were trying to reach my heart.*

Jerusha stopped then and lifted a simple prayer to God. "Jenny is Your daughter, Lord, and You have a plan and a purpose for her life. If it is Your will, let me be a vessel for You to work through to help her."

As she finished her prayer, a picture came to her mind, clear and distinct. It was the quilt that she made for Jenna but that ultimately became Jenny's salvation. Suddenly, a great urgency came over her. She rose from her prayer and went to her sewing room. The old cedar chest stood against the wall. She knelt before it and opened the lid. Pieces of fabric and batting filled the chest, and the faint, comforting smell of cedar rose up to greet her.

She took some of the pieces out and laid them aside until she came to the parcel wrapped in plain brown paper and tied with string. She lifted it out reverently and placed it on the floor, untied the string, and opened the package. There was the Rose of Sharon quilt, the most beautiful quilt she had ever made. Tenderly she spread it out on the floor. There was something about just looking at the quilt that built her faith, something of both of her daughters that comforted her and gave her hope. The red silk rose in the center with its hundreds of petals glowed in the light, and the rich blue silk backing set it off like a jewel. It was still a beautiful quilt even though it was ruined.

Then she heard a voice within her, the same comforting voice that had led her through the storm so many years ago, the voice that showed her the truth about herself as she waited in the cabin for Reuben to come. A familiar, deep peace filled her soul.

Jenny's life is like this quilt. Though it is beautiful, it is not whole. Pieces are missing, and stains must be washed away. You have been chosen to be part of that cleansing. You are a key to Jenny's happiness and wholeness.

Startled by the clarity of the words, she answered out loud. "But I can't do anything. I'm here alone. Reuben and Bobby are the answer."

Again the voice came to her. *I will say again—Jenny's life is like this quilt. Your hands will give you the key to your prayers, and through them her life can be made whole.* Kumme, dochter! *There is work to be done.*

Hope leaped up in her heart. Suddenly she gathered up the quilt in her arms and stood up. It was clear to her now. Jerusha knew what she must do.

◇◇◇

Jenny Springer lay in darkness. The motion of the car under her made her sick to her stomach. It seemed like they had been driving for hours. When they took her from Johnny, they tied her hands and feet and gagged her and then shoved her in the trunk of the sedan. The men warned her not to make a sound. As she lay bound in the trunk, she had a hard time breathing through the gag, but by some strenuous effort with her face she worked the corner of the cloth up to make an opening to breathe through. Then she slowed her rapidly beating heart by taking deep breaths.

When she was calm again, she began to think about her situation. She knew she was in the hands of dangerous men who didn't care whether she lived or died. She also knew that once Johnny gave them the money they would probably kill both of them. Johnny's only hope was to get help before that happened, and her only hope was to somehow get away from these men.

The analytical part of her mind tried to take over the emotions roiling through her. And then out of nowhere a scripture verse popped into her head. *The name of the LORD is a strong tower: the righteous runneth into it, and is safe.*

A deep sense of shame crept over Jenny. She was a Christian girl, yet she hadn't really asked the Lord about anything for weeks.

I should have talked to You about Jonathan and about leaving home, but I didn't. Instead I just let my impulsive heart take over, and now here I am. I don't even know if You still hear me, but if You do, I need Your help.

There in the darkness a small light of hope began to burn in Jenny's heart. A conviction settled on her that her God had heard her prayer.

Sometime later Jenny felt the car slow down and turn right. She guessed that they were leaving the Interstate, and she wondered if they would stop for a break. She had been in the trunk for a long time and was very uncomfortable. The car stopped and then turned left, and she heard traffic passing under her.

We must be going over an overpass to Moe's place, wherever that is.

Jenny thought about where she might be. The only area between Ohio and New York that could provide the solitude needed for a hideout was the Pocono Mountains. She had seen where the Poconos were on maps of Pennsylvania when she researched the Pennsylvania Amish, and she knew there were some fairly remote areas up in those hills. She tried to estimate how long they had been driving and decided it must have been at least three hours. It was an eight-hour trip to New York from Apple Creek, and she and Johnny had driven for more than two hours before they were stopped, so now they must be somewhere in eastern Pennsylvania.

The road beneath the car no longer had the smooth feel of the Interstate, and she could feel a few bumps that might be caused by potholes. The car swung through a sharp turn, and she knew they had turned onto a back road off of Highway 80 and headed into a sparsely populated area.

About half an hour later she felt the car turn off the paved road onto dirt or gravel. The road became very bumpy and rutted, and Jenny bounced around roughly in the back. After a few minutes the man driving the car pulled to a stop. Jenny heard the men climb out, and then the trunk opened. One of the gang, a younger man, helped her out and untied her.

Jenny looked around. They were in a clearing deep in the woods. Brush and brambles filled the spaces between the trees. Ahead was a low, ramshackle building with a wooden porch running along the front. A pile of logs and split wood sat by the front door, and smoke rose from a chimney on the shingled roof.

Dusk was coming on, and it had started to rain lightly. A chilly wind whistled through the tops of the big maple and beech trees, a portent of snow. The leaves on the trees had turned red and gold at the approach of winter and were starting to fall off. Under different circumstances the beauty around her would have thrilled Jenny, but now it all seemed dark and dreary.

A fat, balding man with a whiskered face came out on the porch. "Hello, boys. Did you bring me a present?" He leered at Jenny.

The young man stepped protectively in front of Jenny, an act that was not lost on her.

"She's a little insurance we're holding onto until Sal collects some money our friend from San Francisco stashed back in Ohio," Luis said. "As soon as he lets us know he has the cash, we may give her to you as partial payment for letting us stay awhile."

Jenny's heart sank. The fat man grinned at her again. "She's a pretty little thing," he said.

The young man glanced at Jenny, his eyes troubled.

He isn't happy about this. He must have a good heart.

He stepped over and said something quietly to Luis. Luis looked surprised and then smiled. "Well, Moe, you may have to work it out with Jorge here. He seems to have a little interest in the girl too." Luis laughed wickedly and slapped Jorge on the back. "You're gonna make your bones yet, kid."

Moe looked surprised, and then he laughed. "Tell you what kid. I'll arm wrestle you for her."

Jorge stepped over in front of Moe. He towered over the fat man and pushed up against him.

"Tell you what, Moe. How about you don't lay a finger on her until I'm done with her." He put his hand on Moe's shoulder and squeezed, and Moe winced in pain.

"Okay, kid, okay. I was just foolin' around. I didn't know you had a romantic interest in the little darlin'. Hey, Luis, call the kid off."

Luis laughed again and slapped Jorge lightly on the cheek. "A real ladies' man, just like your Uncle Luis, eh kid?"

Jorge didn't say anything, but he took Jenny by the arm and led her inside. The interior of the house was dark and filthy. A wood-burning stove in the corner was glowing red. It was raised off the floor by a several bricks covered with soot and small pieces of wood. A large table with rough wooden chairs around it stood in the center of the room. A big, worn-out couch sat against the back wall, and water-stained acoustic tile sagged from the ceiling. A single bare bulb hung from a wooden beam. A few throw rugs were scattered on the floor. The kitchen area was off to one side, and a fluorescent fixture with one tube burned out and the other flashing dimly hung over the sink.

Something cooking in a pot on the stove smelled good, and Jenny realized she was very hungry. Jorge pushed her toward the back of the house. They went down a hallway to a small door. Jorge opened it and pushed Jenny inside.

"Don't worry," he whispered, "I won't let them hurt you."

Hope began to wash the fear out of Jenny's heart. In this dark and dangerous place, she may have found a friend! Jorge stepped out, and she heard the lock click. She was alone and still alive.

"Thank You, Lord," Jenny whispered. Then she looked around.

She was in a small room, almost a closet. A grungy mattress lay on the floor with a blanket and a gray-striped pillow piled on it. A tiny window high up on the wall let in the last of the daylight. There was no latch on the window, but it was held tightly closed by several small, flat bars of metal screwed into the sill around it and then into the window frame. It seemed to Jenny like the room may have been used as a prison before.

There was a light switch on the wall and a single bulb on a cord dangling from the ceiling. A dirty spiderweb festooned a high corner by the ceiling, and a filthy piece of thin carpet covered part of the wood floor. She switched on the light and then quietly walked over to the back wall and tried reaching the window. It was almost above her outstretched fingers. Besides, it was too small to crawl through even if she could get out the screws that held it shut. Jenny sank down onto the mattress. It was filthy and stained with only the single, dirty blanket to cover her. She leaned against the wall and pulled the blanket around her shoulders.

"Oh, Papa, I'm so sorry," she sighed—and then she began to weep, quietly so as not to draw attention to herself. The silent sobs shook her shoulders as all of the events of the last few days overwhelmed her.

◇◇◇

Jerusha held the Rose of Sharon quilt in her hands. She stared at the stains and the rips and the place where she had torn the batting out to start the fire that had kept her and Jenny warm through the freezing nights. In spite of the damage, the quilt was still beautiful. The words came to her again.

Jenny's life is like this quilt. Though it is beautiful, it is not whole. Pieces are missing, and stains must be washed away. You have been chosen to be part of that cleansing. You are a key to Jenny's happiness and wholeness.

Jerusha began to examine the quilt, seam by seam, piece by piece. She picked up a pencil and a pad of paper and started to make a list of all the repairs she needed to make. She noted the colors, fabrics, and sewing techniques she would have to reproduce. Jerusha was a master quilter, and her grandmother had taught her to save fabric from quilts she worked on in case of future necessary repairs.

She looked in the chest and began to gather her supplies. She pulled out a piece of muslin and set it aside. She would need the muslin to try out stitches and repair techniques before she used them on the fabrics. At the bottom of the chest lay the remnants of the two bolts of silk that she had used to make the rose and the background, and a large piece of the cream-colored backing. She laid everything out and made sure she had what she needed to start. Jerusha stretched the Rose of Sharon quilt out flat on the sewing room floor. She sighed. There was so much to do. The quilt was stained. Pieces of the rose petals were torn off or frayed. One whole corner was ripped open and the batting torn out.

"Where do I start, Lord?" she asked. "There's so much to be done here."

Then a verse from one of her favorite psalms came to her. *I will praise thee; for I am fearfully and wonderfully made: marvelous are thy works; and that my soul knoweth right well. My substance was not hid*

from thee, when I was made in secret, and curiously wrought in the low-
est parts of the earth. Thine eyes did see my substance, yet being unperfect;
and in thy book all my members were written, which in continuance were
fashioned, when as yet there was none of them.

"I must start with the secret parts," she said out loud. Then with a
prayer on her lips she began to repair Jenny's quilt.

Chapter Twenty-One

Answers

◇◇◇

"I must start with the secret parts," Jerusha said out loud again. She looked at the corner she had torn open. The batting inside was shredded, and a large piece was missing, the piece she had used to start the kindling on fire that first night in the cabin. With her rotary scissors, she began to carefully trim away the matted and torn parts until the batting was ready to splice.

She had used a double layer of soft batting to make the quilt warm and heavy, so she had to use a double piece basted together to patch the tear. The original quilt had been difficult to sew, but the finished product had been a masterpiece. Now she placed the square piece of double batting on the corner and arranged it so that it made a new corner but overlapped the old batting. Carefully she cut through the four layers of batting in a serpentine pattern. When she was finished, she butted the two pieces together and, using a whipstitch, began to join them. She had learned about using a curved cut when splicing batting years before, and she knew that the serpentine line would distract the eye and render the splice almost invisible. When she was finished she would hardly be able to tell the corner had been torn.

As she worked she began to pray, and soon she realized the Lord was leading her in a conversation. It had been a long time since she had heard the trusted voice within her spirit.

When I finished creating Jenny in the secret place of her mother's innermost parts, she was perfect. But after she was born, things happened to her that were not My plan for her, and she was torn inside, just as this batting was torn. The hidden parts of her were damaged when she saw things a little girl should not have to see. I have been waiting to heal those torn parts all these years, and now the time has come.

Jerusha then knew that she had been given an awesome responsibility when Jenny came into their lives, and yet as the years had gone by, she had forgotten that Jenny was not her birth child and that there was a part of her that Jerusha knew nothing about.

"I should have prayed more. I should have asked You about Jenny's past. Reuben and I should have understood that the missing part of her is a big part of who she is. O Lord, will You forgive me for being so blind?"

Tears began to course down Jerusha's cheeks as she laid the quilt down, knelt, and humbled herself before her God.

◇◇◇

Bobby sat at his desk. Johnny Hershberger sat across from him. It was dark outside, and the streetlights were on. It had started raining, and Bobby could hear the hissing of car tires in the water as they drove by. It had been two hours since they found Johnny, and Bobby could see that he was exhausted.

Bobby watched him. He wouldn't be a bad-looking kid if he'd lose the ponytail. Bobby noticed there was a tiny gash on his earlobe where the bullet from his rifle had nicked it on its way to Sal's hand. Bobby smiled. *I cut that one pretty close. Guess I need to get back on the range and practice a little.*

Bobby cleared his throat. "So tell me the story one more time, son. I want to make sure I have all the details."

"But, Sheriff! Jenny's out there with those drug dealers. She's in danger. If Sal doesn't contact the rest of the gang soon they'll—" He stopped cold at the thought.

Bobby looked at the young man sternly. "Look, John—"

"Jonathan. My name is Jonathan."

"Okay, Jonathan," Bobby said. "I want to point some things out to you. You're in a lot of trouble. First of all, you're wanted back in San Francisco in connection with a murder."

"I already told you, I was just the driver," Johnny said. "I needed some money to leave town, and it seemed like an easy way to make it. I didn't know Shub was going to rip them off."

"Be that as it may," Bobby said, "you are an accessory and a witness. Some folks back in Frisco have some questions for you. Then there's the little matter of the fifty grand. If you weren't part of the shakedown, how did you end up with the money?"

"Look, I didn't know I had the money. Shub threw the briefcase in the car when he got shot. I took off and left town that night. I didn't even know what was in there until a couple of days later. After they almost caught up with me in Cleveland, I got scared and hid the money."

"That's all well and good, and we'll sort that out later. Now here's the biggest part of my problem with you," Bobby said quietly. "You have put Jenny in grave danger with your foolishness. Because of you, she's in the hands of bad men. If anything happens to her, you'll wish you'd never come to Wooster. I can promise you that."

Johnny shrank under Bobby's gaze. "Sheriff, I'm truly sorry. I know what I've done was incredibly stupid, but I love Jenny and was just trying to help her. She needs to find out about her past, and it's tearing her up inside. It seemed like nobody in her family was willing to help her. I mean, she helped me find out about my past, and when she did, I started to understand things about my life that have always puzzled me. It was like a door opened and I was able to walk into a place that I always longed for but never understood why. When she asked me to help her, I couldn't turn her down. Later I realized that instead of helping her, I had put her in danger. I was telling her the truth about why I left San Francisco when Sal and his men caught up with us. I'm so afraid for her. You've got to do something. You can put me in jail, I don't care, just find her."

Bobby looked at Johnny for a few moments without saying anything. Then he spoke.

"Jonathan, I want to find Jenny, but I need to get these guys to cooperate. I've booked them and sent their information to San Francisco and New York, and I'm just waiting to get a response. This Sal character is a tough bird, and I don't think we can crack him, so I want to work on Maxie. If I can tie him into the killing in Frisco, I may be able to shake him loose. We've still got a little time before the gang gets suspicious. Just settle down and let me handle this."

Bobby made his voice sound confident, and he could see Johnny begin to relax a little. But inside, Bobby wasn't so sure it would work out. He reached for the intercom button and punched Bull's extension.

"Yeah, Boss."

"Bull, have you got any info back from San Francisco or New York?"

"Something's just coming over the wire now, Bobby. I'll check it out and bring it in."

"Good," Bobby said and clicked off.

In a few minutes the door opened, and Bull walked in. He laid a couple of sheets of paper on Bobby's desk. "Nothing from New York, but we got something on the LDX from the guys in San Francisco that may help us. It seems that a thirty-eight-caliber bullet killed

Johnny-boy's friend. I noticed that Maxie carried a thirty-eight snub nose. If we can make him think we've linked his gun to the killing, we might get him to talk."

"We can try it," Bobby said. "Maxie might crack. Get him in the interview room."

Just then the intercom buzzed. "Boss, Reuben Springer is here."

"Send him in, Jill."

In a moment the door opened, and Reuben walked in. When he saw Johnny, he walked over and stood in front of him, towering over the boy.

"Take it easy, Reuben," Bobby said. "I've been talking to Jonathan here, and I'm pretty sure he's an innocent party in all this. Stupid, but innocent."

"I'm not going to do anything, Bobby," Reuben said quietly. "I just wanted to take a look at the person who has put my daughter in such danger."

"Mr. Springer, I'm really sorry," Johnny said. "I didn't think about what I was doing. Jenny asked me for help, and I couldn't say no. She was really hurt that you had her shunned, and she felt like her family didn't understand what she was going through. I should have kept my nose out, but I couldn't. I…I love her."

"If you put her in such danger, you don't know the meaning of that word," Reuben said.

The boy stood up and faced Reuben. "Maybe you don't know what that word means either, Mr. Springer," he said. "You're the one who punished her for wanting to find out about her birth mother. At least I thought I was helping her find out about the things that mean the most to her. You sure weren't!"

Reuben jerked as though an invisible hand had slapped him. He reached out and took Johnny by the lapels of his jacket and pulled him up close.

Bobby got up. He had seen that look in Reuben's eyes twice before—once a long time ago when Reuben had taken on the biggest bully in Wooster and knocked him cold, and again in a trench on a steaming tropical island.

"Careful, Reuben," Bobby said. "That's my prisoner you have your hands on."

Reuben and Johnny stared into each other's eyes. This time Johnny held Reuben's gaze. Reuben was breathing hard, and his hands held Johnny in an iron grip. Then his grip loosened and he let go as he turned away.

Then he said, "Maybe you're right. Maybe I failed her. I was doing what I thought best."

Bobby looked at Reuben's back with surprise. It wasn't often he had heard Reuben offer up anything remotely like an apology.

Bobby clicked the intercom. "Bull, is Maxie in the interview room?"

"All nice and comfy," Bull answered.

Bobby walked over to the case in his bookshelf and opened it. He took out the picture of the three soldiers and put it in his pocket. Then he turned to Reuben.

"Reuben, I may need your help. This Maxie is a tough case, but we may be able to crack him. If I ask you to come in the room I want you to do exactly as I say and don't say anything, okay?"

Reuben looked surprised. "If you think I can help, I'll do anything you want."

"Okay, I want you to wait in the hall, and if I need you, I'll call you."

"What about me?" Johnny asked. "Can I help?"

"Well, if you believe in God, you might try praying," Bobby said. "In the meantime, stay here and try to stay out of trouble."

Bobby picked up the papers on his desk, and he and Reuben went down the hall to the interview room. He left Reuben outside and went in. Bull was standing in the corner with his sunglasses on, doing his best impersonation of a bad cop. Maxie sat looking at the wall, his face impassive. Bobby slid into the chair across from him.

"Well, Maxie, are you ready to tell us where the girl is?"

"I ain't saying nothing," Maxie said. "I want a lawyer."

"Well, unfortunately, we're a small town. Not too many lawyers to choose from," Bobby lied. "Besides, I haven't charged you yet, so I have seventy-two hours before I have to do anything to you."

Out of the corner of his eye, he saw Bull grin.

Bobby placed the sheets of paper on the table in front of him. "These reports are from San Francisco. They implicate you in the murder of a drug dealer about a week ago. The man was killed with thirty-eight-caliber slugs, a special type with an exploding tip. Actually, just like the bullets we found in your gun."

"Lots of people use a thirty-eight," Maxie said.

"Yes, that's true," Bobby said. "You know, Maxie, I'm not much of a betting man, but I'm guessing when we run tests on your gun, we'll match the bullets with the ones they took out of Shub Jackson's body. What do you think? Want to take the bet?"

Maxie kept his mouth shut.

"I also think if you start talking and give us the location of the girl, I could speak on your behalf when they're considering whether they should put you in the gas chamber at San Quentin or just give you life," Bobby said.

"You can't pin that on me," Maxie said. "I wasn't the only guy shooting."

Bobby saw that he had gotten into Maxie's head, and he pushed the point. "I'm going on the assumption that we're going to match your gun to the killing. It will go better for you if you tell us where you've hidden the girl."

Maxie stayed silent, so Bobby went on. "Well, I wasn't going to do this, but you leave me no choice, Maxie."

Bobby looked at Bull.

"Bull, will you bring Mr. Springer in?"

Bull played along. "You sure you want to do that, Boss?"

"I'm sure, Bull. Bring him in."

Bull opened the door and motioned for Reuben to come in. When Reuben walked through the door, his broad shoulders almost touched the frame on either side, and he had to remove his hat to keep it from being knocked off. He stood silently at Bobby's side, towering over the table and glaring at Maxie with cold steel in his eyes.

"This is my friend, Reuben Springer, Maxie. He is the girl's father, and he's not happy with you."

"So what?" Maxie asked. "I've seen these guys before. They're wimps."

"Well, I want to show you something," Bobby said.

He reached in his pocket, pulled out the picture, and placed it in front of Maxie. He pointed to Reuben in the photo.

"Actually, my friend here wasn't always what you call a wimp," Bobby said. "In fact, he won the Congressional Medal of Honor on Guadalcanal."

Maxie looked at the picture and then at Reuben. "Why's he dressed like that, then?" Maxie asked, pointing at Reuben's hat and overalls.

"Reuben joined the Amish church so they could help him keep his temper under control," Bobby said with a straight face. "Don't you want to know how he won the medal?"

Maxie hesitated.

"He killed fifteen Japanese soldiers with his bare hands. He gutted them with bayonets, knocked their brains out with a rifle butt, and choked the life out of some of them. I watched the whole thing from my side of the trench. I had been hit with shrapnel and couldn't move. Reuben saved us. I never saw anything like it in my life. Reuben went... well, I guess berserk would be the best word."

Maxie looked at Reuben. Reuben stared back.

Bobby turned back to Maxie and spoke in a calm voice that belied the tension in the room. "You see, Maxie, I have a personal connection to all this. I want to see Reuben get his daughter back. His daughter is very dear to me too, so I'm not going to worry about bending a few rules to get the information I want."

He looked over at Bull.

"Got a problem with that, Bull?"

"Not me, Boss. Jenny's my friend too."

"What do you mean by bend a few rules?" Maxie asked.

"Well," Bobby said slowly, "I was thinking that Bull and I would go get some of that coffee he just made and take a little break. Meanwhile, I thought I'd leave Reuben here to ask you a few questions."

"Hey, you can't do that! I got my rights!" Maxie said.

"I don't think we're going to worry about that right now, Maxie. What do you say, Bull? Up for some coffee?"

Bobby got up and headed toward the door with Bull close behind him. Reuben started to move around the table toward Maxie, his hands clenched into fists.

"Hey! Hey! What is this? You can't leave me here with him!"

Bobby heard the chair screech on the concrete floor as Maxie got up. Bobby put his hand on the doorknob and looked back. Maxie was backing away from Reuben.

"Wait! Don't go!" Maxie shouted. "I'll talk. I know where she is. I'll talk. Just don't leave me in here with him."

Bobby smiled to himself and then turned around.

"Okay, Maxie, sit back down and compose yourself. I'll talk to Reuben for a minute."

They stepped out into the hall. Reuben was shaking. "It's a good thing he broke," he said. "Good for him and good for me."

Bobby looked at his friend. "Why's that?" he asked.

"I might have killed him," Reuben said quietly.

Chapter Twenty-Two

Darkness

◇◇◇

Jenny sat on the grubby mattress with her legs tucked under her, thinking about what to do. She started cataloging everything she knew about her situation, looking for any way of escape. The room itself seemed secure, and it would be hard for her to find a way to get out unless she could get a key. She knew she was in the Pocono Mountains at a remote cabin. If she did escape, she would have to stay off the road and find her way out through the woods until she got back to civilization. She suspected she was north of the Interstate, but she didn't know the exact direction back.

The one bright spot was that for some reason, Jorge seemed protective of her. Maybe he had ulterior motives of his own, but when she had looked in his eyes, he seemed to be sincerely concerned for her.

It must be that we're close in age. He can't be over twenty or twenty-one.

Just then she heard the key in the lock, and the door opened. It was Jorge. In his hand he had a bowl, and a blanket was folded over his arm.

"I brought you something to keep you warmer. There will be some snow on the ground in the morning. I brought you some stew. Are you hungry?"

Jenny nodded. She realized the room had gotten chilly. She took the blanket and put it around her shoulders.

"What are you doing with that goofy hippie?" Jorge asked. "You know him from San Francisco?"

"I'm not from San Francisco. I'm from Apple Creek, Ohio. I just met Jonathan a few days ago. He was helping me. I was going to New York to try to find my birth mother. I lost her when I was little, and then an Amish couple adopted me. I've been living with them ever since."

"Amish?" Jorge seemed genuinely surprised. "Aren't they the guys with beards who ride around in buggies?"

"Yes, but there's more to it than that," Jenny said. "Being Amish is about having a relationship with God. Not associating with the world helps us to stay focused on our faith."

Her own words cut her to the quick. She realized with regret that the last thing she had been doing was staying focused on her faith. And now, because of that, she was in danger.

"I know what it's like…not to have a mother," Jorge said. "I never knew mine. Uncle Luis told me she was a prostitute who got killed by her pimp. He's taken care of me ever since."

"Is that why you're with these men?" Jenny asked. "You don't seem like you're really one of them."

Jorge bristled at her words. "Of course I'm one of them! I can take care of myself. Besides, Luis is my family. I owe him."

"Even if it means you might go to prison?" Jenny asked.

"What are you talking about?"

"Jonathan said that your gang killed a man out in San Francisco."

"So what?" Jorge asked. "The punk tried to rip us off. He deserved what he got."

"But if they catch you, they'll put you in prison," Jenny answered. "You don't belong with them, Jorge. You could make something of your life."

"So who says they're going to catch us? And what do you mean I don't belong here? I got a good life. And Uncle Luis is all I got."

Jorge looked sharply at Jenny. "You're too smart for your own good. You're just trying to get to me. Uncle Luis was right—you can't trust women." A change came over Jorge's face, and suddenly he looked very angry. "You need to get wise, girl," Jorge said. "You should be nice to me instead of trying to trick me. You be nice to me and I'll be nice to you."

Jenny felt a stab of fear as he stared at her. He looked her over slowly, and a look she had never seen on a man's face passed over his. He knelt down on one knee and touched her hair. Jenny shivered at his touch.

"Maybe you should be my girlfriend," Jorge said quietly. "Maybe I should move my stuff in here."

Suddenly Jorge grabbed Jenny by the arm and jerked her up, pulling her close. There was a wild look in his eyes. He bent his head and tried to kiss her. Jenny twisted in his grasp, but he was too strong. He pulled her tighter and forced his lips onto hers. She kept her mouth clenched and pushed against him. Slowly he overpowered her and pushed her backward onto the mattress. He half fell on top of her and held her down. Then he started to fumble at her clothing with his hand.

Jenny pulled her mouth away from his and screamed. It startled him, and he jerked back. Just then there was a knock on the door.

"Hey, what's goin' on in there, kid? Is she fightin' ya? Just slap her around—she'll figure it out quick enough."

Luis laughed, and Jenny could hear the other men laughing in the background.

"Go away, Luis, this is my business," Jorge shouted.

"Okay, kid, okay. Just don't wear yourself out. We got things to take care of tomorrow."

Jenny heard him chuckle, and then his steps receded down the hallway. She lay on the mattress, panting like a dog with Jorge on top of her, her whole body trembling.

"Please, Jorge, don't do this. *Please!*"

Jorge slowly came back to his senses. A red flush swept over his face, and he rolled off her. He got up and looked at her with a mixture of pity and contempt. He pointed his finger at her. "As long as you're still alive, you're gonna be with me. No one else."

Jorge walked out and locked the door behind him.

Bobby sat with Maxie in the interview room. A phone sat on the table between them. Maxie was rubbing his hands together and sweating. Reuben leaned against the wall, his arms folded across his chest. Maxie kept glancing at Reuben. Then he looked at Bobby and began to speak.

"Before I do anything, you gotta promise me you'll protect me," he said. "Sal will kill me for ratting him out."

"I've already talked to the sheriff in San Francisco," Bobby said. "It seems that the Federal boys are in on this now. Your gang has been bringing in lots of marijuana and cocaine from across the border, and that puts you and your friends in DEA jurisdiction. They gave me their word that if you give us the names of the big boys, they'll go easy on you and put you in the witness protection program. It kind of sticks in my craw to let a rat like you out of his cage, but Jenny is more important to me. So that's the deal."

"Okay, okay, what do you want me to do?" Maxie asked.

Bobby picked up the phone and handed it to Maxie.

"Call your boss. Tell him you had some car trouble and that you're waiting in town while it gets fixed. Tell him Sal rented a car and he's taking Johnny out to the place where the money is hidden. Tell him Sal thinks they should wait to decide what to do with the girl until he gets back there with the money. You got it?"

"Yeah, yeah, I got it," Maxie said sullenly, "but I don't know if he'll buy it."

He took the phone from Bobby and dialed a number. Bobby could hear a man's voice answer. Maxie dutifully went through the story Bobby had given him. The man at the other end must have asked Maxie to confirm what he just said. "Look, Luis, I'm just tellin' you what Sal told me. I'm not the brains of this outfit, I'm just the muscle. I do what I'm told, so that's all I know. No, he's not back with the money yet, I told you. Okay, Luis, I'm just doin' what Sal said. I can't help it if we blew the water pump. Yeah, yeah, okay, we'll see you tomorrow."

Maxie put the phone back on the receiver. He looked shaken.

"What's up, Maxie?" Bobby asked.

"Luis is a smart guy," Maxie said. "I don't know if he bought my story. I know he's suspicious. He wanted to talk to Sal as soon as he gets back. That means you don't have a lot of time."

◇◇◇

Jerusha lifted her face from her prayers and looked at the quilt. While she prayed, she had a sense that Jenny was in great danger.

"Lord, tell me how to pray for my girl," Jerusha said. "Speak to me."

And again the quiet voice spoke into her heart. *The* LORD *is nigh unto them that are of a broken heart; and saveth such as be of a contrite spirit.*

Jerusha began to pray again. "Lord, speak to Jenny's heart. Help her to put away all pride and self-sufficiency. Help her to know that she can't do this alone, that she needs Your hand to guide her. Give her wisdom, revelation, and knowledge, and keep her hidden under the shadow of Your wing."

◇◇◇

Jenny lay on the mattress. She had turned off the light and waited in abject fear for Jorge to return. She had come to the end of herself, and there was nowhere else to turn. She thought about how convicted she felt while she was telling Jorge about the Amish faith.

I haven't spoken to You or asked You about any of this, Lord. I keep wanting to, but it's as though my pride gets in the way. Help me to pray, Lord.

Then, to Jenny's surprise, words began to form on her lips as she lay on the dirty mattress.

"God, I've tried to be self-sufficient and do everything by myself. I thought I could fix everything on my own, but I can't. If You're listening…I'm in desperate trouble. I need You to intervene, or I'm lost. Help me, please."

In the next room she heard the men laughing. Jenny knew that the crisis of the moment was upon her. Jorge—or worse, one of the other men—would return soon, and then all would be lost. She rose from the bed and desperately looked around the room again for something, anything she could use to escape.

She went back to the window. As she looked more closely, she could see that water had been leaking in between the bottom frame and the windowsill. There was a patch of dry rot starting in the wood around the flat metal bar that held the bottom shut. She could just reach it, so she pushed on the bottom edge of the window. The window was loose in the frame and wiggled slightly. She pushed again. The metal bar moved a tiny bit. She pushed again, and the screw that held it in the frame popped out a fraction of an inch. She pushed her finger under the edge of the bar and pulled. The screw pulled out of the partially rotten wood, and the metal bar hung there, attached to the frame by the other screw. She held the bar and worked it back and forth, up and down, prying at the second screw.

In a few seconds, it pulled loose, and she held the bar in her hand. She went over to the door. The lock was old fashioned and had a large keyhole. That meant that the lock was a simple latch instead of a dead bolt. She turned the light off so she wouldn't attract attention if she got the door open. In the darkness she inserted the flat bar between the door and the doorjamb and moved it around until she felt it push against the bolt. She carefully put pressure on the bolt and pried. The bar grabbed against the bolt and moved it back ever so slightly. She pushed and pried again. The bolt moved again, and the metal bar slipped between the bolt and the door.

She pried once more, and the bolt slid back with a quiet click. Jenny slowly opened the door a crack and looked down the hallway toward the main room. She could hear the men. Their talk was coarse, and they seemed to be egging Jorge on toward something Jenny didn't even want to think about.

She looked around. The light from the front room lit the hallway dimly, and she could see a door at the end of the hall. She opened her door and slipped silently into the hall and made her way to the door. The men laughed again, and she gently turned the knob. To her relief, the door opened.

A light brush of snow was silently drifting, and a pale quarter moon gave a ghostly light through the passing clouds. Not enough snow had fallen to stick yet, and the ground was still bare. Jenny started to open the screen door and slip out when she heard a sound behind her. She looked around and gasped. Jorge was standing at the head of the hall-way, a wicked grin on his face.

"Goin' somewhere?" he asked, his words slurred. He looked at her with bloodshot eyes and then lurched toward her.

Chapter Twenty-Three

Call to Arms

◇◇◇

Bobby, Reuben, and Johnny sat in Bobby's office. Reuben looked grim, and Johnny sat on the edge of his chair.

"So, what are we going to do, Sheriff?" Johnny asked. "We don't have much time. Those guys aren't going to fool around. If Sal doesn't contact them soon, they'll hurt Jenny."

"I know, son," Bobby said, "and we're going to get out there as soon as we get some help. Maxie told us where the hideout is, and I've contacted the local authorities. But it's going to take a few hours to get some men together. I don't know anything about that area."

"Where is it?" Reuben asked.

"It's near a place called Bear Lake, off Interstate 80."

Johnny's eyes widened. "Bear Lake?"

"That's right, son. Why?" Bobby asked.

"I used to spend my summers up there! My Uncle Jim lives in Wilkes-Barre, and he has a cabin up in the mountains near Thornhurst. He used to take me fishing at Bear Lake. I've ridden my bike and hiked all through that area. You can get there from 80 or Wilkes-Barre. It's pretty rugged and there are only a few roads up there. What road is it on?"

"It's on a road called Stone Tower."

Johnny stood up. "Sheriff, I know right where that is. You go out of Wilkes-Barre on Bear Lake Road. Then you turn on Tannery Road and go toward Thornhurst. Before you get there you're behind Bear Lake, and then you come to Stone Tower Road. It takes you up the hill. There's a place up there where you can park and hike down to the back side of the lake. There are some old cabins up there, but I thought they were closed in the winter."

Bobby and Reuben looked at each other in amazement. Jonathan went on.

"We can take a plane into Wilkes-Barre, and I could take you right there. It's only about forty-five minutes, maybe a little longer in snow."

Bobby interrupted Johnny. "Wait a minute, Jonathan, who said you were going?"

Johnny's face was animated and his hands waved. "Jenny's in danger, and we're wasting time. I can take you right there. We have to go now, and we have to move fast."

"Can you handle a gun, Jonathan?" Bobby asked.

Johnny reached for his wallet and pulled a card out from one of the compartments. It signified that he had received an Eagle Scout marksmanship merit badge.

"Number one in my troop," he said with a grin.

Bobby frowned. He was silent for a moment, and then he decided. "Okay, Jonathan, I'll take you along. We better get going."

"Wait a minute, Bobby," Reuben said quietly. "Aren't you forgetting something?"

"What?" Bobby asked.

"Me," Reuben said. "You're not leaving me behind."

"But, Reuben," Bobby said, "this is going to be dangerous. I need everybody armed."

"You're talking about my daughter. A long time ago I told you that

THE ROAD HOME 211

I knew that there were some things worth fighting for. I haven't had
to make a choice like that in a long time. I know my faith constrains
me, and I believe what Jesus said about killing other men, but I also
remember that He took a rope and whipped the men who were making a mockery of His Father's temple. I don't want to kill anybody, but
if it's a choice between hurting the men who have Jenny and saving my
daughter's life, then so be it. If it means that they throw me out of the
church, I'll live with that too. Besides," Reuben smiled, "I'm a much
better shot than you."

Bobby stared at his friend. Then he grinned. "Reuben, you never
cease to amaze me. Okay, you two, raise your right hands."

Bobby commandeered a Cessna six-seater at the Wooster airport for
the ninety-minute flight to Wilkes-Barre. The pilot was an old friend
and was happy to help. Bull stayed behind and called the Wilkes-Barre
police to organize a group that would be waiting for Bobby.

When the plane landed, the local men met with them outside the
terminal. The local sheriff had five men with him and told Bobby the
Pennsylvania State Police were headed up the mountain from Interstate 80 already.

The sheriff, Gary Wagner, was an affable older man. His smile
belied a toughness that Bobby picked up on right away.

"You a vet, Gary?" Bobby asked.

"Hundred and First Airborne," Gary answered. "Normandy, Oper-
ation Market Garden, and the Battle of the Bulge. I was at Bastogne
with McAuliffe when they demanded our surrender and he told the
Germans, 'Nuts!'"

"USMC First Division," Bobby said. "Guadalcanal."

Bobby nodded at Reuben.

"Both of you?" Gary asked, looking at Reuben curiously.

"Yep," Bobby said. "Reuben's a CMH winner."

"Bobby, you don't need to tell everyone," Reuben said with an embarrassed smile. "Besides, you did your part as well."

Sheriff Wagner stepped forward and shook Reuben's hand and then turned to Bobby and shook his. "Proud to serve with you, Gyrenes. Now brief me on what's going on—and who's this kid?"

"This is Jonathan Hershberger. He was with Jenny when she was kidnapped. Reuben is Jenny's father. I brought Jonathan because he says he's been up to the area where the hideout is and knows the trails through the woods. His uncle owns a place up there."

"Who's your uncle, son?" Gary asked.

"Jim Connors," Johnny said. "He lives here in Wilkes-Barre."

"Jim Connors Chevrolet?" Gary asked.

"That's him," Johnny replied.

"Jim's a buddy of mine. We're in Rotary together. Why the long hair, son?" Gary asked with a smile.

"It's a long story that I don't have time to tell right now," Johnny replied. "We need to find Jenny."

Gary laughed. "She your girlfriend, Jonathan?"

Reuben stiffened. Johnny was smart enough to pick up on the tension. "No, sir, she's…she's just…my friend."

Reuben relaxed, and the men returned to the business at hand. Bobby pulled out a map of the area and spread it out on the hood of the sheriff's cruiser.

"Maxie had only been to the hideout once. All he remembered was that it was on Stone Tower Road. What do you know about it, Jonathan?"

"There are two ways to get up there," Johnny said. "One is to go up Tannery Road until you get to Stone Tower and then on up. There are only two or three old cabins back in the trees along Stone Tower, and one of them is probably the hideout. But if you drove up there, they would hear you coming a long way off.

The other way is to come in from the Bear Lake side. There's a fire road around the lake and a path up the hill where a stream comes down a ravine. The ravine runs behind the cabins and then goes under the road and down the east side of Stone Tower Road. The ravine is pretty steep, but there are ways to get up to the back of the cabins. I used to fish that little creek in the spring, and I did a lot of exploring up there. It would only take us about thirty minutes to get there once we got around the lake. We could get right up on the hideout without being seen, and it's more hidden than going up Tannery."

"Okay," Gary said. He turned to one of his men. "Call the PSP and have them block off Stone Tower at the bottom. We'll take the helicopters up to the Lake. There's a big cleared field on the west side. Have the police meet us there. We'll go in the back way and contact the PSP by radio and have them move up Stone Tower. Remind them that the perps have a prisoner and won't give up easily. If we do this quietly we should catch these guys between us and get the girl out before anything happens."

He turned back to Bobby. "Did you deputize these men?"

"Yep, and they can both shoot if they need to."

Reuben winced. Sheriff Gary turned to his men. "Okay, let's go."

◇◇◇

Jorge leered at Jenny.

"Where ya going?" he asked. "Don't you like me? I just want to have a little fun. You can be my girlfriend now. Once you get to know me better, you'll like me."

Jenny froze. Jorge moved toward her, almost stumbling.

Suddenly a voice spoke to her spirit. *Run!*

Jenny turned and burst through the screen door and into the darkness. Jorge shouted something, and the screen door banged again as he ran out after her.

"Come back here, you tramp! Come back here, Jenny, or you'll wish you did!"

Jenny ran like the wind across the open space behind the house and dashed into the woods. Her heart was pounding as branches whipped her face. Suddenly she heard a crash and a curse behind her. Jorge had fallen.

Jenny ran on. The clouds had cleared for a moment, and there was some light from the sliver of moon for Jenny to see by. She burst through a clump of Scotch broom and came to a trail that ran to the left and the right. She followed it left and continued running down the trail.

I've got to lose him. I've got to get off the trail.

Behind her she heard Jorge shouting her name. The path was uneven, and several times she came close to tripping.

Give me hind's feet on high places, Lord.

She came to another fork. There was a small ditch beside the trail, and the fork crossed over it. She took the fork to the right and jumped over the ditch. The snow had started to fall, and she had to slow down to make her way.

Faintly in the distance she heard Jorge shout her name. She had to slow to a walk in the thicker brush. The bushes leaned over the trail and grabbed at her jacket. The air was freezing, and her hands were starting to get numb.

She had to let her eyes adjust so she could see the reflection of the faint light off the packed dirt of the trail. She went slowly, deeper and deeper into the woods.

A big hollow stump appeared beside the trail like a silent man. Her heart jumped into her throat. She took a deep breath and kept going as quickly as she could. The woods grew thicker and darker around her until she could barely see. She stumbled forward blindly, feeling for the edge of the path with her feet. Every few minutes the streaming clouds opened and allowed the moon to light the way ahead. Then at last they closed completely, and the snow began to fall, soft and thick. Jenny stopped and listened. Jorge's voice had died away, and now the woods were silent around her. She heard a flapping sound, and a dark shape passed close by her with a screech. Jenny jumped and took another deep breath. It was only an owl.

Even though the night air was freezing, Jenny was covered with sweat. Her face felt flushed as she stared into the darkness, trying to see the trail ahead of her. A root caught at her foot, and she went down on one knee. She had to find a place to hide. She moved forward again, taking one step and then another. The snow was falling faster. She took one more step, and when she put her foot down, nothing was there. She pitched forward and fell down into the darkness.

CHAPTER TWENTY-FOUR

The Blood

◇◇◇

JERUSHA LOOKED DOWN at the Rose of Sharon quilt with satisfaction. The place where she had sewn in the new batting was barely visible. She felt as though she were back at the beginning of an incredible journey, one that had taken her from darkness to hope, from despair to faith, from pride to dependence. As she worked she spoke aloud.

"When I made this quilt, I was focused on myself—my pain, my grief, my loss. When You sent me Jenny to restore what I lost in Jenna, I only received the blessing for me. It didn't occur to me that You had given me to Jenny as a blessing and a hope to her."

Jerusha thought about the dreams and nightmares that had plagued Jenny all her life. Often in the early days, when Jerusha had awakened to the sound of her adopted daughter screaming in the night, she had been concerned. But Jenny had been so volatile as a child that as the years passed, Jerusha had come to discount the dreams as just a part of her daughter's temperament. Now she saw that the dreams were born of some terrible event, something that had torn Jenny inside.

Like the torn batting in the quilt.

Jerusha examined the quilt again. She noticed all the colored pieces that were either torn or missing, and she was glad she had saved the original silk material. The quilt had hardly been used, so there were no worn places, but the seam where she had torn open the corner was frayed, and the cream-colored cotton backing had also frayed where she pulled the seam apart.

As she examined the stitching, she recalled how her tiny, even stitches had amazed her grandmother. Most quilters would use about seventy thousand stitches on a quilt. Jerusha had used more than ninety thousand in her first complete quilt when she was eleven years old. She remembered her grandmother's words as she looked over the work.

"*Ja*, your stitch is so small and even," said her grandmother. "It is as though you have been quilting all your life."

Her thoughts flew back to the wonderful days when she had learned the art of quilting from her grandmother. Those had been the happiest days of her childhood, and she could hear *Grossmudder* Hannah's voice speaking gently to her as she helped cut the pieces for a star quilt, the first Jerusha had been allowed to work on. She remembered watching as her grandmother cut the chosen pieces of fabric into perfectly matching parts.

"If the quilt is going to be even and symmetrical, the pieces must be true," she said.

She let Jerusha try her hand, and even on her first try Jerusha cut the pieces straight and perfect.

"*Ja, das is gutte,*" Grandmother said. "You will be a fine quilt maker, my girl."

Once the pieces were cut correctly, *Grossmudder* had pieced them together with pinpoint accuracy.

"If the quilt is not aligned properly, even in just one small part, the whole thing will look off-balance and might pucker," she told Jerusha. "If the design is to be even and pleasing to the eye, each individual piece of fabric must be stitched together just right. You must trust your own eye and sewing skills for measurement and accuracy. *Der Schöpfer-Gott*, the Creator, has not given this gift to every quilter."

As the memories flooded over her, Jerusha began to see something she had never noticed before. For her, the completed quilt had always been the purpose for her life, and the process of making the quilt had only been a means to an end. Now she began to see that the process was everything, and the finished quilt was only the revealing of the work that had been put into the quilt.

"You are the Master Creator, Lord, and You put each life together the same way my grandmother made a quilt. You cut each piece that fits into the fabric of our lives, and You stitch them together perfectly. You always have a plan for each of us. And You planned each part of our lives to fit together perfectly."

Jerusha began to see the correlation. Each piece of a life had to be laid in perfectly, and if the pieces were uneven or not stitched together properly, the result would not fulfill the Creator's purpose for that life.

Jerusha remembered something Reuben had taught her. They had visited a neighbor's farm one day and watched as the men helped their neighbor tear down the framing of what was to be a new barn and start over.

"Why are they tearing the barn down?" she had asked.

"Brother King made a mistake when he laid the foundation," Reuben said. "It wasn't level and true. It was pointed out to him when the first wall went up, and the men had a great deal of difficulty plumbing it up. When a foundation isn't laid properly and you build on it, everything in nature, even gravity itself, conspires to drag that wall down. But if the foundation is true, then when you build on it, gravity pulls the wall straight down onto the foundation, and it will stand for years, supporting itself."

She had wondered about Reuben's words that day without really understanding, but now as she looked at the quilt, they became clear.

Everything in Jenny's life had been built on a poor foundation, so even nature had worked against her, robbing her of peace and joy and leaving her with a sense of incompleteness.

That is what happened to Jenny. The foundation of her life wasn't laid in straight and true, and she has been struggling to build on that poor foundation.

Jerusha went back to the quilt and began working on the corner stitching. She had used cotton thread on this part of the quilt because it was kinder to the fabric. She got out a number ten needle and a leather thimble. She had used the thimble since she was a girl. It was her favorite, and as she used it over the years, she had worn the dimples down in such a way that it allowed her absolute control of the needle. The thimble was open on the end so that she didn't perspire inside it and cause it to stick to her finger.

She used a traditional rocking stitch that she had modified slightly so that she sewed toward herself instead of from left to right. That way she could see the stitching as she worked. Carefully she began to stitch the torn corner closed. Where a small piece of the backing was missing, she carefully patched in a new piece by sewing it over the frayed area. She stitched exactly where she had stitched before and buried the knot in the material so that it was invisible. After she finished, she examined the seams and stitching throughout the quilt for any other areas she could repair quickly.

After a few hours of work, she heard a knock on her door. Curious as to who might be visiting at this hour, she went to the door and opened it. Hank Lowenstein was standing there.

"Hello, Jerusha," Hank said. "I just came over to tell you that Reuben called. He asked me to tell you that he went with Bobby to find Jenny. They had to fly over to Wilkes-Barre, Pennsylvania. I didn't know Jenny was gone, so the message is a little cryptic to me. Is there anything I can do?"

Jerusha felt a cold fear try to creep into her heart. She whispered a silent prayer and then said, "Jenny's in trouble, Hank. I can't tell you all the details, but I would certainly appreciate your prayers. Reuben will probably try to stay in touch by calling your phone. I hope it's not a bother."

"Bother! Why, Jerusha, you know we love Jenny. Reuben can call anytime day or night, and we'll come over and let you know what's happening. And we'll be praying too."

"Thank you, Hank," Jerusha said. "I certainly appreciate it. And we know that you love Jenny. Thank you for that also."

Hank tipped his old worn baseball cap and went back over the little bridge that crossed the creek between the Springer farm and the Lowenstein place. Jerusha watched him go with a sick feeling in her heart. *Lord, keep Your hand on Reuben and Bobby. Don't let them be hurt. And please let them find Jenny.*

Jerusha walked back to the sewing table and stared at the quilt. Her hands were trembling, but she thought, *I can't help Jenny by worrying. I've got to keep occupied so I can keep my mind busy.* She sat down at the table and picked up the quilt. And then the deep, peaceful voice spoke to her spirit again.

I have things to show You, Jerusha—things that will help Jenny, but they will help you also. All of your life, you have been in My hand, and yet You still don't really understand Me. The quilt is the key to understanding.

The revelation came with such startling clarity that Jerusha gasped. She nodded and looked over the quilt one more time. The next parts she had to repair were the torn rose petals. She pulled out the piece of red silk and laid it on the table. Then she carefully laid a piece of paper over one of the complete petals and traced the shape. It needed to be exactly the same. She took her scissors and cut out the pattern. Then she laid it on the red silk and began to trace out the five petals she needed to replace the torn ones on the quilt. As she did she spoke out loud again.

"Lord, I know You're speaking to me through the quilt, but I don't understand yet. How does fixing the quilt show me how to help Jenny? Even though it's repaired, the quilt is not the same as it was when I first made it. No matter how skillfully I repair it, it has still been damaged."

Again the still, small voice came to her. *The red silk, Jerusha—what does it represent?*

"I always felt that the red silk was like blood, even Your blood, the precious blood of Christ. But what does that mean?"

Everyone in this world has been damaged, Jerusha. Since that moment when My son Adam decided to go his own way, humans have been damaged and useless to My purpose.

"Dead in their trespasses and sin?" Jerusha asked.

Yes, Jerusha, all men are dead in their sin. But I, in mercy and grace, so loved the world I created that I...

"You sent Your Son, Jesus."

Yes, and what did He do, Jerusha?

Suddenly the thing that the Lord was showing her became clear, like a bolt of lightning into her mind. "He shed his blood!"

Yes, and when He did, what happened, dochter?

"All things were made new. The old creation passed away, and a new creation was born."

In that moment of clarity, Jerusha's heart filled to overflowing with the wisdom and love of her God. She picked up the piece of red silk, the petal of the Rose of Sharon quilt, and she stared at the beautiful deep red color.

Like a rose...or the blood of Christ.

Again the peaceful voice came. *Jerusha, how are you going to repair the torn petals? Are you going to take the old ones away and put new ones in?*

"No, Lord, I'm going to put the new piece right on top of the old one and sew it on using the same stitch I used before."

So the new piece will…will what, Jerusha?

"The new piece will completely cover the old one and hide all the torn places and the imperfections of the ruined piece."

So you are not going to remove it. You are going to…

"I'm going to cover it, Lord. But what…?"

And then like the sun rising over the eastern hills on a quiet spring morning, the answer came.

"Oh! All my sins and imperfections and all of Jenny's, they are… they are covered."

By what, Jerusha?

"Oh my Lord, by Your blood…by Your blood!"

And then Jerusha knew the answer, and she understood for the first time in her life that the same power that had raised Christ from the dead was in her, and in Reuben, and in Jenny. And the blood that was shed to release that power into the world was fully and absolutely capable of healing her daughter's life and making Jenny whole and complete. The wonderful revelation overpowered her. Jerusha put her head down on the table and began to sob. And as she did, a great weight was lifted from her, and the blood of her Savior began its marvelous work.

CHAPTER TWENTY-FIVE

Astray

◇◇◇

SLOWLY JENNY RETURNED TO CONSCIOUSNESS. For a moment she didn't know where she was. She tried to think, and then it started to come back to her. She had been running through the woods. The branches were grabbing at her face, and she couldn't see where she was going. She tried to remember why she had been running. Then it all came back in a rush. Jorge—she was running from Jorge! She was in the cabin and then she got away.

She put her hand out into the darkness and began to grope around her, trying to discover where she was. She remembered stepping off into space and falling and then landing in something, a tree or a bush that broke her fall by snagging her with the branches. She had hung there for a moment, and then the branches broke under her weight, and she had fallen and rolled into something hard. And then there had been blackness.

Now, awake, she could see that she was at the bottom of a hill or cliff. The ground beneath her was hard and uneven, full of rounded objects that she guessed were stones. She felt between them with her hands. They were surrounded by something smooth and cold. It was sand. The stones were ice cold and covered with snow. She became aware of the sound of running water a few feet away. Then she knew that she was lying at the edge of a creek and that she must have fallen down into a ravine or a gully.

She was laying partway on a large rock, and as she shifted her weight, she moved and slipped down the side. Her body jerked spasmodically, and an excruciating pain from her leg made her cry out. Very slowly she shifted herself again, fighting the pain, until she was sitting propped against the rock. The snow had stopped, and the dark clouds that had covered the pale moon began to break up. She had guessed correctly—she was lying in a creek bed filled with different-sized stones that stood up out of the sand like snow-covered igloos. The creek was at a very low stage, and the bed was exposed about ten feet on either side of the sluggish water flowing down the center.

She turned her head gingerly to look around. Behind her a steep bank rose up into the darkness. She couldn't see all the way up, but she imagined it was about fifty feet to the top. She remembered when Jorge had let her out of the car trunk and she had looked down into the ravine on the other side of the road. It had seemed very deep, and the wall below her went almost straight down.

She turned her head back. Across the creek, the ravine widened out, and there seemed to be an area filled with brush and trees between the creek and where the opposite wall of the ravine rose up into the darkness. To the right, the stream came flowing down out of the darkness. To her left, it disappeared around a corner.

The snow clouds streamed by above her, and slowly the sky continued to clear, letting light filter down into the blackness around her. Now she could see a flat place along the other side of the creek. It reflected the light more than the ground beside it, and she guessed that it was a trail. The water was flowing from her right so she knew that downhill was to her left.

That's the way out. I've got to get across the creek and go down that trail.

The throbbing pain in her leg was becoming more intense. She ached all over, but just where else she was injured was unclear. She began to slowly explore her face and head with the tips of her fingers. Something sticky covered the side of her head above her right ear. Blood.

Her fingers moved down to her shoulders. Her left shoulder was sore, but she could move her arm, and she wiggled her fingers to make sure they weren't broken. She worked her way down to her hips and legs. Her left hip was very sore. She struggled to sit further up so she could reach her legs, and once more a bolt of pain shot up her left leg. Gently she pulled her knees up, and the pain from her ankle almost made her scream.

She reached down and carefully felt her anklebones. There was a large lump on the side of her ankle right at the bone, and her foot was twisted strangely. At first she thought it was broken, but then she remembered something that had happened to her when she was a little girl. Running through the field behind her house, she had stepped into a hole and twisted her ankle terribly. It had looked just like it did now. Her Papa had come running when he heard her cries and had gently taken her ankle in his strong hands.

"It's not broken, *dochter*," he said, "but it is dislocated. I'm going to have to pull it hard to make it pop back in. It will hurt very badly, but I must do it."

Jenny stuck out her chin and clenched her fists. "Okay, Papa, I'm ready."

Reuben had looked tenderly at his daughter and then quickly jerked Jenny's foot. The pain had been awful, and Jenny's scream had echoed off the barn. Jerusha had come running to find her husband holding their sobbing daughter in his strong arms.

"She's brave and strong, wife," he said as he held her safely.

Oh, Papa! If only you were here to hold me in your arms.

Jenny knew that she had to do something about her ankle or she would be helpless. She needed to somehow pop the bone back into place, so she looked around, trying to think of what to do. About five feet away, she could make out two stones sticking up out of the sand. They were close together with a small gap between them. An idea came to her. She turned around backward and, using her hands as levers, she scooted along until she felt the two rocks against her back. Then she shifted herself around until she was facing them.

Gingerly, she slipped her foot into the gap between the rocks. She felt the rough granite grating against her skin, and she gasped as the pain struck her leg like an electric shock. The gap was just wide enough for her to lock her anklebone behind the rocks, so she leaned forward and pushed the leg down as far as it would go so it would not slip out. The pain was so intense that she had to lie back on the sand. Beads of salty sweat rolled down into her eyes. She sat back up and was about to jerk her leg when she had a thought. *I'm going to scream!*

She felt in her jacket pocket and found a wad of unused paper napkins. She pulled them out and stuffed them into her mouth. She remembered how bad the pain had been when her papa had set her ankle. She almost stopped, but she knew that if she didn't do this, she would have to lie here until Jorge found her. She stuck out her chin, clenched her fists, and jerked her leg as hard as she could against the rocks. The pain was so intense that she almost fainted. She bit down hard on the napkins as she groaned in agony.

She looked down at her ankle. It had not gone back into place. She had to do it again. Sobs shook her shoulders as she steeled herself to pull again. Once again her fists clenched. She jerked her leg again. This time her ankle slipped up in the crack and pulled from between the rocks. She could feel the stones tear the skin above her ankle as she fell back in the sand, weeping from the awful pain. The wad of napkins fell out of her mouth, and she lay there gasping.

Jenny was quiet for a few moments until the pain subsided somewhat, and then she sat back up. She had to do this. She slipped her ankle back between the rocks and pushed it all the way down, once again feeling the rocks scrape her skin. She scooted up closer to the rocks and bent her knees just a bit so she could get more leverage. She put the napkins back in her mouth, and then with all of her strength she jerked her leg. An excruciating wave of pain shot up her leg, and the anklebone popped back into place. Jenny fainted.

When Jenny came to, the pain in her leg had subsided somewhat. She pulled it out from between the rocks and examined her ankle. The big bump was gone, but she could just barely see that a large deep purple bruise and some bad swelling had taken its place. Her ankle was badly scraped where she had pulled it against the rocks, and blood had dripped down onto her new white shoe. She rolled over onto her knees and then tried to get up by shifting her good foot under her body and slowly lifting herself up without putting any weight on her bad ankle.

She stood there on one leg and tried to put her weight on both feet. Her left leg buckled, and she fell to her knees in the sand. She stayed on her hands and knees until the pain subsided. Then she shifted her good leg under again and lifted herself back up, this time balancing on her right leg. She looked around. A few feet away, a pile of brush had snagged against some tree roots on the bank, probably last spring during a flood. She hopped over to the pile and looked it over. There was a long, fairly straight pine branch in the pile, and she pulled it out. It would make a good walking stick to lean on, but it was a little long. She sat down on a big rock and pulled the end against her knee until it broke off. She looked down at her ankle.

I need something to brace my ankle so I can put some weight on it.

She could make a splint with the piece she had just broken off, but she needed something to tie it onto her leg with. She thought about her shoelace but realized it wouldn't be long enough or strong enough to hold the splint onto her leg. She was about to give up when something caught her eye, a flash of red between the rocks. She hopped over and saw a long red piece of thin nylon rope with a metal handle on one end and what looked like a needle on the other end. It was a fish stringer, the kind that fishermen use to put their fish on to leave them in the stream while they are still fishing. The stringer was wrapped around a rock in what would have been the deepest part of the stream if the stream were full.

Jenny reached down and pulled on the stringer. It was wedged between the rocks and partly covered by sand, but with a few jerks, she got it free. She hopped back to the rock and sat down. She took the thin piece that she had broken off her walking stick and placed it against her leg. Then she started wrapping the nylon rope around her leg and the stick. She started by twisting the rope firmly around the metal handle and then pulling against the knot, keeping the rope tight around her leg. The metal handle wedged firmly against the wood— she knew it would not slip. When she got down to her ankle she used the needle to thread the rope under several of the loops around her leg and then tied it tight. It was the perfect length.

When she stood back up, the splint gave her ankle good support, and she was able to stand on it, not without some pain, but at least it didn't buckle. She leaned on her pine branch, stepped carefully over the narrow stream, and made her way through the rocks to the trail on the other side. Just as she was about to start, she heard a faint voice from the top of the ravine.

"Jenny, where are you? You better show yourself, 'cause I'm not happy with you."

Jorge! Desperately, Jenny looked around. A few feet away, under the trees, was another brush pile on top of some fallen logs. She dropped down and scooted under the overhanging branches until she was out of sight. Up above she heard voices drawing nearer. It was Luis and Jorge. They had a flashlight, and Jenny could see the light reflecting off the trees up on top of the cliff. Jorge was talking.

"I'm sorry, Uncle Luis, but you shouldn't have gotten me drunk. I fell down and she got away."

"Yeah, well I'm not buying it," Luis said. "I never heard of a Sanchez who couldn't hold his booze."

"Maybe we're not all tough guys like you, Uncle Luis," Jorge retorted sarcastically.

Jenny heard the sound of a slap, and Jorge cried out.

"Don't ever talk to me like that again, kid. Now let's find that girl, or you're gonna have more than one thing to be sorry for."

"Okay, okay," Jorge answered.

Their voices faded as they walked up the trail, back toward the cabin. Finally it was quiet again. Jenny realized she had been very lucky to fall off the cliff. The sides were so steep that the men hadn't considered the possibility that she could have climbed down, so they were looking for her in the woods up on top. She breathed a sigh of relief and let her pounding heart slow down. She stood to her feet, leaned on her stick, and began to hobble south down the hill, hoping to find the interstate or at least another cabin.

CHAPTER TWENTY-SIX

Stains

◇◇◇

ONCE JERUSHA WAS FINISHED REPAIRING THE QUILT, she went over it one more time to make sure all of the damaged areas were put completely right. She worked from the top of the quilt to the bottom, examining each section until she was satisfied that the quilt was undamaged and whole again. The red rose, the heart of the design, was totally restored, and the new silken pieces glowed with the radiance that had been so striking when she first made the quilt. After she was satisfied with the repair, she turned down the lights and went to her room. She made herself ready for bed and then knelt down and spoke her prayers.

"Heavenly Father, I thank You for the blessings You have bestowed upon my life—my husband, my daughter, this farm, the plain life we live, and most of all, the eternal life You have granted me through Your Son, Jesus. I also thank You for showing me the wonderful power of Your redeeming blood, the blood that has made all things new. You have told us to be careful for nothing, but I confess to You that I am anxious for Jenny and Reuben, and for Bobby. I place them into Your care tonight. Please be with Reuben and Bobby as they search for Jenny."

As she prayed, her anxiety began to subside, and a peace gradually settled on her. A scripture came unbidden to her thoughts. *He that dwelleth in the secret place of the most High shall abide under the shadow of the Almighty. I will say of the* LORD, *He is my refuge and my fortress: my God; in him will I trust.*

Jerusha began to recite the passage out loud.

"Surely he shall deliver thee from the snare of the fowler, and from the noisome pestilence. He shall cover thee with his feathers, and under his wings shalt thou trust: his truth shall be thy shield and buckler."

Peace flowed into Jerusha's heart.

Early in the morning, the song of a black-capped chickadee singing outside her window awakened Jerusha. The sun was just peeking over the low hills away toward Pennsylvania. A faint touch of frost clung to the bottom of the windowpane, and a slight bite of cold chilled the air, even in the house. Jerusha could feel the coolness on her face as she lay still for a few moments under her warm quilt, listening to the sweet song.

"Chick-a-dee, chick-a-dee."

For those few minutes, the morning held a measure of peace. But then the events of the past days flooded in upon her, and a knot formed in her stomach.

"Oh, Jenny, where are you?" she whispered.

Then the scripture from the night before came to her unbidden. She knew that the Lord had been showing her something about Jenny. *He shall cover thee with his feathers, and under his wings shalt thou trust. That is how You have been with Jenny all her life. You have protected her and guarded her since she was a little girl.*

Everything the Lord had been showing Jerusha about Jenny's life was beginning to piece together.

Just like when I make a quilt. I have the idea, then I do the work, and then I have the quilt.

Jerusha got up and put on her robe. She went to the kitchen, lit the stove, and put on some coffee. When it was ready, she poured herself a cup and went back to her sewing room. The Rose of Sharon quilt lay where she had left it. She picked it up and turned it over in her hands. All the pieces were there, but large stains marred the front and the back. The largest one had been made when she fell into the pond carrying Jenny across the ice, but there were others where the quilt had gotten wet when she had fallen in the snow as she struggled through the drifts on her way to the cabin.

The stains were large and uneven. There were also dirty places where she had lain on the floor of the cabin with Jenny, wrapped in the thick quilt. Sooty handprints reminded her of how she had kept the fire burning. Jerusha sighed. There was still so much to be done before the quilt was fully restored.

"I'm not sure I understand everything yet, Lord," Jerusha said. "I know now that Your blood covers the sins and imperfections in my life, so what are You telling me about these stains? How do they relate to my life? If my sins are forgiven, why is my life still stained?"

Work out your own salvation with fear and trembling.

"What?" Jerusha asked.

Work out your own salvation with fear and trembling.

Once more Jerusha became aware of the trap she had fallen into all her life as a quilter. She had always loved the end result, the finished quilt, but now she was beginning to understand that for the Lord, the work was complete before the foundation of the world. He was the Alpha and the Omega, so He saw the beginning and the end of each life. His attention was always on the process, the things that made a life what it was, and He maintained constant vigilance over the lives of His children to keep them on the path to His planned end.

"So, Lord, when I fall, You are always there?"

I will never leave you or forsake you. I love the church and gave Myself for it that I might sanctify and cleanse it with the washing of water by the word, that I might present it to Myself a glorious church, not having spot, or wrinkle, or any such thing; but that it should be holy and without blemish.

A picture came to Jerusha. She was twelve years old, and her father had given her a new pair of high-top shoes. They were beautiful black leather, handmade by a neighbor, and the finest shoes Jerusha had ever owned. One rainy day, she forgot that she was wearing her new shoes and went outside to play. When she came in, her shoes were covered with mud and stained by the pools of water she had walked through. She thoughtlessly left them on the back porch and went to her room.

Several hours later there came a knock on her door. When she opened it, her father was standing there with her new shoes in his hand. She saw the look of disappointment in his eyes, and then she looked down at the shoes. Instead of being muddy and stained, they were clean and polished, not a speck of dirt on them. They almost looked new again. Her father had said nothing but simply handed her the shoes and turned away.

A rush of shame and sorrow had come over her as her father silently walked down the hall. She had vowed to herself that she would never make that mistake again, but less than a month later she thoughtlessly wore them outside in the fields, and again they were dirty and stained. This time she didn't leave them, but cleaned them herself and tried to polish them. Her efforts didn't produce the desired result, so she had taken them to her father and asked for his help in cleaning them.

Her father had quietly showed her how to clean and polish them. First he wiped the mud off with a damp cloth. Then he placed a small dab of polish on a soft rag and rubbed it gently into the shoes with small circular motions, making sure that each crease and crevice was filled with polish. He set them by the stove for a few minutes until the polish melted into the surface of the leather. Then he sprinkled a few drops of water on the shoes and buffed them with a soft brush. He didn't stop there, but repeated the process two times. When he was finished, he buffed them lightly with a cotton cloth until they shone like new.

"*Ja, dochter, das is gut.*" He had smiled at her. "We learn how to care for the things we are given. The next time, you will clean them."

Jerusha thought about what she had learned. "So we are made new and covered by Your blood, but still we make ourselves dirty by walking in the world? Doesn't living the Amish way keep us from sin?"

The whole world lies under the sway of the wicked one. Your church does not save you. I save you.

"The first time I got my shoes dirty, my father cleaned them for me. The second time, he showed me how to clean them. But from then on, I had to keep my shoes clean or clean them myself if I got them dirty. Is that what You mean by working out your own salvation?"

Yes. I save you and show you the path, but then you must walk it. Each trial is a test. Will you do what I have taught you, or will you go your own way?

Jerusha looked at the quilt. "So even though it is restored and made whole, it can still be stained? And when it is, I must…what must I do then, Lord?"

If you confess your sins, I am faithful and just and will forgive you your sins and purify you from all unrighteousness.

"So, just as a child, I must come to my Father to be cleansed from my sins?"

Yes, dochter. *And I will show you the way, and then you must walk in it.*

Jerusha sat silently thinking. She began to understand that her life with the Lord had been shallow and empty, that she hadn't understood how He really worked in her life to save her, keep her, instruct her, and guide her. She had always believed that her church had kept her from the world, but now she understood that it wasn't her church, but her relationship with Him that kept her. And now she knew that each day, her life could be stained by sin even though she might appear to be doing everything right—sins of omission and sins of commission, sins of pride, arrogance, and so many other things, she would be overwhelmed if she didn't have the Lord to walk with her.

With that in mind, she took the quilt to the washroom. She filled a tub with cold water and stirred in some liquid soap, and a very small amount of vinegar. She placed the quilt in the water, pushing it under the water and making certain the entire quilt was wet. She gently moved the quilt around in the water. Then she left the quilt in the water for about ten minutes. After that, she drained the wash water and filled the tub again. She repeated draining and refilling the tub until the water and quilt were soap free—just clear water and no suds. After the quilt was rinsed, Jerusha blotted it dry with towels to absorb the moisture. Then she hung the quilt over the quilting frame where air could circulate around it.

As she stood looking at the quilt, she could see that the stains were almost gone. There were still a few spots that were slightly discolored, but the vinegar had restored most of the brightness. She began to understand on a deep level what the Lord had been showing her through the quilt. His words came to her again.

The washing of the water by the word...

"No matter how much we try or how many rules we follow, we will never be free from the stain of sin in this life, will we, Lord?" Jerusha asked.

Then without waiting for the answer she spoke, for the word was in her heart. "You made us whole, not by works of righteousness which we have done, but according to Your mercy You saved us, by the washing of regeneration, and renewing of the Holy Ghost. And now when we sin again, You have made a way for us to remove the stain. But, Lord, as I look at the quilt, I still see the stain. Isn't my life like the quilt?"

Yes, dochter, *but when I look at your life, I see the life of My Son, who lives in you. And there is no stain or sin in Him. He has made the way. He has covered you with His blood, and He washes you with His word. That is the way You must walk, and it is the way for Jenny. You must pray that she does not love Me because of you, but because of what I have done for her. She must understand My shed blood and the power of My word to cleanse. That is the key, and that is the way for her to find peace.*

Jerusha began to pray.

CHAPTER TWENTY-SEVEN

The Hideout

◇◇◇

BOBBY AND REUBEN WALKED QUIETLY up the trail through the ravine. Sheriff Gary and his men followed, and Johnny was out front, leading the way. It was dark, and a light snow had been falling intermittently.

From time to time the snow clouds cleared and allowed the dim light from the moon to light the way. They had flashlights but kept them pointed down at the trail as much as possible. They could see a small creek meandering through a wide, flat area filled with rocks and sand to their left. Beyond the creek, the east wall of the ravine rose steeply up into the darkness. To their right, between the trail and the western side of the ravine, was a flat area filled with brush and trees.

Reuben was unarmed, but Bobby and the men behind them carried rifles. They had helicoptered in to the field behind Bear Lake, where they met the local police. Now fifteen men were moving up the trail toward the supposed hideout.

They had been walking twenty minutes when Johnny stopped and motioned for quiet. He slipped back to Bobby's side and pointed to a small dam that blocked the creek. A flat, concrete path led to the other side across the top of the dam.

"The trail to the first cabin goes up over there," Johnny whispered. "It's steep but fairly easy to get up. I know the way, so I should go up first and check it out. The cabin is about fifty yards from the ravine, so it'll take me a few minutes to see if anyone's there."

"Okay. Take a flashlight but use it sparingly and cover the lens," Bobby said. "And be careful. Only go far enough to determine whether they're there, and then come back."

Johnny nodded and slipped away into the darkness. Reuben and Bobby and the rest of the men waited silently. In about ten minutes they heard Johnny coming back down the hill. He came across the dam and whispered to them.

"This cabin is empty. It doesn't look like anyone's been here for a long time. The road into the place is filled with weeds."

"How much farther to the next cabin?" Bobby asked.

"About five minutes," Johnny answered. "It's easier to get to—the original owner built a staircase down the side of the ravine to the creek. It comes up right behind the cabin. The bank widens out on the other side of the creek, so we can cross here and walk up."

"Lead on," Bobby said.

Once again Johnny took the lead as they crossed the dam and began to walk single file along the eastern side. After about five minutes they came to a place where another gully came down from the left and intersected the ravine. Johnny pointed up the gully.

"That's where the stairs come down. The bottom of the stairs has a door that locks from the inside so kids like me couldn't climb up." Johnny smiled. "It's easy to climb over and unlock it from the inside. I used to do it a lot."

The men quietly moved into the end of the gully. About twenty feet up they came to a wooden wall that blocked the end of the gully. Set in the wall was a door. Johnny moved to the right side of the wall.

"Let's see if that old root is still here," he said, reaching up into the darkness. "Yes, here it is."

Johnny grabbed onto something and put his foot on the side of the gully. With a quick pull and a scramble, he was on top of the wall. He let himself down on the other side, and Bobby and Reuben heard a click. The old door opened, and they could see a flight of stairs zigzagging up into the darkness. Johnny put a finger to his lips and disappeared up the stairs. In a few minutes he came back down.

"This is it," Johnny said. "There are lights on in the house and at least two cars in the driveway. One of them is the brown sedan Luis was driving."

Bobby and Gary gathered the men around them. "Call the PSP on the walkie-talkie and let them know that it's the second cabin on Stone Tower Road. How far is it from Tannery, Johnny?"

"It's Jonathan," Reuben said.

Johnny looked at Reuben with surprise, but he couldn't read his expression in the dark.

"How far up, Jonathan?" Sheriff Gary asked.

"A little over a quarter of a mile. The driveway from Stone Tower Road into the cabin is really just a dirt trail that cars can come down, so they need to watch carefully for it. There should be an old mailbox and a green tube where they put the newspaper out in front. The road into the cabin is on the left of the mailbox."

"How do you know all this stuff?" Gary asked.

"I used to hike down to the lake from this side because the fishing's better on the back side of the lake," Johnny said. "I would ride my old Schwinn up from Uncle Jim's cabin. It's about three miles. I'd stash my bike out on the road and come down the stairs to the ravine. In the spring, the creek is full of brownies, and I'd fish my way up to the top. There's another ravine back a ways where the creek comes down from the ridge. It splits there—one fork goes to the lake and the other fork comes down the hill, crosses under a bridge, and goes down a deep ravine along Tannery Road all the way to Bear Creek.

"The old guy who used to live here didn't like me using his stairs. He had some fruit trees behind his cabin, and I used to sneak up the stairs and steal apples and cherries. It really made him mad. I learned all the trails and roads around here so I could keep out of sight."

Sheriff Gary turned to the man with the walkie-talkie. "Okay, give them the directions. Tell them to leave their cars about two hundred yards up Stone Tower and walk up to the mailbox. Then come in quietly and spread out in the trees in front of the cabin. We'll be out back waiting for them to let us know they're there. Then we'll move in. Tell them to remember the girl and to move fast so we can take these guys by surprise."

Johnny led the way up the stairs. They followed several switchbacks up the side of the gully and finally came out on top. Johnny pointed silently as Bobby and Reuben and the rest of the men came to the top. They could see an old cabin about a hundred feet ahead of them. A light was on in one window. Bobby and Gary moved to the front of the group. Using hand signals, they spread the men out in a line in the woods behind the cabin. Bobby grabbed Reuben and Johnny and whispered to them.

"Stay with me and be careful. These guys are dangerous, and they're armed."

The men crept through the woods forming a half-circle behind the cabin. Johnny pointed to the back door to the kitchen and another door on the side of the house. They waited for the PSP to move up from the front.

As they waited in the woods, Bobby remembered being with Reuben in the jungle on Guadalcanal, hiding from Japanese soldiers and spying out their positions. The clouds opened up again, and the dim moonlight cast an eerie glow over the scene. Bobby glanced over at his friend. Reuben's face was impassive. Reuben looked back at Bobby. Bobby had seen that look in his eyes before, and he knew it didn't bode well for the men inside the cabin.

Just then the walkie-talkie crackled and a loud voice said, "We're in position."

The man with the walkie-talkie looked at Bobby with a stricken face. "I must have bumped the volume button," he whispered.

Without hesitating, Bobby signaled the men, and they stood up and ran toward the cabin.

Bobby ran full tilt into the back door and broke it down. His momentum carried him into the kitchen area, but he kept his feet. Gary and Reuben rushed in behind him, followed by Gary's men. The assault completely surprised the two men stretched out on couches in front of the fire. One man started to reach for a gun, but when the sheriff's men leveled their rifles at him, he realized he was outmatched and quietly surrendered. More men came through the doors at each end of the house. Suddenly there was the crash of breaking glass from one of the rooms off the hallway to their left. Then there was shouting from out front.

"Drop your weapons and raise your hands."

There followed low explosions from a heavy-caliber pistol returned instantly by a volley of rifle fire and more crashing sounds. Bobby and Sheriff Gary moved into the hallways and began checking the rooms. Bobby pushed open a door to a small room off the right-hand hallway. Johnny gave a cry, pushed past him, and knelt by the filthy mattress on the floor. He held up a white handkerchief. Reuben was standing behind Bobby and came over to Johnny's side.

"That's Jenny's," Reuben said. "But where is she?"

Sheriff Gary came into the room. "We've got everyone that was in the house. One of them got shot when two of them went out through the front window. He's badly wounded, so we'll have to get him to a hospital. But we didn't find the girl."

◇◇◇

Jorge and Luis were walking through the woods back toward the cabin. They had been searching for Jenny for an hour without success. As they came up the trail, Luis stopped Jorge and pointed to the left. Fresh tracks in the snow led out of the trees and headed straight toward the cabin. Just then they heard a strange crackling sound and a voice. Then in a few seconds they heard a crashing sound from up ahead and some yelling. Suddenly the sound of two gunshots and then an answering volley of rifle shots crashed through the woods. Luis swore and shoved Jorge behind a tree.

"They found us. That stupid Sal must have got caught and squealed!" he growled under his breath and cursed again. "We have to find that girl. She's our ticket out of here."

The two men ran toward the woods where they had seen the tracks. Just behind the first trees they came to a wooden landing at the top of a set of stairs.

"Hey," Luis said, "maybe the girl found these stairs and went down into the ravine. We didn't see any tracks in the woods up here."

Jorge and Luis hurried down the stairs to the door at the bottom.

"It's going to be dawn in a little while," Luis said. "We have to find the girl before it gets light. Take my flashlight and go that way," he said, pointing left. "I'll go down here. Look for little tracks. If you don't see anything in twenty minutes, get back here quick! It won't be long until they go out searching for the girl."

The clouds had cleared away, and there was enough light to see the trail. Jorge ran down the trail to the left, looking for tracks, and Luis ran to the right. In a few minutes Jorge came upon a set of tracks coming up out of the creek bed. The snow had been disturbed, and he could see where someone had lain in the snow. He walked over and looked closer. There were some spots of blood in the snow between two rocks, and something had been pulled up out of the sand.

It looks like she hurt herself. That means she's walking slow.

Jorge ran back to the bank and looked at the tracks. The left foot was dragging in the snow, and there was a strange mark on the left side of the tracks. Jorge could see that Jenny must be using a stick to lean on. He hurried on down the trail following the tracks until he came to a place in the snow where she must have fallen—there was a handprint, and the snow off the trail was disturbed. Jorge had forgotten Luis' instructions about returning, so he continued on. In about twenty minutes he came to an area where the walls of the ravine closed in. The tracks led on down the trail around a corner. Jorge ran around the corner and stopped in bewilderment. Ahead of him, shrubs and trees overhung the trail, and the snow had not come down here. Jenny's tracks led up to the edge of the snow and then disappeared on the hard ground under the tree.

Jenny hobbled down the path leaning on the stick. The nylon line was strong, and it supported the broken pine branch against her still throbbing ankle.

Suddenly she stepped on a hidden rock, rolled her bad ankle, and pitched forward into the snow. The pain was agonizing. She tried to get up and realized she was going to have a hard time going any farther. She looked around for a place to hide. The light from the sun was slowly illuminating the sky. Ahead of her was a clump of bushes, and it seemed that it was darker behind them. She randomly poked the pine stick into the bushes, and instead of the wall of the ravine, her stick encountered a hole in the side of the hill.

A cave!

Jenny knew she had to hide somewhere, but her tracks would give her away. Then she remembered something Uncle Bobby had told her about hiding from the Japanese when he was a scout in the Marines.

"We would walk out to a place where the ground made our tracks hard to see and then walk backward in our tracks until we came to where we wanted to hide," he had told her. "Then we would jump off the trail and walk backward using a branch to sweep our tracks away. The enemy often walked right by where we were hiding and lost us. Some of the Indian guys taught us that in training."

Up ahead the ravine narrowed, and the snow had not covered the trail because of the brush overhanging it. Jenny broke a branch off a Scotch broom and walked up the trail until there was no more snow. She stepped out onto the hard trail and took a few steps. Then she stepped backward as carefully as she could in her tracks until she came to the bush that hid the mouth of the cave. She gathered her strength and jumped off the trail.

Again an agonizing pain shot up her leg. She gritted her teeth and began to inch backward into the bush, sweeping her tracks as she went. She pushed through and found the cave. It had a narrow, low entrance, but it looked big enough for her to wriggle through. She knelt down and crawled in.

Inside, the ceiling rose up into the darkness, and the floor was dry and sandy. She could see a little but not much. The cave seemed to go back a lot farther than she thought. Her ankle was throbbing horribly, and she was exhausted.

Suddenly she heard a rustling sound up in the roof of the cave, and out of the dark, something black came at her. Bats! Jenny's heart leaped up and she almost screamed. The bats fluttered all around her, brushing her with their wings in their effort to get out. She heard their tiny squeaks and felt their bodies hitting her head and shoulders, and then she collapsed in a heap on the floor.

CHAPTER TWENTY-EIGHT

A Quilt for Jenny

◇◇◇

JERUSHA KNELT BY HER BED and cried out to the Lord on Jenny's behalf. The Rose of Sharon quilt was spread out before her, restored to its former beauty. Where the corner had been torn and the batting matted, Jerusha had skillfully pieced in new batting and sewn it with such tiny stitches that unless she looked at it very closely, she couldn't tell it had ever been damaged. All of the ruined red silk rose petals had been replaced, and the mud and water stains had been removed by slow and careful washing. Now it was as she remembered it, the most beautiful quilt she had ever made. Jerusha's thoughts carried her back to the days when she had labored over the quilt, planning her escape from the Amish life and cursing God for taking Jenna from her. She thought at the time that she was making the quilt for Jenna, a memorial to her precious little girl.

How You dealt with my heart, Lord. I was so proud and arrogant in those days. I believed You had killed Jenna because You hated me for my skill as a quilter. Now I know that we live in a sin-cursed world where bad things happen. But I also know that You are the one who gave me my skill and that every quilt I make comes from You and not from me.

She remembered when she had to make the choice between saving the quilt and saving Jenny from the storm. After she made the decision, she realized that the quilt had not been made only for Jenna, her first-born, but also for Jenny, the little lost girl. And as she surrendered her own plans and the bitterness that was killing her, she found a wonderful blessing in the life of the little girl God gave her.

It was like the story of Job. Everything he had was gone, but in the end he repented and blessed God, and God restored everything and more.

Now Jenny was lost, and Reuben and Bobby had gone to find her. But Jerusha wasn't angry with God. No, this time it was different. She trusted Him with Jenny's life, and her prayers ascended to heaven on her daughter's behalf.

◇◇◇

Bobby and Gary and the rest of the men gathered in the front room. Three sullen men were standing against the wall.

"Two guys are missing," Johnny said. "Luis and a younger guy. They must have Jenny." He slumped down in a chair and put his hands over his face. Reuben started to move toward the men, but Bobby put a hand on his arm and held him back.

"I'll talk to them, Reuben," Bobby said.

He stepped in front of one of the men, a fat, beady-eyed, balding guy. "Where's the girl?" Bobby asked quietly.

The fat man just glared back at Bobby. Reuben stepped forward and locked eyes with him. The fat man immediately started talking. "Okay, okay, the girl's gone."

Johnny looked up in surprise. "What do you mean, gone?"

"She got away when we were all out here drinking," the fat man said. "She unlocked the door of the room somehow and ran out the back door. Jorge and Luis went to look for her. They wanted me to come, but I told them to find her themselves. It was too cold out there."

◇◇◇

Jerusha sat at the kitchen table as the first rays of dawn came up over the eastern fields. A kiss of frost had formed on the windows, and the beautiful crystalline patterns etched their magic on the glass. She lit a fire to take off the chill. Fall would soon be coming to an end, and it would be time for the Thanksgiving feast, for weddings, and for the friendly fellowship that the Amish shared together during the long winter months.

Once she would have felt great anticipation, but now her life seemed disconnected from everything but Jenny. It was hard for her to comprehend. She had lived in the simple way, she had been faithful to the *ordnung,* and she had shunned the world. But the world had crowded in on her life for the second time now, and once again her daughter was at the center of the storm. She thought of the Rose of Sharon and how the quilt had been inextricably bound to the lives of both of her daughters. And then it occurred to her— *The quilt is bound to my life too!*

She remembered the days when she had cut the pieces for the rose pattern, more than a hundred perfectly duplicated pieces of silk, overlaid and stitched together to make the beautiful rose in the center of the quilt. She thought about the way the rose had shone in the soft light of dawn, the morning of the big storm before she left for the fair. Not one stitch out of place, not one pucker, each piece perfectly placed and bound together.

You are the quilter of our lives. Your hand places us perfectly into the pattern of Your plan for us—a plan that You have always had in mind.

As Jerusha let the wonder of this revelation wash over her, the deep, peaceful voice that she had come to know again in these troubled days spoke to her spirit.

I sent you the Rose of Sharon quilt to awaken you, to tell you that I was reaching for you. But you had forgotten. You thought that the peace you knew before Jenna came into this world was born from your faith, from your husband, from the land. But it was from Me.

"Because you are the Prince of Peace?"

Yes. And Jenny has never known Me in that way. So she has never known peace. Jenny is looking for something out there in the world to give her peace. But she will only find it in Me.

"Then tell me, Lord, how I must pray for Jenny."

I have a plan for each of My children. But if My sheep cannot hear My voice, they will not follow Me into the sheepfold, where I can guard them and protect them. Jenny needs to hear My voice for herself, not from you or from Reuben. And until she does, she is in great danger. I have no grand-daughters, Jerusha—only daughters. That is how you must pray.

◇◇◇

Jenny waited until the fluttering and squeaking bats were gone. Her ankle was beginning to throb again, and her left side ached where she had landed when she fell off the cliff. The cave was cold, but it was dry. She was lying on a sandy floor. The dim light from the first rays of the sun filtered through the low entrance and lit the cave enough for Jenny to see around her. She could see that the cave was narrow in the front where the roof came down to the entrance but that it widened out the farther back it went.

The floor was smooth sand except where a few rocks stuck out. Back into the cave a little farther, someone had dug a pit, and she could see that a few pieces of burned wood and ashes from an old fire were still in it. Jenny slowly got to her feet and looked around. She could feel her heart beating in her ankle. There were ledges on the wall, almost like shelves, and the stub ends of candles were stuck on them. Some-one had obviously used this place, probably kids.

As she was looking around, she heard a noise from outside. She shrank back against the wall of the cave and cautiously peered out the entrance to see Jorge walking along the trail, following her tracks.

The sun was barely up, but there was enough light for her tracks to be easily seen. Jorge continued walking right past the brush in front of the cave. Jenny's ruse had worked! He continued on up the trail until he was out of sight.

Jenny sank back down on the floor of the cave, her heart pounding. She waited in fear for him to come back. After a few minutes she thought about hiding from him farther back in the cave. She looked along the shelf where the candle stubs were to see if someone had left any matches. There! A small circular metal tube with a screw-on lid was lying beside one of the larger candles. She picked it up and unscrewed the lid. Inside were about ten perfectly dry wooden matches. There were four candles on the shelf. Three of them were burned almost all the way down, but the fourth stub was fairly large. She gathered all of them up and limped to the back of the cave.

There was an opening in the back wall that she could just barely see. She waited in the silence to make sure Jorge wasn't coming back, and then she struck a match on a striker inside the lid of the tube. The match flared up, and she lit the candle and held it aloft as she began to walk down the narrow passage until she came to a blank wall. As she stood looking for any other way out she noticed that the candle flame was fluttering. A breeze.

She raised the candle higher. About five feet up the wall was a narrow opening. It appeared big enough to crawl through, but she couldn't figure out how to get up. Then she noticed a pattern of holes in the wall of the cave leading up to the opening, almost as though someone had cut them for a ladder. She took one of the small candle stubs out of her pocket, lit it, and set it on a rocky projection next to the holes.

Jenny blew out her big candle and started climbing. The first step was easy because she could use her right foot. But when she put her weight on her injured left ankle, the pain almost made her fall off the wall. She gritted her teeth and pulled her weight up using the handholds. Slowly she climbed up the wall until she came to the opening. She put her knee up and used her hands to lever herself up and into the hole in the wall. It was cramped inside, but there was just enough space to turn around in. She leaned partway out and grabbed the smaller candle off the wall where she had put it. It blew out, and then she was in darkness. Jenny rolled over on her back and tried to get the matches out of her pocket. Her ankle was throbbing, and she wanted to give in to the urge to just break down and cry.

The narrow passage she was lying in sloped downhill, and there were loose rocks underneath her back. As she struggled to get the tube of matches out of her pocket, she felt herself begin to slide. She struggled to stop, but when she tried to push her left ankle against the wall, a jolt of pain shot through it and she took her weight off. Desperately she clawed at the walls, trying to get a grip. She slid a few more feet and then, with an agonizing jolt, she jerked to a stop. She tried to move her legs, but the injured one was stuck somehow. She was trapped in the dark.

CHAPTER TWENTY-NINE

A Light in the Darkness

◇◇◇

JENNY LAY QUIETLY, THINKING OF what to do, but there was nothing but to stay here for now, stuck somewhere in the dark pit of a cave. Her mind played back a memory buried deep in her youth of another time when she was trapped. It was in a car, and she was very small. She had been cold, looking out of a car window as the wind howled like raging demons and the snow blew fiercely.

Outside the car window was ice, but there was a hole and water splashing. Then a man's face rose up out of the water. Jenny thought the face would see her, but the eyes were raised to heaven and the lips were moving soundlessly. It was a man with stringy hair, and he was struggling to get out of the water, but the edge of the hole kept breaking. And then he looked straight at her and reached for her—but suddenly he disappeared under the water. The wind howled and the snow slowly covered the window bit by bit until she couldn't see the hole anymore.

The roar of the wind had grown louder, and Jenny felt the cold encase her body…and then something wonderful happened. She heard a sound like a scraping at the window. She looked up and saw something moving outside, brushing and cleaning the snow away from the glass. The movement continued, and suddenly the little girl was looking up into the most beautiful face she had ever seen. The eyes stared back at her, and the mouth opened in surprise. It was her mama! She was kneeling in the snow, looking at Jenny through the window.

Jenny cried out, "Mama, Mama, I'm here! Mama, come find me!"

Jenny could see her mama struggling with the door of the car, but she couldn't open it. Her mama got up and went around to the other side of the car. The door slowly opened, but then everything got mixed up. Her mama was in the car with her, and they were huddled together, and then her mama was gone but she was covered by something like feathers—and then her mama was back and she was wrapping Jenny in something wonderfully warm and soft, and Jenny could see there was a flower, a rose. And then her mama was carrying her through the howling wind, and Jenny was safe and warm in the quilt.

The memory faded, and Jenny returned to reality as a stab of pain shot through her, almost causing her pass to out.

I'm in a cave, and I slid down. I may have fallen a long way. I was dreaming about the car again. I was back in the car by the pond, and I was freezing to death, and my mama found me and wrapped me in a warm quilt.

Jenny thought about the quilt. Her mama had called it the Rose of Sharon. It had been Jenna's quilt, but her mama used it to save her when she was lost in the big storm, and then it was her quilt. She remembered the last time she had seen it a few years earlier. She came home and couldn't find her mama, and she looked all through the house. Then she peeked in her mama's sewing room. Jerusha was sitting in her rocking chair, holding the quilt close to her, tears glistening down her cheek.

"Mama?" she asked.

"Come in, *dochter*," Jerusha said, and she did. She stood at her mother's side and looked down at the quilt.

"That's my quilt," she said. "The one you wrapped me in to save my life."

"Yes, Jenny, this is your quilt," Jerusha said. "It's a strange and wonderful story, how it came to be yours."

Jenny sat down at her mother's feet and laid her head on Jerusha's lap. "Tell me again, Mama," she said.

Jerusha laid her hand gently on her daughter's head and began to stroke her hair as she spoke.

"I made this quilt for our Jenna when I was running away from God and from my faith. This quilt was my way out. But then God led me to you, and I had to make a choice—hold on to my pride and keep the quilt unspoiled, or use it to save you. I made the right choice."

You had to make a choice to save me, and the way you saved me was to ruin the quilt.

"And how did you get me?" Jenny had asked.

"No one knew where you came from or who your parents were," Jerusha said. "By the time the police went to Jepson's Pond to pull out the car, it was already spring. In the bottom of the pond they found the body of a man. He had been there too long for them to take any fingerprints. When they checked on the car, they found that it was stolen in New York City. He may have been your father, but no one knows."

He may have been my father, but he hurt me, and he did something bad to my first mama.

Jerusha kept telling the story. "Well, since you were all alone, we applied to take you into foster care while the authorities looked for any relatives. That was a fruitless search, so we adopted you, and that's how you became our daughter. And a wonderful daughter you have been."

"Mama, did you ever regret having me instead of Jenna?" Jenny asked as she looked up into her mother's face.

"Jenna was a wonderful child. She already had a special relationship with the Lord when she died. It was an easy and pleasant task to raise her."

Jenny wondered what her mama had meant about Jenna already having a special relationship with the Lord. As she lay in the darkness of the cave, she tried to remember the rest of the conversation.

"You were a stronger child than Jenna, more determined and self-willed. God knew that you needed your papa and me to raise you, to bring order to your life, and to give you the opportunity to have a relationship with Him," Jerusha said.

Jenny wondered how being stronger made her different from Jenna. Wouldn't that make her better? And then Jenny remembered a scripture verse she had been taught as a child. *Therefore I take pleasure in infirmities, in reproaches, in necessities, in persecutions, in distresses for Christ's sake: for when I am weak, then am I strong.*

Jenny lay in the dark, pondering what that meant. It didn't make sense to her. She had always been able to solve her problems by exerting her own will. She took pride in her ability to work her way through any difficulty and solve the problem with her mind and her knowledge. Jenny closed her eyes and thought about her childhood. It had been difficult, but somehow she had always found a way to get through the hard times. Or had she? She thought about what her mama had said to her that day as she told her the story of the quilt.

"Who knows what would have happened to you or me or your papa if God had not put us together? We all needed each other."

Jenny considered those words. Her mama said that God had put them together and that their lives might have been different if He had not made them a family. As she lay alone in the cave, she began to see things in a new way. All her life she had believed that people made their own way through life—they used whatever talents they had to face each day and somehow make it through. But now she was beginning to see that behind her life, a hand had been guiding and directing her.

THE ROAD HOME 259

What if the bad man hadn't crashed the car? What if her mama hadn't been out in the storm? What if her mama hadn't made the quilt for Jenna, and what if she hadn't had it with her to wrap Jenny in and save her? The quilt! There was something about the quilt that she needed to understand.

Her mama had told her that she had come upon the beautiful silk she used for the red rose by accident. But was it really an accident? All the pieces that made up the quilt were somehow like her life, stitched together in a perfect pattern, yet done so skillfully that even when she looked closely, Jenny had never seen how it was fitted together. It was just a quilt, wasn't it? But as she thought about it, she remembered how difficult it was for her to even stitch, much less make a beautiful quilt the way her mama did.

Another stab of pain shot through her leg. She reached down and carefully pulled her right leg out straight. Her injured left leg was wedged against something, and she tried to pull it loose, but it wouldn't budge. She gasped with the pain.

She had to get out of this place. No one would ever find her. It was up to her now. She reached out her hands and felt the walls that were close to her on both sides. She was in some sort of a narrow passage that slanted upward toward the place where a dim light was now coming in as the sun outside rose. She had slid down on the rocks when she was trying to find the matches to light the candle. She tried to sit up, but the pain in her side and leg was too much to bear, and she fell back.

She lay there helpless, and it occurred to her that all of the times that she had saved herself had only led up to this moment, and now she didn't know what to do or how to get out of her predicament. She thought of what her mama had said—that she was stronger than Jenna but that Jenna had a special relationship with the Lord. And then, almost like an audible voice, the words came to her. *My grace is sufficient for thee: for my strength is made perfect in weakness.*

Like a light in the darkness it came to her. God had been waiting all these years for Jenny to place her complete trust in Him. He was the Master Quilter who had stitched her life together with her mama's and papa's lives so seamlessly and so perfectly that she had never even seen how He had done it. He had given her mama the quilt, and the story of their lives was written there. She thought about the quilt, torn and stained but still beautiful.

She could see it. God wanted her to let Him be Lord in her life, to put down her plans and her desires. Suddenly she realized that it wasn't finding her real mother that would give her peace, it was finding Him and placing her life in His hands, letting Him wrap her in His love and care.

Just like my mama wrapped me in the quilt.

And again, like an audible voice, the words of a psalm her mother taught her came to her. *He that dwelleth in the secret place of the most High shall abide under the shadow of the Almighty…He shall cover thee with his feathers, and under his wings shalt thou trust.*

And then Jenny remembered the wings, the feathers. She had been freezing in the car, and someone or something had come and covered her with something wonderfully warm that felt like…like…like feathers! And then Jenny knew that He had always been with her and that He had been waiting for her to see how much He loved her and cared for her and how much He wanted her to trust Him completely. And in that moment she put down her burden and spoke to her God.

Chapter Thirty

Reunion

◇◇◇

"Okay, we've got two armed and dangerous men out in the woods looking for the girl," Sheriff Gary said to his men. "Johnson, I want you and Henderson to make sure these three we apprehended are turned over to the state troopers and taken back to Wilkes-Barre. There's an ambulance on its way up the hill. The wounded man will go back in that along with one of the men that came with the PSP."

The sheriff turned to Jonathan. "Well, son, so far your directions have been spot on. So you spent a lot of time up here when you were a kid?"

"Actually, sheriff, that wasn't so long ago," Jonathan said. "I'm only nineteen, and I was up here just two summers ago. I've been coming up here every summer since I was six. I caught my first fish in Bear Lake."

"Good," Gary said. "So what's the lay of the neighborhood?"

"The creek in the ravine behind the cabins comes down from the ridge above the lake and splits—part goes down the north leg of the ravine and feeds the lake, and the other branch goes south down the ravine toward Tannery road, dips under a bridge, and then runs down on the south side of Tannery until it levels out and flows into Spruce Swamp. The woods up here on top are full of brush, but there aren't a lot of places to hide.

"If you get across Tannery and follow the ravine down to the bottom of the hill, you come to a really swampy area, and anybody who walked in there would get stuck bad, believe me. I would park my bike on Tannery and use the ravine to get up the hill and down to the lake because you can't see into it from the cabins up on top. The folks who lived here before weren't very friendly, so I had to be cool and stay out of sight."

"So where might Luis and his partner be?" Bobby asked.

"The ravine cuts the woods in half, so if they were still up on top they most likely would have run into the troopers coming up the hill," Johnny said. "Jenny would have seen the police too if she was up here, and she would have shown herself. So my guess is that somehow she got down into the ravine, and the crooks followed her down there after we came up."

"You should probably have them sweep the woods on top of the hill, starting at the ravine and working east until you come to the road," Bobby said to Gary. "Tell them to send a couple of men up the ravine from the road. The rest of us can get down into the ravine and search it down to the road and over to the lake."

"Sounds good," Gary said. He pointed at Reuben and Jonathan. "What about these two? Do they have guns? It might get a little sticky down there."

"I've deputized them, so they can carry guns," Bobby said. He reached over, grabbed a shotgun that was leaning against the wall, and tossed it to Reuben. Reuben instinctively caught it and then stared at it. He turned and handed it to Jonathan.

"You sure?" Bobby asked.

Reuben nodded. "It's got to stop somewhere, Bobby," Reuben said, and then he smiled. "I'll stick with Jonathan. We'll be okay."

Sheriff Gary looked dubious, but Bobby said, "Okay, pal, but keep your head down. I'm getting too old to be bailing you out of trouble."

Jorge looked around. Jenny's tracks disappeared under the trees where the ravine narrowed, so Jorge went down the trail until the ravine opened back up, and there was snow on the ground. There were no tracks coming out from under the trees. Jorge thought about it for a minute and then realized that Jenny must have backtracked and hidden along the trail. He turned and headed back down the trail.

Luis had followed the trail by the creek for about a half a mile. He saw the tracks of the men coming up the trail, but they all wore large boots. He couldn't find any tennis shoe tracks among them, so he turned back. It had been longer than twenty minutes, and he knew that the police would be looking for them. He started running back up the trail, looking for Jorge.

Bobby, Reuben, Jonathan, and the rest of the men stood at the top of the stairs leading down into the ravine. Sheriff Gary sent two of his men with the PSP boys and the local police to search the woods around the cabins. Then the rest of them, seven in all, headed down the steps to the creek. When they got to the bottom they divided up. Three men went down toward the lake. Bobby, Reuben, Jonathan, and Gary headed the other way. The sun was just coming up.

When Luis came to the bottom of the stairs he stopped and listened. He thought he heard voices talking quietly, and then he distinctly heard someone coming down the steps, so he quickly ran back down the trail looking for Jorge. In a few minutes he saw Jorge coming up the trail. He ran up to him and grabbed him by the arm.

"We've to get out of here," Luis panted, out of breath. "They're coming this way. We have to get down the ravine into the woods on the other side of the road."

"What about Jenny?" Jorge asked. "She's around here somewhere. A little way down the path her tracks went under the trees, but they didn't come out on the other side, so somewhere right along here she got off the trail and hid. There can't be too many places."

"We don't have time to find her," Luis hissed. "We have to go! Now!"

Jorge shrugged, and the two men headed down the trail. They had only gone a few hundred feet when Jorge spotted movement in the woods ahead. He grabbed Luis and pointed. They both ducked behind some brush. Ahead of them about a hundred yards away were two men with rifles. They were coming slowly up the trail, looking into the woods on either side.

"We have to find a way up the bank," Luis whispered.

"I'm telling you, Jenny found a place to hide back along the trail," Jorge said. "If we can find her, she's our ticket out of here. Come on, I have a pretty good idea where she got off the trail. She's not far from here—I know it."

Luis and Jorge headed back down the trail. They came out from under the trees where Jenny's tracks had disappeared.

"She's hiding right along here somewhere," Jorge said, "We have to find her."

The two men frantically began to search among the brush and trees. Suddenly Luis grabbed Jorge. "Back there, behind those bushes."

They pushed through the bushes and spotted the mouth of the cave. Jorge smiled. "Smart girl."

The two men ducked down and went through the cave mouth on

their hands and knees. Jorge pulled out his flashlight and turned it on. He shined it down at the ground. There in the sand were the marks of Jenny's shoes.

"She's in here all right," Luis said. "Jenny," he called softly. "Come on out, we found you."

Jorge shined the light around. The cave opened into a narrow passageway. Jenny's tracks led toward the opening. Luis and Jorge followed. In a few minutes the passage ended at a blank wall. The two men looked around. Then Jorge pointed the light up higher. About five feet up was another narrow opening.

"How did she get up there?" Luis asked.

"By using these," said Jorge, as he shined the light on the steps carved into the wall.

Jorge called out. "Come on out, Jenny, we know you're up there. Don't make me come up there and get you."

◇◇◇

Outside, the four men moved quietly down the trail. Ahead of them in the snow were two sets of tracks.

"Luis and the other guy," Bobby whispered.

They followed the tracks. Then they saw another set of tracks coming up out of the creek bed. Johnny pointed. The tracks were from tennis shoes, and the left leg was dragging in the snow. Jonathan stooped down and looked closer. There were a few drops of blood in the snow by the tracks.

"It's Jenny, and it looks like she's hurt. She's dragging her leg, and there's blood here."

"We have to find her before they do," Reuben said, starting up the trail.

The others hurried after him.

◇◇◇

Jenny lay in the darkness. She had been either dozing or unconscious, and something had awakened her—a bright light shining on the roof of the passage where she had climbed in. She could see that the pine stick that was her splint had wedged in a crack as she slid, and that was what had kept her from going all the way down. Then she heard a voice. *Jorge!*

"Come on out, Jenny, we know you're there. Don't make me come up there and get you."

Jenny's heart began pounding. She looked around. There was no way out except down. She reached over and tried to pull the pine splint out of the crack where it was wedged.

Stop!

Jenny's hand jerked back. The warning had come like a shout. She reached toward the splint again.

Stop!

Then she knew what it was. Once again she was trying to save herself. The words came to her quietly. *My grace is sufficient for thee: for my strength is made perfect in weakness.*

Jenny lay back. "All right, Lord," she whispered. "You win. I'm helpless. I put my life in Your hands."

◇◇◇

Gary and Bobby were in the lead with Reuben and Jonathan right behind. They came to a place where a jumble of tracks led under the trees. The light snow covering had begun to melt, and it was hard to tell if anyone had gone farther. What tracks remained in the melting snow were mixed up and confused. Bobby and Gary moved forward and around the corner, where the ravine narrowed. Jonathan and Reuben followed. They came out the other side, but the confusion of tracks didn't come out from under the trees. Bobby saw the two troopers coming down the path about fifty yards away.

"Gary and I will go see if those guys have found anything," Bobby said. "You two go back along the trail and look to see if Luis and his buddy found a way out of the ravine."

"But, Sheriff, what about Jenny?" Jonathan asked. "If she's hurt, she couldn't climb out of here."

"Well, get in behind the brush along the trail and see if she's hidden somewhere," Bobby said. "We'll talk to these guys and then come find you."

Bobby and Gary headed up the trail. As they did, Jonathan stopped and grabbed Reuben's arm.

"The cave!"

"What?" Reuben asked.

"The cave—maybe Jenny found the cave!"

"What cave?" Reuben asked.

"There's a big cave behind the brush back there. I'll bet Jenny's in there!"

Jonathan and Reuben went back to the pine trees. They pushed their way through the brush and began walking along the face of the cliff. Ahead of them in the wall of the cliff was a dark opening.

"There it is," Johnny said. "You have to get down and crawl in, but it opens up right away."

The two men crawled into the cave.

"Jenny, are you in here?" Jonathan called.

"Yeah, she is," said a voice. "But so are we—now drop the shotgun."

As their eyes adjusted to the dark, Jonathan could see Luis and another man standing at the back of the cave. Luis had a pistol pointed at them. Jonathan slowly put down the shotgun. Luis walked up to him and stuck the pistol in his face. "Well, Johnny the Candyman, I see you got away from Sal. I should have just killed you. I think I'll do it now."

He pulled back the hammer of the pistol. Jonathan turned his head, but before Luis could fire, Reuben spoke.

"The woods are full of armed men. You fire that gun and they'll be here in a minute."

Luis looked at Reuben and then grinned. "You're right, big man. So maybe I'll just beat him to death."

"You're not going to get Jenny again!" Jonathan shouted as he lunged forward and tried to grab Luis' arm.

Luis raised the pistol and struck Jonathan a powerful blow on the side of the head. Jonathan crumpled into a heap. Luis leaned over him to strike again, but Reuben leaped forward and grabbed his wrist. The two men began to struggle for the gun. Jorge had a gun and aimed it at Reuben.

Reuben swung Luis around between them and Jorge leapt forward, trying to get to a place where he could fire at Reuben without hitting Luis. Reuben reached out with his free hand and grabbed Jorge's gun arm. Now the three men were locked in a deadly dance. Slowly Luis and Jorge forced Reuben backward. Reuben struggled to keep the guns pointed away from him, but the combined strength of the two men began to force Reuben to his knees. Luis began to move the gun toward Reuben. Reuben used all his strength, but he knew he was about to be shot. Then Luis felt something cold on his neck.

"If you want to live, drop your gun."

The two gangsters felt the guns in their backs, and they stopped struggling. Bobby, with Gary at his side, reached in slowly and relieved them of their guns. Then he used his leg to sweep Luis' legs out from under him and knocked him facedown in the sand.

"You too," Bobby said to Jorge. "On your face."

Jorge dropped to his knees and lay facedown in the sand. Gary stepped in, pulled Luis' arms behind his back, and quickly snapped on a pair of handcuffs. Bobby handed him another pair, and Gary did the same to Jorge. Reuben looked up at Bobby.

"We're even, old pal," Bobby said with a grin.

There was a groan from the corner and Jonathan slowly raised himself to his knees. A stream of blood ran down the side of his face where Luis had hit him. Bobby and Reuben helped Jonathan to his feet.

"Are you all right?" Reuben asked.

"I'll be okay," Jonathan said. "I have a pretty thick skull."

Just then they heard a distant voice from the back of the cave. "Papa? Uncle Bobby? Is that you?"

Reuben ran to the back of the cave. "Jenny!"

"She's in there," Jonathan said as he ran back. He pointed up the wall to the mouth of the passage. "Jenny, are you okay?" he shouted.

"Jonathan? I'm here, but I'm stuck."

"Don't move," shouted Jonathan. "That channel is a tunnel that goes through into another cave. There's a fifty-foot drop at the end of it. Stay right where you are. I'll come and get you."

Jonathan picked up the flashlight where Jorge had dropped it in the struggle.

"Point this in there so I can see her," he said.

Quickly, Jonathan scrambled up the footholds and disappeared into the opening. Carefully he made his way down the chute until he came to where Jenny lay.

She looked up at him and tears began to form in her eyes. "Jonathan? I didn't think I would ever see you again."

"Just lie still, Jenny," Jonathan said. "I'm going to put my hands under your arms and pull you up. Be very still and let me do it. I don't want you to slip."

Carefully Jonathan grasped Jenny under the arms and began to pull her up the channel. Slowly, inch by inch, he eased her up. When he came to the opening, Jonathan looked down into Reuben's face.

"I've got her, Mr. Springer. I'm going to pass her down to you."

Reuben reached up. Slowly Jonathan pulled Jenny past him until Reuben could take her. Gently Reuben lifted her out and into his arms.

Jenny felt her papa's strong arms wrap around her, and she put her arms around his neck. She could feel his body begin to shake. She pulled her face back and looked at him in surprise.

Reuben pulled her close, and Jenny began to cry with him.

Part Three
THE ROAD HOME

◇◇◇◇◇◇◇◇◇◇◇◇

IN EACH OF OUR LIVES there is a longing, deep rooted and unshakable. It's the longing to return to the place of our birth, the place where we grew up, the place we call home.

Regardless of where we are or what we're doing, the memory of this place of our origin can rise to the surface of our thoughts like a trout rising in a still lake when the sun has just gone down over the mountain, and then a yearning comes into our heart to return, to go back, to turn our steps toward home.

These moments can spring unbidden from the deepest recesses of our being, and when they do, we can be overwhelmed with memories, pictures, and emotions. It's as though we climb the dusty stairs into the attic of our consciousness, open the old chest filled with our past, and take out the quilt of our lives.

In the dim light we kneel in our thoughts and look at all the days we've lived, each day stitched to the one before and the one after. And though each may be different, the whole connection of those days makes a pattern that becomes clear only as we look back with eyes that now know that there is a beginning...and an end.

In this moment, we remember the road we've traveled. As we turn to look, we see our own footprints mixed with those of all who have traveled with us. Then we know that though this road goes on into a future to reach an end we cannot yet see and may even fear, it is also the road home.

CHAPTER THIRTY-ONE

The Agreement

◇◇◇

Dim light crept into the room where Jenny lay sleeping. Outside the window a pine siskin sang a song of praise to the rising sun. Jenny groaned, and her eyes fluttered open. She gasped, sat up, and looked around. Then it dawned on her. She sank back down in the bed and pulled the covers around her. She was home, she was warm and toasty, and most importantly, she wasn't afraid anymore. She was safe in her bed in the room she thought she would never see again.

Slowly she took in her surroundings—the oak chest her papa had made, the chair in the corner, her mama's quilt pulled up close around her. Her mama's quilt! She sighed and stretched, and as she did, a pain shot through her shoulder and down into her leg. She raised the covers and saw the cloth splint strapped on her ankle, and then she remembered her papa carrying her out of the cave and the ride to the hospital and the doctor who had put the splint on her.

"It was just a dislocation, Mr. Springer," the doctor had said. "But we better splint it for a week until we know it's in place to stay."

Jenny lay back and nuzzled the quilt against her cheek. Then she noticed something different about the quilt. She lifted herself up on one elbow and looked down. It wasn't her familiar star quilt, it was the Rose of Sharon quilt—the one her mama had wrapped her in to save her so long ago in the big storm. She looked with amazement at the beautiful quilt. The ripped and tattered corner had been repaired. Even the missing piece of batting had been replaced. The red silken petals that had been torn and frayed were restored, perfectly sewn into the beautiful rose design. And the blue silken backing and the white linen were free of every stain. The quilt was whole again!

As she stared in amazement, there was a soft knock on her door, and then her mama peeked in. Jenny felt tears form in her eyes, and she lifted her hands. Jerusha came quickly to the bedside and took Jenny into her arms. She held her daughter quietly as she softly stroked her short, curly hair. Jenny could feel her mama's heart beating, strong and sure, letting Jenny know that she was in the safest place she could be.

"Jenny, my darling girl," Jerusha said softly as her arms held the girl close.

"Mama, I'm so sorry…I…"

Jerusha pulled back a little and placed her finger on Jenny's lips. "Hush, my dearest, there's no need. We can talk about it later. I understand now, and so does your papa. He's waiting outside."

"Papa," Jenny called out, and Reuben came into the room. His head was bare, and his hat was in his hands. He came to the side of the bed and looked down at his daughter with love in his eyes. She shifted her aching body and held her arms out to her *daed*. He came around and knelt beside the bed. He lifted his arms and Jenny came into them. The soft hair of his beard brushed against her face, and the familiar, beloved smells of the farm in his clothing filled her senses.

"Papa…" Jenny said. "Papa, I'm so sorry I caused you worry. I'm sorry I made you so angry with me. Please forgive me."

Reuben's arms held her tighter for a long moment. "Well, *dochter,* I must admit I was upset when you ran away and very frightened when you were kidnapped. But I was most upset that you would cause your mama such distress."

"Reuben, it's not necessary…" Jerusha said.

Reuben looked at Jerusha, and Jenny saw a look pass between them. Then her papa continued.

"I was upset, as I said, but as I prayed and as we searched for you, I realized that I had been unfair with you. Your mama and I have talked, and she's shared some things with me that helped me understand."

"But, Papa, I was—"

Reuben took Jenny's hand in his. "Let me finish, Jenny. I need to say this."

Jenny looked at Jerusha. Her mama smiled at her and spoke. "Often it is hard for your papa to tell us what's in his heart. Now is one of those times when it is not, so we need to listen."

Reuben smiled gratefully at his wife and then looked back at Jenny. "I didn't understand how much it meant to you to know who your birth mother and father were. And, to tell you the truth, I was afraid that if you did find them and they could offer you more than we can, you'd leave the farm forever and go to be with them. But your mama has pointed out to me that you needed to know these things because your life was incomplete in many ways. We see now that things happened to you before we found you, things that hurt you, things that should never happen to a little girl. Your mama saw it in the quilt."

"The quilt?" Jenny asked.

Reuben looked at Jerusha and nodded. Jerusha went on. "Yes, dearest, the quilt. You know that I made that quilt for Jenna long ago. It was going to be my way to leave the Amish faith after Jenna died and your papa was gone. But then I found you in the storm and I had to choose—save the quilt or save you. I can't believe now that there was ever a moment's hesitation, but in that moment I had a real battle with my pride. I know now that God was reaching for some things deep in me. So I wrapped you in the quilt and saved you. And then it became your quilt too. But in saving you, the quilt got ruined."

"What does that have to do with me?" Jenny asked, looking from Reuben to Jerusha. "And why does my quilt look brand new?"

"While I was praying, I truly believe the Lord spoke to me about the quilt. I clearly heard Him say, 'Jenny's life is like this quilt. Though it's beautiful, it's not whole. Some pieces are missing, and some stains must be washed away. I have given her to you so you can be part of that cleansing. You are a key to Jenny's happiness and wholeness.' When I asked Him what that meant, He told me."

Jerusha looked back at Reuben and smiled. "You tell her, husband."

Reuben held Jenny's hand and looked into her eyes. "The Lord showed your mama that when you were little, terrible things happened to you, things you didn't remember until He started showing you."

"The dreams," Jenny said. "He showed me in the dreams. And I saw my birth mother and the bad man who tried to hurt me."

"Yes, Jenny, you did," Reuben said. "I just wasn't paying attention when you told us about them. I should have listened, but sometimes I can be so pigheaded…" Reuben stopped and swallowed hard before continuing. "When those bad things happened, they hurt you inside and robbed you of your peace. And so all your life, you've been looking, searching, trying to find the answers, but until the Lord intervened, we didn't understand what you were looking for. We just thought you were energetic and high-strung and that you would get over it in time."

"But I didn't get over it," Jenny said, "and I caused you and Mama a lot of heartache and trouble."

Reuben pulled Jenny into his arms again and spoke softly in her ear. "But, Jenny, you were given to us to love and protect and help. Your mother and I failed you in this way because we forgot about the miracle God performed when He gave you to us. We should have remembered every day that there was a purpose and a design in the things

God did for us, starting even before Jenna was born. The Rose of Sharon quilt was part of that. God gave us something to remind us about what happened to you, but we put it away and forgot. And so we went on living as if you were our natural-born daughter without seeing that you needed our help to become complete and whole again. The ruined quilt should have reminded us that there were places in your life that needed healing and restoration. But we were so blind."

Reuben paused, then said, "We want to ask you to forgive us. Will you?"

Jenny looked from Reuben to Jerusha and back again. "But I'm the one who disobeyed and ran away. I'm the one who needs forgiveness."

"Perhaps the Lord is asking us to forgive one another," Jerusha said softly. She moved closer, and Reuben's arm drew her to them. Then they sat together in love's embrace, sharing tears and joy and forgiveness.

After a while, Reuben spoke. "I have something else to say, Jenny."

They pulled back, and Jerusha passed around a handkerchief she had in her apron pocket. Reuben dabbed his eyes and then said, "Jenny, we want to help you find your mother."

Jenny stared at them again, amazed at what she was hearing.

"You've already done some research that may lead us in the right direction. If it means that we have to go to New York, I'm willing to take you."

Jenny could barely speak. Finally she said, "When I was in the cave, hiding from Jorge, I found out that I have never really trusted my life completely into God's hands. I've always tried to solve my own problems. I've always felt strong enough and smart enough to work things out on my own. But I found out that the Lord wants me to stop trying so hard and to let Him be Lord of my life.

"I believe He spoke to me as I was lying there in the darkness. He said, 'If you will only put all of this into My hands, I will show you the truth.' There was one last moment when I wanted to fight Him and get out of danger on my own. I tried to move, but He told me to stop and lie still. Later, Jonathan told me that if I had moved I would have slipped down and fallen a long way into the darkness. I might have been killed. Now you're saying you're going to help me do what I set out to do on my own…Surely God is showing me once again to trust Him. Thank you, Papa. Thank you from the bottom of my heart."

After another moment of silence, Jenny spoke again. "Papa, what about Jonathan?"

Reuben looked uncomfortable but said, "I like Jonathan. Underneath the hippie clothing and ponytail, he's an intelligent and brave young man. He helped me to find you, and I will always be grateful to him for that. As for you and him…"

Jenny lowered her face and looked at her hands. "Papa, I love him. I can't help it, I just do."

"I believe you, *dochter,* but I'm not sure what to do. As things stand, you can't be with him, for he's not Amish. If you must be with him, you will have to leave the church. We can't change those rules. But I can tell you that if your mother and I see that this is something that God is doing in your life, we will not stand in your way."

"Where is he now, Papa?"

"He's staying at Bobby's house. He has been very anxious about your condition and very kind to your mother and me."

"Mama, you met Jonathan?"

Jerusha smiled. "We met while you were in the hospital. He's very handsome. He's also a Hershberger…and therefore my kin. Yet he's not a believer. It's all very strange. I don't know what to make of all this, but somehow I sense the Lord is in it. On the other hand, I do know this—the Bible says that a person who believes in Jesus should not be unequally yoked to an unbeliever. He says that for our own protection. You must search your own heart and listen to the leading of the Holy Spirit. I will support you in whatever you decide."

"Thank you, Mama."

Jenny looked down at the quilt. "Why does it look new, Mama?"

Jerusha softly touched the blood-red rose in the center of the quilt. "God showed me that He gave me this quilt and then let it get ruined as a picture of your life. He showed me that there are things in the foundation of your life that need to be healed, and as I repaired the inside of the quilt, I began to understand."

Jerusha pointed to one of the rose petals. Jenny could see that it was brand new, but she couldn't tell how it had been placed into the quilt.

"When you repair a part of the quilt that's torn or frayed, you don't remove it. You cover it with a new, identical piece. So it is when we come to know Jesus. He doesn't remove the old frayed pieces; He covers them with His precious blood, and all is made new again. I saw that so clearly as I sewed this new piece over the old. In all of it, the Lord showed me that He is fully able to heal you and make you a new creation. You simply must let Him. You can't be His granddaughter, knowing Him only through your papa and me. You must know Him for yourself and be His *dochter*, and He will make you whole. As a remembrance of what the Lord showed me, I added something to the quilt."

Jerusha pointed to a spot in the middle of the rose pattern. Sewn into the rose with stitches so tiny that it was almost invisible was a small key-shaped piece of red silk.

"When we forget that Jesus is our help in time of trouble and that we must turn to Him for everything, we can look at this quilt and remember that He is the key that unlocks all hidden things."

Reuben took Jerusha's hand. "We need to let you get some more sleep. We'll talk more about these things when you're rested."

They both hugged Jenny once more and then left her alone.

Jenny sat for a while propped up on her pillow. Then she lay down and closed her eyes. She had a lot to think about.

CHAPTER THIRTY-TWO

A Key in the Lock

◇◇◇

JENNY HOBBLED INTO THE KITCHEN on her crutches. It was a bright fall morning about a week after her rescue in Pennsylvania. She was eager to get the splint-wrap off her ankle, but the doctor had told her she needed a few days more to heal. So she had been hopping about the house like a little robin, her black prayer *kappe* perched on her head with the ends of her now short, curly red-gold curls tumbling out in disarray.

The kitchen table was full of notes and papers and military registry books that Bobby had brought over. She flopped down in a chair, picked up a pencil, and began sucking the end as she went through her notes. Just then she heard the front door open. She hadn't expected her mama and papa back so soon. She called out to the next room. "Mama? Papa? Are you home now?"

Boot heels clicked on the wooden floor of the front room. Jenny looked up to see Jonathan standing in the kitchen doorway, a nervous smile on his face.

"Jonathan! What…what are you doing here?"

Just then Reuben's broad shoulders filled the doorway behind Jonathan. He put his hand on Jonathan's shoulder.

"I brought him, Jenny."

"Hi, Jenny," Jonathan said awkwardly. "How are you?"

Suddenly her hands were shaking. She had never expected to see her papa with Jonathan. A flaming blush suffused her face, and she lowered her eyes.

"I'm fine, Jonathan. Are you well?"

She felt foolish as she asked it. She wanted to fling herself into his arms, but her papa was there, and…well, what if Jonathan didn't feel the same about her anymore? And besides, since she had met with the *bisschop* and repented, she had made up her mind to be more obedient to her parents and try to fit the mold of a good Amish girl. So she sat silently as Jonathan answered.

"I'm fine too," Jonathan said. "I was worried about your leg, and I asked Sheriff Halverson if he would contact your dad for me…so I could…uh, find out how you're doing. Mr. Springer was kind enough to invite me here to see for myself. The sheriff dropped us off."

Jenny looked up, and their gazes locked. She felt herself being drawn into the deep blue of his beautiful eyes, so like her papa's.

Reuben sensed their awkwardness and gave Jonathan a nudge. "Sit, Jonathan. We welcome you to our house. We won't forget how you helped rescue our Jenny."

"Or how I got her into trouble in the first place?"

Reuben smiled. "I'm glad the good Lord doesn't hold all my youthful foolishness against me, Jonathan. And since I've been forgiven those indiscretions, it's only right that I forgive yours. I won't forget how you guided us to Jenny and how you stood up for her against those men in the cave. *Alles ist gut, der gut endet.*"

Jonathan looked at Reuben strangely.

"My grandfather used to use that expression," he said. "It means all's well that ends well."

Reuben nodded toward a chair across from Jenny, and Jonathan sat down. He looked into her eyes until Jenny blushed and looked down.

"I have a question to ask you, Jenny," Jonathan said.

"What is it?"

"The cave…how did you find the cave—*my* cave?"

"Your cave?" Jenny asked.

"Well, when I was a kid I used to call it that. I found it in the ravine one summer when I was twelve. The man in the cabin up on top had a cherry tree on his property, and I used to sneak up and pick cherries. He didn't like that. One day when I was up in his tree, he came out of his cabin and yelled at me, and I jumped down and ran down the steps. He was really angry and yelling that he'd make sure I never came up there again. I could hear him coming after me, so I ran down the ravine. As I was running, I tripped on a rock and fell flat on my face. I couldn't get up, so I crawled under a bush by the creek and scooted up against the cliff wall behind it. I was going backward, and I wasn't looking where I was going, and I fell right into the cave. I heard the guy running past down the trail, but he didn't see me."

"That's kind of what happened to me," Jenny said. "I was limping down the trail, and I fell and hurt my ankle again. I couldn't go on, so I needed to hide. I just poked my stick in the bush and found the cave."

Jonathan looked perplexed. "It's so strange that you found it," he said. "I used to go there when I was a kid. It was like a fort or a hideout. I don't think anybody else knew about it when I was going there. That channel you were stuck in is actually a narrow tunnel that goes through into another part of the cave. It's about fifteen feet long and pretty steep. At the end it goes right over a cliff. I had my old Boy Scout flashlight when I first crawled down there, but I still nearly fell off. You can maneuver around and step down onto a ledge at the end of the channel. The ledge widens out, and then there's a path that gets you down into the deepest part of the cave. You were lucky you didn't just slide right off into the dark."

"I don't think it was luck," Jenny said. "My splint, the one I tied on with the stringer I found, got wedged in a crack when I was sliding, and I got jammed in between the walls. When I tried to get it out of the crack, I heard a voice tell me to stop. I tried to pull it out again, and I heard the voice once more, so I just lay there waiting for help. If the splint hadn't been tied on my leg, or if I had pulled it out of the crack, I guess I would have slid right over the cliff."

Reuben had pulled up a chair and sat looking at Jonathan and Jenny. "Do you want to know what I think?" he asked.

"What, Papa?" Jenny asked.

"I think the Lord guided you through the whole journey. I think He took you to a place that Jonathan already knew about so Jonathan could help. I think He showed you the cave. And it makes me wonder just exactly what He is doing in your lives."

Jenny nodded, sure Papa was right. "When I was in the cave, I wanted to do what I always do. I wanted to help myself to get out of the situation. But I was helpless. I couldn't do it. And then I realized that I have never let the Lord be God in my life. I have always known about Him, but I've never really known Him. And so when I came to the point that I couldn't help myself, I just stayed where I was and put my trust in Him. And then you found me."

Jonathan sat silent while they were talking. Jenny glanced over at him. "What is it, Jonathan?"

Jonathan paused for a long moment and then spoke as though he were sorting out his thoughts as he spoke them. "I don't know exactly what to think about all this," he replied. "When I was growing up, I never went to church. My parents never talked about religion, and even my grandfather seemed to have bitterness toward God. He always used His name as a cussword. I guess when I was growing up I asked myself the same questions most kids ask—why am I here, and what's the meaning of life? I never found the answers in Long Island.

"I was still searching when I went to San Francisco. I did some drugs and thought I had found the way until one day I took some LSD and had a wake-up call. I was sitting in my room, watching all the patterns in the air and thinking I had finally discovered a new reality. It was all so beautiful. Then I closed my eyes and saw the same patterns on the inside of my eyelids. I realized in that moment that nothing had changed in the world around me. What I was observing was the effects of a chemical inside my body. I hadn't discovered real spirituality or a new reality after all, and I really felt stupid. I tried it a couple more times, but in the end it was just a waste of my time. So now I really don't know what to think about all this spiritual stuff."

"Perhaps you should consider taking a look at God as the source of reality, instead of all these other things, Jonathan," Reuben said.

"Well, I have found myself praying the last few days—and there was that dream I had."

"What dream?" Reuben asked.

"I had a dream about Amish men working in a field," Jonathan replied, "but at the time I didn't know they were Amish. It was the night before I left San Francisco, and I dreamed about being in a field with men who were farming with hand tools and horses, and they were wearing clothes like yours and looked like you, Mr. Springer. And then I ended up in Apple Creek and somehow I met Jenny, and after I did I saw Amish men working in a field, just like my dream. Then Jenny showed me that my family used to be Amish. I don't know what to think about all this, Mr. Springer. I guess it has to be just a coincidence, doesn't it?"

"Maybe it's not, Jonathan," said a soft voice.

Jerusha stood in the doorway. She had come in from the outside and was holding her coat in her arms. Jonathan started to get up, but she waved him back into his seat.

"I once heard that coincidence is just God choosing to remain anonymous," she said.

Jonathan looked at her with a puzzled look. "You mean that God has been in this all along and I just haven't known it?"

"It's worth considering, son," Reuben said. "Don't you think?"

Jonathan nodded slowly.

"Wife, Bobby's coming back soon to pick up Jonathan. Don't you think it would be a good idea to have him stay for dinner so we can look at some of the notes that Jenny has made?"

"An excellent suggestion, husband, and of course that includes you, Jonathan."

"Are you sure, Mrs. Springer? I don't want to be a bother."

"Jonathan, we would like to get to know you better. We would like to find out who it is that our girl has become so fond of."

"Mama!" Jenny said, with a fresh blush.

Jerusha smiled. "We would be honored if you would join us, Jonathan."

Jenny looked up at Jonathan and had the strangest feeling that he belonged right here with her and her family.

◇◇◇

After dinner, Bobby Halverson pushed his chair back from the table. He groaned and put his hands on his belly.

"I'm trying to keep in shape, but if I have any more meals like that in the near future, I'm going to lose my boyish figure." He then turned to Jenny. "Have you found anything in those registry books I got from the VFW?"

"I haven't had a chance to look, Uncle Bobby. I've been organizing the notes I wrote down when I talked with Mr. Schumann, the man who wrote the article about the crash."

"I know Bob," Bobby said. "What did he give you to go on?"

"We think we have a service number for a naval officer. We found it in the large tattoo of the Statue of Liberty that the man in the pond had on his shoulder. Mr. Schumann made a drawing of the tattoo when we spoke. The number was under the statue on the man. It had Roman

numerals—IVIII IIIVI. We figured it must be 153,351. That's why I
had you bring the books. They have a list of all the service numbers
from the time they started issuing them until they stopped."

Jerusha cleared dishes from the table while Jenny fetched the books
that were stacked on a bench by the back door. Reuben, Bobby, and
Jonathan gathered around while Jenny opened the first book. It was
titled *National Personnel Records Center, Military Operations Branch,
Service number index and registry of retired, deceased, and discharged military personnel—volume I.* She glanced through it and then closed it
and picked up the second volume.

"That one has the numbers that were issued before World War Two,"
Jenny said. "This one has the ones issued from the time the war started.
Let's see, 153,351."

She turned the pages, licking her finger each time to help. She kept
going until she came to a page that started with 153,000. Slowly Jenny
ran her finger down the page until she came to 153,351. A name leaped
up at her.

"Pharmacist Mate Joseph K. Bender, Patterson, New Jersey. Born
nineteen twenty-two. Dishonorably discharged from service, September, nineteen forty-two."

A chill came over Jenny. His name was Joseph. Joseph, Joe—she
remembered that name—Joe. The face of the man from the dream
came to her. She could see the evil in his eyes as he tried to get her out
of the car. She saw the fear on his face when he fell into the pond and
his open mouth calling for help as he sank beneath the water.

Jerusha put her arms around Jenny's shoulders. "What is it, *dochter?*"

"I don't know," Jenny replied. "I just feel strange about it, that's all.
As if it's familiar…but how can it be? Do you think this man could be
my real father?"

CHAPTER THIRTY-THREE

More Answers

◇◇◇

"PHARMACIST MATE JOSEPH K. BENDER, PATTERSON, New Jersey. Born nineteen twenty-two. Dishonorably discharged from service, September, nineteen forty-two."

Jenny leaned over the table, read the name aloud again, and then looked at her mama.

"Dishonorable discharge, Mama. I've always been afraid my birth father or mother was a bad person. Now that I see it, I seem to remember the name Joe. I think Joe was the man in the car. He was a bad man, and he tried to hurt me. Why would he do that if he was my father?"

Her mama put her hand on Jenny's shoulder. "Let's not jump to any conclusions, Jenny. We don't know if that was your father. Isn't that right, Bobby?"

Bobby nodded. "We don't even know if Joseph Bender was the man in the car."

"What else can you do then?" Jonathan asked.

"There was a license plate number—SN12-66," Bobby replied. "Sheriff Cowsill, my predecessor, traced it to a stolen car in New York. He left a file on the case that I've gone through a couple times down through the years. Sheriff Cowsill tracked down the name of the person who owned the car and called him, but the guy wasn't very cooperative, so Arnold didn't follow up. If we can somehow connect Joseph Bender to the car, then we can place him at the scene of the crash. But that still wouldn't prove whether he's Jenny's father or not."

"I just don't see how we can find the answer," Jenny said, sinking back in her chair. "I never should have gotten you all into this. It's hopeless. Why can't I just be satisfied with the family God gave me?"

She put her head down in her arms on the table. Reuben awkwardly patted her shoulder. Jerusha pulled up a chair next to her daughter and put her arms around Jenny's shoulders. She laid her head close to Jenny's.

"Remember what I shared with you—what the Lord showed me when I was praying for you?"

"You mean about the quilt?"

"Yes, *dochter*," Jerusha replied. "I believe these things are true. There are places inside of you that need to be healed, and the way that will happen is by you finding out the answers to your questions. Don't you see, Jenny? All these things have been happening for a reason. There must be an answer, and I believe it's right here in this room. It's no mistake that your papa's best friend is the sheriff. Your Uncle Bobby can help us discover things we couldn't possibly find on our own."

"I'll do my best to help, Jerusha," Bobby said. "We do seem to be at somewhat of a dead end here, and I can't promise anything, but there are a couple of things I can do."

Jerusha went on. "Your papa and I want you to be whole and free, Jenny. We want you to fully know the life that God has planned for you." She paused and looked at Jonathan, and then she continued. "Even if that means that you leave us."

Jerusha laid her head back down on Jenny's shoulder. "Wherever God takes you in this life, my darling, your papa and I will always love you, and your home will always be here with us."

THE ROAD HOME 291

Jenny turned into her mama's embrace. The two women clung to each other and cried softly while the men looked at each other uncomfortably.

◇◇◇

The next day Bobby sat in his office going over the notes his predecessor had compiled on Jenny's case. The details of the autopsy, the report on the wrecked car, and the articles by Bob Schumann were spread out on his desk. Sitting on top of it all was the license plate number of the car and a phone number. He had checked the area code and discovered that it was a Manhattan number. He had called the number twice already without success.

He sighed and picked up the phone again. He dialed the number one more time, but he wasn't really expecting an answer, so he was surprised when a gruff voice spoke from the other end of the line.

"Talk to me," the voice said.

"Is this James Radford?" Bobby asked.

"Yeah, and I'm not interested in any insurance," said the voice.

"Mr. Radford, this is Sheriff Bobby Halverson from Wayne County, Ohio. I can assure you I'm not trying to sell you insurance."

There was a pause, and then Radford spoke. His tone was not friendly. "How do I know you're a sheriff?"

"I can give you the number of the Wayne County Sheriff's office. You can check it out and call me back on your dime, or you can just trust me and answer a couple of simple questions," Bobby replied.

"Is this about the car?" Radford asked gruffly. "That happened a long time ago."

"Actually, it is about the car," Bobby said. "I understand that you were the owner of a nineteen forty Ford station wagon that ended up in a pond outside of Apple Creek, Ohio."

"As I said, that was a long time ago," Radford said. "It was a piece of junk anyway. Besides, I didn't put it there, it was stolen from me."

"I know that, Mr. Radford, and I'm not accusing you of anything. I would just like to find out more about the car if I can."

"Why?"

"A little girl was discovered in that car fifteen years ago. We're attempting to track down her birth parents. Your car is one of the few clues we have. Can you tell me anything about it?"

There was a pause. Then Radford answered. "Another guy called me about fifteen years ago. He said he was the sheriff."

"Yes," Bobby said. "That would have been Arnold Cowsill. He was the sheriff before me. He said you weren't very cooperative, so he never followed up. Now I'm following up."

"Well, what if I don't want to cooperate with you?" snarled Radford.

Bobby paused, and then he followed a hunch. "Look, Mr. Radford, I don't want to get into unpleasantries with you. Let me just say that I have much more of a concern about this case than Sheriff Cowsill did. The girl who was found in the car is very dear to me. I have a vested interest in her well-being. And let me also say this. I am willing to come to New York and speak to you directly, but I won't be as pleasant as I am today if I have to do that. I also have access to the most modern databases and can do a very thorough background check on you if I need to. If something unsavory appears on your record, I would be... shall we say...compelled to turn it over to the New York authorities."

Bobby knew he was taking a chance but he pressed ahead. "Now, if I can just get a few answers over the phone today, I will be most appreciative, and you and I can go our separate ways."

There was a pause and then Radford answered. "What do you want to know?"

"Is there anything more than I already know that you can tell me about the car?"

"Well, I don't know if this will help, but they caught the guy who stole the car."

"What?" Bobby exclaimed. "We assumed the man who stole the car died in the pond."

"Yeah, one of the guys died in the pond."

"One of the guys?"

"Two guys stole it and used it to rob a bank. The one they caught was inside the bank while the other guy was outside with the motor running. The guy inside got shot by a guard and was captured. The other guy got away."

"Do you know the name of the man who was caught?"

"Yeah, Sammy Bender."

"Bender! His name was Sammy Bender?"

Radford paused. "Yeah, Bender. Ain't that what I said?"

"Okay, Sammy Bender. So what else?"

Radford waited for a moment and then went on. "I had to testify at Bender's trial. The rat tried to implicate me as the other guy, but I had an airtight alibi."

Bobby's thoughts were whirling. Bender! The dead man's name was Bender. Maybe this Sammy was a direct connection to Joseph Bender.

"Do you know where this Sammy Bender is now?"

"Yeah, he's up at Sing Sing. He got seventeen years because he wounded a bank guard and a teller in the crossfire. I was glad to see him put away. The guy steals my car and then tries to frame me. Jerk!"

"Why didn't you tell Sheriff Cowsill about this?" Bobby asked.

"When Bender robbed the bank, someone got the license number of the car and traced it back to me. When they tracked me down, Bender told them I was the driver. If I hadn't been out of town on a fishing trip at the time with my pals, he would have framed me. So when the sheriff from Ohio called, I thought they were still trying to stick me with the heist, and I clammed up. It took a long time for the whole thing to come to trial, and Bender finally admitted that I wasn't with him, but he wouldn't rat out the other guy."

Bobby smiled. Radford obviously had a shady background, or the cops wouldn't have been so eager to nail him. He decided to try one more thing. "So did you know this Sammy Bender before he stole your car?"

There was another long pause.

"Mr. Radford?" Bobby asked.

"Yeah, okay, I used to see him and his brother around. We ran in somewhat the same circles."

Bobby smiled. He had been right! Radford was most likely shady too.

"Oh, and one more thing," Radford said. "The eyewitness saw a woman and maybe a kid in the back of the car."

"A woman and a small child?" Bobby asked.

"Is there an echo in here?" Radford snarled. "That's what I said."

"Thanks a lot, Mr. Radford," Bobby said. "You've been a big help and—"

Radford interrupted. "Are we done?"

"Sure," Bobby said. "Unless you can think of something else, I think that will do…for now."

There was a click as Radford hung up. Bobby looked at the phone and then smiled. Maybe they were getting somewhere.

Jenny sat with Jonathan on the swing on the front porch of the Springer house. She wanted Jonathan to put his arms around her and hold her, but her parents were inside, so they sat apart. Jenny pushed on the porch with her feet, setting the swing in motion.

"I used to do this when I was a little girl," she said. "I had so much energy, I would swing for hours. Mama would sit over in that chair and sew or read her Bible. I never seemed to have enough time to read as much as she did. I was always on the go, like a shooting star buzzing across the horizon. When I had swung long enough, I would do this."

Without thinking about her sore ankle, Jenny pushed really hard with her feet, and the chair swung far up on the backswing. When it came forward, Jenny jumped from the swing and sailed over the porch steps and landed on the lawn. Her bad leg buckled under her, and she went down on her face in the grass. Jonathan got off the swing and knelt beside her.

"Jenny, are you okay?" he asked. "You need to be more careful of that ankle."

Jenny lay still, her heart pounding, afraid to look at him for fear her heart would burst in her chest. Then she rolled over and looked up at him.

"Jonathan, do you love me?" she asked simply.

Without caring if her parents saw, Jonathan enfolded Jenny in his strong arms and held her close. Jenny's words came out in a rush.

"I'm so afraid, Jonathan. I cry at the least thing. Everything is mixed up and crazy. I love you and yet I'm Amish—but am I really? And if I am, I shouldn't love you because we come from different worlds, and I belong here but I belong to you and…and…oh, Jonathan, can you help me? I don't know what to do."

Jonathan held Jenny in his arms without saying anything. There was the sound of a cough behind them, and they looked around. A tall, older man wearing an old baseball hat was standing on the lawn, self-consciously shifting from one foot to the other.

"Hi there, er…I didn't mean to interrupt, I mean…well…"

Jenny sat up and rubbed her tears away with her coat sleeve. "It's all right, Mr. Lowenstein. This is my friend Jonathan. He helped me get home. Jonathan, this is our neighbor, Mr. Lowenstein."

Jonathan got to his feet and shook Hank's hand. "Nice to meet you, sir."

"You too, son," Hank replied. He looked at Jenny. "Jenny, is your pa around? Sheriff Bobby just called, and he said it's important that Reuben call him right away. Can you tell him?"

"I will, and thank you, Mr. Lowenstein."

Jenny looked at Jonathan, and then Reuben came out on the porch. "Hello, Hank," he said.

"Howdy, Reuben. Just came over to let you know that you should come over and call Bobby. He said he has some interesting developments concerning Jenny to share with you."

CHAPTER THIRTY-FOUR

The Visit

◇◇◇

JENNY WATCHED OUT THE CAR WINDOW as the Pennsylvania country-side rolled by. Uncle Bobby was driving, and her papa sat in the passenger seat. Jonathan sat with her in the back. They were trying to be respectful to her papa by not sitting too close, but Jonathan had slipped his hand over to hers about an hour before, and she took some comfort in his touch.

They had been on the road for what seemed like hours, and Jenny was tired. So much had happened to her in the past two weeks. Her ankle still hurt, and she had a nagging headache. Her hopes had risen when Uncle Bobby told her about the man who might know about Joseph Bender. But since then she had slipped back into a dark mood. Even Jonathan had been unable to cheer her up. Now she sat staring out the window, lost in her thoughts.

"Jenny?"

Jonathan's voice brought her back from her musing. "Yes?"

"We just passed the place where they captured us."

A chill ran down her back as she remembered how close she had come to death, or worse, at the hands of Jorge. She leaned forward to speak to Bobby. "What's going to happen to Jorge? I feel sorry for him. At first he seemed nice, but he couldn't break away from his uncle's influence. Then he tried to…hurt me."

"I'm afraid Jorge is going to spend a few years behind bars," Bobby said. "He's over eighteen, so they'll try him as an adult. He wasn't in San Francisco when Jonathan's friend was killed, but he has been involved in a lot of other crimes. The state will make sure he gets indicted along with the rest of them."

"Shub wasn't my friend," Jonathan said. "I just knew him. I'm really sorry I ever got involved with him."

Jenny felt irritated at Jonathan's response. She wondered why he couldn't just accept the truth that he had done some really foolish things out in San Francisco. Jonathan heard her sigh.

"Are you okay, Jenny? You seem awfully—"

"Uptight?" Jenny asked, with a half-smile.

Jonathan smiled back. "Yeah, really uptight, man," he said in an exaggerated hippy drawl.

That produced Jonathan's desired effect—a smile at last. He looked at her face and took her hand again. "Look, Jenny, I know that everything that has happened in the last two weeks has taken a toll on you. I just want you to know that I'm so sorry I ever got you into this mess. I've done some really dumb things and messed my life up pretty good. But in the midst of all this I'm beginning to believe that maybe there might really be a God after all.

"I mean, just think of all the things that have happened. How did I end up at that traffic light just in time to almost hit you? How did we end up finding out about my family? How did you find the cave? The list goes on and on. And it seems like every time I pray, I get an answer. I've never gotten answers before—not with Buddha or Krishna or any of the drugs I took. Maybe your mom is right. Maybe God is trying to tell me something."

Jenny didn't know what to say to this admission.

In the front seat, Reuben smiled.

Bobby Halverson sat at a metal table in a grim, olive-green room at Sing Sing prison. The single fluorescent light above his head made the setting even starker. The man across from him was slouched in his chair, staring at Bobby. A guard stood at the door, and another was outside looking through the observation window. It was obvious that the prison officials considered Sammy Bender worth watching.

"So what do you want from me, copper?" Sammy snarled.

He was a scruffy, heavyset man with bad teeth. Longish black hair curled down his neck, but he was balding on top. The sleeve of his prison issue T-shirt was rolled up and held a pack of Camels. Bobby looked closely at the man. Underneath the Camels, Bobby could see a large tattoo on Bender's shoulder. Bobby recognized it. It was the same tattoo the man in the pond wore on his shoulder.

"Sheriff," Bobby said, "I'm a sheriff."

"Like Sheriff Matt Dillon?" cracked Sammy. "Hey, Chester, woo-woo." Sammy guffawed at his own joke.

"Not exactly," Bobby said patiently. "Matt Dillon is a TV marshall. I'm a real sheriff, and I'm here on official business."

"Yeah? What official business?"

"I want to know about the bank robbery that put you in here. I want to know about the car you were driving, and I want to know about the man who was with you."

"What man?" Sammy asked. His eyes blinked several times, and he fidgeted in his chair.

"We found the stolen car in a pond outside of Apple Creek, Ohio, in the spring of fifty-one," Bobby said, ignoring Sammy's question. "There was a dead man in the pond with the car. Interestingly enough, he had a tattoo just like yours on his arm."

Sammy jerked upright. "Joe's dead? I mean…the guy is dead?"

He looked away from Bobby and grimaced as he realized he had given himself away.

Bobby smiled pleasantly. "Now that we know you knew the man, I just need a few details. The man had been in the pond for a few months, so there was no way to take fingerprints. But his tattoo, the one that matches yours, was still intact, and there was a military service number under the statue. Based on that number, we believe the man was Joseph K. Bender, a former naval officer, and since he has the same last name as you he must have been related. Is that true?"

Sammy slumped back down. "My brother," Sammy muttered. "Joe was my brother."

"Go on," Bobby said.

Sammy looked stunned. "So Joe's dead. I always thought he got away to California."

He sat in thought for a few moments.

"So the man's name was Joseph K. Bender?" Bobby asked again.

"Yeah, yeah," Sammy grunted. "It must have been Joe. We did the heist together. He was outside the bank waiting for me in the car. I messed up and let the teller trip the alarm. The cop on duty shot me. I got off a couple of shots and I guess I hit him and got the teller too. I never blamed Joe for running. I would have done the same."

Bobby took a chance. "What about the woman and child that were in the car with Joe?"

Sammy looked at Bobby with surprise. "You know about Rachel?"

It was late in the afternoon. Bobby had called and asked everyone to meet him in the restaurant at the motel where they were staying in downtown Ossining. He promised that he had some exciting news. Jenny, Reuben, and Jonathan were waiting in a back booth when

Bobby arrived. Jonathan was sitting next to Reuben, and Jenny sat across from them by herself. Bobby walked over to the table and sat down next to Jenny. A skinny teenage waitress came over and asked if he wanted coffee. He nodded, and she left to get him a cup, giving them a strange look as she went. Bobby smiled. It wasn't often that you found a sheriff, an Amish man, a short-haired Amish girl, and a hippie all seated at the same table.

Jenny looked at Bobby expectantly.

"The man in the car was definitely Joseph K. Bender," Bobby said. "He was Sammy Bender's brother. They grew up in Patterson, New Jersey, and started getting into trouble when they were teenagers. Sammy knew about the tattoo on Joe's shoulder and confirmed that the number was a service number. It seems that when the war came, they both enlisted and got a tattoo. Joe got picked for officer training, so he added his service number under the Statue of Liberty. Not that it makes any sense, but then these guys aren't noted for their smarts."

"But the report said he got a dishonorable discharge," Jenny said. "What about that?"

"From what Sammy said, Joe did pretty well during his first year as an officer. He was trained to be a pharmacist mate, which is like a petty officer. He was assigned to a battleship in the Pacific. I guess he got wounded in one of the battles. It wasn't bad enough to get him discharged, but he did need pain pills while he recovered.

"Sammy says he got hooked on the medication. He got caught stealing narcotics from the infirmary, and they drummed him out of the service. He ended up in New York and graduated from pain pills to morphine and then to heroin. Sammy got tossed out of the service for slugging a superior officer, and he hooked up with Joe. Their life of crime went from there and ended up with the bank robbery."

Jenny felt sadness overtake her. So her father was a dope addict. That thought was foreign to her, but she tried to understand it anyway.

Bobby saw the look on her face and took her hand. "Jenny, I've got some news for you."

Jenny looked up. She felt the possibilities for her life getting smaller and smaller. What could Uncle Bobby say that could possibly help?

"Joe Bender was not your father."

Jenny looked at Bobby with a blank stare. "Not my father?"

"No, he was not your father."

Jenny felt the darkness beginning to lift from her spirit. "Not my father," she repeated softly.

Jenny looked at Reuben. He was so strong and handsome. He had always been there for her. He had protected her all her life, cared and provided for her, carried her when she had fallen, encouraged her when she failed, and always loved her. What had she been thinking? Tears formed in her eyes. She saw her papa's jaw working as he tried to keep his emotions from showing. Jonathan stared at both of them.

Jenny got up slowly and went around the table. She stood in front of Reuben and picked up one of his big, strong hands. She put it next to her cheek and felt his calloused palm against her face. Then she kissed his hand and looked into his eyes.

"Of course he's not my father," she said to Reuben. "You are."

Reuben's arms came around Jenny, and he pulled her close. "Jenny, Jenny, my *dochter*, my precious *dochter*," he said softly.

Jonathan and Bobby looked at each other and then turned away so they wouldn't show each other the tears welling in their eyes.

◇◇◇

Jerusha suddenly smiled. She had been sitting at the kitchen table, praying for her family. She opened her Bible to the Psalms and was reading through them. She stopped when she came to Psalm 68:6. The words leapt up at her. She reads aloud, "God setteth the solitary in families: he bringeth out those which are bound with chains."

A great weight lifted from her heart. She stood up and walked to the front door, opened it, and walked out onto the porch. The sun was just setting in the west. The smells and colors of fall assaulted her senses, and her faith began to rise up. Away in the east, her daughter and her husband were finding answers, and all things were working together for good. Jerusha smiled again. The words of her beloved *Lobleid* came to her lips. Her clear, sweet voice lifted in song.

"*Lässt loben Ihn mit allen unseren Herzen! Weil Er allein würdig ist!*"

"We praise Him with all our hearts! Because He only is worthy!"

CHAPTER THIRTY-FIVE

A Missing Link

◇◇◇

"How do you know Joe Bender wasn't Jenny's father?" Jonathan asked.

Before answering, Bobby got the waitress's attention by holding up his coffee cup. She scuttled over and poured them all a fresh round.

When she left, Bobby said, "After Sammy gave himself away when he heard that Joe was dead, he loosened up and pretty much spilled the beans about everything. As I understand it, when Joe Bender came back from the Navy, he was addicted to the pain pills they gave him when he was wounded in battle. Sammy said that Joe tried to go straight, but he couldn't hold down a job, and the addiction pretty much took over his life. He was already using heroin when Sammy got kicked out of the Navy and met up with Joe in New York. They started doing robberies, small stuff, knocking over liquor stores and breaking into houses so Joe could support his habit.

"In nineteen forty-nine, Joe and Sammy lived in a crummy apartment in Manhattan near Fifty-Second Street. From what he said I gather there were a lot of nightclubs there and plenty of drugs. Heroin seemed to be the drug of choice, so it was easy for Joe to get some. Joe got friendly with some of the big-time musicians and became a heroin dealer. He and Sammy lived a pretty sad life, hanging out in the clubs by night and holed up in their apartment during the day, taking drugs. Sammy said that one day Joe had been out buying some drugs, and he showed up back at the apartment with a young woman and a little girl."

Jenny looked at Bobby, wide-eyed. "Was the little girl…me?"

"Yes, Jenny, I believe it was you. The young woman's name was Rachel, and the little girl's name was Jenny."

"Rachel…Rachel," Jenny said the name slowly. It might sound familiar, but she couldn't be sure.

Bobby went on. "Joe found Rachel sleeping under a stairway behind his supplier's apartment. Sammy said that when Joe brought her home she was mixed-up and very sad. She wouldn't say much about herself except that she had only been in New York a few months. She had one suitcase and a tote bag for the child—that's all. Sammy did find out that she came from somewhere in Pennsylvania, but other than that she was very private about her past. She came back to the apartment with Joe because she needed a place where she could get her little girl off the streets.

"Sammy said that after they had been there a few weeks, Joe got Rachel to try some heroin. He told her it would make her blues go away. I guess it did, because Sammy said Rachel got hooked pretty quickly. After you and Rachel had been with them several months, Joe and Sammy pulled the bank job, Sammy got caught, Joe and Rachel got away, and that's the last that Sammy ever saw of them."

Jenny felt like she was staring at a thousand-piece picture puzzle with most of the important pieces missing. Rachel was her mother, maybe. At least the way Sammy told it, Jenny wasn't Joe's child. She had already been with Rachel when Joe found them. But how could they find out who Rachel really was? Jenny put her chin in her hands. Then a thought came to her. *This is the way, walk ye in it.*

Jenny looked at her papa and then took his hand. She remembered when she had been lying helpless in the cave and had to learn to trust the Lord completely.

"Papa," Jenny said, "will you pray? I feel very uncertain, but still I know the Lord is leading us. We just need to fit the puzzle together."

Reuben held out his hand. He looked at Bobby and Jonathan. Jonathan took Jenny's hand and held the other out to Bobby. Bobby awkwardly took Jonathan's and Reuben's hands, and the four of them bowed their heads.

"Lord," Reuben prayed, "You have gotten us this far, and You have showed us part of the mystery. Would You help us now to uncover the things that will fill in the gaps? We ask it in Jesus' name."

"Amen," Bobby said a little too loudly.

Reuben smiled at him. "No atheists in foxholes, eh, Marine?"

Bobby returned his friend's smile and said, "There's one other thing that might help us. When Sammy got busted and knew he was going to jail, he called his mother and had her come clean out their apartment. She might know something about Rachel. Sammy gave me an address and a phone number. She lives in Patterson, New Jersey."

They were parked next to a dusty playground across the street from a ramshackle bungalow in Patterson, New Jersey. It was a hot fall day, almost Indian summer, and Jenny had rolled the window down in the car. Her uncle Bobby and her papa were standing on the porch of the bungalow talking to an elderly woman.

"Jenny, Jonathan, come on in," she heard her papa say. She and Jonathan looked up and saw her papa motioning to them to come.

The old woman looked at them sadly. There were still tears in her eyes, but she had composed herself and dabbed most of them away with a hanky, and now she sat slowly rocking in a chair by the window. The room was musty and stale, and paint was peeling off the walls in several spots. A rickety old table sat in the small dining room next to a doorway that led into the kitchen. A small upright piano stood against the wall, with hymnbooks piled on top next to a small brass lamp. Above the piano on the wall was a needlepoint. It showed the sun's rays behind the words, "I am the resurrection and the life."

Next to the piano was a plain wooden bookshelf. On the top shelf were three pictures. One was of a smiling blond boy with a missing front tooth, and another was of a younger boy with dark curly hair. The third was a picture of the two boys seated together on the front step of the bungalow. The blond boy had his arm around the younger boy's shoulder. They were both smiling.

"I used to hold him in my arms and rock him to sleep when he was a baby, right here in this very chair." Magdalena Bender reached into a pocket of her apron, pulled out the hanky again, and dabbed her eyes.

"You know, you try to help them become men, you do everything to teach them right from wrong, and still they turn out like Joseph and Samuel. It wasn't easy after their father ran away in the Depression. If I hadn't owned this house, I would have been out on the street. Oh, Joe, my poor boy. I read to him out of the Bible every day. He used to love the stories."

Bobby and Reuben had pulled up chairs, and Jonathan and Jenny were sitting on a dilapidated old couch.

"Mrs. Bender, can I ask you a few questions?" Bobby asked. "About Joe?"

"Why, yes," Magdalena said.

"Sammy said there was a young woman with Joe when they robbed the bank and that she had a young child, a girl, with her. Do you know anything about that?"

"That would be Rachel and Jenny," Magdalena said.

"You knew my mother?" Jenny blurted out.

Magdalena turned and looked at Jenny intently. "Rachel was your mother?" she asked. "You're Jenny?"

"I'm Jenny," she said. "But I don't know who my mother was."

"Come here, child," Magdalena said.

Jenny got up from the couch and came close to the old woman.

"Come down here where I can see you," Magdalena said.

Jenny knelt down by the rocking chair while Magdalena searched her face intently. After a few moments, she said, "Yes, you are Jenny. I know those eyes and that red-gold hair."

"But how do you know me?" Jenny asked.

"Whenever Joe got tired of having you around, he used to bring you out here and leave you with me. You were such a good little girl. Rachel didn't like it when Joe made her do it, but the poor girl was so beat down that she just did what Joe said. I think she was glad when you weren't around to see what Joe had done to her. She was such a sweet thing. I felt so bad when Joe told me she died."

"You were there when she...died?" Jenny asked. She looked around at her papa and Jonathan.

"Well, not exactly, child. It was the day before Thanksgiving, nineteen fifty. I remember the day because the big storm was moving through—biggest in a long time. There were all kinds of warnings on the radio, and I was really worried that I might not have enough coal to keep from freezing. Joe called me late that afternoon. He said he was calling from a pay phone in Stroudsburg. He was crying, and he kept saying, 'She's dead, Mom, Rachel's dead.' I kept asking what was wrong and he just kept crying. I asked him why he was in Stroudsburg, but I couldn't make any sense of what he said. He kept saying that Sammy was shot and Rachel was dead and he had to get away to California, and then he hung up. You can imagine how I felt. After a week or so, Samuel called to tell me about being shot and arrested. He wanted me to bail him out, but I didn't have any money, and besides, the police got the judge to say that he couldn't be bailed out."

"Why didn't you call the police about Rachel?" Bobby asked.

"Sammy said not to tell them anything about Joe because Joe had got away. Joe used to call here all the time acting real crazy and saying the strangest things, so I thought he and Rachel had got away to California. I didn't want to see my other boy in jail too, so I just kept quiet. I wasn't sure your mama was really dead, child, but I think I knew all along. I guess that's why I felt so bad about her."

"Is there anything else you can tell us, Mrs. Bender?" Reuben asked.

"Well, I don't think so…" She paused. "Wait," Magdalena said. "There is something."

She stood up slowly and went into her bedroom. They could hear her opening a drawer, and then she came back in the room. In her hands she held a small blue book. Magdalena sat down and opened the book. In between the cover and the first page was a photograph. Magdalena took it out and handed it to Jenny. It was a small black-and-white photo, faded around the edges but still clear. There was a young woman in the picture holding a small girl in her arms. The woman had mid-length dark hair and a sweet, lovely face. She was wearing a cheap-looking dress and flats. The little girl was wearing a thin summer dress and a coat.

Reuben looked over Jenny's shoulder. "That's you, Jenny," he said.

Jenny looked again. It was the face from her dreams. The woman's eyes looked so sad, and her face was set as though she didn't want anything of herself to show in the picture. Jenny's heart went out to her. The picture was taken in front of Magdalena's house, and Rachel was standing by the front steps. Afternoon shadows were creeping toward her up the sidewalk, and Jenny could see the shadow of the head of the person taking the photo. Magdalena was standing on the porch, smiling. The little girl was turned in Rachel's arms looking directly at the camera. Jenny devoured the photo with her eyes. It was her mother and her!

Then Magdalena handed Jenny the blue book. Slowly Jenny opened it. The pages had once been blank, apparently to be used as a diary or journal. About half of the pages had been torn out. On the inside cover someone had written something at the top, but Jenny couldn't read it because it had been crossed out so thoroughly that it was illegible. Under that, written in neat cursive was the name Rachel St. Clair.

CHAPTER THIRTY-SIX

The Journal

◇◇◇

JENNY STARED AT THE LITTLE BLUE BOOK. Her heart was racing as she reread the name—Rachel St. Clair. The handwriting was strong and smooth, evenly spaced, in cursive letters that slanted slightly to the right. The stubs of the missing pages were smooth, as though someone had torn them out in one piece. The book was obviously a journal or a diary of some sort because the entries were dated. Jenny read the first one.

> *April 23, 1950. Today I arrived in New York with Jenny. I have a little bit of money and got a room in a hotel in Manhattan. The room is tiny and smells of cigarettes, but it will have to do. Jenny has been awfully fussy. I know she misses Robert very much. Tomorrow I will go to see Robert's parents. Robert told me where they live. It's in someplace called the Upper East Side, right on the East River. I hope they are as kind as Robert said. Surely they will love their granddaughter and want to help her. Robert, I miss you so much too.*

Robert! Somehow the name seemed so familiar. Why did she remember that name? Robert! But was his name St. Clair or something

313

else? And why did she miss him? Suddenly Jenny was overwhelmed. She closed the book and looked at Reuben.

"Oh, Papa," she said as the tears started in her eyes. "I don't think I'll find the answers I've been looking for, just more questions. I'm anxious and tired, and I just want to go home."

Reuben met her gaze and smiled. "This is a difficult time for you, I know. But, Jenny, I've never known you to be a quitter. Your mother knows that you need to follow this journey to its end if you ever want to really know peace. I believe that too, and your Uncle Bobby and I and even Jonathan have been put into your life to help you now."

"Don't give up, Jenny," Jonathan said. "You'll find the answers, I know you will, and then we…I mean, you can go home. I remember how much it meant for me to find out who I really was and where I came from. You did that for me, and I'll never forget."

Jenny looked at Jonathan. He had changed so much since she had met him. He somehow seemed older and more serious about his life. The hippie ways and the devil-may-care approach to life were fading away, and yet he was still the same person she had fallen in love with. Maybe Mama was right after all. She had given her heart to this man, and she knew it would always belong to him, even if they couldn't be together. She reached over and took Jonathan's hand.

His eyes, I love his eyes!

"Thank you, Jonathan, for encouraging me," she said. "I don't know how everything will turn out, but I want you to know that you'll always be my friend."

"There are a few more things we can do to answer your questions, Jenny," Bobby interjected. He turned to Magdalena.

"Didn't you say that Joe called from Stroudsburg the night he told you Rachel was dead, Mrs. Bender?"

"Yes," Magdalena answered. "Like I said, he was always calling me up and acting crazy, so I took most of what he said with a grain of salt.

But when he told me Rachel was dead, I somehow knew it was true. And yes, he did say Stroudsburg. I remember that."

"Then I propose that we go to Stroudsburg and check the police records," Bobby said. "We may be able to find something about her death. Joe called home the day before Thanksgiving in nineteen fifty. That means that right after he called, he started on his way west and crashed at Jepson's Pond sometime that night. Jerusha found Jenny in the car on Friday. So if any women were found dead in Stroudsburg, it would have to be within a very narrow window of time. That should be helpful. If we leave now we can get to Stroudsburg in a few hours. I'll phone ahead to the local authorities."

Everyone got up to go. Magdalena struggled to her feet. She looked at Jenny sadly. Jenny could tell that Magdalena was distressed, and a great feeling of pity came over her. She hesitated but then gave Magdalena a hug.

"I'm very sorry we had to bring you the news of your son's death," she said as she held Magdalena close. She could feel quiet sobs shaking the old woman's body.

Jenny spoke again. "I feel like you're a part of my life. I want to thank you for taking care of me when I was little. I'm wondering if it would be all right for me to write to you and let you know how everything turns out."

"Why, that would be wonderful, child," Magdalena said. She took Jenny's hand and looked into her eyes. "Your mother loved you very much. You were the only bright sunshine in her life. I don't know what happened to her before I knew her, but she was always so sad and quiet. The only time I saw her smile was when she was with you. I'm angry with Joe for what he did to her, but there wasn't much I could do about it. Joe made his own choices in life, and they turned him bad. I'm sorry he's dead, but somehow I always expected someone to come knocking on my door to tell me. I'm glad it was you, just so I could see you again.

You've grown up into such a lovely young woman. I hope everything turns out all right for you and for your young man."

"My young man?" Jenny stammered, pretending not to understand.

"Why, dear, I may be old, but I'm not blind. Surely you are going to be married to Jonathan someday?"

Jenny blushed. She bent over to whisper in the old woman's ear. "I hope so, Mrs. Bender, but I just don't know how it will work out."

"Pshaw," Magdalena said with a laugh. "The Lord knows even if you don't. I've been around long enough to pick up the hint when He drops one. Now you go find out about your mother, and don't forget old Magdalena. Trust in the Lord with all your heart, and lean not on your own understanding. Then He will direct your path."

Jenny hugged her again. "I will, Mrs. Bender. Thank you."

As they drove away, Jenny could see the old woman on her front porch, waving with one hand and wiping her eyes with the other.

◇◇◇

"I don't know, Sheriff," the woman behind the receptionist desk at the Stroudsburg police station said to Bobby. "That's a long time ago, and of course we've had a lot of turnover in our department since then."

It was three o'clock in the afternoon. Bobby and Jonathan were standing in front of the reception desk. Jenny was exhausted, so they had left her and Reuben at a motel downtown, promising to come get them if anything turned up.

The receptionist, an older woman dressed in the uniform of the Stroudsburg police, paused a moment to think and then brightened.

"I can call Bill Martin," she said. "He was our lead detective in nineteen fifty and still comes around to do training. He might be able to help you."

The woman got on the phone and dialed. The two men could hear it ringing, and then a tinny voice said, "Martin here."

"Hi, Bill," the woman said. "This is Ethel down at the station. I have Sheriff Bobby Halverson and a friend of his from Wayne County, Ohio, here. They're trying to find out about any unsolved deaths or unidentified bodies from…"

She put her hand over the receiver and looked at Bobby. "When was it again, Sheriff?" she asked.

"Thanksgiving week, nineteen fifty," Bobby said.

"Right!" Ethel said.

She spoke back into the phone. "Thanksgiving week, nineteen fifty, Bill. What? Oh, okay, I'll have them wait."

Ethel put down the phone and motioned to some chairs against the wall.

"Bill will be here in about twenty minutes, if you care to wait."

Bobby and Jonathan sat down in the chairs. They were both tired but willing to wait. In about twenty-five minutes a short, burly man walked through the door. He was balding and wore a jacket that was a little too big for him. The man walked over and stuck out his hand.

"Bill Martin," he said brusquely.

Bobby got up and took the offered hand. "Sheriff Bobby Halverson. This is my friend, Jonathan Hershberger."

"How can I help you, Sheriff?" Martin asked.

"We're trying to trace a woman, Rachel St. Clair, who may have died here in Stroudsburg around Thanksgiving Day, nineteen fifty. We can't be sure if she was here at all, but we were hoping that if she did die here, there might be some record or perhaps an investigation that you would have notes on."

"Nineteen fifty, eh?" Martin said. "That's a while ago, but I can look through the records. Come with me."

Martin waited for Ethel to buzz him into the back part of the station house and waved Bobby and Jonathan ahead of him. They walked down a hallway floored with gray-and-white checked linoleum. The sound of their shoes echoed off the walls as they passed several offices. When they arrived at a door at the end of the hallway, Martin pulled out a key and led them into a small, windowless office with a desk and two chairs. He waved them to the chairs and sat behind his desk. A picture of Martin in uniform with a group of men holding rifles hung on the wall behind the desk. Under the picture was a caption—"Pennsylvania State Police Rifle Team." The other walls in the room were bare.

"Sharpshooter?" Bobby asked, glancing at the picture.

"What? Oh, yes. I was captain of the State Police Team in nineteen fifty-eight. That picture was taken at the Pennsylvania State High Powered Rifle Championship."

"I was a Marine Corps sharpshooter-sniper in World War II," Bobby said. "First Marine Division, Guadalcanal."

Jonathan spoke up. "So that's why you didn't take my head off when you fired through the car window at Sal."

"Yes, but I nicked your ear, and I remember thinking that I probably should get back out to the range for more practice," Bobby laughed.

Bill Martin stared at them with a puzzled look.

"It's okay, detective," Bobby said. "It's a long story."

Martin shrugged. "Now, what was the woman's name again?"

"Rachel St. Clair," Bobby replied. "She was with a man named Joseph Bender. They were fleeing a bank robbery in New York. Bender died in a car crash on or before Thanksgiving Day, nineteen fifty, in Apple Creek, Ohio. We know the car he was driving was in New York on Monday of that week, and we know the woman was with him, as well as a small child. A friend of mine found the little girl in the car the day after Thanksgiving, but she was alone. It was in the middle of the big storm that year. During the storm, the car sank into the pond. When the police recovered the car from the pond in the spring, they also found Bender's body, but there was no one else in the car or the pond.

"Bender had made a call to his mother before he died, claiming

Rachel St. Clair had died in Stroudsburg, probably from a drug overdose, which would explain why he was alone with the little girl. We're
hoping you might have a record of that death."

Martin thought for a moment. "It seems there was a Jane Doe
about that time. It wasn't my case; Jerry Hanks handled it, but he
passed away last year. I can go check the cold case records."

"That would be great," Bobby said.

Martin got up and left the office.

"Maybe I shouldn't have mentioned that you almost shot my ear
off," Jonathan said.

Bobby laughed. "Yeah, it did seem to get his attention, didn't it?"

In a few moments Martin came back. "I looked in our cold case
files, but for some reason they only go back to nineteen fifty-six. I'm
sorry, but I don't think I can help you."

Bobby and Jonathan looked at each other with disappointment.

"Are you sure?" Jonathan asked.

"Yes, I looked everywhere in our file room, but there was nothing
before January first, nineteen fifty-six."

The three men walked back down the hallway. Bobby and Jonathan
shook hands with Martin and started to leave.

"Did you find what you wanted?" Ethel asked.

"No," Bobby said, "we didn't."

"Oh, I'm sorry," Ethel said.

"For some reason our cold case files only go back to January of fifty-
six," Martin said.

"No, they don't," Ethel said. "They go back a lot further than that."

"Hmm…I couldn't find them," Martin replied.

"They're up in the attic," Ethel said. "Remember? We had that horrible flood in fifty-five. Almost the whole town was underwater. We
moved all the records to the attic to keep them dry. And then we left
them up there because we didn't use them that much."

"You're right," Martin said. "I completely forgot that we did that. Wait here."

Martin went in the back and came back in a minute with a tall ladder. He went out in the reception area and set it up. Bobby looked up and saw a trapdoor in the ceiling he hadn't noticed before. Martin climbed up and pushed the trapdoor open. He reached up into the darkness. There was a click, and a light came on. Martin climbed the rest of the way up the ladder and scrambled up into the attic. In a few minutes he came to the edge of the trapdoor with a box in his arms.

"I think I've got it," he said.

Bobby climbed up and took the box from him and handed it to Jonathan, who set it down on a chair. Martin went back into the attic and returned with a small suitcase and another bag. He handed them down and then climbed back down out of the attic, and the three men gathered around the chair. The box was labeled with black indelible marker on the end. "Jane Doe—overdose—Mill Wheel Motel, November 21, 1950." Martin took out a file and opened it. On top was a photo labeled "Coroner's Report." The photo showed the body of a young woman with dark hair lying faceup on an examination table. The woman was the same one that was in Magdalena's photo—Rachel St. Clair.

Chapter Thirty-Seven

Robert

◇◇◇

EVERYTHING WAS LYING ON THE BED in the motel room—the suitcase, the bag, and the journal. Jenny held a copy of the picture Uncle Bobby had brought from the police station. She had been staring at it for a long time. She looked at the other picture they had gotten from Magdalena. This was how she wanted to remember her mother—alive and holding her close.

"Once we confirmed that the woman in the coroner's report photo and the woman from our snapshot were the same woman, Bill Martin turned all this stuff over to us," Bobby said, nodding toward the suitcase and bag on the bed. "They were glad to clear out some space and close out one of their cold cases."

Jenny looked at Reuben. "It's so sad that someone's life comes down to a suitcase and a bag on a motel room bed." She sighed deeply. From the moment she had seen the coroner's picture of her mother and known for sure that Rachel was dead, she felt a strange heaviness come over her, and her shoulders started aching. A slight headache throbbed behind her eyes. She felt detached and isolated from everyone in the room, as though they were all strangers.

She lifted the bag and set it on the dresser by the bed. It was made of canvas with two handles and a zipper. Slowly she pulled the zipper and looked inside. A familiar face stared up at her. She couldn't connect for a moment, but then it came to her in a rush.

"Bear!" she exclaimed. "Bear!"

Jenny reached into the bag and pulled out an old brown teddy bear. One of the button eyes was missing, and there was a tear on one of the seams, but it was Bear. *Her* bear. He had comforted her when she had been afraid, staying close to her in the darkest nights. She turned to the three men who were watching her.

"This is Bear," she said slowly. "Except for my mother, he was my closest friend. I don't know how I know that, but I do."

Jenny held the old bear close. Despite the slight musty smell, there was another fragrance she remembered, one that had comforted her at night so long ago. Memories began to flow in her mind. She was in a rocking chair with her mother and Bear, and there was a red-haired man with them, and everything felt right and good. The man's face was kind, and he was looking at her with love in his eyes. Who was he? Was he Robert? Jenny felt as if she had opened the lid of an old chest in an attic and found…what?

She dug farther into the bag to find a child's underwear, a small flowered T-shirt, and two small dresses. At the bottom was a plastic zipper bag. Slowly she examined the contents—a small comb, a brush, a bar of soap, a washcloth, and a toothbrush. She felt a deep sadness and a yearning she couldn't express.

For some reason, thoughts of her mother brought Jerusha to her mind. Suddenly Jenny wanted to just go home and crawl up in her mama's lap and sit for hours wrapped in Jerusha's arms. Those arms had always been her refuge and her strong tower of safety. Now she felt confused and defenseless. Tears began to run down her face.

"I didn't think it would be this hard, Papa," Jenny said.

Reuben came behind her and wrapped his arms around her. "I'm here, *dochter*," he said. "It's all right. We've been led to this place by *du lieber Gott*, and now, with His help, we will be able to put to rest the questions you've carried for so long. He is doing this for the good of us all."

Jenny sighed. "You're right, Papa," she said, "but I feel so strange… so anxious."

"You're grieving, Jenny," Jonathan said quietly.

"Grieving?" Jenny asked.

"Yes," Jonathan answered. "Grieving shows up in a lot of different ways—physically, emotionally, even spiritually. But it's good. You need to go through it."

I'm grieving! Of course I am.

She picked up the journal her mother had kept. She had put it aside while Bobby and Jonathan had been at the police station, not able to read more, fearing she might read something she really didn't want to know. Now she turned to the second entry and began to read it.

"Would it be too hard for you to read it out loud?" Jonathan asked gently.

"Of course not," Jenny said. "I'm sorry, I know you all want to hear it."

She began to read out loud.

> *April 24, 1950. This morning I took the streetcar from the hotel to Fifth Avenue to see Robert's parents at the address he had given me. It was difficult to find, but I finally got to the house. It's enormous! It sits right across from a big park. The streetcar man said the name of the park is Central Park. My heart was beating when I went up to the door. There was a big knocker, so I knocked on that, and after a while a young woman in a black and white uniform came and answered the door. I told her who I was and who Jenny was and that I wanted to see*

Robert's parents. She looked very surprised. She told me to wait and closed the door.

After a while another young woman came to the door. She said her name was Augusta, and she asked me what I wanted. I told her who I was and she smiled a strange smile at me. I asked if I could see Robert's parents, but she was very cold and suspicious. She told me that Robert's father had died shortly after he heard about Robert, and his mother was in seclusion and would not see anyone. I told her about Jenny, and she just laughed. She said that I was just another fortune hunter who had heard about the family's tragedy and wanted to cash in. She told me to go away, and then she closed the door in my face. I knocked again, but no one came.

After a while I went back to the hotel. Tomorrow I will take the proof and show her.

"Robert, that was his name—the red-haired man. I think remember him," Jenny said softly. She read on.

April 25, 1950. Today I took the papers and went back to the house with Jenny. Instead of a girl in a uniform, a big man in a black suit answered the door. He told me that Miss Augusta had warned him that I would be coming back, and he told me to go away. I begged him to let me see Robert's mother, but he told me if I didn't go away he would call the police. Then he closed the door. I knocked and knocked. After a while a car pulled up in front of the house and two men got out. They didn't say anything to me. They just put me in the car and drove away from the house. Finally one of them asked me where I lived. I told him the name of the hotel and they took me there. When I got out they warned me that if I went back to the house I would be arrested and put in jail. Robert! Why did you leave me? I need you!

May 5, 1950. For the past week I've been trying to call Robert's mother, but every time I get the house, whoever answers hangs up on me. Finally yesterday they told me that they knew where I was staying, and if I ever called again, they would send the police and take my little girl away and put me in jail. My money is almost all gone, and the man at the hotel told me I have one more day to pay him.

God, why have you abandoned me in this horrible place? I feel so hopeless. I wish I had listened to Daddy. I miss them all so much, but I can never go home. What can I do?

May 6, 1950. Today something frightening happened. While I went to a restaurant with Jenny to get something to eat, someone came into my room. It was very odd because the door wasn't broken and the windows were locked. I knew someone came in because all of Robert's papers were gone. I have the most important ones hidden though, and they didn't find them. I think that the woman, Augusta, sent someone to my room to make sure I couldn't prove anything. I had my diary in my purse, so they didn't get it, but I'm going to take the pages about Robert out and hide them too. Maybe I can still find a way to see Robert's mother.

Jenny noticed there was one more entry. The handwriting wasn't as smooth, and the ink was smeared as though it had gotten wet.

May 10, 1950. I've been out on the streets since the two men came with the hotel man and put me out. I've been sleeping under the stairs behind an apartment building. Today I met a man named Joe. He said he would let us stay in his apartment and that he would help me to

The letters faded away. The pen had run out of ink. It was the last entry in the book. Jenny threw herself on the bed and began to sob.

Jonathan and Bobby looked awkwardly out the window while her papa sat beside the bed and patted her shoulder. After a while she composed herself and sat up.

"I'm sorry," Jenny said.

"You're allowed," Jonathan said.

"Well," Jenny said, "my mother said she hid something from this Augusta woman. She probably didn't hide it at the hotel because she knew she was going to leave. So if it's not gone forever, perhaps it's here."

Jenny got up, pulled herself together, and picked up the suitcase. It was an old leather one that looked as if it had been part of a set. She had seen others like this in catalogs. Usually there was another, bigger suitcase and a steamer trunk. She opened the suitcase. It was lined with a flowered material and smelled musty, like an attic. There were straps to hold the clothes, and along both sides were pockets with elastic along the top. Jenny looked through the things inside. There were some clothes, an old magazine from 1950, a brush and comb, and a few other odds and ends. There was nothing else in the suitcase.

Jenny started to close the lid, but Jonathan stopped her. "My mother had a suitcase like this. It was part of her luggage set. She used it when she and my father took trips."

"I thought it looked like part of one of those sets," Jenny said. "I've seen pictures in a catalog."

"This one has a special feature," Jonathan said. "There's a hidden compartment. Jonathan lifted up the two side pockets and pushed his fingers underneath. Hidden behind them on both sides were two fabric loops attached to the bottom of the suitcase. Jonathan slipped his fingers into the loops and pulled upward. The whole bottom of the suitcase lifted out to reveal a small compartment underneath. In the compartment were two envelopes.

Lying on top of them was a picture. It was her mother with a handsome, well-dressed man who was holding her close. They were both looking at the camera and smiling. Jenny's mother was obviously pregnant. Jonathan took the first envelope out of the hiding place and opened it. He pulled out a sheaf of papers. They were the same size as the journal.

"The missing pages," Bobby said.

Jonathan opened the second envelope and took out the papers inside. He unfolded them and showed them to Jenny.

Jenny gasped. The first one was a birth certificate dated January 6, 1947. The name on the certificate was Jennifer Constance St. Clair. It was from a hospital in Lancaster, Pennsylvania. There was a tiny footprint. The names of the parents were written on the certificate. Robert William St. Clair and Rachel Mary St. Clair. Her parents! There it was, right before her eyes. The second document was a marriage license. It was dated September 14, 1946. There were two names—Robert William St. Clair and Rachel Mary Borntraeger.

"Papa, isn't Borntraeger an Amish name!" Jenny exclaimed.

Chapter Thirty-Eight

The Truth Will Set You Free

◇◇◇

Jerusha walked slowly back home from the Lowenstein farm in awe of the mercy and goodness of her God. She could see how the hand of God had been working in their lives all the way back to the day Jenna had died. Step-by-step He had brought them to this day, and now the wonder of His wisdom and love filled her to overflowing.

A fresh layer of snow blanketed the ground as she walked toward the bridge spanning the creek between her home and the Lowenstein place. A crisp bite was in the air, and her boots crunched in the white powder beneath her as she walked. The wind carried a fresh, clean taste, and Jerusha could almost feel a heavy darkness lifting from her daughter. She knew in that moment that all was well with Jenny.

Henry had fetched her when Reuben called from Stroudsburg, Pennsylvania, to tell her the news. They had found evidence that proved who Jenny's mother was, and the most amazing thing was that Jenny's mother may have been from an Amish family in Lancaster County, Pennsylvania. Reuben, Jenny, Bobby, and Jonathan were going to Lancaster to see what they could find out, and then they would be home.

Rachel. Jenny's mother's name was Rachel. It was all too much for

Jerusha, and she stopped on the bridge and watched the creek flow by beneath her feet. A scripture came to mind. *O the depth of the riches both of the wisdom and knowledge of God! How unsearchable are his judgments, and his ways past finding out! For who hath known the mind of the Lord? Or who hath been his counsellor? Or who hath first given to him, and it shall be recompensed unto him again?*

Weil seiner, und durch ihn, und zu ihm, alle Dinge sind: zu wen, Ruhm auf immer sein. Amen.

◇◇◇

July 4, 1946. Today my new life begins. I moved into Robert's apartment downtown. He is ready to get married right now, but I want to be sure. So much has happened, and I'm afraid. What if Robert doesn't really love me? What if he's just doing his duty as far as the baby is concerned? Now that the war is over and the future of St. Clair Manufacturing in Lancaster is uncertain, Robert has talked to his father about converting the plant to peacetime use.

There are whole fields of planes and tanks that were ready to go overseas, and then VE day came. Robert says they can tear them apart and use them for scrap metal. There's an automobile plant in Butler that needs lots of steel. Robert's father likes the idea and says Robert can stay here and organize it. I'm so relieved!

Robert's father doesn't know about me yet. I think Robert is afraid to tell him. He says he's going to marry me first so that when the baby is born he can give our baby his name, and his father will have to accept it, but I wonder if he will ever tell his parents about me. I love Robert so much, but sometimes I wish I had just followed my father's way. Everything is so different, and I miss my home and my mama and papa so much.

Jenny sat at the restaurant table with her papa, Jonathan, and Uncle Bobby. She was putting the torn pages of the journal in order. She took the page she was reading and put it in its place. There were about 70 loose pages, and they had gotten mixed up somehow. Everyone had taken a small pile and sorted them into years, then months, and then days. It had taken them about half an hour. The pages started in early 1946 and ended with the last, terrible entry in 1950.

The men looked at Jenny expectantly as she tapped the pile into an even stack and then looked up from her task. The waitress brought them all some more coffee. Jenny took a deep breath and began to read.

> *March 23, 1946. Today was a terrible day and a wonderful day. I had whiskey for the first time and it was awful. And then I met a boy. Well, actually a man. He is not Amish, but he is wonderful.*

As Jenny read, it was as though her mother's story began to come to life in her mind. She could see it as if it were a movie.

Rachel Borntraeger walked unsteadily along the road toward her farm. She was getting cold and tired. Her head ached, and she felt sick to her stomach. The March wind had died down, and the chill that had come as the sun set didn't feel so biting. It had actually been almost balmy earlier in the afternoon. There was a hint of spring in the air, and some of the plum trees had already started to blossom. It had been a mild winter, and the snow had melted off a few weeks before.

Rachel wished she had never gone with Rebecca and those boys from Leola. She remembered the bitter taste of the whiskey and how it hit her stomach like a kicking mule. The boys had laughed and tried to kiss her. Rebecca had gone along with the game, but Rachel had climbed out of their car and started home. Rebecca had called her a *spielverderber* and stayed with the boys, but Rachel didn't care. She felt awful. *Rumspringa* was definitely not what everyone made it out to be. Her stomach gave a lurch, and Rachel stumbled off the road and into the bushes to relieve herself of the unwanted substance in her belly.

When she finished, Rachel wiped her lips with the sleeve of her dress. Her mouth had an awful, bitter taste, and her *kappe* was askew. She knew she looked a mess. What would Papa say? She felt so ashamed. In this sad state she wandered disconsolately home in the middle of the narrow road.

The car was upon her before she could even react. The horn blared, and she could hear the tires screeching. She looked around in shock as the car came straight at her. Then the front of the car swerved to the right and then back to the left as it went around her, and then it went into a slide. The rear end swung around, and the car went off the road backward into a thicket of bushes. Rachel stood enveloped in a cloud of dust in the middle of the road. She heard the door open, and an angry voice yelled through the dust.

"What are you doing in the middle of the road? Are you trying to get killed?"

Rachel felt her temper rise. "Well, if you didn't drive like a *wahnsinniger* down such a narrow lane, perhaps you could have seen me in time!"

A figure appeared out of the dust cloud. The voice belonged to a very tall young man with flaming red hair. He was wearing white linen slacks, a white shirt, and a pullover sleeveless sweater with a big letter *P* on it. His shirt was open at the collar, and his loose clothing didn't hide his athletic build and broad shoulders. The man was about to shout something else when he saw Rachel. He stopped and stared at her, and then his face changed, and he laughed out loud.

"Are you drunk?" he asked.

"What if I am?" Rachel retorted, her words a bit slurred.

"But you're, you're…"

"What? You don't think the Amish drink? And besides if I am, it is *wonnernaus.*"

"What does that mean?" the young man asked.

"None of your business," Rachel replied.

"Well, I'm just asking," the young man said.

"No, none of your business is what *wonnernaus* means," Rachel replied.

Suddenly Rachel realized how she must look. There she was, the prim and proper Miss Rachel Borntraeger, standing in the road, *kappe* half off her head, face flushed, *kutz* on her chin, and shouting at this *Englischer*. It struck her as extremely funny, and she began to laugh. The young man looked at her in amazement, and then he began to laugh too. Finally the young man pulled himself together and reached out his hand.

"You're right," he said. "I was going too fast. I just got this car, and we were taking her for a test run. I got a little carried away. I hope you will forgive me for almost killing you. My name is Robert St. Clair."

Rachel looked at his face distrustfully, but she could see that he was genuine in his apology, so she reached out her hand to introduce herself. Something strange happened, though, when his hand closed around hers. A little shock ran up her arm, and a hot flush rose into her cheeks. She stared at him without saying anything. He was extremely handsome, with strong, regular features and a cleft in his chin. His hair was bright red and combed straight back. He was at least six inches taller than her, and his eyes were the most intense blue she had ever seen. She felt herself being drawn into them, and she stood silent as he stared at her too.

Rachel was a beautiful girl, even in her present state. Her dark hair was pulled into a bun under her *kappe*, but it framed her lovely face and her deep violet eyes and set off her pale skin. Her plain clothing only made the loveliness of her features more evident, and Robert was speechless for a moment. Finally he found some words.

"And your name?"

"I'm Rachel Borntraeger. I live in Lancaster. My father is the bishop of the Amish church, and I am…"

Rachel stopped. She was talking too much, but for some reason she wanted to tell this man everything about herself. Their reverie was broken by a shrill voice from the car.

"Robert, are you going to stand out there all night, or are we going to get this car out of the ditch and get going? We'll be late to the country club."

Robert released her hand, and the electricity stopped. He turned his head and looked over at the car, and then he looked back at Rachel and smiled sheepishly.

"That's Julianne. She's my date tonight. We're going to a dance at the country club. Benny Goodman is playing." He paused. "But I wish you were my date instead."

Rachel blushed but managed to say, "*Ja*, well. You should get going to the dance then."

"Will I see you again?" Robert asked.

Without even thinking Rachel spoke. "I work at King's Mercantile store on Fridays and Saturdays."

Then she turned and headed home. Robert stared after her and then slowly turned toward the car.

"Robert!" came the shrill voice. "Let's go!"

Robert turned back and watched Rachel as she walked away up the road. Then he shrugged and walked toward the car.

March 26, 1946. Today I saw Robert again. I was working at the store and then he was there…

Rachel had seen Robert again the next Friday after the incident on the road. She was working in the back of King's Mercantile, stacking bolts of cloth on the shelves, when suddenly she felt someone standing behind her. She had turned and he was standing there, staring at her. She suddenly felt hot and weak, as if she could faint. She reached out and took hold of the post that held up the shelf full of cloth. She stared back at him.

"I've been thinking about you," Robert said simply and quietly.

Rachel flushed again. That strange feeling came over her that she had experienced on the road. She wanted to tell him everything. She tried to hold her tongue, but she couldn't.

"And I, you," she answered slowly.

She felt as though she had just handed a complete stranger the key to something she had locked away for safekeeping all her life.

"Can I see you after you finish here?" he asked.

She hesitated, but just for a moment. Then she surrendered. "Yes, but you must meet me where no one will see us. My father is the bishop, and it would bring great shame to him if—"

"If he knew you had gone outside your religion?" Robert asked.

"Yes," she said with a shrug.

"My apartment is about eight blocks from here. Will you come there?" He pressed a slip of paper into her hand.

She nodded without speaking, and he turned and walked out of the store.

> I opened the paper and read the address. Then I went back to my work. I don't know what is happening to me except that my heart is his and his is mine. I can see it in his eyes, I hear it in his voice, and I feel it in his touch. I will go to him today and whatever happens, I will be his.

◇◇◇

Jenny set the pages down. Her mother had loved her father, and he had loved her. It was enough.

Chapter Thirty-Nine

The Road Home

◇◇◇

May 26, 1946. Today is the saddest day of my life. My papa found out I'm pregnant with Robert's child. Papa is so proud, and I have hurt him so deeply. I have never seen him so angry. He did not say a word to me but gathered my things…

"Papa! Please! Papaaa!"

Rachel beat her fists on the door of her home. The door was shut, and she had heard her *daed* lock it and slide the wooden bar into place after he pushed her out. The shades over the windows were drawn, and the house was dark. The unseasonably warm sun beat down on her back as she knelt on the porch, pounding futilely on the wood. She knew her papa and mama were standing on the other side of the door, just inches away, but they didn't say a word.

"Please, Papa! I'm sorry. Don't do this! I need your help."

Her papa answered her from behind the door. "You can keep the child but you must give the *Englischer* up and never see him again."

"I can't do that Papa, I love him." She sank down in a heap on the porch and wept, great sobs torn out of her gut as if by the talons of evil birds. Her clothes and personal belongings lay scattered on the porch and out in the yard behind her. As she lay there, she heard a car pull in the driveway. A car door opened, and then she heard footsteps coming quickly up the gravel path.

"Rachel! What is it?" It was Robert. He knelt down beside her and drew her into his arms. "What has happened?"

"Papa...Papa has...put me out of his home."

Robert stood up and knocked on the door. "Bishop Borntraeger, it's Robert St. Clair," he said. "I would like to speak to you."

A grim voice answered from the other side of the door. "Take the girl and go. She is yours now. She is dead to me. I'll speak no more of this matter."

◇◇◇

I heard Papa's footsteps going away from the door, and then there was silence. Robert knocked again and again, but the house was quiet and still, like a tomb.

Jenny put the page down. Her hands were trembling, and she looked at Reuben. "My poor mother," she said. "She must have been heartbroken."

"It is hard being an Amish father and a bishop," Reuben said. "Unless he had *ein herz aus stein*, I'm sure it was a difficult time for her papa also."

Jenny started to reply, and then it came to her. Her papa had feelings too! She thought back to all the times she had clashed with Reuben over the years, and it occurred to her that Reuben had always done everything with her best interests in mind. Even though she might not have liked his decisions, they had always been made out of love. The revelation was like a bright ray of sunshine on a stormy day. Instead of snapping at him, she took his hand.

"Yes, Papa, I'm sure the situation was very hard for Rachel's whole family."

Jonathan asked, "Can you read a little more?"

The four of them had gathered in the restaurant at the motel the morning after they had found the missing pages of Rachel's journal. They'd had breakfast, and now Jenny was reading to them as they sat together drinking their coffee. Jenny picked up another page and began to read.

> *December 12, 1949. I can't bear this. Today two policemen came to my door. They asked me if I was married to Robert St. Clair.*

◇◇◇

Rachel sat in her rocking chair with her daughter. Jenny had Bear and was holding a book that had pictures of animals with their names printed in large letters.

"Cow," Jenny said, pointing at the picture.

"Yes, cow," Rachel said, pointing at the letters. "That's my good girl."

Rachel looked around their small apartment. She and Robert had been married for three years. The time had been difficult, and she was estranged from her family, but they had each other. Robert had his family problems too. Robert had called his father after Jenny was born and told him about Rachel and the baby. His father had been furious. Rachel heard him shouting over the phone.

"Yes, Father," Robert answered. "I know I should have come to you, but I love her, and I want to bring her home so you can meet her."

There were more angry words from the other end of the line.

"I know you could have fixed it, but I wouldn't do that to Rachel. I love her, and I love my baby."

The conversation had ended with Robert's father shouting something and hanging up. Robert's shoulders slumped as he hung up the phone. That had been three years ago, and Robert's father still refused to meet her. Robert had gone to New York several times but had always returned without winning his father over.

"Mother is heartbroken, but Father won't let me bring you and the baby home. He's still hurting over my brother Frank's death, and it's made him bitter and hard-hearted. Even though I'm the oldest son, he always favored Frank. When he was shot down over Germany, Dad never recovered. Now he thinks I did this just to get his attention."

So they had made a life for themselves like two marooned sailors on a desert island. Rachel's papa refused to see her, and Robert's father was just as difficult. It was a terrible situation, but they had each other, and somehow that was enough. And then one day, everything changed.

> *My heart turned to stone. They said they were very sorry, but Robert had been killed in a car accident. He was driving home from the plant and a trailer-truck ran through a red light and hit his car. He died instantly. Oh God, I can't bear this.*

◇◇◇

"So that's why Rachel went to New York," Jonathan said. "She couldn't go back to her family, and she had nowhere else to turn. And then Robert's family rejected her, and she ran out of money and ended up out on the street. And that's how she met Joe Bender. Of all the bad luck."

◇◇◇

Reuben and Bobby had talked it over and decided they needed to make one last journey to tie up all the loose ends. So now they were in the car headed toward Lancaster, Pennsylvania. Jenny sat in the back-seat staring out at the night sky. Everything was so different! Her life had changed so dramatically in just a few weeks. She had met Jonathan and fallen in love, she had been shunned, and she had run away.

She had been kidnapped by drug dealers and rescued, she had been restored to the church, and she had found out who her birth mother and father were.

But the most important change was her new relationship with the Lord. She no longer felt as though her prayers fell on deaf ears, and she knew they never had. Jesus had been with her all her life. He had saved her in the storm, He had put her mama and papa in her life, and He had guided her and guarded her all these years. And now He was bringing her to the end of a journey she had been on since she was born. Jenny had a strange feeling she was going to find the answer to all her questions in Lancaster. Suddenly she giggled. Jonathan glanced over at Jenny with a quizzical look.

"What's so funny?" he asked.

"I just was thinking how *verrückt* my life has been the last few weeks. Not what you would expect from an Amish girl."

Jonathan looked away.

"What is it?" Jenny asked.

"It's nothing," Jonathan said. "I've just been thinking some things over."

"What things?" Jenny asked.

"I'd like to tell you when we can speak privately," Jonathan said quietly.

Jenny looked at Jonathan, and an uncertain feeling came over her. She had been so sure that everything would work out.

Jerusha spread the quilt out on Jenny's bed to look at it. Except for a few tiny, almost invisible stains where the main part of the quilt met the border, the Rose of Sharon quilt looked almost as it had the day she finished it. Now she thought back to the day she had finished restoring it for Jenny. The Lord had impressed her to add one small thing to the quilt. She had taken a scrap of the red silk and cut out a small, key-shaped piece of the fabric. At first she wondered where to place it, and then she knew.

She had pulled the quilt to her until she had the red rose in her hands. Carefully she placed the key-shaped piece in the very center of the petals. Then using her tiniest stitch, she sewed the key in place. When she finished, she had examined her work. Except for the outline of the stitches, the key was almost invisible against the matching red rose. Now she looked at the key again and ran her fingers lightly over it.

"The quilt is the key," Jerusha spoke out loud. "Thank You, Lord, for revealing Yourself to me through Jenna's quilt. And now it is truly Jenny's quilt, and I know Jenny's life will be whole and complete."

Jerusha carefully folded the beautiful quilt and wrapped it in the brown paper. As she did, a memory of Jenna came to her. One day when Jenna was four years old, some of Jerusha's friends and their children came to visit. After the women visited for a while, Jenna came into the house from playing in the yard with tears in her eyes.

"*Was ist los, dochter?*" Jerusha had asked.

"Jonas hit me, Mama," Jenna said.

Jonas' mother got up to fetch her child. "I will make sure to spank him, Jerusha," she said.

"Please don't spank him," Jenna said. "I forgive Jonas."

"But Jonas did a bad thing, Jenna," Jerusha replied. "He deserves a spanking."

"We all deserve a spanking," Jenna answered softly. "But God forgives us, so I forgive Jonas."

The women stared at Jenna with surprise, and then Jerusha took her little girl into her lap and held her.

"You are kind, my darling, and you are right. We all do deserve a spanking, but God in His mercy has forgiven us."

Jerusha smiled at the memory. She remembered being in awe at the wisdom her daughter had shown. And then she realized she was smiling. Jerusha put her face in her hands and began to cry—not with grief, but with tears of joy. Now she knew that the quilt was indeed the key, not only to Jenny's healing, but to hers as well.

Jenny stood at the desk of the county clerk and held out the birth certificate. The lady behind the desk glanced up at her with a questioning look.

"Can I help you?" she asked.

"Yes," Jenny said. "This is my birth certificate. I'm adopted, and I'm trying to find out more about my birth mother."

"Well, dear, I'm afraid that adoption records are sealed."

"I'm an unusual case," Jenny replied. "I'm not looking for adoption records because I wasn't given up for adoption. My mother died, and I was stolen. The man who stole me was killed in a car wreck. There was no way to trace me, so I was given to the people who rescued me. My adoptive parents are helping me to locate my birth mother. So there are no legal impediments keeping me from finding out about her. What I'm looking for are any records you might have on my birth parents."

Bobby stepped forward. "She's right, ma'am. I'm Sheriff Bobby Halverson from Wayne County, Ohio. I can assure you she's telling you the truth."

"Well…" the woman said skeptically. Then she reached out and took the paper from Jenny. "Let me see what I can do."

CHAPTER FORTY

Journey's End

◇◇◇

JENNY AND JONATHAN sat next to each other in two molded plastic chairs in the waiting room of the Lancaster County courthouse while the receptionist went to talk to her supervisor about Jenny's request. Jonathan had been very quiet the past two days, and Jenny felt a little disconnected from him. Her papa and Uncle Bobby had gone to get some coffee from the break room down the hall, and Jenny and Jonathan were alone.

"What was it you wanted to talk to me about, Jonathan?" Jenny asked.

Jonathan looked at her and then lowered his gaze and began to speak. "I've been thinking a lot about…about…"

"About what?" Jenny asked.

"Well, about us," Jonathan said softly. "And a lot about me. First of all, I want to tell you that I love you with all my heart. I always will. You're the most amazing girl I've ever met. You helped me to find a part of me that's been missing all my life, and I'll never forget you for that, but…"

Jenny's heart lurched in her chest. She suddenly felt cold. "But what?"

"But I just don't think it is going to work out between us."

There! It was out in the open, and Jonathan looked relieved.

Jenny clenched her hands. "But why, Jonathan?"

"Jenny, you're Amish. I'm not. You love your mama and papa more than anything. Your dad is a wonderful man. I wish my father had been like your papa. Reuben is strong and brave, and yet he's kind and gentle too. He loves you so much. And then there's your mom. She's your rock whether you realize it or not. I know she prays for you every day. Without her to guide you and love you, I think you would be very lost.

"If I take you away from them, I just don't see how it would work out. You would be shunned, and they couldn't speak to you or associate with you. In the beginning we might be happy, but after a while you'd miss them terribly. And the life away from the Amish community is so different. You would always feel out of place. Instead of a family who loves and cares for you, all I can offer is a father who cheats on his wife and a mother who's an alcoholic. It just wouldn't be right."

Jenny started to protest, but Jonathan shushed her. "Let me finish. I've thought this all through and I want to say it the right way." Jonathan turned in his chair and took her hands in his. "Even though it doesn't seem that it will work out for us, one thing I can say is that I've been watching this God of yours at work, and the past few weeks have blown my mind."

He frowned, and paused. "That's not how I meant to say it. It sounds dumb, so let me start again." He took a deep breath. "I've been amazed at the things that have happened through all this. Actually a better word would be astonished. I can't just call it coincidence anymore, but I haven't known what to call it. When I was a kid, I never really thought about God, and no one told me about Him anyway. I heard my grandfather use His name as a cussword, but for sure that didn't help me find out anything about Him. Then when I got older, I read books that filled my head with a lot of philosophical nonsense. I tried to apply it to my life, but I found out it just wasn't true. I went out to San Francisco to put my great wisdom to the test, and all I found was a bunch of people who just stayed stoned all the time and did nothing productive. It was like they refused to grow up and take responsibility for their lives."

Despite the somber tone of Jonathan's words, Jenny giggled.

Jonathan drew himself up and tried to look solemn. "What's so funny? I'm trying to be serious."

Jenny squeezed his hands and smiled. "I know, Jonathan, and I don't mean to make light. It's just that as you were talking I was thinking about the day we met. You thought I was in a costume for a play, but the costume you were wearing was much more...well, it was silly. You looked very strange. And that van." She giggled again.

Jonathan looked at her for a moment, but then his stern expression cracked and he smiled too. "Okay, you're right. I looked very weird and, boy, did you let me know it. But hear me out, please. This may be the most important thing I've ever said in my life. I never had anyone who really loved me. Not my dad or my mom, nobody. And then I met you, and for some reason I'll never understand, you loved me—without question, without reservation, holding nothing back, you loved me. I've been thinking about that a lot.

"How did I get to San Francisco from Long Island, and then to Pacifica with Shub, and then to Wooster, where I met the first person who ever loved me and the first person I ever really loved? How does that happen to two people who are so far apart one day and then totally entwined together the next?

"And then when I thought about the incredible gift that your love is to me, I realized that someone must love me a lot to give me such a precious thing. Someone big enough and powerful enough and merciful enough to take someone like me, who doesn't deserve anything, and give you to me, just to show me how much He loves me. And then I knew. It has to be God. No one else could do it—not karma or destiny or coincidence, but a real, loving, kind merciful being who cares enough about two little people in all this wide world to bring them real love. Your God must be real. And not only is He real, He loves me, and you are the proof of that. So I have decided that whatever it takes, I want to follow your God. I don't know how, but if you'll show me, I'll do it."

Jenny looked at Jonathan and was about to reply when someone put a hand on Jonathan's shoulder. Jonathan turned and looked up. It was Reuben. They had been so engrossed in their conversation they hadn't noticed him walk up. Jonathan stood up and faced him.

"I heard what you said, Jonathan, and it pleases me," Reuben said. "Only a fool says there is no God. Jenny can explain to you what it means to be a Christian. It's very simple. It can be summed up in one sentence: 'Thou shalt love the Lord thy God with all thy heart, and with all thy soul, and with all thy strength, and with all thy mind; and thy neighbor as thyself.'"

"Mr. Springer, I do want to be a Christian. But I also want you to know that as much as it hurts me to say it, I'm willing to give Jenny up to keep her from losing you and her mother and her way of life."

Reuben put his hands on Jonathan's shoulders. "I hear what you are saying, Jonathan, and I admire you for it. Now let me tell you something. I have watched you since we met, and I've come to respect you and, yes, even love you. You are a brave and decent young man. You have cared for my Jenny selflessly, and you've been respectful to me and to her mother. You're a man that I would be proud to call my son. But the most important thing is this—Jenny loves you with all her heart. There is nothing I can do about that. So I want to ask you this. Will you wait until we've finished answering Jenny's questions and then sit down with me? I may have a solution to your problem."

Jonathan stood with a dumbfounded look on his face. "Mr. Springer, you don't know how much it means to me to hear you say that. I'll do anything, if it means that Jenny and I can be together." He turned to Jenny. "Anything, Jenny, because I love you. I've loved you from the first moment I saw you."

Jenny reached out and took Jonathan's hand. "And I you, Jonathan."

Just then Bobby came walking up with the receptionist and another woman.

"This is Mrs. Bronstein," the receptionist said. "She's my supervisor, and she can help you."

"I've talked with Sheriff Halverson and see no reason why we can't release the information concerning your birth mother," she said sweetly, smiling at Jenny. "Since there was no court action removing you from your mother's care, and since you were adopted as an unknown child by the Springers, there are no court orders sealing any of your parents' records. So here they are." Mrs. Bronstein held up the folder. "If you'll just come with me, we can take care of this in short order."

They followed her down the hall to a conference room with a large table. Everyone took a seat. Mrs. Bronstein opened the envelopes and took out the papers. "Just give me a minute to look these over," she said.

Everyone sat silently as Mrs. Bronstein scanned the documents. Finally she spoke. "Your father was Robert St. Clair of New York. I don't have much more information than that because he was born in a different county. However, your mother is another story. Her maiden name was Rachel Mary Borntraeger. It's on the marriage certificate that Sheriff Halverson gave me. She was born in Lancaster County, Pennsylvania, May twelfth, nineteen twenty-eight. She was not born in a hospital, but her midwife filed the birth certificate. I have it here. She was eighteen years old when she married your father. Her parents are

Abel and Eliza Borntraeger. They live just outside Lancaster in a village called Paradise."

Jonathan's jaw dropped, and Reuben laughed.

"Of course they do!" Reuben said.

◇◇◇

The car drove slowly into Paradise. They were looking for Leacock Road. Bobby saw it first and turned left off the highway. They drove past snow-covered fields and stately barns. A horse-drawn buggy was coming toward them, and Bobby stopped and rolled down his window. The man driving the buggy pulled up. He looked at Reuben with curiosity,

"Hi, neighbor," Bobby said. "We're looking for Abel and Eliza Borntraeger's place. Can you help us?"

"Bishop Borntraeger? *Ja.* He's the next turn to the right. His barn is a big bright red one, just there. He lives alone now. His wife died ten years ago."

"*Ja,* friend. We're thanking you," Reuben said.

They turned right at the next road. The sign by the mailbox read Borntraeger. They drove slowly up the long dirt road. Finally they pulled up in front of the farmhouse. It was a simple two-story structure painted light blue. A porch with a carved railing ran along one side of the house. Dead flowers stood in the snow in two little gardens on either side of the front steps. Suddenly fear gripped Jenny's heart.

"Oh, Papa," Jenny said.

"What is it, *dochter?*"

"What if…?"

Reuben smiled and touched his finger to his daughter's lips. "*Du lieber Gott* has brought us this far. Now is not the time to stop trusting Him."

They all got out of the car and walked up on the porch. The house faced west, and the sun was setting over the snow-covered hills behind them. Their footsteps made a hollow sound on the porch. Jenny stood close to her papa, slightly behind him, while Bobby knocked on the door. They waited for a long time, and then they heard slow footsteps from inside the house. The door opened, and an old man looked out. He was very tall, with a white beard and a stern face. Wrinkles lined the area around his eyes. He looked at them curiously.

"*Ja*? Can I help you, then?" he asked.

"Bishop Borntraeger?" Bobby asked.

"*Ja*," the old man said.

"Sir, we are here on an interesting—"

The old man waved his hand at Bobby to silence him and stepped out onto the porch. The setting sun was shining in his eyes. He squinted, and then he looked straight at Jenny. He put his hand above his eyes, shading them from the sun, and looked again.

"Rachel?" he asked slowly. "Rachel, have you come home then, girl?"

Jenny stepped shyly out from behind her papa. "I'm Jenny," she said.

"Jenny?" The old man said her name slowly. "But…I don't understand."

"I'm Rachel's daughter…*Grossdaddi*," Jenny said, twisting her hands nervously.

The old man stepped forward until he stood right in front of Jenny. "You are my Rachel's little girl?" he asked.

"Yes, *Grossdaddi*." The word had a wonderful feel as it came from her lips.

The old man put his hands on her shoulders. He gazed into her face for a long time. "*Ja*, you are her daughter," he said finally. He paused and then he spoke slowly. "Will you…forgive me?"

"Forgive you, *Grossdaddi*?" Jenny asked.

"*Ja*," the old man said as tears formed at the edges of his eyes. "I was wrong to be so hard on my daughter…on your mother. It took me a long time to realize that."

The old man looked around at the people standing on the porch. "Where is she?" he asked.

"Rachel…my mother is dead, *Grossdaddi*," said Jenny.

The old man looked at Jenny, and then he smiled through his tears. He reached out and pulled Jenny close. His strong arms held her tight, and Jenny's arms crept around him. And then she was holding onto him with all her strength.

"*Grossdaddi*," she said as her own tears coursed down her cheeks. "Of course I forgive you."

She could feel him crying as he said her name over and over. "Jenny…Jenny…"

And at last Jenny knew that she was home.

Epilogue

◇◇◇

My precious Jenny,

It's the end of another long day here in Paradise. I've been in the fields since daybreak with Grandfather Borntraeger. As soon as the thaw came and the soil started to warm, we began preparing the ground for spring planting. This is the hardest work I've ever done, yet at the same time it is the most fulfilling. Your grandfather is a kind man, but he is very strict and does not put up with any complaining or questioning of his methods.

Since I'm so new to this, he must teach me as we work. I feel like a little boy all over again, but he is very patient with me, even when I make mistakes. Since your grandmother died before we met him, he has been alone, and I think he is happy to have the company. We talk together late into the night by the fire, and he teaches me from the Bible and prepares the soil of my heart. In many ways I feel like my life is like the ground we are working every day. He takes me with him to church and has introduced me to the families as his little lost sheep who has returned. They are very open to me, especially when they hear that my name is Hershberger and understand that my family was originally Amish.

I'm beginning to comprehend so many things, especially about God and His Son, Jesus. The Bible is a wonderful book. Did you know that God made the first man out of dirt? I wonder if that's why I feel so at home on the land? When I'm out in the fields with Grandfather Borntraeger, walking behind the plow, I feel as though my life finally means something, as if this is the most natural and real way I could ever be.

Grandfather explained to me that cultivating the soil not only prepares it for planting the seeds but also helps to keep the weeds from mixing in with the crop. I understand that my life has many weeds, and as Grandfather plows my mind with the word of God, it helps to prepare my heart for the words of Jesus to take root and grow. As I work, I remember the words of a song I heard the Amish men singing when I first came to Apple Creek.

"Let him who has laid his hand on the plow not look back! Press on to the goal! Press on to Jesus Christ! The one who gains Christ will rise with Him from the dead on the youngest day."

That is who I want to be—the one who has laid his hand to the plow and will not look back.

But enough about me. How are you, my dearest Jenny? I must say that the most difficult part of this is not being with you. When your father sat with me and suggested that I consider joining the Amish church, I don't think I understood what it really meant, but I did see that it was the only way for us to be together and that it was, for me, the right way.

I do know that until I'm baptized I can't court you, and that makes me impatient sometimes, but Grandfather Borntraeger says I'm learning things sehr schnell *and that it will probably only take two years for me to fully learn the Amish ways. It's hard because every moment we're apart is like an eternity.*

Grandfather says that you and your mama will be coming

after spring planting to visit for a week. I can hardly wait to see you.

It's getting late and I must get to bed, but before I go I want to pray a prayer for us that I learned from Grandfather Borntraeger.

As You have loved us, holy Father, so may we obey You out of childlike love.

Just as we acknowledge Your fatherly love, so may we love our neighbors as ourselves.

Let us do nothing contrary to this love, and so do right by our neighbors.

We ask, holy Father, that we may enjoy in moderation all You give us to fulfill our needs and not misuse it due to extravagance or evil impulses. Give us a sensible heart, one faithful with Your gifts and not overly concerned for food, drink, or earthly nourishment. Instead, teach us to put our faith in You and to yearn for Your divine help and grace.

Give us a humble, broken spirit, a penitent nature, true gentleness, and a hunger and thirst for Your righteousness. Amen.

> *With all my love,*
> *Jonathan*

My dearest Jonathan,

How proud I am of you and all that you've done in these last months. When you told me you were going to study to join the church, I knew then that du lieber Gott *had a plan for us all along. When I saw that you were willing to change your whole life to be with me, I was honored and humbled. But mostly it made me love you so much more…if that were possible. You are a good man, and I know you're doing well under* Grossdaddi's *teaching. He and I write at least once a week, and he tells me that you are* schmaert *and* mudich. *Please don't let it go to your head, but* Grossdaddi *has become very fond of you, and no wonder.*

I want to thank you, my dearest, for helping me to locate my grossdaddi. *Finding him has put a seal on my life. The questions are all answered, the journey is over, and all the fear is gone. Now I finally know the truth. I am Amish—I always have been and always will be. And now I will marry an Amish man, and my life will flow on in the unending ways of our people.*

It's like the quilt my mama made for Jenna, the one she wrapped me in to save me so many years ago. Every piece of the quilt fits together in a perfect pattern, and none of it is haphazard or unplanned. Every color means something, and the whole quilt tells a story. So it is with my life. God has always been with me, and He has always been with you. Each piece of our lives was planned before we were born, and God has fitted it together perfectly, every stitch in place and every piece in perfect relationship with the one next to it.

And now I wait for the day when we can begin courting and the story of our lives will be complete and whole. I love you, Jonathan, I always will. I wait now with peace and great joy in my heart for the day that we will be married.

As you rest tonight, may the good Lord's merciful eyes be on you. May He cover you with His divine protection and shield. May He judge, rule, and bless all of your undertakings for His glory. Amen.

I will see you after spring planting.

Yours forever,
Jenny

Discussion Questions

◇◇◇

I. The Importance of Family

Jenny Springer is struggling with the fact that she is adopted. Not knowing her real parents causes bitterness between her and her adoptive parents. In today's society with a prevelance of divorce, blended families, and adoption, many families are struggling with the same issues.

1. Do you have a similar situation in your family? Or perhaps friends who have adopted a child?
2. How are you or the family you know dealing with it? Are you (or they) letting the Lord guide as to how the situation is handled?
3. How are the children responding?

Scripture References: Psalm 68:5-6; 82:3

II. Family Ties

In chapters 13 and 14, Jonathan learns that his family was originally Amish. It changes his whole perspective on life.

1. How important is it for children to know their family history?
2. Does knowing your family roots give you strength or does it even matter?
3. Do you ever have a deep longing to go back to the place where you grew up?
4. Why do you think that is?

Scripture References: Deuteronomy 19:8; Luke 15:13-24

III. Understanding the power of God's love.

In chapter 24, when Jerusha is repairing the quilt, the Lord shows her several important things about Jenny's life.

1. What did the Lord show Jerusha about building a proper foundation in your child's life?
2. When Jerusha replaces the torn rose petals, what does the Lord show her about the shed blood of Jesus?
3. What did the Lord show Jerusha about the stains of sin in our lives?

Scripture References: Isaiah 1:18; Romans 4:7; I Corinthians 3:10-15

IV. Listening to God

In chapter 30, Jenny has to finally surrender to following God's way instead of her own. If she doesn't, it could mean her death.

1. Have you ever come to a point in your life where you would only make it through if you stopped doing what you wanted to do and let God take over?
2. How did you respond to the test?
3. What was the outcome?

Scripture References: Isaiah 58:11; Hebrews 3:7-8

About Patrick E. Craig

◇◇◇

Patrick E. Craig is a lifelong writer and musician who left a successful songwriting and performance career in the music industry to follow Christ in 1984. He spent the next 26 years as a worship leader, seminar speaker, and pastor in churches and at retreats, seminars, and conferences all across the western United States. After ministering for a number of years in music and worship to a circuit of small churches, he is now concentrating on writing and publishing both fiction and nonfiction books.

Patrick and his wife, Judy, make their home in Northern California and are the parents of two adult children and have five grandchildren.

> Be sure and watch for book three in the
> Apple Creek Dreams series,
> *Jenny's Choice.*

- Exclusive Book Previews
- Authentic Amish Recipes
- Q & A with Your Favorite Authors
- Free Downloads
- Author Interviews & Extras

AMISHREADER.COM

FOLLOW US:

Visit **AmishReader.com** today
and download your free copy of

LEFT HOMELESS

a short story by Jerry Eicher